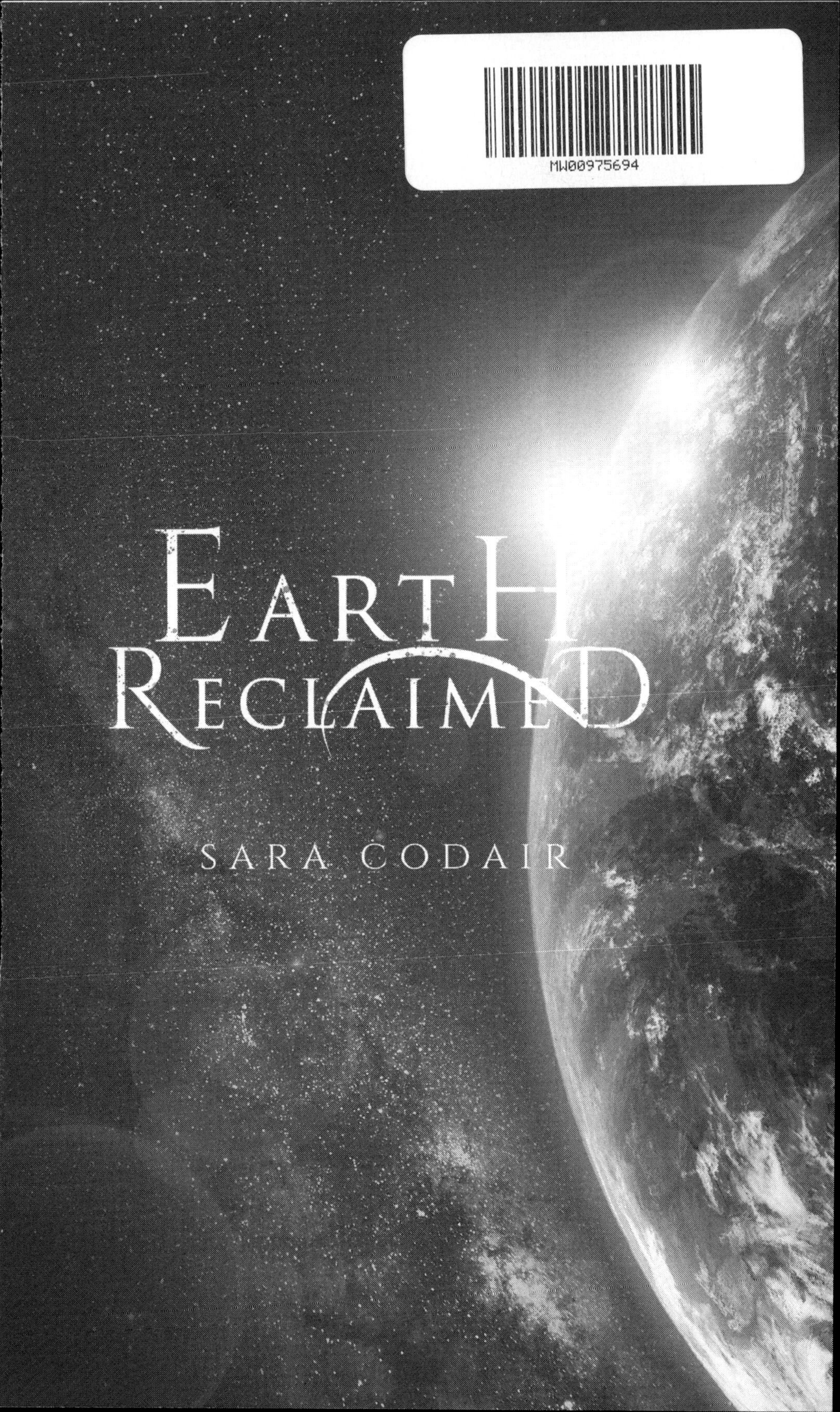
EARTH
RECLAIMED
SARA CODAIR

EARTH RECLAIMED

www.aurelialeo.com

Codair, Sara

Earth Reclaimed / by Sara Codair

ISBN-13: 978-1-946024-78-7 (ebook)

ISBN-13: 978-1-946024-76-3 (paperback)

ISBN-13: 978-1-946024-77-0 (hardback)

Library of Congress Control Number: 2020932008

Editing by Lesley Sabga

Cover Design by Fantasy & Coffee Design

Book Design by Knight Designs (www.authorzknight.com)

Printed in the United States of America

First Edition:

10 9 8 7 6 5 4 3 2 1

AUTHOR NOTE

When creating the world for *Earth Reclaimed,* I was torn between creating a queer normative world where things like transphobia no longer existed, or one where the queer characters faced the kinds of discrimination that plague us in the present day. I'm bad at picking, so I made it a little bit of both. There are moments of joy in this book, moments of power, where people who happen to be nonbinary and trans are adventuring and exploring. However, there are some scenes have potential to be triggering.

The alternate future Earth Seren and Erik inhabit is a varied, complex landscape. There are towns where queerness is accepted, and in some cases, is the norm. Towns that show a future I dream of. And there are others where people are very homophobic and transphobic. As Seren and Erik travel, they, as a nonbinary person and a trans man, encounter both acceptance and hate. There are instances where they learn about violence against trans people, are misgendered, experience violence themselves, and have their gender questioned by those who don't understand it. Throughout the book, Erik and Seren are fighting to keep hate from infiltrating their home and corrupting a new nation struggling to form.

Other potentially triggering events depicted in this book include violence, sexism, depictions of anxiety and panic attacks, death, discussion of murder, and discussion of climate disasters.

Please take care while reading, and if you decide this book isn't for you, that is okay.

For the Earth, and and for everyone working to keep it healthy.

CHAPTER ONE

The invitation was both freedom and a tether. It represented everything Seren wanted and didn't want: the chance to travel and the weight of a responsibility that would eventually confine them to Valley-Port and bind them to its magic.

And it wouldn't leave them alone.

It had most definitely not been in their pocket when they got dressed this morning. Yet, when they stuck their hand in there, searching for a bag of berries and nuts, the invitation was there, and the snacks were not.

Every muscle in their body tensed as they slipped the card out of their pocket and looked around. Afternoon sun glistened on the lake in front of them. Behind them, on a deck grown out of the oak tree Seren and their family lived in, an oblong table was set for a lunch that should've started twenty minutes ago, but Ambassador Freeman was running late. When he arrived, he'd expect to hear Seren's decision.

Anxiety snaked through their chest so tight it felt like their heart would burst. They whipped the invitation towards the still lake.

Wind suddenly gusted.

The invitation flew back and slapped them in the face.

Seren's hands shook as they grabbed it and took depth breaths. Why did the Elementals want them to go so bad? Seren plopped down on the end of the dock, dangling the feet over the edge and re-read the invitation. It was ridiculous that such a tiny piece of recycled paper could have such a large impact on their life.

The offending card was addressed to their mother in and embossed mossy letters:

Greetings, Assana McIntyre,

Your presence, your heirs, or that of an alternate representative fully authorized to make legal decisions on your behalf, is requested at the First Constitutional Convention of Newly Unified North Eastern States (NUNES) on the 14th day of June in Merry Basin of the Lakes Region during the 176th year after The Flood.

Seren and their mother had been dreaming of war and catastrophic storms since the invitation arrived. Seren didn't know if it was actual prophecy, or if a threatening message the Elementals were slipping into their slumbering minds. But they had a feeling if dozens of small, sovereign states couldn't agree on a constitution and peacefully unite as one nation, something bad would happen.

This was one of the reasons Seren didn't want to go. The Elementals wouldn't let Assana leave Valley-Port, but there had to be someone more qualified to represent her than her seventeen-year-old heir. Sure, Seren could raise their hand and vote the way their mother instructed, but they'd be next to useless in the debates.

The wind picked up, conjuring whitecaps on the lake, and Seren could feel it in their head, rustling their brains. Silverware clattered. A coarse cloth napkin blew off the table, right to Seren's face.

"Stay out of my head!" Seren glowered over their shoulder. They couldn't see the nosy wind elemental, but the results of its annoyance were plenty visible: the flapping tablecloth, the overturned chair, and whirlwind of napkins. Their heart raced. Their palms sweated. They crumpled the invitation in their fist.

"Maybe if you just told them what you decided, then they wouldn't need to search your mind for answers," said Assana.

"I haven't decided." Seren spun around and hugged their knees to their chest. They hadn't heard their mother approach, but there she stood, staring down at Seren with her hands on her hips. Her knee-length, bark-colored hair and patchwork skirt swished in the breeze. Her eyes, bluish-gray like the lake on a cloudy day, were narrowed. The skin around them was the color of sand, with a heron's footprint on the edge of each eye.

Assana smiled. The heron-prints deepened around her eyes, but her face glowed as if kissed by the sun. She ruffled the feathery tufts of brown that crowned Seren's head and sat down next to them. "Then I suppose you'll be happy to hear you can put your decision off for a few more hours."

Seren rubbed their temples then dragged their nails across their scalp. "That is more time I can torture myself. Did you finally hear from him?"

"The message was garbled, like he was far away, but he should be close." Assana frowned, staring out at the lake. "All I could understand were 'uncooperative winds' and 'rough water'."

"Didn't he check in last night from Port's Mouth?" Seren tried to pull their thoughts together. They'd spent most of the night pacing around their room and running along the lakeshore. It was a blur of movement and anxiety, but they swore their mom had talked to Freeman via the communication basin.

"Yes. With a crystal-clear message." Assana tucked a strand of wild hair behind her ear and focused on Seren. "Something isn't right."

Seren bit their lip. "Do you want me to go looking for him?"

"Normally I would send Reggie and David out, but they only just returned from a long trip and need rest," said Assana. "Don't venture too far out into the ocean. If you don't see him within a few miles, ask Atlantik if She knows where he is and return home."

Seren stood. Breathing came easier, but their muscles were still tense. Getting out on their boat always made them feel better but communicating with Elementals was always a risk. They were the reason mages like Seren and their mom could do amazing things, but any interaction with them meant that they could get in your head and make you their puppet. Outside of training with their mother, Seren only initiated contact with Elementals and used their powers in emergencies. And they weren't sure if this counted as one. Yet.

CHAPTER TWO

Seren threw the invitation over the side of their boat while they sped across the lake. It just flew back. They dropped it in the water while they were puttering through one of the river's many no wake zones and it hovered in the air then fluttered back to the boat. When they got to the island where they knew their partner, Erik, usually took his lunch break, they dropped it on the river bank. Surprisingly, it fluttered to the damp ground.

"Seren?" A familiar voice, followed by the crunching of feet on rocks and shells, drew their attention.

Seren walked away from the invitation, almost certain it would find its way back into their pocket and stood. The Elementals all seemed to want Seren to go. And it made them more determined not to. They desperately wanted to see the world outside Valley-Port, but it's not like they'd have to explore if they were rushing to get to a convention. And once they got there, they'd be cooped up indoors with politicians.

"Erik!" Seren walked over to a young man just a little taller than them. Soft, dark curls, wind-tousled from a morning on the docks, framed his tanned face. His eyes were deep brown, like the nutrient rich riverbank.

His eyebrows arched, but a grin brightened his face. "I thought you were supposed to be having lunch with your mother and Ambassador Freeman and letting him know if you were going to NUNES."

"He's delayed. It's going to be more of a supper." Seren stepped closer to Erik. They were here to ask for help, but part of them didn't want to find Freeman. Part of them just wanted to sit on this riverbank listening to Erik talk about the chaos of working on the docks in Little Port while he ate his lunch.

Erik uncrossed his arms and pulled Seren into a hug. Warmth flooded their body. He smelled like salt. The ocean. The rush of the incoming tide. His head titled as he pulled back. His nose wrinkled. Laughter bubbled out of his mouth until it shook his entire body.

Seren turned around slowly. A fiddler crab scuttled towards them, holding the invitation up in its large claw.

Grinning, Erik glanced back and forth between Seren and the crab. "Did you make up your mind yet?"

"No." Seren crouched down and plucked the invitation out of the claw and stuffed it in their pants pocket. "But I'm looking for Freeman. He sent a really sketchy message about being late."

"His ship is anchored within sight of the jetty. It didn't seem like it was in trouble when my shift ended, and the winds weren't too bad." Erik's grin inverted to a frown and his forehead wrinkled. "We have a berth prepared for him, and a small vessel to take him upriver to your mother's house, but he didn't respond when we hailed him."

"That's strange." If he was that close, then the message shouldn't have been garbled. Seren and their family lived about five miles inland of Little Port, and the messages between the two places were always clear. "Maybe he isn't on the ship."

Erik's eyes widened. "That would explain why he ignored us."

Seren's chest tightened. It explained some things, but they couldn't think of a reason for him to not be there. Sea monsters never came within sight of shore. Ambassador Freemen was skilled enough to talk with the ocean Elementals and use their power to shield his vessel against rough weather, so unless he angered them, he had nothing to fear from the sea.

The only other people out there were the women who lived on the solar barges, the BREAD (Biological Recovery, Exploration, and Development) Team. They had survived The Flood on some big ship called the ARC and had come looking for land last year. They'd expected to find a barely salvageable wasteland and had been shocked to find a thriving community and ecosystem. However, most of them refused to accept magic had protected everyone. They came to land for trade and information, but tensions were high. They thought ambassadors were religious zealots, and some ambassadors feared their technological advances could trigger a second flood. What if Freeman was one of those?

Seren looked up and made eye contact with Erik. "I could use some help looking for him."

Erik was a mage, but where Seren, an ambassador, could communicate with any elemental, and as a result, work any kind of elemental magic, Erik could only connect with water Elementals and, as a result, exert some control over water. He was very familiar with the two that lived at the mouth of the river and even interacted with the larger ocean elemental, Atlantik.

He glanced up at the sun, shining high in a clear blue sky streaked with thin cirrus clouds and then down at the sandwich he'd just taken out of his satchel. "I'm working a double today. I need to be back at the docks in an hour."

Seren scooted closer and leaned their head on his shoulder. "I'll stop by and hi on my way back."

"Stay safe," Erik said as Seren stood up.

"Always." They smiled, but it felt forced. A weight pressed down on their chest. As they walked towards their boat, a white and blue skiff beached on the river bank, the weight grew heavier.

Seren came alive on open water. The smile never left their face while wind tousled their short hair. They pushed the throttle forward. Engines were rare and hadn't been produced since before The Flood. The Mother wouldn't allow it, but with the help of a local metal mage who could repair its parts and convert it to run on alternative fuel sources, their family had kept this one going for a long, long time, which meant Seren didn't have to rely on air and water Elementals to make their boat go fast.

The bow rose as Seren crested a wave and then slammed down, splashing sea water in their face. Grinning, they licked the salt off their lips. They slowed so the boat didn't slam so hard with each wave. A sloop loomed ahead of them. The sails were down. It rocked in the chop. Every time Seren tried to get close, the waves would get bigger and the wind stronger, literally pushing their boat away from the sailboat. Someone, or something, did not want them going on it. Freeman could've left a ward around the ship to prevent it from being stolen or tampered with. Or the Elementals didn't want them near it.

They tightened their grip on the wheel, frustrated. They shouted at the ship, asking if Freeman was on board, but knew no one would hear with the howling wind. They sped up, trying to get closer, and nearly capsized when a wave rose out of the water and slammed the side of their boat. They tightened their grip on the wheel and backed off. The water calmed down.

Seren grit their teeth and took a deep breath, trying to suppress rage and frustration. They wanted to punch the wheel. Stomp their feet. Throw a tantrum like a child. But what if Freeman or his staff were on board? What if they saw?

There was one way to figure out exactly what was going on, and Seren did not want to do it. But their mom would be upset if they came home without trying. They took slow breaths, opening themself to the elements. Wind and waves filled their mind and reached out towards the ship. It was alive. Its boards retained a ghost of the sentience of the trees they came from. There were a few people on board, but none felt like ambassadors. None felt old or powerful enough to be Freeman. None of them were connected to the wind or water in a way that would stir it up, and Seren did not sense any wards around the ship either.

Biting their lip, Seren focused on the water. Below the ocean's churning chaos were awarenesses, several that were tied into deeper, vaster one. Seren sent their mind down into the water, seeking the larger awareness, Atlantik, the spirit of this ocean. Well, at least a part of her. The ocean was massive, and the being Seren sometimes spoke with was a fragment of it.

Seren held an image in their mind. They'd met Ambassador Freemen once before when he'd traveled down the coast to meet with Assana while NUNES was still being planned. Assana had made Seren sit through hours of tortuous meetings where they talked about the pros and cons of uniting all the little sovereign regions into one larger nation and how to go about doing that. Pressure grew in Seren's mind as Atlantik turned her attention toward them. That ancient, all knowing presence sent chills down their spine.

Ah, Seren. I thought you'd never ask.

Was that you keeping me away from his ship? Seren thought at Atlantik, thankful they were willing to use words today.

Indeed. Had you reached out to me as soon as you crossed into my waters, that wouldn't have been necessary.

You almost flipped my boat. You could've killed me.

Laughter ripped through Seren's mind. If you perished, it would've been your own fault for refusing to use your powers. For refusing to seek my aid.

That was not reassuring at all. Unlike the Elementals that lived alongside humans on land and lake, Atlantik was not bound by Survivors Accord. They were free to drown reluctant mages if they chose to and didn't need to rely on one to act. In turn, the humans who lived on the sea, like the women from the solar barges, were not bound by the same rules as the people who lived on land.

Do you know where Freeman is? If Atlantik wanted Seren to ask for help so bad, She better have some useful information.

Can you show me?

I will guide you, wordy child.

Thank you, Seren thought at the elemental, even having another presence in their mind made them uneasy as they pushed back on the throttle, especially when opinion flooded their head that they should turn the engine off, which Seren reluctantly did. A current of water broke from the ocean's normal movement and surrounded the boat, pushing it forward.

Seren wasn't sure what they expected to find, but it was not the old mage standing in a row boat, raising a wall of water between him and a solar skiff. Freeman was ancient. With skin like a weathered tree bark, hair reminiscent of cirrus clouds, sunken black eyes, and posture gnarled like an ancient apple-tree, he looked old enough to have been alive before The Flood. This was definitely him. And his energy was clearly tied to the wave threatening to crash on the solar skiff.

"Ambassador Freeman, what in the Mother's name are you doing?" Confusion and rage pounded Seren like waves. They wanted to wrestle control of the wall from him and send it crashing down on his dinghy. But that was a terrible idea.

He glanced over his shoulder and squinted. "Seren, what are you doing here?"

"You're late." Seren growled. Squeezing the wheel hard even though they weren't even steering. They could make out two figures on the retreating solar skiff, but they were far away to make out details aside from one was blonde and tall and the other had shorter, darker hair. The boat, if Seren had to guess, was about twenty-feet long, and mostly open. The skiff had a center console for steering.

Solar panels the canopy and the sides of the hull. There were also panels strapped in the boat. Most were to power more dock lights in Little Port, and some were for private homes, including Seren's. They were looking forward to being able to read at night without relying on fungi, fireflies, or fire magic.

"And you didn't answer my question. What are you doing?" Seren growled through clenched teeth.

"Those witches are trying to contaminate the land with those solar panels." With a wave of his hands, he sent the wall of water forward.

"Witches?" Seren reached out through their still open connection with Atlantik and wrapped their will around the water, halting it. Barely. The effort conjured an ache in their head as if waves were sloshing their brains around. "They're scientists, and they're not contaminating anything."

Freeman pushed the wall forward. Seren opened their mind further, drawing more strength from Alantik. With the power came a sense of amusement and sharp anger. Disappointment. Atlantik wasn't giving him any power, but he was old and skilled, and she wasn't resisting him either.

Why are you allowing this? Seren thought, struggling to hold him back. Their lungs and throat felt filled with burning seawater, but Seren couldn't tell if it were a side-effect Altantik's power or their anxiety about it. But they needed that power. If Atlantik wasn't backing them, then resisting Freeman would've been like a little kid trying to physically push back against a large adult.

Atlantik didn't answer.

"Freeman, let go," Seren shouted. "Assana and I traded a fair amount of food for those solar panels."

"What?" Freeman spun towards Seren, focus shifting from the wave.

"Using solar power for lighting reduces our dependence on magic and frees certain mages to do other things." Seren took advantage of his distraction and pulled harder. The wall of water inched away from the solar skiff. Freeman pushed it back.

Seren swore if he didn't let go of it, they would dump it on him then scoop him out of the water, preferably unconscious, and bring him back to the lake for the stupid, delayed dinner. Assuming they could get control of it. Assuming they didn't pass out from the effort. "The Little Port fire mage can spend more time making glass if he isn't busy dealing with the dock and street lamps all night."

"The Elementals tolerate it?" Freeman asked, face all wrinkled up.

Seren tugged the wall of water closer to him. "Yes. They accept it. Encourage it, even."

Freeman frowned. "Do you know what else those women do?"

"Mind their own business? Trade? Research?" Satisfaction mingled with appalled rage as Seren gained control of the water while Freeman tried to make sense of their reply. Their stomach churned. They felt like they were about to vomit up a whole damned ocean, but they held on. They couldn't let him hurt those people.

"They grow their children in vats. They want to cut down trees and poison the earth with their experiments." Freeman tried to regain control of the water, but he couldn't get a grip on it. and made eye contact with Seren, snarling. "Tolerating their nonsense will get us all killed."

Freeman didn't look so all powerful now. He looked like a tired, cranky old man.

Seren held the water over him. They didn't trust him. He could've killed those people if he'd hit them hard enough with that wave. And if they didn't make the shipment today, Seren might not get to see their solar panel fully installed before they left for NUNES.

But if Seren set it lose on him, they weren't much better.

They pulled it down slowly until it had shrunk to the size of the other waves, but they held onto control of it.

They were going to NUNES. Not because the Elementals wanted them to, but they couldn't risk an attitude like Freeman's going unchallenged. If he'd kept his backwards views hidden until now, how many other ambassadors were doing the same?

"You know what will also get us all killed," Seren shouted. "Starting a war by trying to drown scientists from the BREAD team, which is planning to join the new government."

Freeman grimaced. "I cannot believe Ambassador Root is letting them."

"They have every right to be there." Seren used the currents to push their boat closer to his. If Freeman hated them so much, he'd probably end voting opposite them on everything to spite them or to make it as hard as he could for them to join. How many other ambassadors had such distrust of these people and their science that they would try to hurt them?

More than you would expect, Atlantik whispered in Seren's ear. Why do you think we want you to go?

Seren assumed "we" meant the other Elementals. So they were conspiring. Lovely. But they had a point.

"I'm going NUNES, by the way." There would be one mage voting against this anti-science bullshit. Seren was young and terrified of Elementals and their magic, but they were a future ambassador. They could commune with Elementals as much as some ancient man. Maybe some of the mages who might be on the fence about certain things would listen to Seren. Maybe they could be something of a mediator between two factions. Maybe they'd actually be good at it.

"Well, I'm happy to hear that," he said, nose wrinkled. Clearly, he wasn't happy. "I suppose we should both be heading back to your mother's house."

The boats lurched as a current of seawater pushed them back towards land. Seren surrendered control of the water back to Atlantik. Assana would be happy Seren decided to NUNES. The Elementals were happy. But Seren's insides buzzed with nerves. Exhaustion weighed on their shoulders. What if NUNES was a complete disaster? What if getting representatives and leaders from a whole bunch of different little states ended with more division than unity? If there was a war, even a small one, would that trigger a second flood, one that wouldn't leave any survivors? As Altantik's currents guided them home, a crushing weight settled on Seren's chest. They were pretty sure they knew the answer to that last question.

CHAPTER THREE

The river was sleepy, clinging to a blanket of fog like it didn't want to wake up and start the day. But Mother Earth was a relentless taskmaster. The sun rose and burned off the fog. The tide changed. Wind stirred up waves. Only on rare, doldrums days, when the clouds and fog refused to move, was everything allowed to be still.

Today was not one of those days. As master of tides and docks, Erik was going to be busy. He opened his mind to the river, listening to the water as it rushed out to see and gauging the mood of the Elementals. Something had them stirred up. Merri and Mac felt rough and choppy like the waves slamming into the rocks on the jetty.

But it wasn't so rough that it would keep people on land, especially since many of the fishers were also mages. Some loaded boats with bait, while others checked their nets. Johnny Wind, the ancient mage and unofficial mayor of Little Port, was already perched on his favorite bench, watching the day unfold.

So far, Martin was the only dockhand to show up on time. He was a burly man with dull gray hair, a freckled white face, and brown eyes. He'd worked on the docks since Erik was small, and Erik had thought the man would be furious when Bob Bottom retired and put Erik in charge instead of Martin because of Erik's connection to the Elementals. Martin never complained. Dockhands came and went, but Martin was a constant as fixed as the tides.

A group of the leather-clad strangers loitered on the docks. The symbol on the side of their boat gave Erik chills. Someone had painted the turkey vulture's wrinkled head blood red and its outstretched wings a glossy black. It clutched a piece of carrion in its beak, dripping blood.

Altzis. Erik had heard rumors about them, and none of them were good. This was the first time any had landed in Little Port.

Creaking wood and squawking gulls obscured parts of their hushed conversation, but the words Erik heard made him cringe.

Dead.

Imposter.

Deserved it.

Words grew clearer as Erik inched closer. Each sentence was laden with hate. Things he had only read about in the old books he collected, relics from before The Flood. It was a kind of hate he never experienced in Valley-Port but had read about, had heard tales about from the most ancient mages still alive. Words directed towards people like him, trans people. They'd only booked the transient slip for a few days, but Erik wondered if there was a way to make them leave sooner.

"Magistrate should've been thanking Donny, not locking him up," said one of the men as the group started walking in Erik's direction.

Erik's palms sweated; his breaths came quick. If these people realized Erik was like the victim they thought deserved to be murdered, how would they react? Erik took a few deep breaths, reminding himself that Assana had been very thorough when transitioning his body to its current masculine state. If anyone in town remembered he'd been assigned a different sex once, they never mentioned it. He was Erik, a young man with a talent for controlling river currents. The Altzis would never know.

"His men will get him out soon enough. No one else knows how to drive that clunky boat of his."

If he could work up the courage to talk to them, maybe he could find out where the murder happened and where the killer was imprisoned, so he could warn them about possible breakout. There were no prisons in Valley-Port. Very few states had them, so if he got a general idea of where it was, someone would be able to narrow it down.

"You think they'll let the Burnt Falls Chapter into NUNES if they find out what he did? Sounds like a lot of these people don't see things how we do."

Erik's stomach dropped. People who approved of murder were going to NUNES? Different morals were one thing, but endorsing murder crossed a line. He hoped this group was the exception, not the rule, when it came to Altzis.

"Dom isn't a delegate," said one of the men. "Root doesn't need to know who the captain is. He only cares about that delegates show up on time."

Erik needed to talk to Assana and Seren. If these men hated people who transitioned from one end of the gender spectrum to the other, he didn't imagine they'd be kind to someone who existed in the middle of it. Erik took a deep breath and tried to clear out his mind. He could use the river to send a quick message, but Seren wouldn't see it unless they were near the lake or the communication basin. He focused on the river. Merri and Mac were close by, ignoring one boaters' requests.

"You would look much prettier with a smile on your face." One stranger raised his voice, leering at angler as she double-checked her reel's mechanisms, just a few boats down from where Erik stood.

Tina didn't look up from her task, but even from a distance, Erik saw her freckled cheeks turn red and her wind-burned nose wrinkle.

"I'll buy you dinner later if you come back to my room after." The man looped his thumbs through his belt loop.

Erik's hands balled into fists. He needed to make these men leave, but fear was a heavy mooring, keeping him from stepping forward. He looked for Martin. He was helping someone load a wooden boat with freshly repaired lobster traps.

Tina can handle herself, he thought, struggling to justify his inaction. She doesn't need me. If she defends herself, they'll know women like her aren't easy targets.

Tina snorted. "I don't know who you think you are, or where you are from, but men don't talk to women like that around here."

"Well, I ain't from around here." The man stepped into Tina's boat.

"Obviously." Tina crossed her arms. The current sped up around her as she reached out to Merri. "Get off my boat."

Erik grinned. Merri was cooperative and mischievous. Maybe he'd scare the Altzis out of town.

The man arched his eyebrows. "No."

"Get out or I will make you." Tina's her energy mixed with river elemental's.

Erik didn't know if the man just didn't take the threat seriously, or if he thought he could overpower her, but as he took a single step towards her, she conjured a wave that pushed two Altzis flat on their backs on the docks and swept a third into the river.

Johnny Wind broke out into honking laughter, shaking Erik's panicked daze. Erik was dock master, and these men were harassing someone in his domain. Burying fear deep inside, he strode towards them.

Tina pushed off the pier and the two men who remained on the dock pulled their friend out of the water. His salt and pepper hair was plastered against his white face. Rage lit his eyes.

"What are you looking at?" spat the soaked man, glaring up at Erik.

Erik crossed his arms. "You and your companions are

trespassing. This section of dock is for resident fishers only. Please either go to your own vessel or to shore."

"Who do you think you are, boy?" He picked a piece of seaweed off of his cheek and flicked it at Erik, but the wind caught so it landed a few feet to his left.

"The dockmaster." Erik squared his shoulders. "I run these docks and liaise with the Elementals. And you need to leave."

The man snorted. "What are you, fifteen?"

"Nineteen," Erik blurted before he could stop himself.

"I have a daughter your age." The man plopped a heavy hand on Erik's shoulder like they were old friends. It conjured a feeling akin to maggots squirming under Erik's skin. "How about instead of chasing us away, you apologize for that bitch who pushed me in the river."

"You deserved that for verbally harassing her and violating her space." Erik wanted to back away, but he stayed still, not wanting the man to see any sign of weakness. "Now get off my dock."

"And what are you going to do if I refuse?" The man leaned forward, close enough that Erik could smell his rotten breath. "It's not like you have any jail or sheriff in this immoral hovel you call a port."

Erik blinked. "We don't have them because we don't need them. Now leave. This is your last warning."

A vein bulged on the man's forehead. His hands balled into fists. "Are you threatening me?"

Erik opened his mouth, but no words came out. He had never been in a fight before. If it came to blows, he had no chance of winning against three men, all taller and bulkier than him. At least, not without the river's help. But he couldn't run away either.

"Just leave, please." He stepped closer to the edge of dock and turned sideways, so his back was to the water, which was angrily slapping on the dock. He glanced around. The other dockhands had finally showed up, but they were all busy helping people. It seemed like no one at all noticed the brewing confrontation between Erik and the Altzis.

No. Someone had noticed. The waves slapped this section of dock harder than another, and when Erik let his head go quiet for a moment, he could feel Merri and Mac swirling around, angry, ready to defend him if necessary. Their power rushed through him, bolstering his muscles and chasing away his fear.

The Altzis' mouths moved, but all Erik only heard the rush of water in his ears.

One man raised a fist, but as he swung, Erik pulled waves against the dock and the man stumbled and missed. He growled, lunging for Erik with range in his eyes. Sun glistened off the naked blade in his hand. Panic shot through Erik. He called water out of the river to knock the knock the man over, to restrain him until he could go get help. The water rose like an arm and knocked the man down, but it didn't hold him off the dock. It dragged him into the river. Merri and Mac pulled him down deep and sent him shooting out towards the rock-infested stretch of river between the harbor and the ocean.

"Erik, what are you doing?" Martin put his hands on Erik's shoulder, shaking him. "Make them give him back!"

Erik blinked. Rage still rushed through him like a Nor'easter's frigid storm surge. That man people like him and supported murders. Murdering people like him. That was forbidden. Like War. Those humans could not be tolerated. They must be drowned.

"Boy, is it you who wants him drowned, or is it the river?" Johnny Wind's voice, louder and clearer than Martin's, was cold wind chasing Merri's and Mac's thoughts out of Erik's head. Martin stood on the edge of the dock, focused on the river. Johnny Wind waved a brown hand in Erik's face. "Erik, stand up to them."

Erik shook his head, separating his feelings from the river's rage as he plunged his awareness further into the water. *You've made your point. Give him back.*

At first, he didn't think the river would to listen to him. It didn't always. But when he bared feelings, how much it would hurt to know he was responsible for someone's death, the currents shifted slowly, pushing the man back to the surface, and shoving him up onto a rocky island.

If there is a next time, we won't give him back. The words came with a rush of anger. A splash of mischief. It didn't matter what laws people came up with at NUNES. The delegates could vote all they wanted on the constitution's wording. They could make laws and courts. But at the end of the day, the Elementals had their own twisted sense of justice, and that would always prevail.

Erik opened his eyes and glared at the two Altzis. "You better go get your friend before the tide comes in."

"I'll help." Martin put a hand on each of the men's shoulders and steered them away.

He turned around and stormed off to the other side of the docks.

People called to as he passed. Those without magic struggled to get off the dock in the suddenly swifter current. He helped, but he was distracted, wanting to get as far away from the Altzis as possible.

If they said another foul word to him, threatened him, or even looked at him wrong, he didn't trust himself not to shove them back in the river. Not with the sound of water angrily rushing in his head, not with the way the currents had sped up and how eddies were spinning all over the river. Merri and Mac were angry and would be churning on the edge of his awareness until he went inland.

He wanted to run to Seren and tell them what happened. Hug them. Talk. Figure out how much of that rage had been inside him and how much belonged to the river. But Seren was back at the lake, getting ready to leave for NUNES. And his work day had only just begun. He couldn't leave the docks, but he could try to find out more information about the Altzi. And someone he needed to check in on knew more about them than anyone else here.

Thankfully, the solar skiff was as far from the Altzi boat as it could get.

"Erik, are you okay?" Tav, one of the few BREAD researchers from the solar barges who was not a woman, stood an inch taller than Erik with a lanky build, a jaw right in the middle of round and blocky, olive skin, and dark spiked hair. They wore dark gray pants and a light coat that hung to their knees made of a tightly woven, almost shimmery fabric.

"Yes." He was not all right at all, but Tav, like their aunts, did not believe in things like sentient river spirits, though as the one who spent the most time on land, they were starting to recognize magic here, even if they were reluctant to call it that. "How are the repairs coming? Is there anything I can get you?"

"Slowly." Tav glanced over at the flat boat covers in reflective panels.

"Should I extend your reservation?" If they stayed, Erik could offer to buy them lunch in exchange for more information about the Altzis. They'd been in a lot of ports up and down the coast. They'd asked for the slip as far away from the Altzis as possible.

"My aunt wants to leave today, but I'll be shocked if the boat is seaworthy by sunset," said Tav. "We're already behind schedule, and my aunts are acting like it is a race to get to NUNES. A potentially lethal one."

"Lethal?" Knots twisted in Erik's stomach. Seren was about to enter that race. Seren who was naïve, stubborn and terrified of their own power.

A horn honked. Someone shouted Erik's name. He ignored it.

"The Altzis know they're outnumbered by people who disagree with them on almost every item. But they think if enough of us suffer tragic accidents on the way there, then they can control the vote." Tav glared across the water, to where Martin was rowing out to rescue the Altzi from the island the river had stranded him on. "But the Altzis didn't damaged this boat."

"So instead of accepting many people might disagree with them, some Altzis and mages are resorting to violence to get their way?" They sounded like toddlers. Not adults. Not leaders. Maybe Seren shouldn't go. Maybe Valley-Port needed to stay as far as possible from this new government.

"Some of the more extreme followers of your religion think we're going to bring on a second apocalypse with technology." Tav crossed their arms and stared down at him.

"I'm stuck on this mooring!" Someone shouted. Erik closed his eyes, asking Mac to slow down so their rope slackened.

"It's not a religion. At least, not to me," Erik told Tav. "The Mother is a sentient planet with the ability to trigger extinction on a whim, not a goddess. The Elementals are powerful too, but I don't worship them. I work with them."

Though he supposed, some people did see The Mother and Elementals as deities. And if the old books were to be believed, there had been a lot more religions before The Flood. There were theories about what happened to the lost ones, but no one knew which were true. "What do you know about the Altzis?"

"They're the type of selfish power-hungry monsters who trashed this planet a couple centuries ago." Tav's hands balled into fists. "They worship 'The Mother' and Elementals like a lot of people here, but they have a very rigid life style and moral system that they want to make *everyone* follow. They think if they vote for a strong central government and gain control of it, then they'll have the power do it."

Erik shudder. He didn't know what the Altzis stood for, but based on the little he'd seen of them, he didn't think he'd like it. He made eye contact with Tav. "The mages aren't all zealots, you know. You should try to get you aunts to work with us, not against us. We stand a better chance of outvoting the Altzis if we stand together."

"I agree," said Tav. "But you also need to convince your people to trust mine."

A ringing bell alerted Erik to a boat struggling to get into the harbor because the river was raging. A second struggled to reach their mooring ball. A third kept overshooting the slip they were trying to enter. Chaos had broken out in the few minutes he'd taken a break. Martin was out helping the Altzis and all the other dockhands were busy. He had so many questions, but he had no more time to ask them.

He reached out to Merri, instructing him to help the person at the mouth of the river, and ordered Mac to help the person stay close enough to their mooring ball to tie up. Erik strode towards the slip. He wasn't sure how much he could really help, but he would do whatever he could to help unify the mages and the sisterhood and stop the Altzis from grabbing power.

CHAPTER FOUR

Seren tried to focus on the roaring engine. On the briny droplets landing on their nose, the golden glow of late afternoon sun, and the rowboats and sailboats they soared past. They studied the old houses and pines lining the river. They had survived wars, storms, and floods, including The Flood, which purged the Earth of many technologies that were slowly killing Her and thinned the warring human population. It was only within Seren's lifetime that some more advanced technologies, like electricity and solar panels, reemerged. And if NUNES failed, if people started fighting instead of uniting, it would all be washed away.

This trip was no longer about going to some big, boring political convention and voting the way mom had told them. Now they had a purpose: try to convince the mages and BREAD that they actually wanted the same things. They had things to say. They had to make people listen to them.

"So this is going to be your first time North of Little Port, right?" David's voice startled Seren.

"Yeah, more or less." When they got caught up in the wind, it was easy to forget about passengers.

"Port's Mouth has everything Little Port has but more of it. More people. More travelers. More food." David sat on the bow of the boat, letting the wind whip the braids of his red hair and beard. He leaned forward and brushed braids out of his eyes.

Seren tightened their grip on the helm. What he said was true, but Port's Mouth and beyond was foreign territory. Merry Basin, where esteemed Ambassador Tristan Root was hosting NUNES, was at least a three-day rise and they were going to have to pass through some dangerous places on the way. The twins hadn't mentioned the danger directly, but their weapons were poorly concealed. "So what kind of trouble are you expecting?"

"Monsters," grinned Reggie at the same time David said, "Hopefully none."

The twins were cross between bodyguards and security officers. When it came to trade with other states or territories, Reggie and David were security guards for the trip. Or the only people on it. They'd seen more of the world than anyone else in Valley-Port.

Reggie sat in the stern, sprawled out on the back bench.

Ignoring Reggie, Seren made eye contact with David. "I've never seen you so heavily armed."

David frowned. "Your mom did tell you about the Altzis, right?"

Seren nodded. Assana had explained that the Altzis were people with values completely different than theirs. For decades, they were hemmed in by raging waters and carnivorous trees. But in the past few years, the waters calmed. Paths opened through the forests. The people ventured beyond their homes. They clashed with a lot those they encountered, but they also found and united with like-minded individuals and together, that group united under the name Altzi. But different didn't mean dangerous. "Are they really that bad?"

"The human monsters are the scariest kind." Reggie appeared almost identical to David, but their jaw was a little rounder, they had no beard, and shorter hair. "But when it comes to humans, your mother tries to see the good in everyone. If I say, 'this people-eating three-headed bear I ran into is threat, tell people to avoid Gnarly Path,' she listens. If I say these people are dangerous and want to force their beliefs on everyone, she says they're misled or misunderstood."

"The bear only had two heads," said David.

"Then it was three eyes," said Reggie.

Tension grew in Seren's shoulders. They slowed as they entered one of the rockier, shallow parts of the river that was tricky to navigate at low tide. Especially since the pesky stone Elementals liked to move them around.

Seren's hands twitched. If they didn't need both hands on the wheel, they'd be running their nails across their scalp or picking their lip to distract themself from the tension in their chest. Erik had a recent run it with the Altzis and was still really upset by. It was why they were leaving this afternoon instead of tomorrow morning. They were going to check in on him, and the twins were going to investigate all the harassment complaints that had come in about the Altzis in the three days they'd been in Little Port and make sure they left first thing in the morning when their slip rental expired.

Seren's voice cracked as they forced words out of their tight throat. "Do you think the Altzis would really attack us?"

"We'll be fine," David said softly.

Reggie snorted. "There are monsters everywhere, Seren. I can't predict which types we'll see on this journey."

"You're not helping." Every muscle in Seren's arm was tense. A storm of unformed thoughts raged in their mind.

"I'm here to make sure the monsters don't eat you, not to comfort you." Reggie stretched their arms and yawned. "Coddling is more my brother's thing."

Seren grit their teeth. In theory, there were plenty of ways they could use magic in self-defense, but the idea of exposing their mind to an unknown elemental was worse than the thought of baring it to one they knew. What if the elemental didn't want to be used to protect Seren? Or worse, what if it did, but decided the only way to defeat the attacker was to kill it? Seren remembered how the whites of their mother's eyes disappeared once. How all feelings but anger fled their expression. They saw someone slowly sinking into the dirt as tree roots twined around their limbs and dragged them down. That day, Seren had sworn they would never let an elemental use them for harm, justified or not.

By the time Seren reached Little Port, the sun's golden rays were turning red, and the wind picked up. White caps crested waves as they navigated around fishers returning from a day at sea and ghostly schooners that haunted the wider sections of river. When Seren got close enough, they heard the ships singing to each other. They didn't use human language, but the creaks and groans the forest made when the wind blew through it.

Seren didn't know what each sound meant or if they could even be translated into human speech, but they could sense the ships, or the fragments of dead Elementals trapped in their boards, were angry about something as three lined up around Seren. The ships didn't resume their original courses until Seren tied up.

"Seren?" Dark hair curled around Erik's face like seaweed in a tide pool. His lips were magnets, pulling Seren's mouth towards his.

"Who else gets a schooner escort every time they drive down this river at dusk?" Seren turned off the engine as David tied *The Whaler* up to the dock. "Please tell me you're here to greet me and not working again."

Erik grinned. His cheeks burned red as boiled lobsters. "I'm supposed to be done, but Martin is late."

"Is he okay?" Seren didn't need the hand Erik offered, but they took it anyway because they liked the way his rough skin scratched theirs, especially when their palms were itchy from the steering wheel's vibrations.

"I think so." He didn't let go of Seren's hand when they got onto the dock. "He sent a message saying he'd be here by nine."

Seren took in Erik's stained, damp clothes and wind-tousled hair. "What time was he supposed to start?"

"Six," Erik said. "But he's never been late before."

"The more important question is, how long have you been here?" David stood beside Seren and put a hand on Erik's shoulder.

"You don't want to know." Erik scratched his head and yawned. "You're staying at the Compass Rose, right?"

Seren nodded, making a mental note to talk to their mom about how short-staffed the docks were. She could transfer one of the water mages from fishing to dock work.

"I'll come see you as soon as I'm done." Erik's grip on Seren's hand tightened. His gaze drifted over to Reggie and David, and all the bulges under their tunics. "Why bother covering the weapons if they're that obvious?"

"Assana said she didn't want to see our weapons." Reggie smirked. "Technically, she didn't see them."

Erik rolled his eyes, but his grip on Seren's hand was almost painful. "You're expecting trouble."

"We're prepared for it." David glanced up the river at the slowly setting sun. "And hoping our preparations are unnecessary."

"You keep telling yourself that, brother." Reggie crossed their arms.

A bell clanged.

Erik jumped. "I have to go. Merri and Mac have been riled up this week."

He let go and walked towards the river, pausing a moment to glance back at Seren, like he was trying to communicate something with his eyes in a language Seren didn't know. Then he turned around and ran off, leaving Seren alone with the twins, who were glaring at each other. Fantastic.

Seren shook their head and walked up the cobblestone street, towards the Compass Rose Inn, one of the few non-fishing businesses in town that had been in operation since before The Flood. Half the point of coming here was to see Erik.

They passed pubs filled with string instruments and raucous laughter, cats lurking on fences waiting for small prey, and well-lit warehouses where people cleaned fish meat for eating and ground the bones into fertilizer. The warmer, orange light came from magic-fueled lanterns, while the cooler lights were bulbs powered by energy cells that had been charging all day in the sun.

The Compass Rose Inn was a three-story building with lights glowing behind thinly shaded windows. The smell of chowder and pies made Seren's stomach growl. The young woman staffing the front desk checked Seren, David, and Reggie in promptly and gave them the last table in the crowded dining room. Seren recognized a handful of people from their regular trips to the port, but the strangers were the ones that got their attention. They'd never seen the tall woman with white streaked blonde hair, wrinkle-free white trousers, chrome jewelry, and a matching shirt, nor had they seen the younger, spikey-haired person sitting beside her.

A spark of envy flared in Seren—they honestly couldn't guess the person's gender. Like Reggie, no matter what kind of binder Seren wore, breasts always gave their assigned-at- birth-sex away. Seren could've used their connection to Earth to alter their body, but the magic scared them more than their breasts. Body alterations took time, and the longer Seren stayed open to magic, the more they risked being overtaken by it. Assana would teach Seren how to work that kind of magic, but she wouldn't do it for them.

Part of Seren wanted to walk over and ask them if they were the ones who were delivering the solar panels. The shipment hadn't made it inland to the lake yet, but Seren had noticed some of the new panels hung on the way in. They considered apologizing for Freeman's bad behavior, but then remembered Erik saying those people didn't believe in magic. Maybe they didn't realize he conjured that wave.

A loud belch, followed by a string of curses drew Seren's

attention away from the scientists. The table is full of loud, bald men with the weathered skin and leather clothing. Seren had never seen someone wear that much leather. Deerskin and wool were far more common. Leather was mostly used as tools and safety equipment. No one wore entire suits made of it.

Reggie glared at the men. “Those are the Altzis.”

“I can’t wait for them to be gone. Hailey, the server, made eye contact with the twins as she tucked a honey-colored curl into her gull’s nest of a bun.

“They’ll be gone tomorrow.” Reggie smiled at her. “My brother and I are investigating them and making sure they leave on time. Anything you want to tell us about them?”

“Lots of things,” whispered Hailey. Everything her face, from her heart-shaped forehead to her apple-blossom lips was cute and Reggie had had a hopeless crush on her for a year but refused to act on it.

One of the Altzis whistled. When no one responded, he shouted something about a refill.

Reggie’s eyes narrowed. Their hands balled into fists.

“I’ll take my meal upstairs,” said Seren. “Whatever your special is tonight, please. No rush sending it up.”

It was Reggie and David’s job to deal with Altzis here. Seren didn’t know if anyone in this group was a NUNES delegate, but in case they were, Seren didn’t want to be involved in any kind of confrontation that might complicate negotiation with them later on.

Seren spent the next two hours alternating between reviewing Assana’s notes and the constitutional articles they’d be voting on at NUNES, reading the antique book they’d bought for Erik, and pacing around until Erik finally showed up.

He looked like he was about to collapse as he stepped through the door.

Seren closed the book and rushed up to hug him. "Are you okay?"

"No." He leaned his head on theirs. "I'm exhausted and scared."

"Tell me everything." Seren held his face away from theirs.

Erik closed his eyes. "Seren, I almost killed one of them."

"You or the Elementals?" Seren thought the latter was much more likely.

"Both?" He let go of Seren, walked over to the armchair they'd just vacated and plopped down, not even noticing the book on the table next to it.

Erik was really out of it if he didn't notice a book.

Seren understood why as he told them about the Altzis, followed by a tale of Seren's worst nightmare come to pass. The story raised the hairs on their arms and conjured a churning in their stomach. Erik tried to defend himself using elemental power, but the Elementals took over and tried to kill someone. Still, the story ended better than Seren expected.

Seren took deep breath and put a hand on his shoulder. He was shaking. They opened their mouth to say something, but every phrase they thought of sounded wrong.

"You were right," he said and put a hand over theirs. "About the Elementals."

Seren took a deep breath. "Maybe. But they listened when you told them to stop. They let him go."

He brushed hair out of tearstained eyes. "That's not what I expected you to say."

"But it's true." And that was what mattered in the end. Seren sat on the edge of the arm chair, wrapped their arm around Erik and pulled his head against them.

Erik peered up through curls that had fallen over his face. "I'm afraid the Altzis will hurt you. I'm afraid of what will happen if you have to fight them."

"That's why Reggie and David brought their guns." Seren tried to sound confident, but trepidation cracked in their voice. No one had ever tried to hurt them before. No one had ever openly hated them.

The Altzis cracked how they saw their reality and made they feel like they were wading into a strange river in the dead of night, unsure about what lurked below the surface of the still water.

Erik leaned his head against Seren's ribs, and they just held each other. The silence wasn't awkward, but it wasn't comfortable either. They'd both lived in a bubble and now, they'd glimpsed what lived outside, and it wasn't at all what they thought it would be. As the silence stretched on, questions slithered through Seren's mind until one found its way out of their mouth. "Did anyone around town seem open to their ideas?"

"Most aren't, which is why they keep harassing people." Erik hugged them tighter. "But Martin has been spending a lot of time with them. And acting weird. I think he is buying into their nonsense."

"Oh no, Erik. Is that why he was late?" It was bad enough to have the Altzis around. Seren couldn't stand the thought of them sewing hate in this community.

"I think so." Erik's voice cracked. "If they can't convince people to live like them, they want to force it on us. They think they can use NUNES to do that."

Seren opened their mouth to say that was ridiculous but stayed quiet as their thoughts caught up. The items they were voting on would determine how much power new government would have and in what areas they would have the most power. If enough people voted for the most power to be held by the central government, and the Altzis got control of it, then they could control the justice system, education, healthcare, and even how people could use their magic. And if they were as transphobic and homophobic as Seren had heard, they could outlaw same-sex marriage. They could make it illegal to transition. They could deny people basic human rights based on who they were and who they loved.

Seren's heart raced. They shook their head. That would never happen. Not with all the ambassadors attending. Not with NUNES being hosted by Root at Merry Basin. People wouldn't stand for it.

Not unless the mages and scientists were too busy fighting each other to notice what the Altzis were up to. Seren had to make sure that didn't happen.

Erik stood up and wrapped his arms around Seren. "You really need to be careful while you're traveling, Seren. My friend Tav, who is part of the BREAD team, called this a lethal race."

That phrase sent chills rattling through Seren. Not only because it was dangerous for them, well that too, but also because it painted a picture of three groups on the brink of war. They thought of the dreams they'd had recently, dreams their mom had. Rain, thunder, raging rivers, and surging tides. What if NUNES turned into a literal battle ground instead of a political debate? Would that count as a war? Would that be the end of all humanity?

"Seren? What are you thinking?" Erik moved his hand up to their cheek, leaving a trail of warmth in its wake.

"This is too big for me." Seren put their hand over his. "I want freedom. I want to see the world beyond Valley-Port. I don't *want* to go play politician with real adults. But it's what I need to do, and I'm terrified I'll fail."

"What made you decide to go?" He asked, lips closer to theirs.

"Freeman attacking the solar skiff. The way he talked about technology. I thought as a mage who favors technology, I might be able to bring people together." Seren's lips twitched, like one side wanted to frown and the other smile. "That and the Elementals were going to torment me if I didn't."

"I'd come with you if I could." Erik leaned his forehead against Seren's. "I could help the BREAD researchers and the mages understand each other."

Seren smiled. "You'd be good at that."

"Can I kiss you, Seren?" Their lips were practically touching already.

"Yes," Seren breathed, leaning forward into a kiss they hoped would give their racing thoughts a rest. If there was a chance they might not come back, then they were going to enjoy the next couple hours with Erik as much as they could.

After Erik left, and thin pine walls failed to muffle Reggie's bear snores, Seren ghosted into the washroom and turned on the sink's spigot. The cloudy water grew clearer as it surged through the pre-flood piping that pulled it in from the same network of underwater wells that seeped into all of Valley-Port's rivers and lakes.

When the sink was full, Seren drew power from the elemental that drowsed in Little Port's groundwater. They borrowed just enough energy to use the water to make a connection to the communication basin Assana kept in her houses' observatory.

"You're up late," yawned Assana as her face appeared in the rippling water.

"I can't sleep," said Seren. "I'm scared."

"Fear is wise, but if it controls you, it can lead to folly." Assana reached forward with long, branching arms, as if she were going to hug Seren through the water. "No matter what you encounter out in the world, remember that you are a child of Earth advocating for peace and symbiosis."

"I love you." Seren brushed the image of their mother's arms with their fingertips, wishing they could hug her and hide in a moment of being mother and child, not leader and heir.

Assana smiled. "Keep an open mind. Listen to understand. Stay safe and stay in touch."

"Of course. And you stay safe here," said Seren, struggling to figure out why they thought Assana might face trouble of her own.

When Assana laughed, her whole face brightened. "Nothing is going to hurt me here. You are the one venturing off into the wild."

CHAPTER FIVE

As far as Seren knew, just outside of Little Port, at the mouth where the river met the ocean was and always had been treacherous. Sandy beaches on either side made it appear benign, but with its currents zigzagging around rocky islands and sandbars that were only visible during the lowest tides, anyone unfamiliar with it was sure to get wrecked. But even without assistance from the Elementals, Seren knew the location of every rock and shoal. This place was familiar. Normally, it was the gateway to the wild, open ocean where they could escape the crushing responsibility of being their mother's heir.

This time was different.

This time, they were carrying that weight with them as they raced into unfamiliar territory, towards a debate and vote they weren't prepared for. Their chest tightened. They were just a teenager. Maybe they'd been raised to be a politician, but they weren't ready for this. Not when so many of the delegates were older and hostile. Not when one of the groups vying for power wanted to strip them of basic human rights. The enormity of it made their breath come fast and their chest ache.

"It looks pretty rough out there." David stood on the bow, shielding his eyes from the sun as he glanced out at the sea.

A herd of harbor seals lounged on black rocks, gulls lazily circled overhead and cormorants dried their wings on the ends of the jetty. Inside the jetty water churned. Just off shore, an Osprey dove towards the white-capped ocean and pulled a fish from the waves. Had the bird been a second slower, a wave would've knocked it out of the air.

"She can handle it." Seren patted *The Whaler's* hull. They'd gotten caught in waves much worse than this. And if they had to, Seren could draw power from Atlantik to protect them. Knowing the old ocean elemental, she'd probably be offended if Seren didn't seek her help.

"We have enough time to delay another day and see if this wind dies down," said David.

Reggie winked at Seren. "Hmmm, you could spend the afternoon with Erik since he actually has the day off."

"I want to get there early and try to get a better idea of people's opinions before the voting starts." Seren pushed the throttle forward as they entered the currents rushing into the channel with the tide. The boat plopped up and down over waves crowned with frothy tiaras.

The further they got from Little Port, the rougher the water got.

David hadn't braced himself properly as the bow slammed down and wound up falling onto the floor.

Reggie laughed. "You just wanted them to turn back so you wouldn't fall on your ass."

Seren hit another wave. A spray of cool, salty water crashed down on them, and when the boat leveled out, Reggie sat on the floor with David. "You might want to stay there. Or get a better grip on the rails."

The soaked twins glared. Reggie looked like they were going to puke. "I hope it's not like this all the way to The Port's Mouth."

The wind howled at their backs, angry and cold, urging them

onwards. Seren opened a crack in their mind, sensing rage beneath the surface of the ocean's power. The sky was an ominous lead gray, ready to burst open and drench them with cold water.

"Is there anywhere to pull ashore?" shouted Reggie. They were fearless when fighting a monster, but terrified of storms.

"There is a little harbor halfway between Little Port and Port's Mouth," said David.

"Or you could beach it," said Reggie.

Their voices were hoarse, barely audible over the growling engine and howling wind. Seren answered them by pushing the throttle forward as *The Whaler* climbed a swell and slammed down the other side. The twins groaned. The cycle went on and on. Without drawing power from the ocean, Seren listened, sensed the currents, the rise and fall of each wave just before they hit it.

Maybe they should've been afraid, but each time a wave failed to flip their twenty-foot skiff, it was a victory. Proof that they were good at something. Seren held the wheel and throttle as tightly as their sweaty palms would allow. The vibrations and jarring made their skin itch, but they didn't dare take a hand off of the wheel to scratch. They were on their feet, never losing balance no matter how hard the waves tossed their little vessel.

"Seren, can't you use magic to make this hurt less?" asked Reggie.

"I would if I could," added David. "I'm using all my power to dull my pain sensors and control my fear enough, so I don't shit myself."

"We're fine. I can handle this." At least, they could if the twins stopped distracting them.

Then, as if the elements were determined to prove them wrong, the wind, which Seren already guessed was blowing close to gale force, intensified. The waves tripled in size.

"Seren! Do something!" screamed both twins simultaneously.

It was time to draw power from Atlantik. Their little boat was not made for waters this rough. For a moment, their chest sized up as they thought of what Merri and Mac had done with Erik. But this situation was different, and if they didn't do something, they'd capsize.

Closing their eyes, they reached for the magic all around them.

It's about time. Atlantik's voice swished in their mind. *Did you not learn from last time?*

Are you making the storm?

Laughter slapped through their head like waves hitting rocks. *I'm giving you a head start. Don't waste it.*

The voice faded to the angry roar of the wind.

Seren realized they couldn't use magic to calm the storm. That probably be counted as wasting the head start, and the might not even be able to if Atlantik fought them on it. Yet without calming the waters, they couldn't stay in them, so they raised the boat above it by creating a bubble of air around the ship. It rose up above the wave and rode the wind from one crest to the next instead falling and rising with the sea.

"Kill the engine," shouted Seren.

They didn't see who answered, but the grumbling outboard shut off. It was eerily silent inside the bubble. They could hear the twins breathing, but the wind and waves were merely muffled splashes.

"This is amazing," whispered Reggie.

Seren opened their eyes. The waves were a blur of blue and white about ten feet below them. The tightness drained for their chest. They felt light. As inflated as the bubble. A grin bloomed on their face. Maybe they didn't use magic a lot, but when they did use it, they did amazing things.

"How fast do you think we're going?" asked David.

Laughter shook their body. This was ridiculous and beautiful and exhausting. Raw energy poured them from the ocean to the bubble, already making their head feel might and their body wobbly. They couldn't maintain this long. "I'm...I'm guessing we're travelling at whatever speed the wind is."

"Amazing. I didn't know you could do stuff like this." David grinned, eyes wide with wonder.

"I've never done anything quite like this," muttered Seren. They'd made bubbles before when they had rescue people stranded on vanishing sandbars or in sinking boats, but they'd never made *The Whaler* fly.

But Seren could already feel their own energy draining as it mingled with Earth's magic.

Reggie peered over the bow. "We'll be at the Port's Mouth in no time."

Seren hoped Reggie was right, because the wobbling in their legs had nothing to do with the waves.

CHAPTER SIX

According to their pocket watch, only fifteen minutes had passed since Seren conjured the bubble, but it felt like hours. They maintained it as long as they could, gradually letting go of the magic as their boat passed between the lighthouses and rocky islands that broke the biggest swells.

"Hold on tight," they warned as they released their hold on the last thread of magic, allowing the boat to drop the last inch into the crest of the wave. It landed with a plop, and then it slammed down into the trough.

"Are you trying to kill us?" shouted Reggie while David muttered curses under his breath.

David and Reggie resumed their cursing, but Seren didn't have the energy to complain. The waves weren't as big, but they were still tossing the boat about as Seren maneuvered inland towards an area littered with rocky islands. Based on the charts they'd seen for these waters, there were more rocks just below the surface. It resembled the entrance to Little Port, but three times as big with more chaotic currents. And unlike Little Port, there weren't two mischievous Elementals playing in the water. The spirit of this river slumbered.

Slumber sounded good. Seren yawned, blinking twice as much as they should. They wanted to curl up in a soft bed under their favorite quilt and sleep for hours. They started to take a hand off the wheel to rub their eyes, and then they saw a large black rock as foamy water receded. They put their hand back on the wheel and turned just in time to avoid it. Carefully not to accidentally poke the sleeping elemental, Seren sent their mind slightly below the surface of the water, feeling the currents and the places they moved around rocks.

"Please tell me your eyes are closed because you are using magic to navigate and that you aren't falling asleep at the wheel," said Reggie.

"I am." But Seren opened their eyes anyway. The waves shrunk as they entered the channel that would through islands. Land stretched out on either side of them.

The one benefit of the rougher than usual waters was that there were very few boats out. An old schooner slipped off its mooring, even though no one visible was at its helm, and pulled up along Seren's portside, curiously groaning. With its triple mast and long hull, the schooner towered over the twenty-foot skiff. Seren tightened their grip on the wheel, neither steering too close nor too far away from their escort.

As much as Seren wanted to drink up their surroundings, they only caught quick glimpses of the antique mansions and brick row houses.

"Do you want one of us to drive?" David asked.

Seren shook their head as hard as they could, hoping the movement would jostle their mind awake. They hated letting anyone else take the helm. *The Whaler* was Seren's boat, passed down through generations. According to Seren's father, when their ancestors created wards to fight the floodwaters in the region that would become Valley-Port, they made a special ward to protect that boat. It was as much a legend as heirloom. More importantly, *The Whaler* was one thing Seren could control and not worry about it controlling them back.

Plus, the water wasn't exactly calm. Even as the mouth narrowed into an actual river, the waves still battered the hull. Rocky cliffs topped with rows of old brick buildings lined the river. Water splashed against the wet jagged rocks.

And unlike in the ocean, the waves came from all different directions. Sometimes, a trio would merge together, forming mini maelstroms whose currents pulled the boat off course towards rocks or lobster traps. The schooner helped keep Seren out of the stray currents on their portside, but they were unprotected on the starboard.

"That is the biggest one I've seen," said Reggie, daring to stand up and point at a maelstrom off to the starboard.

Seren watched the water swirl and swirl. It sucked in a piece of barnacle-covered driftwood which went around and around and around. It pulled their boat closer and closer. Seren turned the boat hard and slammed the throttle forward.

"Look out!" Reggie screeched as Seren overcompensated and found themself heading straight towards the schooner. They turned again, this time with much less force and got themself back into deeper water.

"See, we're fine." Seren wiped sweat off of their brow as they glided past the maelstrom, then noticed the schooner was as far to their port as it could get without running aground. They started to follow its course, but the river curved. Seren swerved to avoid a concrete pier, a relic from a bridge long gone.

On the other side of the pier Seren came face to face with an image of themself: a bedraggled teenager in a baggy gray sweater, standing with their hands clinging to a black steering wheel. Seren blinked and shook their head, afraid that they'd fallen asleep. Gaping, they raised a hand, and so did the ghostly version of themself.

"Seren, turn before we hit the solar barge!"

Seren didn't know which twin said it, but the warning jolted them alert and make them realize that they weren't dreaming, hallucinating, or having an out of body experience—they were staring at their reflection on a wall of solar panels rising off of ship six times the length of *The Whaler*.

"How can they maneuver something so big through here?" Seren yawned, shaking their head. They needed food. They needed rest. They couldn't fit between the schooner and the solar barge, so they turned hard starboard. *The Whaler* jerked in the current as Reggie scrambled for the horn and squeezed it, as if the lumbering vessel would be able to do anything even if it did know there was a puny skiff in its way.

The Whaler slid by the barge just close enough for Seren to reach out and touch it if they dared take their hand on the wheel. They stared, mesmerized as dozens of panels like the ones that lined Asana's roof sailed past them.

A screeching groan ended the daze.

A thunk made Seren jump.

Their boat stopped moving abruptly, sending them flying onto David and Reggie. The engine quit.

"Is everyone okay?" Seren sagged as the adrenaline faded.

"I will be once you get off me," muttered David.

"Damned rocks." Seren picked their foot up to stomp but caught themself before they did more damage. They stumbled towards the back of the boat, unlocked the engine and tilted it out of the water. All three of the propeller blades were cracked and bent. Seren glared at the currents swirling around them. The boat wasn't moving. They ran their hands through their hair, tugging fuzzy tufts. Their throat burned. The threat of tears stung their eyes.

The solar barge glided away. So did the schooner.

"You think you can get us out of here on a magic bubble?" asked Reggie.

"The wind is blowing the wrong way," said Seren, not admitting they were too dammed tired.

They were barely staying awake as it was, and the cord of magic felt like a leash and collar tightening around their throat, tugging them back home. They interlocked their fingers behind their back and stretched. They paced around the boat and splashed salt water on their face, trying to wake up.

Seren sat down on the bench in front of the wheel. Their knees bounced. They wrapped their arms around themself, shaking. They were drained, in a stormy river, farther away from home than they'd ever been. They did not want their first impression on the people in this town to be that they were weak and in need of assistance. They were the child of one of the most powerful mages in the region. Their mother might never leave Valley-Port, but she had a reputation. And if Seren wanted people to take them seriously at NUNES, they didn't want to their journey to be seen as the incompetent, fumbling teenager they were. They had to find a way to get out of this without help.

Very, very slowly, the siphoned energy from the sleeping river elemental and used it to guide currents around their boat. Luckily, the tide was coming in, so the dominant current mostly pushed them in the right direction, but Seren used magic to nudge it around rocks and old pillars until eventually, they glided into the dock.

The twins didn't wait for the disheveled dockhand. Reggie leapt out while David stood on the bow and tossed them a rope. They secured it and then David threw a line from the stern, which Reggie pulled until the boat was parallel with the docks.

"Do you need a hand?" asked a person with so much hair and so many sweaters that Seren couldn't guess at what they looked like underneath all the layers

"Only if you want us to move," said Seren. "The boat is leaking slowly, and my prop is smashed. I'll probably need to make hull repairs."

"We can pull her out on the slack tide tomorrow morning," said the dockhand, pushing tangled red curls away from their face. Their voice was husky and chapped from a life on the docks.

"Mama," cried a little kid, running down the dock. "Did you see Old Lila?"

"I did, darling." The dockhand knelt down to be closer to the child's height. "That schooner hasn't ever moved before!"

Seren extended their hand. "My name is Seren and my pronouns are they/them."

"Call me Barb. She/her." Barb stood and shook Seren's hand.

"I have a reservation for a slip for two hours, but I need to extend for at least a day, so I can repair my boat." Seren clasped their hands tight behind their back. They hoped it was only a day. "And do you know of any inns?"

"The Meadmaker," said the Barb at the same time as Reggie and David.

"I'll secure the boat. In the morning, assuming this storm passes, you can assess the damage and tell me how long you plan to stay," said Barb. "We'll square up then."

"Thank you." Seren's stomach growled.

"My little Alex, who's pronouns are she/her, can show you the way to the Inn." Barb ruffled her child's hair. "But keep your eyes open. There are lots of strangers in town, and some have wandering hands."

"Will Alex be okay walking back here alone?" asked Seren.

"Alex will stay at the Inn and help her Aunty Tilly out in the kitchens until I finish up my shift down here." Barb paused and made eye contact with Alex. "And if she even thinks about trying to leave to go explore Old Iron Lila, she will have potato duty for a month."

Alex rolled her eyes. "Follow me, new people. If you see any men wearing cow skins with ugly symbols, ignore then, unless you are ready for face punching."

"But what if I like face punching?" teased Reggie.

Alex shrugged. "Aunty Tilly got punched by one of them. She still has a black eye, but the other guy has two, and him and the other Altzis stay away from the Meadmaker!"

"Well, that makes me happy I'm staying there," said Seren.

Alex gave Seren a grin filled with half-grown adult teeth.

As they got closer, Seren noticed men lurking in shadows. At least one had a turkey vulture painted on his jacket. Every time Seren looked, there were more Altzis, gradually closing in on the group. A chill swept through their body. Their heart raced as the men circled like wolves.

"Are we almost there?" David's hand slid down the bugle at his waist.

"Two more blocks," said Alex

"Stay close," said Reggie.

They made it about ten more steps before the circle of men closed on them.

"You're Seren of Valley-Port, right?" A man, tall and lean like a fir tree, leered at Seren.

They squared their shoulders and made eye-contact. "Who is asking?"

The man stepped closer. "My boss wants to have a conversation with you."

"I don't know who Seren is, but my friends and I are late for work, and you're in our way." Reggie squared their shoulders and stepped between Seren and the man.

"Liar." The man unsheathed a large knife at the same time David, Reggie, and half a dozen Altzis pulled their pistols.

Seren shifted their weight and bent their knees, ready to do something, though they didn't yet know what. Cobblestones covered the street. The surrounding buildings were brick. In theory, as an ambassador, they could work magic with any element, but aside from talking to trees, they'd only trained with air and water. They shook their head. Their thoughts were running in the wrong direction. They should be thinking of a way to resolve this without violence. Seren took a deep breath.

"Put the guns down and we can talk." Seren studied each of them men. No one moved. "Threatening me won't accomplish anything."

The tall man who first spoke adjust his aim, leveling the gun at Seren's head. "You come with us and talk when you meet the boss."

"Jared," whispered a man from the shadows.

"Baxter? What do you want?" Jared didn't look away from the twins' guns.

Seren wished they knew how to metalwork. Then guns wouldn't be a threat at all. They closed their eyes, feeling the air around them. It was dead and still. A wind elemental might have been able to help, if it came to a fight. Of course, if Seren asked it to knock the men off balance, the Elemental could've taken control and used Seren to do a lot more damage.

"There's a child with them. A little girl. Seeing this violence will harm her," whispered Baxter.

Jared rolled his eyes. "It will teach her..."

"All the wrong lessons." A white-haired man Seren assumed was Baxter stepped out of the shadows and put a hand on Jared's shoulder. Seren hoped he'd make the others leave. "Now is not the time or the place to fight. Spare the child's innocence."

Jared's eyes narrowed.

Everything was still. Seren's heart thundered. The tension made their skin crawl. They didn't know who these people were or why they approached with threats if their boss really only wanted to talk.

"He's not going to be happy with us. Jared sheathed the knife and stomped away. His men put their weapons away. Everyone but Baxter melted into the shadows.

"I'm sorry." Baxter walked away with his eyes cast to the ground.

A dozen responses bubbled inside Seren, but they didn't utter any of them, afraid the men might come back to abduct them. The group of Altzis terrified Seren, but this Baxter had saved a lot of lives. Reggie and David wouldn't have let them take Seren without a fight.

CHAPTER SEVEN

Erik had watched Seren drive off dozens of other times, but something felt different. His only connection to Earth's power was through the tides, but sometimes, he got hunches about things. He suspected this was one of those intuitive feelings, though to be honest, he had a hard time telling what ideas were Earth whispering to him and what was anxiety triggered by the world around him.

There were plenty of triggers. David and Reggie had loaded their sacks and the boat with more ammo than he had ever seen, and the Altzis were only part of the motivation for the extra bullets.

"Those Altzis are like bad pennies." The deep voice startled Erik from his thoughts.

"What do you mean?" Erik peeled his eyes away from the river and focused on Johnny Wind. The old man reminded him of a tree on a mountain summit, bent over from years of exposure to the harsh winds.

"Don't tell me none of those pre-flood authors you read uses the old euphemisms."

Erik shrugged. The pre-flood books used a lot of phrases he

didn't understand. Sometimes he deciphered them. Other times he didn't.

Johnny Wind winked. "It means they'll be back."

Erik nodded. "I'm surprised they get away with so much. Hopefully they won't be around long."

"These men aren't anything new. They're mimicking groups that have come before them." Johnny Wind grimaced. "If The Mother put any thought into her purge instead of blindly slashing us with her rage, She could've made sure no mention of those groups survived."

"Are they just as dangerous?" Erik had read about old hate groups. Whenever they appeared in books, they were the kind of villains that gave Erik nightmares. If he had read about them, then others could have too. But why in The Mother's name would people want to imitate the kind of villainy that caused The Flood in the first place?

"Their ideology is. It was contained, but it's leaking, and their support is growing. People find it easier to blame The Flood on those who are different from them because it alleviates the guilt of their ancestors. They twist history to their own will, believing in some alternative truth."

Erik picked at his cuticles, trying to decipher the mage's words. Before he could come up with a question that might lead to clarification, Johnny Wind continued, "A storm is coming. You and Seren are our best chance at weathering it."

Erik didn't argue with him and his abrupt change in subject. Seren, whether they wanted to admit it or not, was an heir and a powerful mage with a direct line to The Mother's power. It wasn't entirely surprising that they would get caught up in something big. But Erik? He was just a regular dock worker with a tight bond to two small water Elementals. He couldn't communicate planet. He had no political status. He wasn't even going to NUNES. How could he help with whatever metaphorical storm Johnny Wind was talking about? He turned to ask, but the man was gone.

Erik watched the sunrise over the choppy harbor, hoping Seren was doing okay with the rough waters. The wind howled. Seren could handle rough seas better than anyone he knew, but Seren only used their connection when Assana made them or there was a life or death situation. Though, Erik thought, if he were Assana's child, disobeying her would be pretty close to a life or death situation.

Assana was kind. She hadn't asked anything of Erik and his family helping him transition. However, the woman controlled the very air they breathed in the Valley-Port region. Crossing her would be a bad idea.

The wind picked up, tousling his hair and almost knocking him off the dock. He grabbed a railing to steady himself. The river writhed with foamy white caps, raging towards the ocean where he could just make out enormous waves swallowing the jetty. Life or death it was. Seren would use their magic and they would be fine.

Confident with Seren's ability to take care of themself, Erik braved the gangplank and tested his balance on the bouncing docks. He held a hand out to each side, imagining that he held a railing even though there wasn't one on the floating sections. He stood still with his eyes closed, feeling the tugs of the current. Once his mind attuned to them, he knew which ways the dock would rock before it did, so he could plant his feet correctly and not fall. He stood a few steps further out, and he reached out to Merri and Mac for help, but they ignored him. So with a push of his own energy, Erik directed the worst currents away from the dock and out to the middle of the river.

This ability was why at nineteen, he was the dock master instead of someone more experienced. Most of the dockhands could feel the currents. Some could talk to Merri and Mac. But Erik was the only one who could actually control the river. Of course, as soon as he stopped willing the currents away, they would come right back, which meant today, he needed to stay on the docks, out in the wind, until boats stopped coming in or else risk a crash that could not only harm the people on the incoming vessel, but also wipe out a section of the docks and the boats tied up there. The wind would keep some people off the water. The Mother provided for her children, but She didn't always make things easy. There were always a handful who didn't eat if they didn't fish.

By lunchtime, Erik was shaking. June was a fickle month—one where it could be sweltering hot or snowing. He guessed today was in the fifties, but the whipping wind made it feel far colder, and the spray from a river that still had a few licks of winter didn't help. At least the river calmed enough that it didn't need his constant attention.

One helper left for lunch. One went home for the day. Another's shift hadn't started. Erik refused to leave the water and Martin had volunteered to take second lunch even though it was his turn to take first lunch. Erik wondered what motivated the man to willingly delay his meal, but it was hard enough to focus and shiver. Talking would be too much of an effort.

Martin was never one for conversation anyways. He stood at the other end of the dock clutching a pole and staring at the waves. He wasn't moving, and Erik couldn't hear anything but the howl of the wind and the slap of waves battering the docks until eventually, he noticed something else: a roaring hum, and a splashing that was out of time with the harsh tempo Earth was playing. "We've got an incoming vessel! One that's not on the schedule."

Martin nodded, turned and made eye contact with Erik. His mouth was open in a grin that showed all his crooked, yellow teeth. That smile, along with the thumping and hum of the incoming vessels, made Erik shiver.

He reached out through the water, feeling the shape of the boat.

"Let's put them in twenty-one A," said Erik, walking over to an empty slip to make sure all the ropes were still tied tight to the dock.

"All right." Martin's grin widened. "I'll wave them in. You do your magic."

Erik's spine quivered like an earthquake intensifying as it

traveled from one end of the fault line to the other. The chugging got louder. Erik turned his head towards the sound. A ship traveled up the river, propelled forward by two massive wheels rotating on its port and starboard side. It was blood red, and in the middle was turkey vulture with outstretched wings. Altzis. "Seriously? More of these jerks?"

Now Merri and Mac decided to wake up, but instead of helping, they slammed the boat with currents and waves that dispersed as soon as they came within three feet of it. Great. The Altzis had a water mage. A powerful one, if they were holding the Elementals back so effectively.

"I kind of like them."

Erik jumped. Martin stood right behind him, close enough now that he could feel that man's hot breath on his neck.

"Martin, I thought you were waving them in." Erik stepped sideways.

"That isn't necessary." Martin brushed a rough thumb across Erik's cheek. It felt like it left a trail of maggots behind that squirmed everywhere the thumb had touched. "They're smart, practical men. They don't put up with imposters like you."

"Imposter? What are you talking about?" Cold snaked through his body. Did Martin remember how he had looked as a young child? Had he told the Altzis? The very people who celebrated the murder of trans people?

Martin laughed, and it wasn't a sound that suited him—it reminded Erik of an engine in desperate need of corn oil. "Your daddy and I were friends. I remember how excited he was to have a baby *girl.*" Martin's lip curled up at the word girl then he continued speaking. "Assana might be able to make you grow hair on your face and give you the strength of a man, but I know what you are. And I know if she hadn't messed with your biology, I'd be in charge of these docks, earning double the wages and rations."

"My gender had nothing to do with my position," said Erik. His muscles tightened, and his stomach churned. Gender didn't affect someone's ability to be a good dock master. It didn't affect their ability to be good at any job.

"It's not fair." Martin gazed out at the river. "The Altzis *get* that. Nature has a plan, and us humans shouldn't interfere. We shouldn't accuse her of mistakes"

"Assana is an ambassador. She doesn't interfere. She helps us commune with the Earth." There were so many more things Erik wanted to say, but he wasn't sure how to make Martin understand. Transition wasn't interference. It wasn't a correction. Nothing about his body had been a mistake. But transitioning had replaced discord with harmony; dysphoria with euphoria.

Martin turned and looked in Erik's eyes. "The Earth talking to Assana is like you talking to an ant. How often do you talk to ants, Erik?"

"No." Erik shook his head. How could anyone who lived in Valley-Port for forty years think this way? The Altzis had only been here a few days. They might have influenced him, but in order to buy in that quickly, he had to already have agreed with them on some level.

"Erik, there is so much you don't understand about the world." Martin patted Erik in the back and moved hand up.

Something pricked Erik's neck.

The world tilted. His connection the currents faded until he couldn't feel the water all.

"Martin, what did you do?" Erik raised his hand to his neck and felt blood.

The dock swayed, and the world darkened. He fell, expecting to be swallowed by the cold river, but hands grabbed him and hauled him away. He tried to resist, but he couldn't move. Rope twined around his useless hands, and then his sense of touch vanished. He was completely numb, floating in the black silence of drug-induced sedation.

CHAPTER

EIGHT

The Mead Maker Inn made the Compass Rose look like a cottage. Its red brick walls loomed five stories above the ground. The oversized windows revealed people eating on the first floor, and reading, and sleeping on the floors above.

An old person in a tattered apron and black eye patch opened the door and ushered Seren's group inside. There was no foyer or check-in counter, only an open area with wide floors and a bar that wrapped around from the right wall to the rear one.

Alex introduced the person as Aunty Tilly, who promptly said her name was Matilda. After exchanging pronouns and discussing payment for a meal and a room, she seated them at stubby rectangular table and plopped a menu down in front of them that had a dozen different kinds of fish on it, as well as turkey and venison, much to Seren's delight.

Seren ordered turkey stew. David ordered white fish. Reggie got turkey skewers. While they waited for food, Seren surveyed the area. Dented and stained tables were spread through room in no particular order. Almost all of them were full of people eating and drinking. Their voices echoed in the cavernous room, making Seren miss the cozy, low ceilings of the Compass Rose.

Thankfully, there were no Altzis. However, Seren recognized the three BREAD representatives they'd seen in Little Port. Seren wondered if they had navigated through the same storm, or if they had left sooner. Seren considered asking but decided against it. If their method harmed Earth, then the knowledge wasn't worth the temptation.

Seren didn't recognize anyone else. They looked at the twins. "Do you two know anyone in here?"

"Scott, the man with the ginger curls and beard in the right-hand corner, is a smith and metal mage," said David. "Bought a sword from him once. It was really high quality. Then Reggie lost it in a bet."

"Only because you were too distracted by that cute, blonde person from Broken Mill and fell flat on your face when you easily could have walked across that rope."

"They were cute," said David.

"I know," sighed Reggie.

Seren watched the two of them, bemused. "Are there any cute people here that you two should warn me about?"

They shook their heads. "We're on the job out of our home territory. The trip in Broken Mill was for supplies."

"Because you two never flirt with Hailey."

The twins blushed.

"That's different," said Reggie. "Little Port is part of Assana's territory. Normally, it's really safe."

"Whatever you say," said Seren.

Soon, the food came, and the trio was too busy eating to talk or do anything but devour steaming deliciousness. They were so focused on their food that they didn't notice the people surrounding their table until one, tall, blonde-haired woman with icy blue eyes cleared her throat.

"Umm, hi," said Seren, too tired formalities.

"My name is Dr. Fullerton, she/her pronouns." She pointed to an even taller woman with sleek black hair and dark eyes. "This is Dr. Zhao. Her pronouns are she/her."

The younger person, who Seren assumed was Erik's friend Tav, remained at the table across the room, probably guarding the canvas bags under the table. Seren swallowed their food and hoped nothing was stuck to her teeth. "I'm Seren, they/them pronouns please, and these are my friends, David and Reggie."

Dr. Zhao crossed her arms. "You almost crashed into are barge today."

"I'm sorry." Seren kept eye contact with the woman, though the smell of the stew tempted them to ignore her and eat. "The water was rough, and I was getting tired. I'd already navigated through a storm."

"Are you on your way from Valley-Port to NUNES." Dr. Fullerton ran a hand through her hair.

"Yes," Seren said hesitantly. After the encounter with the Altzis, they weren't sure if they really wanted to broadcast their identity. They hadn't had any direct interactions with these people, but Erik knew them, or at least he knew the younger one at the table.

Dr. Fullerton's cold eyes bore into Seren's. "Did you try to hit us on purpose."

"No." Seren tensed.

"A couple weeks ago, Tav and I were attacked by one of your people just outside of Little Port." Dr. Fullerton narrowed her eyes. "I saw your boat approach his shortly after the attack."

Seren's throat tightened. When Seren arrived, they'd been too far away to make out details of the people on board. How had Dr. Fullerton recognized them? "He was late for a meeting with my mother and I, so I went out searching for him."

Seren wanted to say that didn't know what he did, but they were terrible at lying. They wanted to apologize, but then that would mean admitting they knew what he did. And he owed them an apology anyway. Not Seren.

"Do you know why he attacked?" asked Dr. Zhao.

Seren inhaled slowly. They wished their mother was here. She'd know how to answer in a way that would smooth things over instead of making them worse. Relief flooded through them when David cleared his throat.

"Ambassador Freeman is from another territory and was merely stopping by to confirm the representative Valley-Port was sending to NUNES, and to drop off a packet of charts and paperwork too heavy for birds to deliver." David made eye contact with each of the women. "After he concluded his business, Seren informed Asana of his transgression, and my sibling and I escorted him out of Valley-Port with instructions not to return. We don't know why he attacked, but we do not approve of that behavior."

It was exactly the type of thing Seren should've said. And the fact that they hadn't said anything? That they had frozen? It meant they weren't ready for this. Agreeing to go had been a mistake. Who was going to listen them if they couldn't even think of the right words once the pressure was on?

Dr. Zhao tucked a strand of hair behind her ears. "He believes we are a threat and should not be welcome at NUNES. Do you feel the same way?"

"No." Seren bristled, thinking of his narrow-minded remarks. "Of course you should attend."

"Do you believe our science will trigger a second flood?" Dr. Zhao stared at Seren so intently they felt like she could see right through them.

Seren sucked in a deep breath, squeezing the top of their arms. "As long as you don't harm the earth, then you have nothing to fear."

Dr. Fullerton tilted her head. "But you do believe in the Mother, like he does."

"Yes. I have the same connection to the Mother and her power. One day, I'll be an ambassador too." Sometimes Seren wished they didn't have that connection. Then they wouldn't have to worry about one day inheriting their mothers' position and being trapped in Valley-Port. They wouldn't be here under the scrutiny of these adults, they wouldn't be going to vote on a constitution, and they certainly wouldn't be the one tasked with bridging the gap between magic and science.

Dr. Zhao and Dr. Fullerton stared at each other. But Dr. Fullerton spoke. "Would it anger the mother if we were to bring a group of people to shore, clear land, and build our own community?"

"Yes." Seren folded their hands on the table to keep from fidgeting. "If you tried to cut down trees, you'd anger the Mother and forest Elementals."

"So if we offered to buy land in Valley-Port, your mother would decline our request? She would not allow us to settle there?"

Seren shook their head. "I said you couldn't cut down trees. If you want to bring people to Valley-Port, you would have to speak to Assana. There is some vacant housing in Little Port she could assign your people, but if that wasn't enough, she'd have to ask the forest Elementals if they were willing to grow more homes."

"You truly believe that?" asked Dr. Zhao.

Seren nodded. "Have you ever ventured inland from Little Port?"

Both women shook their heads.

"You should come see the land you want to move into before you make assumptions about it." Seren glanced down at their plate. Their stomach growled. "Are there any other questions I can answer for you?"

Both women shook their heads.

"We hope to speak with again, Seren," said Dr. Zhao before her and Dr. Fullerton walked back to their table.

"That was something." David resumed devouring his baked haddock and crab.

"Do you think she believed me, about the trees?" Seren stuff their mouth full of turkey and broth so thick it was really gravy. "Erik said they don't believe in magic."

Reggie shook their head. "That trio's been hanging out here for a few months, traveling back and forth between here and Little Port. They come on land to eat and trade, but they never head inland, and stay long enough to see what the mages can do."

"And when they do see something, they struggle to accept," David added.

As far as Seren knew, the only reason humans survived was because Earth had given Her ambassadors the power to shield their land and people from the storms and tides. They stared at the twins, hoping they would say something to help them make sense of it all. "How could people survive The Floods without any magic?"

"They're smart," said Reggie. "I assume their technology saved them."

Seren frowned down at their now empty plate. "How did they predict storms, catch fish, and navigate?"

"The same way people did before The Flood. With machines and math that makes my head hurt," answered David.

"It's all numbers—enough to make me sick." Reggie mined throwing up, eliciting a snicker from David.

Seren rolled their eyes, utterly perplexed. "So they understand nature so well they predict storms, but they can't accept the Earth is sentient and that trees can be convinced to grow homes for people?"

David shook his head. "They believe what they see and what they can explain. To them, calling it magic means you're too lazy to try and figure it out."

"They called me lazy once." Reggie studied the room, making eye contact with the wait staff. "Nobody calls me lazy."

Frustrated, Seren stared up at the ceiling. Thick spider webs stretched from beam to beam. In one web, a spider the length of Seren's thumb wrapped a fly up in a lethal cocoon. One thing bothered Seren more than anything else.

Mother Earth flooded the planet to rid Herself of poisonous technology, yet these women, isolated from the rest of the world for generations, continued to use advanced technology. Johnny Wind often complained The Mother's wrath was more like a blind giant trampling the earth than a calculated strike. A few folks with limited power questioned Her sentience, but a majority of people feared and rejected that notion. Perhaps the ambassadors overestimated Mother Earth or maybe they didn't know nearly as much as they thought.

CHAPTER NINE

Erik woke in a room so dark he touched his eyes to see if they were open or closed. Hot and damp air clung to his skin like slug slime. The floor below him was metal. The chug chug of the paddle wheels pounding through water reverberated through the floor and in turn, his bones.

"Damn you, Martin," he cursed, but not enough sound came out to fully form words.

His hands and legs were untied, so he groped around the cell. It was just a little longer than him, but not high enough for him to fully stand. There was an iron door at one end with no handle on the inside, and no matter how hard he pushed and kicked, it wouldn't budge. He tried until his limbs ached and his head spun. He had no clue what these people wanted with him, but based on the stories he heard, it wasn't anything good. This boat had come up the river a few days after the first one left. Could this be the one who had been locked up for murder? Was Erik going to be his next victim?

If they were heading out into the ocean, he doubted he'd live to find out. The boat was clunky, better suited for churning its way up and down rivers with steam-powered paddles than braving the ocean during a squall. Unless the water mage on board was exceptionally talented, the steamship would go down, and he'd slowly suffocate in this little box unless he was somehow able to reach Seren.

They could technically communicate with each other through water since both of them had the ability to manipulate and communicate with it. However, because of Seren's fear of their own power, they seldom used it socialize.

"I'll talk to you when I'm in town," they said every time he mentioned it. When they first started dating, he had been suspicious that they were seeing someone else back at the lake, but as time went on, he learned to trust them and settled for talking to them when they could meet in person. The times he had communicated with Seren through the water had been urgent situations, like when he'd capsized his boat and Atlantik ignored his request for help.

His current situation was as urgent as it got. He had to try to reach Seren. It wouldn't work unless Seren was looking at water connected to the water he used. The stronger the connection, the clearer the picture. When Seren was on the lake that flowed into the river, they had a good connection, but if they were at an inland stream that only trickled into the lake, and dripped diluted by other waters, the image was distant and rippled. It was a long shot, but it was his only hope.

He focused on his breathing until all thoughts left his mind but those searching for water. He searched and searched, but he only felt steam condensing on steel walls. He knew there was water below him, but no matter how hard he focused, he couldn't get past the steel.

His rate picked up, but he crushed the rising panic. Was he still drugged? Or was there something about this room that prevented him from reaching the water? He pressed his palms against the walls, and traced every inch of wall, floor, and ceiling. He couldn't sense any symbols carved into the metal. If they were drawn, it was too dark to see.

He was trapped. But he refused to panic.

He slowed his breathing down, praying to the Mother, Elementals, and every half-forgotten deity he could think of he didn't run out of air before his captors opened the door.

CHAPTER TEN

Even though the sun was just beginning to rise, Port's Mouth was already waking up. Windows opened, letting fresh morning air into houses. Seren's stomach grumbled when they smelled baking bread. They wanted to stop and eat all the food every time the smell of eggs wafted out from a kitchen and teased their nose.

Seren pulled a handful of nuts out of their knapsack and chewed on them. Getting their boat out of the water was their first priority. Breakfast could wait. They shared the nuts with the twins, who were also longingly eyeing the cafés and kept trudging down to the boat.

Barb waited for them on the docks. Mist rose off the water and curled around her feet. Seren grinned, happy to see that the water smooth like glass and not full of waves and maelstroms. "It's almost a different river than the one I came in on last night."

"The Piscataqua River doesn't stay quiet long, but she sure is a wonder when she does," said Barb, gazing out at the water.

Barb untied the stern line and tossed it to Seren. Then she undid the bowline and took it herself. "Let's walk her to the ramp."

The task sounded simple. However, there were dozens of other boats tied up to the wharf. Had it just been a straight pier, it might have been a quick task, but seven additional sections of dock shot out to the right and left, meaning they would walk towards land on one straight section, then out, around, back in, and straight again. While doing this, they had to move *The Whaler* around all of the other boats, which meant going out on them.

"Wouldn't it be easier if I rowed to ramp?" Seren perched on the edge of the dock. "The leak is slow—I'm not going to sink in the short span of time it would take to get to the ramp."

Reggie stood beside Seren with their arms crossed. "You see anyone rowing there right now?"

"That is odd." Early morning when the water was one of the best times to go fishing. If they were on the water anywhere between Lake Attitash and Little Port, there would be dozens of people out in small craft and kayaks, casting lines and nets. "Why is nobody out?"

The twins glanced back and forth between Seren, Barb, and each other. Reggie paled. David bit his lip. "We'll tell you when we get *The Whaler* up on dry land."

"Make sure you don't fall in." Barb shuddered and stared at the water for a minute before getting back to her task.

Seren wanted to argue, but if something scary lurked in the water, they agreed they'd rather not know until after the risk of falling in had passed. If they knew what it was, they would spend more time searching for it than focusing on what they were doing.

The process of moving *The Whaler* around all the other boats and sections of dock seemed to take forever, but during that time, Seren didn't see any reason to avoid being in the small boat on the water. By the time they got to the end, people were making their way down with oars, fishing poles, and tackle boxes. The sun was visible at the mouth of the river, looking like it was just a few stories above the water, even though they knew it burned light years away.

Seren leapt from the last boat—a small wooden trawler—to land. Dried barnacles and seaweed crunched under feet. "So if the water is so dangerous now, why not wait until later to pull the boat out?"

The twins, then Barb, landed on shore beside Seren and they started walking the boat to the ramp. Seren could see Alex there now, waiting with two donkeys.

"Would you want to pull the boat out in chop even half as rough as what you pushed through last night?" asked Barb.

Seren shook their head, and a breeze caught the tips of their hair and ears. It stirred little ripples in the water.

"Did you see any of them?" asked Alex, wide-eyed, bouncing on her heels.

"See what?" Seren hoped someone would finally tell them what they had been avoiding.

A mischievous grin broke on Alex's face. "Whenever the slack tide is at dawn, sea monsters come into the river to have a feast! There are the Thousand Jellies. No one can tell if they are really one jellyfish or a thousand separate ones. The venom is so strong that no one who gets close enough to touch it lives to tell the tale."

"We have work to do," scolded Barb, but as they hooked the ropes up to the donkeys and lined up the rollers, Alex entertained them with tales.

"I didn't see any jellies." By the time Seren was half way across the dock, the water had been clear enough to see down to the bottom.

"You wouldn't have seen it," said Alex. "Not unless it was dark out or you were looking right into its massive, stringy red eye."

"Then how do you know it exists?"

"It exists," said Reggie. "David almost fell into its eye once."

"Almost got pushed." Shivering, David wrapped his arms around himself. "Thankfully, my twin grabbed me by the ponytail with one hand. The man who pushed me lost his balance and fell into the eye. I'll never forget the sound of his screams as the tentacles wrapped around him and dissolved his flesh."

Alex shuddered at the end of the story, and Barb glared at David.

If it was Reggie who told the story, Seren might have assumed they were exaggerating. David was usually the more serious one. But jellyfish wasn't the part of the story that sent chills down Seren's spine. It was the violence. The attempt at murder.

Seren let the last roller thud to the ground as a knot twisted in their stomach.

Mischief gleamed in Reggie's eyes. They were probably waiting for Seren retort with a complaint about the lack of warning. But the tale of death reminded Seren why NUNES mattered. The more people traveled between region, the more they fought with each other, and they couldn't just go back to being isolated, not when there were whole towns and territories where people struggled to eat and make it through harsh winters. Uniting people and sharing resources was their best shot at keeping the peace. Their best shot at surviving.

Barb shouted, "Haul Barney, Haul Baily," and the two donkeys brayed and started walking forward, pulling the whaler out of the water. As it rolled up onto the wooden rollers, Seren swore they saw drips that were more the texture of a jellyfish's guts than water drop off and slither back into the river.

"Did I ever tell you about the Gator-Dragon ?" Reggie picked up a log and moved it in front of the whaler.

"The sea is full of genetic masterpieces," said a chilly voice.

Seren looked up and saw one of the BREAD representatives walking down to the landing.

"'Monster' is such a crude term," said Dr. Fullerton. "Those creatures are creations—the work of human geneticists who should be praised as heroes, but their bones lie in an unmarked, water-logged grave."

"Whether they're made by humans or The Mother, they are still monsters," said Barb. "We could use an extra pair of hands, if you wouldn't mind helping."

Dr. Fullerton crossed her arms. "Last night in the tavern, we heard rumors you came in on a flying boat."

Seren ran their hands through their hair, waiting for their brain to switch from fighters and sea monsters to Dr. Fullerton showing up and wondering who else had been in that storm to even see their boat fly.

"We've been trying to master flight for decades. Before The Flood, humans used all kinds of flying machines," Dr. Fullerton continued. "We want to bring them back. Honestly tell us how you made her fly, and we will help you repair her."

"It was magic," said Seren even though they doubted the women would believe her. "I closed my eyes, reached out to the Earth's power, and used it to make a bubble of air that lifted the boat above the waves. The wind blew us the rest of the way here."

"I'm serious. How did you make it fly?"

"I'm being serious too." Seren stared into the woman's eyes, begging her to believe them.

"It's true," said David and Reggie simultaneously. "We were on the boat and saw them do it."

"Can you do it now?" whispered Dr. Fullerton.

Seren stared at woman, waiting for her to blink and break eye contact. She didn't. Seren's throat itched at the idea of using magic, but they hated being called a liar, and it would be easier for the mages and people from the solar barges to communicate if the BREAD Team at least acknowledged that mages were real. The snippets of intelligence they had about the Altzis implied they were going to vote in favor of the central government having more power and then in turn use it to their own benefit. In most cases, Assana had instructed Seren to vote on middle options. Give the government too much power and people risk losing freedom but give it too little and it won't actually do anything. Seren thought they were fine without a central government, but Assana said that not all areas were as prosperous as Valley-Port, and by uniting as one nation, the more prosperous regions, mostly ambassador lead, could help the ones where people struggled to survive with limited magic and technology. Seren had no clue how Dr. Fullerton's people planned to vote, but Seren hoped to get their support to make sure no one group ended up with too much power.

Seren's hands coiled behind their back. They closed their eyes and opened their mind. Their skin crawled with ants and no amount of scratching could relieve the itch.

Ignoring wormy noose on their throat and the churning in their stomach, they reached out to Earth's raw power. They wrapped themself in it like a blanket and let it mingle with their own energy. Pushing the power out, they shaped it into a slithering snake. They guided under the boat, blew air out of their mouth and pictured it inflating until the boat hovered two feet off the ground.

"Impossible!" Dr. Fullerton rushed towards the boat.

"There must be some kind of propulsion under here." She laid on her back and slid under the boat.

"Don't!" shouted Seren through gritted teeth.

"What's going on?"

Feet scurried down the street.

"Aunty Rita, what are you doing?" Tav skidded to a stop just past the boat.

"Get out from under there before they drop it on you," said Dr. Zhao.

"They're not going to drop it," said Tav.

"Not on purpose, but I can't hold it much longer." Sweat dripped down Seren's temples. The bickering distracted them. The boat quivered and dropped an inch.

Tav and Dr. Zhao rushed forward and pulled Dr. Fullerton away.

"What were you doing?" asked Tav.

Relieved, Seren lowered the boat back onto the rollers and sunk to the ground, not caring that damp seaweed soaked through their pants.

"Looking for some kind of propulsion system." Dr. Fullerton frowned at the boat while she brushed dirt and seaweed off of her pants.

"Did you find one?" Dr. Zhao stepped in front of her and gently wiped mud of her cheek.

"No." Dr. Fullerton took Dr. Zhao's hand then turned towards Seren. "Tell me how you did that?"

"The same way I did last time. I reached out to the Earth's energy and made it do what I wanted."

"That's not how things work," snarled Dr. Fullerton.

Seren grunted. It was more complicated than their words implied, but getting into more detail about The Mother and Her relationship with the ambassadors would only make these people think Seren was even more full of it.

"I think they believe what they're saying." Dr. Fullerton put a hand on the Dr. Zhao's arm.

Dr. Zhao smiled. And then they started arguing about Seren like they weren't standing right there.

"Ahh—maybe they're modified like the Thousand Jellies or the Gator Dragon."

"They could've been given an implant a birth. If their mother always told them it was magic, then they would believe it."

"It is magic!" Seren stood up. "No one put a chip in my head or modified my DNA. I have a connection to The Mother and her magic that lets me manipulate the elements."

They all stopped talking, steered at Seren, and walked away muttering about samples they would need to take from Seren to determine if they were genetically modified, had cybernetic implants, or both. They wanted to know what Seren's brainwaves looked like.

"If they touch you, I will shoot them," said Reggie.

"Science can't stop bullets," said David. "Can it?"

"They can make armor that stops bullets," said Barb. "I've seen it action. An Altzi shot Dr. Zhao. Her vest caught his bullet. It left a big bruise, but it didn't break her skin."

Seren shuddered. More fighting. More violence. This was why the

Elementals were riled up. Why Merri and Mac were so quick to try and drown the Altzi that threatened Erik.

Reggie smirked. “If those women touch Seren, I’ll shoot them in the head.”

“You shouldn’t be shooting anyone,” said Seren. The Altzis seemed like the biggest threat, but they weren’t solely responsible for the violence. Reggie and David were technically on their side, but they played a part in the growing violence too. There was no group to blame, and Seren suspected trying to blame anyone at all would make things worse.

CHAPTER ELEVEN

Hinges screamed as the door opened. Erik crouched. His head spun from hunger and dehydration, but he wasn't going down without a fight. He lunged, ready to kick, bite, punch, and claw past his captors. If he could make it to the deck, he could jump overboard and try to contact Seren or Assana. If he was lucky, help would arrive before he drowned.

He got three steps before a gushing burst of salty water punched him in the chest, forcing air out of his lungs and his feet out from under him. His back and head slammed against metal. Feet pounded on the floor, and hands hauled him up and out towards the light. Sun seared his eyes, which had grown accustomed to the utter blackness. He flailed, trying to get free, but it was useless. He was weak from spending Earth knows how long in that cell. His assailants were strong and twice his size.

"What do you want with me?" he hissed with his parched voice.

The men laughed. Spots and glares distorted their faces. He closed his eyes and opened his mind, mentally reaching for the tides. Feeling them rush through his mind calmed his racing heart. Based on the speed, depth, and direction, they were halfway between Little Port and the Port's Mouth and far enough offshore that he couldn't swim back if he were to jump overboard. However, he was close enough to the water that he could use it. He called the stronger currents to ever so subtly shift the boat towards shore while also sending a picture out on the water, him in captivity, and sent it to Seren, hoping they were close enough to the ocean to see it.

"Martin swore you were a little girl when you were born. Is that true?" asked a man with a gruff voice.

Erik didn't respond. His throat was dry. His mind was split between the message for Seren and altering the tide.

"My name is Domhnall," said the gruff voice. "Will you tell me what your name really is? Erik is not a girl's name."

"I'm not a girl. I never have been." The fact that someone had labeled him as female when he was born didn't mean he had ever been a girl.

Domhnall grinned, revealing a mouthful of crooked yellow teeth. "Either Martin just wanted to get rid of you, or your local ambassador is more powerful than most."

"Martin wanted my position as dock master," said Erik. It was the truth, and maybe it would convince the Altzis to let him go.

"I believe you, but his jealousy doesn't mean he lied about your birth sex. Tell me, Erik, who are you really?"

A group of men hulked behind Domhnall. Erik ignored them and stared into Domhnall's eyes. Their color reminded him of bread mold. "I am Erik, a master of tides and docks."

Domhnall cocked his head. "How long have you been a man?"

Erik didn't blink. "Always."

"You're speaking truth." Domhnall's brow furrowed. "Sensing lies is the one magical gift The Mother blessed me with. I sense no lies in your words."

Hope buoyed in Erik. "Does that mean I can go?"

Domhnall laughed. "No. I'm afraid my introduction may have been misleading."

Hope transformed into a heavy dread that crushed Erik until he could barely breathe. "Why am I here?"

Domhnall stared at him.

Thoughts raced through Erik's mind as he tried to figure out what these men wanted with him. He'd never even met an Altzi until a few days ago. "Is it because of the man I almost drowned?"

Domhnall tilted his head, but he didn't speak. Sun glisten off his bald head. His chapped lips pressed together. He didn't blink.

Erik's heart raced. Maybe this was some kind of retaliation. "He attacked me first. I just defended myself. I didn't know the Elementals would take it so far."

Domhnall stepped forward. "Now that bond you have with those Elementals is interesting. Will you tell me more about it?"

Confusion jumbled Erik's thoughts. "Are there not Elementals where you come from?"

Domhnall signed. "Boy, I know what Elementals are. I want to know about your Elementals. Merri and Mac, right?"

"They can be mischievous, but are fairly cooperative to people they like," Erik said slowly. What if they wanted revenge against Merri and Mac for almost drowning the man. Erik had never heard of people hurting Elementals, but that didn't mean it wasn't possible.

Domhnall narrowed his eyes. "How strong are they?"

Erik's breath snagged as he inhaled. "Why do you want to know?"

Domhnall put his hand on his hip, beside the hilt of a blade. "Because I do. Answer my question."

Erik had a feeling that no matter what his response was, he would regret it. He suspected Domhnall's intentions were malicious, even though he didn't know what they were. They wouldn't have bothered with the kidnapping if they thought Erik would be willing to give the information they sought.

He took a deep breath. "No."

One of Domhnall's thugs punched him in the face.

Erik reached out to the water. *Hurry, Seren. I need help!*

The largest thug kicked his shins. Another punched him in the stomach. He tried to only think of the tides and the water. He managed to drown out the questions, but soon, the pain became too much. It filled his mind like the ocean flooding a tide pool until everything hurt. He lost his sense of the tides. He let go of the image he was trying to send. He just wanted it to stop.

"Answer my question." Domhnall snarled at him while two men held him upright. "How strong are Merri and Mac?"

"Strong," Erik whispered before the man could land another blow. "If they chose to, they could keep any boat from entering the river. They could push all the docks out to sea. They could rise up and swallow the homes along the river. They could drown anyone brave enough to set foot on the banks and control people like me if they chose to. They relinquished the other man because I *asked*, not because I commanded it."

"I appreciate your cooperation," said Domhnall. Instead of hitting him, the man patted him on the back and guided him over to another. "Get him some water and bread when you bring him to the brig."

The brig was a luxury compared the cell Erik had been in previously. Sure, it had bars on three sides and a wall on the fourth, but it had a cot, a bench, a pot for him to piss in, and a small table with bread and water. Most importantly, it had light. It wasn't much, but after spending an eternity in darkness, the sunlight trickling through the porthole was heaven.

After devouring the food, he lay on the cot, trying to think beyond his throbbing body. Everything hurt, but the ache in his heart was the worst. The Altzis he met earlier in the week had been narrowed minded jerks. He worried they'd hurt him because he was trans. But there was something bigger at play than hate if they wanted to know about the strength of the Elementals that lived at the main entrance to the Valley-Port region.

He knew the slightly more humane cell was some kind of reward for saying what the Altzis wanted. Leaving him in the dark to starve for a day or two before interrogating him had been a tactic. This was only the beginning. He hadn't heard about the Altzis interrogating people, he had read enough salvaged novels where the villains, and sometimes the protagonist, tortured people for information. In many of those novels, the victims either escaped, got rescued, or died. Unfortunately, knowing didn't do anything to help him resist.

No good would come out of giving them what they wanted, but unlike the heroes in the old novels, he had no experience with violence, and no idea how to resist. Maybe he just lacked the will. Maybe in real life, nobody resisted.

Exhaustion overpowered fear, and Erik drifted into dreamless sleep.

Screeching hinges jolted him awake.

He tensed, but he didn't have the energy or the will to stand. If they were going to bring him back to the deck, they would have to drag him.

A reedy girl tiptoed into the room. Her gray dress was filled with more air than flesh, probably a hand-me-down from someone larger. A matching bonnet half slid off of her head.

"Hi." Erik titled his head towards her. If she were a slave or another prisoner, maybe she could help him escape.

The girl jumped, bowed her, and continued to the chamber pot.

Dark circled and bruises blended with the shadows the bonnets cast on her face. Her huddled posture and down cast eyes told him she was afraid. But was she more afraid of him or whoever sent her in to his cell?

"What's your name?" Erik's abdomen muscles burned as he sat up.

The girl poured the chamber pot's contents into a bucket and left. Someone shut and locked the door behind her. She put it down just outside the cell and threw her arms around one of Domhnall's oversized thugs.

"Thank you, sweetie," the man whispered. "If I could've, I would've done it myself, but Domhnall will hurt you if I disobey him again."

Erik couldn't see the girl, but her shadow nodded. "Daddy, what did the man do?"

"You're too young to understand."

"Is he as bad as the man who hit me when Domhnall made me deliver food last week?"

"No, sweetie. I would've bribed one of the older girls to clean the cell if he was."

"But he is still bad?"

"It's complicated." Footsteps echoed as the man walked away.

Erik made a mental note to learn more about that man. If he had reason to go against Domhnall, maybe he could become an ally. Maybe he'd want to get his daughter away from Domhnall and the other thugs.

Erik slipped in and out of a fit full sleep and the door hinges screamed as it flew open and Domhnall strode into the room with a dozen knives on his belt. Erik nearly shit his already soiled pants. Domhnall sat down next to Erik with a grin saying, "You said Merri and Mac cooperate with those they like. What qualities do they like in a person?"

Erik didn't respond.

Domhnall unsheathed his largest knife. It was wide near the hilt. The blade curved, getting narrower and narrower until it formed a point that gleamed in the sun.

Every ounce of Erik's intention to resist faded. "They like people who respect them, the land, and other people. They like confidence. Tenacity. Kindness and love. They do not like people who harbor hate in their heart."

"Good, it seems like you're a smart boy." Domhnall took the knife out of his belt and started sharpening it on a whetstone. "Isn't it fascinating how Elementals have different morals and personalities?"

Erik stared down at the floor. He might not have the courage to resist Domhnall, but maybe he could learn a few things before he escaped. "What are the Elementals like where you come from?"

Domhnall grinned at Erik. "Many sleep but the wood Elementals of the Quaking Forest only allow the bravest men to hunt, and the one in the ancient apple tree hungers for the flesh of sinners."

"Sinners?"

"Those who take what isn't theirs. Those who resist the role The Mother gave him. Those who twist and abuse Her power, like the witch, Assana."

"Assana?" Erik closed his eyes. He hated the way this man said "witch". He wanted to correct the man and tell him that she was an ambassador and knew more about Earth than anyone else, but the steady *slink slink* of the knife on the whetstone was like a mind control machine from an old science fiction novel. It bypassed his consciousness, telling the unconscious, instinctual part of his mind how sharp the knife would be and how much it would hurt slicing his skin open.

"I've heard all kinds of stories about her twisting trees into houses and changing people's sexes." Domhnall wrinkled his nose. "We are not meant to change the gifts the mother gave us. Tell me, Erik, what is the most terrifying thing you have seen her do?"

"Execution." The word felt like choking on barnacles. There had only been three executions in his life time, and for each of them, it was the Elementals in control, not Assana, but Erik left out that fact as he describe each one in detail. He didn't want her to sound weak. He wanted to scare Domhnall.

But if hearing about people being fed to trees, drown, or having air sucked out of their lugs scared him, he didn't show it.

"I like your honesty." The man put the whetstone on the bench and sheathed his knife. "So tell me more about Assana. What are her strengths? What are her weaknesses?"

Between questions about the river Elementals and Assana, Erik had a sinking feeling the Altzis were planning to invade Valley-Port. He needed to warn Seren and Assana, but when tried to reach out to the water, he only felt an ache in his head. The harder he tried, the more it hurt.

CHAPTER
TWELVE

After walking on cobblestones for ten minutes, Seren was convinced they were one of humanities worst inventions. Why had The Mother allowed them to survive The Flood? The rocks were uneven, making Seren feel like they were walking in a slow boat meandering through choppy water.

As if that wasn't bad enough, their stomach ached liked they'd been punched half a dozen times, and they couldn't tell if it was from overuse of magic, a pulled muscle, or eating too many breakfast sandwiches. The discomfort and the exhaustion made them wish they were home with a book or snuggled up with Erik.

Seren paused at a cross road, leaning up against a wall with their eyes closed. One road led down to the river, where Seren could use magic and the river to send an update to Assana. They could use the tides to chat with Erik, who would probably be down at the docks in Little Port, just about to break for lunch. The other road led to a post office that delivered messages via trained gulls, hawks, or owls for a hefty fee.

"The post is a waste of resources for you," muttered David as Seren turned towards the post office.

"No more magic," was the only justification Seren could come up with. Thinking about opening themself back up to Earth and Her power made them queasy. They'd rather pay to have a bird deliver the letters.

Neither David nor Reggie tried to dissuade them again.

Seren relaxed for the rest of the walk, taking slow breaths and trying to picture Erik out on the docks, skin glowing gloriously in the afternoon sun while he guided boats in and out of Little Port. They imagined amusement flickering in his eyes as he read about using ropes to guide *The Whaler* to shore, and how anger would redden his cheeks when he read about how the twins neglected to tell Seren about the Thousand Jellies. Seren kept those thoughts in their mind as they walked over brick roads and more of those cursed cobble stones to an old warehouse full of salvaged motors.

Seren had never seen so many engine parts in one place. The rusty metal building was large enough to house a schooner if it could ever be coaxed off the water, and small engine parts filled the whole thing. There was a whole wall full of propellers.

Grinning, Seren ran over to it, scanning for one that would fit theirs. The motor had been old long before The Flood, so by now, the thing was ancient, but then, most of the motors still running were. Anything with an electric start was either no good or needed to be retro fitted. The only useful ones were simple engines that could be converted to run off of used cooking oil and fermented waste. The others were melted and repurposed.

"There's nothing like this at home," said Seren, zooming in on the blue propellers.

"Port's Mouth is a big city and was a busy port long before The Flood," said David.

"Look up in the seventh row, three props from the left end." Seren pointed at a prop that resembled the one they broke.

"We'll go get the owner and find out how much it is. Hopefully Assana thought ahead and gave you enough coin."

"She did," said Seren, "but she told me not to tell you how much because she thought it would make you want to bring more bullets."

"I guess we're even then," said David as he walked out of the building.

"For what?"

"For not telling you about the Thousand Jellies. Now come on, we still need a shaft and a gear box."

Seren gazed at the prop one more time, memorized its exact location and followed Reggie over to the section where the shafts were kept. By the time David got back with one of the marina's workers, Seren had located everything they needed but the gearbox.

Much to the twins' dismay, Seren didn't even try to haggle. After paying, they clutched the propeller as close to their body as they could without hurting themself, made Reggie carry the shaft, and David the spare spark plugs. Seren trotted across the boatyard towards *The Whaler*. "Do you think Scott is awake and human now? Can we go see if he can make the gearbox?"

Reggie peered up at the sun. "It's still before noon, but it's worth a shot. If we end up waking him, at least we know he'll be sober."

"So, yes," said David. "We can go see Scott and get him to fix your gearbox but promise me you will haggle and not just pay what he asks."

"Fine. I'll promise, but I'm not leaving his forge without my gears."

David grimaced. "Just make sure he doesn't know how bad you need them, or he'll ask for something utterly ridiculous simply because he can."

Scott's smith shop was dark, hot, humid and reeked of burning metal and alcohol, but none of the ovens, bellows or other pieces of equipment was even in use.

"He smells like he just pissed his pants," said David.

"How should we wake him?" Reggie arched an eyebrow at David. "Dump a bucket of water on his head? Poke him with his irons?"

"Scott?" called Seren walking over to the sleeping smith. "Will you wake up?"

"That won't work," laughed David.

Reggie kicked Scott in the ass. He jolted awake, pulling a pistol out from the folds of his ale-stained shirt. "Who's there?"

"It's customers, you big oaf." Reggie smirked at him with their arms crossed. "We have a job for you."

He blinked, tucked the gun into his belt, and rubbed his eyes. "What can I help you folks with?"

"I need my boat's lower gear box fixed," said Seren. "I can't find a spare anywhere in town."

"How'd it break?" he said through a yawn.

"I hit some rocks. I got replacements for everything but this." They took the broken gears out of their bag and showed them to Scott.

"You got a problem with magic?" he asked.

"Only when I'm the one working it." Seren scratched their throat.

"So you've got gifts yourself?" he made eye contact and took a step closer, looking more alert than he had a few seconds ago.

"Some." Seren didn't want to elaborate in case he asked them for some kind of service trade. "What does magic have to do with making new gears?"

"The quickest way to fix it is with my magic. Cheapest way is to make molds and cast them the traditional way."

"Can you elaborate on the difference in time and price?"

"I'd have to take some very precise measurements, so getting mold right could take a week or two, and..."

Seren shook their head. If they waited a week, they'd miss NUNES. If they missed NUNES, there would be one less voice advocating for Earth, one less person who saw the value of magic and science, and a greater chance the Altzis would sway people to their side. "I need a replacement now."

“Then you’ll want me to use magic. As a user yourself, you probably understand it has a cost beyond money.”

“All too well.” Seren had used magic more in the past two days than they normally did in two months, and it was starting to take its toll. It choked them, pulling them back towards home. They wondered if the smith had a similar problem, and that was why he always drank.

“What kinds of things can you do?” asked Scotty.

Seren placed the gearbox in an empty spot they found on a cluttered table and crossed their arms. “We’re not here to talk about what I can do, but what you can do. You haven’t even looked at the part I need repaired.”

“I don’t need to,” he snapped. “I can feel it—how it was, how it is and how it wants to be. If I use my power, I’ll have it good as new in an hour, but I’ll be left exhausted and defenseless. Money isn’t going to stop anyone from raiding my shop while I’m sleeping off the magic.”

Seren frowned.

Reggie laughed. “And what was protecting your shop while you were passed out drunk? We walked in here without tripping any alarms.”

Scott’s cheeks reddened. “I may have been too drunk to properly set the wards last night.”

“I see. Would a night of unlimited free drinks be sufficient payment?” asked Seren.

David grimaced. “Be careful what you offer. This man has a hollow leg.”

“I get plenty of mead doing repairs for Matilda,” he said. “And material is not something I need more of right now. Tell me about your powers.”

Seren looked at David and Reggie. They nodded. Seren clasped their hands tight behind their back and took a deep breath. “I’m not sure what I can really do, since I only use my magic when my mother makes me or if I am in a life or death situation.”

Reggie folded their arms. "Levitating the boat for Dr. Fullerton wasn't life or death."

"Kind of was," they muttered. Seren may only be one vote, but something in their gut said that one vote mattered. This whole mission was life or death for everyone on the planet, and convincing BREAD that mages were more than zealots or charlatans brought the one step closer saving humanity from Mother Earth's wrath.

"So your talent is with air?"

"Air and water, mostly. I can make things levitate for short amounts of time, but I get worn out quickly." Their abilities with plant magic weren't developed enough to mention. They could talk to trees, but they couldn't get them to do anything.

Scott smiled. "What's the biggest thing you ever levitated?"

"My boat," said Seren.

Scott's grin widened. "If you can retrieve the metal printer from the marsh for me, then I will fix your gear box."

"I'm not going into the marsh," said David.

"We survived last time." Reggie snorted. "And Seren has a thing for marshes. Remember when they were a kid and tried to make marsh perfume?"

Seren's cheeks flushed. They liked smells other people hated and aside from the ocean, marshes were their favorite place to relax. "What's a metal printer?"

"A machine makes metal parts efficiently than a person without magic can."

"But you have magic, so why do you need the machine?"

He shrugged. "Why do you avoid using your magic?"

"It has a price," they whispered.

"Exactly," said Scott. "I'll pay the price and use my magic for you as long as you use yours to get me something that means next time someone comes in here with broken gears, I don't have to choose between getting the job done quickly and using my magic."

"Then we have a deal," said Seren.

Scott extended a hand for them to shake and proceeded to

describe where the machine was supposed to be. The more he talked, the creases around David's frown deepened and Reggie's wild grin grew. What could really be so bad about a marsh?

"That could've been worse," said Reggie.

"But the Marsh?" David shuddered.

Seren froze. "Don't tell me there are giant jellyfish or gator whatevers there too."

"There are no monsters," said David. "Unless you count the Elemental as one."

"The Great Salt Marsh is rather particular about who She allows to pass and who She sucks up for breakfast." Reggie licked their lips. "And that is She with a capital S. She has a rather high and mighty sense of herself."

"Lovely. And is there a specific time when it is safer to go there?" Seren ran their hands through their hair. They loved marshes. They did *not* love arrogant Elementals.

The twins shook their heads.

"You don't have to do this," said David. "There are junk shops all over the city. One of them might have the part you need."

"Searching through the shops will take forever. How bad is the Elemental?"

David and Reggie looked at each other, one frowning and the other beaming.

"We crossed the marsh once, and survived, but the person who was chasing us didn't. Like we said, She is picky about who She lets cross," said David.

"Though it does help if you ask first," added Reggie.

"If it gets my boat fixed and me out of this town, then it will be worth it." Seren resumed their trek, turning their back on the smithy and diving into the herd of people wobbling over the cobblestones like drunken sheep. Scott had given them a pretty good description of what he wanted and where he last spotted it, but Seren found themself wondering if it would still be there when they got to that part of the Marsh.

The Port's Mouth was a bigger city than any Seren had been in before, but it still didn't take that long for them to walk across the whole thing. The change between city and wilderness was drastic. They walked to the end of a street crowded with a rainbow of different houses, and it ended with a wall of birch trees. It was impassible, save for a narrow game path.

"Do I ask permission to enter here or wait until we get to the Marsh?" asked Seren.

"Both," said Reggie. The trees rustled in agreement even though there was no wind.

"All right then." Resisting the impulse to scratch their already raw throat, Seren opened their mind to the magic. Old trees creaked slowly while saplings rustled with impatience. None of the trees appeared to move much, but Seren felt branches of awareness reaching towards their mind. Power curled around their throat like living, snaky vines. They sucked in ragged breaths and clenched their fists, determined to resist the pressure pulling them downwards.

"Can we pass through to the Marsh?" they said out loud while visualizing themself, David and Reggie walking through the forest, staying on the path, and not touching anything. The trees rustled with a breeze Seren couldn't feel, revealing a path just wider than David's shoulders.

Thank you, thought Seren before shutting most of the magic out of their mind. Vines released their throat but snaked under the imaginary door that shielded their mind from magic. They couldn't quite shake the feeling of being watched as they stepped forward onto the path. Tree branches swung out and pushed them forward and closed the path behind them.

Seren sucked in air like they had just surfaced from a long underwater swim. With each step they took forward, the trees picked up their roots and shimmied on to the path behind them.

Through the vine holding their magic-blocking door open, Seren could sense the trees pushing them on. Whenever the wind blew, it seemed as if the birches were saying, *Hurry up. Get through and get out. Hurry up.*

"Is it just me or does the land around the Port's Mouth seem more hostile than the land at home?" whispered Seren. They knew whispering wouldn't really make a difference in a forest, especially with their mind a little open to the magic. It was a two-way channel. If they could sense the forest's mood, the forest could sense theirs, and possibly influence it.

"The forests south of the port are dormant enough for people to hunt in and travel though, but there are no more ambassadors north of the city until we get to Merry Basin," said Reggie. "Earth must fend for Herself."

"That makes sense." Seren's shoulders sagged and their pace slowed down. When Assana got old and retired, Seren would take her place. They wouldn't just be in charge of the people, but of placating the Earth and keeping monsters out of the river. Power came with a price, but before they could fret about the cost, they had to survive this trip.

CHAPTER

THIRTEEN

After an hour of trudging through a humid, buggy forest in which they didn't dare swat away the swarming insects, Seren, David, and Reggie emerged onto a rocky outcrop overlooking a vibrant salt marsh that stretched onto the horizon. It was high tide, so the marsh was flooded, but the green tips of the grass were tall enough to be visible above the water. Rocky islands rose out of the wider rivers, and a few were large enough to hold trees. Bits and pieces of rusty metal poked the landscape like wicked thorns.

"We should've brought a canoe," Seren said, not wanting to trample the pristine wetland. Walking on it would risk crushing small crustaceans or damaging the grasses that sheltered them from the sun at low tide. Wading through the rivers would be equally dangerous to the local flora and fauna.

Even if they dared threaten the delicate ecosystem with their feet, they would be putting themself in danger. The marshes at home were infamous for muck one could sink into up to their knees and random holes in places no one would expect. Assana said the treacherous mud was a defense mechanism that kept clumsy humans from tromping through on foot and killing innocent creatures. They never traversed a marsh without some kind of boat.

Seren crossed their arms. "Don't tell me you two walked through here last time."

Reggie smirked. "Why don't you ask it if you can cross?"

Sighing, Seren once again opened their mind to the magic around them. Communicating with it wouldn't tire them out like using magic would, but it still left their mind exposed. The forest's rustling and creaking was quieter, further behind them, and drowned out by the buzzing mass of life and death sprawling out in front of them. Marshes were both a graveyard and incubator. Plants, crustaceans, mammals, birds, and fish all died there. Bodies sunk into the muck, releasing nutrients that nurtured eggs, larva, and living plants. Some larvae were eaten before they had a chance to grow. Others grew into fish and insects that fed birds and mammals. Seren got lost in the brilliant hodge-podge of life and death before they even set foot in the marsh.

They pulled their mind far enough back to themself so they could feel their blood pumped through their veins by a beating heart. They retreated further, into synapses firing and gray matter until they were conscious enough to picture them and the twins crossing the marsh. They envisioned an abandoned boat floating up to them, the hollowed-out trunk of a tree that died of age, or a raft made up of sticks. Anything to get them to be able to cross the marsh without hurting it.

"We would like to pass through and remove a piece of machinery we believe is polluting your waters," said Seren, adding their vision of what Scott described and drew for them. "Can you take us to it?"

A breeze conjured ripples on the still water below them. The ripples formed a circle, like someone had thrown something in the water, except no one had. Something rose from inside.

A head came first. It was roughly human shaped, but instead of hair, green grass crowned it. Instead of skin the muck from the bottom of the river coated the body, and the eyes were water reflecting the forest. She had no nose, but nostrils that were like a snail, and a slit of a mouth was filled with barnacles instead of teeth. She smelled like low tide. The odor made David and Reggie cringe, but Seren inhaled deeply—low tide was their favorite smell.

"It has been a while since one so attuned to The Mother visited my land," said the creature in a voice that seemed to alternate between hissing and gurgling. "What may I call you?"

"Seren McIntyre. My pronouns are they/them. And what may I call you?"

The creature grinned, revealing more of her barnacle teeth. She stood so her whole mud body was visible above the water. "You may call me Great Salt Marsh. She/Her."

Seren tried to not stare and failed. Great Salt Marsh definitely made herself female, right down to the lumps where a human's breasts would have been. Seren blushed.

"You find this form pleasing?" asked Great Salt Marsh.

Seren nodded, wondering if their reaction would make Erik jealous.

"Fascinating. And why do you wish to remove one of the machines I have imprisoned in my collection?"

"I made a bargain with a blacksmith. He said he'd repair my boat's motor if I got him this machine."

"And why do you need your motor repaired?"

"Humans are gathering up north to form a government for this region. There are two factions who have an agenda The Mother does not approve of. I plan to make sure those two factions do not sway the majority of representatives and to stress the importance of maintaining the Survivors' Accords."

"The idea that they need reminding at all perhaps shows The Mother's lack of logic. Perhaps She left too many humans alive."

Seren swallowed hard. "I seek peace and harmony. Not more death."

"And what about your companions?" The Great Salt Marsh stepped out of the water and sauntered over to the twins. "They smell like the dead. Last time these two passed through my land, their adversaries did not make it through, and I suspect that was their reason for leading those men into my waterways in the first place."

Seren watched David and Reggie squirm. They stared with their jaws clenched. Seren shrugged. Violence came easy for Reggie and David. They had to atone for their own transgressions. Seren bit their lip and tapped her foot, anxious to get on with their quest. The more time they lingered, the more time the other factions would have to sway people away from the accords.

The twins remained silent while Great Salt Marsh walked circles around them, sniffing their hair and their lips. "Your charge grows impatient. What do you have to say for yourselves?"

"We defend Assana," said Reggie in one exhale. They sucked more air in and continued. "And by defending her, we defend the Earth. The Mother drowned her children to ensure their continued survival as a species. Predators kill to eat, and to defend their territory. We kill those who threaten our survival. The men we led through here would have poisoned both Mother Earth and the minds of Her children had we let them live, but we were not strong enough to kill them alone, so we sought your assistance."

"It's true," said David. "They were killing whales for oil and leaving the carcasses to rot, had plans to dig deep into the earth and suck up her black blood, and attacked us when we tried to stop them."

"Very well." Great Salt Marsh glided back to the water, letting one muddy finger linger on Seren's neck before slinking down the rock and into the water. She waved her hand. Grasses parted. A rustic canoe carved out of a fallen tree flowed towards them. "You may pass."

Great Salt Marsh held the canoe still while Seren and the twins got inside it. There were no paddles.

"You do not need those," said Great Salt Marsh. "My currents will take you to the object you seek." She gave the canoe a push and sped down the wide channel, leading them directly to the machine.

Seren cursed when they saw it. The thing was huge—the size of a small shed.

"I can see why your levitating powers appealed to him," said David, staring at the machine while the canoe stayed still even though the water rushed past it with the outgoing tide.

"I didn't think I'd have to carry it the whole way back," said Seren. "I thought it would be something I could just lift out of the mud and tow without magic."

"Things are never that simple with Scott," said Reggie.

"We warned you he'd ask for something outrageous," said David.

"I'm going to need a big dinner tonight," muttered Seren. Their hands shook, and their throat constricted at the thought of using magic so heavily again, but they didn't see any other option. They needed their gears, so they could get to NUNES on time.

Seren closed their eyes and let the magic in.

They expected the wave of life and death they'd felt earlier, but they weren't prepared for the rush of mischief, one that couldn't quite mask the betrayed rage flaring beneath it. Great Salt Marsh was part of Earth, yes, but she had a mind of her own. Her will seeped into Seren's. Alien malice made Seren's skin crawl. Energy flooded Seren's spirit and bolstered their limbs, making it easy to surround the boat with a bubble of excited molecules.

Great Salt Marsh purred at how they didn't waste any energy, but just used enough to get the machine to float on the surface of the river. She stroked Seren's spine with warm, tingling energy that tempted them to fall into Great Salt Marsh and let her consume them.

The boat jerked. The twins tripped and fell over. Currents surged, pushing the boat forward, past where the machine had been and away from the point of entry. The speed was one they were more likely to see in a raging river, not a salt marsh. It carried them through the winding channel and what resembled like a graveyard of machines jutting out left and right.

"Seren, what's going on?" asked Reggie as the boat sped towards a rocking outcropping.

Seren shook their head, struggling to remember how to speak through the storm of Great Salt Marshes consciousness. They could barely hear anything other than the swish of water and the rustle of grasses in the wind. They focused all their attention on keeping the machine floating close to the speeding canoe.

"Seren, I think we're going to crash.

"She—she's maneuver going to," stuttered Seren. Their jumbled response was the best they could manage.

The twins screamed, but right before the boat crashed, the water rose up and carried them over the rock, and then it plopped them down into the river. They sped forward on a straight vein of water until it met Piscataqua, where Great Salt Marsh spat Seren and the twins out like a drunk purging her stomach from a night reveling in the cups.

David and Reggie panted and cursed, swearing they were never setting foot in the Marsh again. Seren's body sagged, cut off from the marsh's energy, and their spirit rose, free from the marsh's tether. The river currents still guided the boat in the right direction, but now Seren only had the normal magic to rely on and not the enhanced version they experienced in the marsh. Their head ached like a family of mice were gnawing on their brains and their hands trembled, but they kept the bubble of air around the machine until the little canoe crashed into the side of brown dinghy. They gave one final push, got the cursed thing up on dry land, and passed out.

CHAPTER FOURTEEN

Seren didn't stay unconscious long enough. They knew this because their brains still felt like mice had gnawed them on, but now an earthquake had chased said mice away.

"Seren, wake up!" The voice was somehow both a shout and a whisper. Seren wondered if it would to make their skull crack open.

"Come on, wake up. We're outnumbered and need your help."

"Go away," yawned Seren, deciding the voice belonged to David. Whatever the problem was, he could handle it.

David didn't go away.

"We're not exactly in the best position," David shook Seren, "but we can handle it if you give us a diversion."

"No magic," they whined, flailing their arms to get him off. They didn't open their eyes, but knew they hit their target when their elbow collided with his nose.

"Snap out of it!" he shouted.

Seren flailed harder, though it didn't seem to do much. They were too drained to do any real damage.

David stopped addressing them directly and muttered a stream of curse words. Seren hoped that meant he got the message and would leave them alone.

A sharp, barking bang ripped through their ears, a hundred times louder than David's voice. His body landed on top of them as they tried to sit up, jolted back to consciousness by the gunshots.

"Stay low," he whispered, rolling off them, laying on his stomach beside them and peering over the edge of the canoe.

Shaking and blinking, Seren scooted next to him and peered over the canoe wall. From there, they saw Reggie duck behind the salvaged machine as a group of Altzis shot at them. Seren clutched the canoe's wall so tight their nails left crescent marks in the wood.

When the Altzis stopped shooting to reload, Reggie peeked out from their cover, fired a few shots, ducked, and fired a few from the side and ducked again. A cry of pain and a splash of blood and bone followed the bang of each shot. Seren clenched their jaw and pressed their lips together so they wouldn't vomit. They couldn't tear their gaze away from the gore in front of them.

One man's knee exploded. Another clutched his bleeding stomach. A third lay unmoving with a hole in his head. Three more were on the ground, stunned, but not bleeding anywhere Seren could see. Was The Mother okay with this violence? Or were skirmishes like this the beginning of the end? Seren feared finding out.

"Reggie has it covered." Seren stood while their brain failed to comprehend the significance of what they saw. David pushed them back down just as something hot whizzed over their heads.

"They have snipers and most of them are wearing bullet-stopping body armor," whispered David.

"Where?" People and buildings were everywhere. The presence of too much spent adrenaline in their body made it hard to focus.

"Up the hill on the buildings, and I think there might be one in the crow's nest of the galley being restored on the dry docks. We don't exactly have the best vantage point down here."

"And what, exactly, do you think I can do to help?" Chills coursed through Seren's veins. They neither wanted to kill, nor be killed. They wanted the fighting to stop. They wanted to find a way to make sure it didn't happen again.

David's lips screwed up in a weird smile. "Ideally just magically make them stop breathing."

"It doesn't work like that, and even if I could do that, I wouldn't. Magic is a tool Earth gave us, so we could survive without inventing things that poison Her. It's not a weapon meant for killing." Seren wasn't sure about the last part, but David didn't need to know that.

"Even if you're killing people who wouldn't mind poisoning Her?"

Seren bit their lip so hard it bled. "I'm not a killer."

David stiffened. "Fine. Can you get them all looking away from us? Just get their attention focused on something that isn't us, so Reggie and I can take care of them before we run out of bullets."

"I might pass out again." Seren looked around as much as they could without actually getting up. They assumed the men with the guns didn't know they were in the boat, or else they would be shooting through it.

Seren closed their eyes, opened their mind to the magic. Dozens of human life forces filled the area around them, but Seren couldn't figure out if they were all enemies or if some of them were bystanders trying to stay out of the crossfire. Assana would've been able to tell. Seren didn't have the wildest inkling about how to read their energy and had never been interested. Simply pondering mind-control made Seren shiver. It was obvious reminder that Earth could control ambassadors if She chose to.

Seren opened their mind wider, letting the magic flow in even though it hurt. It made their chewed-up brain feel like hermit crab trapped in a too-small shell, and their insides feel like hot metal pipes were expanding inside them, all while being pulled towards a magnet in the general direction of home.

They were about to give up and let it go when bullets plopped into water just off of the stern. Seren pulled more magic and reached out with it as they exhaled, ignoring the risks and spiritually diving deep into the river.

The Elemental slept, buried deep under the currents, rocks, and wreckages, but its sleep was not so deep that it didn't notice Seren prodding it with their mind, asking for its help. The river tossed and turned like Seren might do if a fly landed on their back. Seren latched onto the energy and pulled it up and up until a wall of water rose behind them. The banging guns and plopping bullets stopped. Humans ran, shouted, and screamed as Seren let the wall of water edge closer to the city.

"It's working," said David. "They're running for higher ground."

Seren stood and stretched as the river did the same thing, looking for the men who dared harm one of Earth's ambassadors. They reached down with a watery arm and swatted those men, knocking them down and surrounding them with water until they gasped for breath. When Seren's lips moved and sound came out of their mouth, they didn't recognize their own voice.

"Mother Earth may have returned to sleep, but She slumbers lightly. Revolt against those She left in charge and you will all suffer!"

"That's enough," said David. His voice was muffled, like it sounded when Seren was swimming in the lake and someone else called to them. They tried to lower their outstretched arms, but they wouldn't budge. They tried to answer David, but the words wouldn't come out. Liquid chains bound Seren to Piscataqua's will.

All Seren could do was open their eyes and turn enough to see the giant wall of water behind them. Piscataqua's vaguely human face glared out from the wall as people, both bystanders and Altzis alike, ran for high ground. Seren wasn't entirely sure if it was their own feelings or the river that reveled in their fear and raised the wall higher, wondering how hard to let it slam down. They could throw it hard enough to smash boats against the brick walls of buildings or fill lungs with water until hearts stopped beating like they had done in the great flood. It would be fun, a show of power and a good way to remind the people that they did not own the planet. The planet owned them.

Anger bubbled in Seren's soul. Poking a slumbering Elemental was a risk, and they did it anyway. Innocent people would pay for their foolishness if Seren couldn't gain control. They twisted their body and soul, writhing until the Elemental's grip loosened enough for Seren to inhale on their own.

"Most people know the consequences, and respect them," breathed Seren. "Most people are innocent. Please don't punish them for the crimes of a few."

The river opened its human-shaped mouth and made a *glup-glub* noise that was as close to a laugh as an ancient river spirit could get. "My child, I think you are the one who is innocent, but I will spare them, for now."

The river yawned and sank back down to her banks, only spilling over to shore enough to wet the feet of the closest humans and tickle the belly of an old galley.

"What the hell was that?" Reggie stormed down the beach.

Seren shook. Reggie glowered at them, red-faced with their hands balled into fists. David swayed pale and ghostly.

Seren sunk to their knees, leaned over the edge of the canoe and vomited.

"I mean the wave was brilliant. It scared them shitless. But by The Mother, it scared me shitless. For a minute, I thought you were going to flood the whole damned city. I thought you were going to drown *me!*" Reggie slammed a fist against their chest.

"She wanted to," whispered Seren through a hoarse, dry throat. "She was going to remind everyone who was boss, but I stood up for them."

"She?" David's voice and hands shook equally.

"The river Elemental. She was sleeping and I woke her up." Seren stumbled out of the canoe and collapsed onto the damp riverbank, shivering. How close had they come to killing hundreds of people? Was the river's rage a reflection of the Earth's?

Reggie put a hand on Seren's shoulder. "It's okay. We're all alive and the river is merely a river again."

Seren shook their head. Nothing was okay. Back home, the Earth felt like a mother's embrace, simultaneously warm, comforting, and smothering. Here, barely a day's boat ride away, it was hostile and angry, wanting to wipe out humans as if they were parasites, not as much as a part of the ecosystem as everything else alive on the planet.

"Seren, we should leave." David slid his arms under Seren's shoulders and them up.

Seren nodded, attempting to put weight on their wobbly legs. They stepped forward even though they wanted to run home and cry to their mother. But Seren wasn't a child anymore. They were adult, out in the wild world for the first time, facing down powerful predators they hadn't realized existed.

CHAPTER FIFTEEN

After spending hours telling the Altzi boss, Domhnall, how Assana could not only manipulate elements like wind, water, fire, and earth, but also use Earth's magic to modify any living thing that consented to be shaped, they gave Erik water. He hesitated to drink. He hadn't been able to feel the river since he ate the food and drank the water that had been in his cell.

But his throat ached with thirst.

Fading light from the window glinted off of Domhnall's knife.

Erik drank.

Whatever was in it acted fast, sucking him down through a spinning void until he floundered in a haze of dreams where Seren summoned walls of water and cyclones. Sometimes they released the water back to the river. Other times they let it crash over him and all the other blurry figures watching in helpless horror.

The dream spun on until cold water poured over his head. Domhnall dragged a stool into Erik's cell and sat beside him. He took out his knife and began to sharpen it. The *schink schink* of the blade meeting whetstone kept time for the litany of questions.

"How often does Assana modify people's gender?"

"I don't know." Erik stared out his window. He could just make out an expanse of ocean and the first hints of dawn lightening a dark sky.

Domhnall leaned forward until his nose nearly touched Erik's. "Has she ever persuaded or forced anyone to have their bodies altered?"

"Never!" Erik was horrified by the thought of one person trying to force another to do anything, let alone make changes to their body.

Domhnall's lip twitched in amusement. "Aside from sex-changes, what other kinds of modifications does she make?"

Erik was about to answer none, but then he thought of Reggie and David. Their earth magic allowed them to modify their own bodies, to an extent, but Assana had amplified that. "There are two people she made faster and stronger."

Domhnall arched an eyebrow. "Only two?"

"That I know of." Erik's breath snagged. He was giving away too much, but he didn't want to get hurt again. Sleep had done little to dull the ache in his bones and muscle. Maybe if he could get some information in return, it would be okay. It would balance out if he shared it when he escaped. "Do you strengthen people with magic?"

Domhnall scowled. "I've told you it's a sin to modify what The Mother created."

"I'm sorry." That wasn't actually a no. He couldn't rule out the possibility. But maybe he could play off of Domhnall's rigid morals, act like he was buying into them. "Are you going to save us from Assana's wrongful use of magic?"

"Perhaps I am." Domhnall leaned forward, eyes narrow, a grin tugging on his lips. "If I were to liberate the people of Valley-Port from Assana, what would stand in my way most?"

"The people and the Elementals love Assana." Erik suppressed a shudder. Domhnall was planning an invasion, but if Erik wanted to warn anyone, he needed to escape or go without water. "I'm not sure which would be a bigger threat. But you'd be fighting both. Many would work together."

A tentacle of power brushed Erik's spirit, evoking a burning tickle that made him squirm like an eel in a net.

"You're telling the truth." Domhnall leaned back. Domhnall's mental tentacle stilled, but it didn't retreat. "Have you ever seen Assana fight?"

Erik shook his head. "No."

"Kill someone?"

"Just the executions I told you about." Erik squeezed his eyes shut. He hoped Domhnall didn't make him recount those again.

"Have you seen anyone in Valley-Port fight?" Domhnall held his blade up and inspected the edges. It was at least eight inches long and looked like it could slice through bone.

"No." The closest thing to a fight he'd witnessed was Reggie and David sparring with each other. Some people had come close to blows in arguments over fishing spots, but when things got heated on the docks, Merri and Mac took it upon themselves to cool things down, literally. Erik smirked, picturing a wave rising out of nowhere and soaking to arguing fishers.

"What is so funny?" Domhnall brushed the sharp edge of his knife across Erik's raw knuckles. With almost no pressure applied, it stung worse than jellyfish venom.

The little joy the memory had conjured fled as blood spilled out of Erik's knuckles and pooled in his blisters.

Domhnall smirked. "Tell me what you were thinking of."

Erik told him about Merri and Mac's methods of preventing fights.

"Erik, I can sense there is something you are not telling me." Domhnall pointed his wicked blade at Erik. "I'd rather not use this knife, but I will."

Erik's leg bounced. He picked at a scab on his hand. He didn't want to tell him about Reggie and David, Valley-Port's only soldiers.

At least not without getting something in return. Domhnall had answered the last question he asked. Maybe he'd answer another.

Erik peered up to his eyes. "Can we trade?"

"Trade?"

Erik took a deep breath. "I'll tell you about Reggie and David. You tell me what else you want with Valley-Port, aside from saving us."

Domhnall wiped Erik's blood off of his knife and sheathed it. He stared at Erik with his eyes narrowed. Just when Erik thought he would never answer, he said, "My land was plentiful once, but the population has grown too large for it to sustain us. Valley-Port is one of the most prosperous states in the North East. We need its resources, and in return, we will teach the people a better way to live."

Without the constant *schink schink* thoughts formed more clearly in Erik's mind. He wanted to ask Domhnall why he thought Valley-Port was so prosperous in spite of its "sinfulness" but worried that question would get him hurt. Thankfully, that was only one of many things he wanted to ask. "Isn't half the purpose of NUNES to facilitate a more even distribution of resources? To make sure prosperous regions share with those struggling to support their people?"

Domhnall unsheathed a new dagger and picked up his whetstone. "Tell me about Reggie and David."

"I've been told that as a child, Reggie was always into fights, and trying to tame their violent energy seemed futile, so Assana harnessed it." Each word a heavy chain of guilt wrapping around Erik, dragging his thoughts to the depths of a murky river. "Assana assigned Reggie to apprentice to one of her peacekeepers as a child. Their twin insisted on joining, even though he did not share their hot tempter or passion for fighting."

"Are these the people Assana modified for strength and speed?"

Erik stared at the threads fraying on the edges of a hole in his pants. "Yes."

Domhnall picked up his whetstone and began sharpening the dagger. "Tell me all you know about them."

The sun rose as Erik told Domhnall everything he knew of David and Reggie's history, trying to avoid details of their strengths and weaknesses with stories of Reggie's pranks and their fascination with monsters. But Domhnall always saw through Erik's distractions and asked pointed questions to keep him on topic. Erik talked until his throat was parched and his head was light. He suspected Domhnall might have kept him there all day and had the man with the daughter that cleaned the cells not strode down the hall, warning Domhnall of an approaching boat of wounded men.

Domhnall stood. "How were so many wounded?"

"They had a run-in with the heir from Valley-Port and their bodyguards." The man glanced back and forth between Domhnall and Erik. "It started out a gunfight, but then the heir woke the river elemental and almost drowned half the city."

Chills shot through Erik. His muscles tensed. Bile rose in his throat. What had Seren done? What had it cost them? Were they alive?

"Almost?" Domhnall arched his eyebrows.

"It was a warning. Stop fighting or die." The man scratched the back of his head. "And when they stopped shooting and our people fled, they also backed off."

Erik exhaled slowly. It sounded like Seren was alive, and that they hadn't fully lost control of whatever elemental they tangled with to fight of the Altzis. It also meant they were close.

"But from who? The kid or the river?"

The man shrugged. "Ask the men who were there."

Domhnall stared at Erik, but his words were clearly meant for the other man. "I need to wrap up here, then I will hear their tales."

The man left. Domhnall handed Erik a cup of water and a hunk of bread. "You did well today. Keep up like this, and you may survive the trip to NUNES."

NUNES. Erik almost smiled. They weren't just near Seren but

heading to the same place as them. Hope grew inside him, like fluffy clouds on a summer afternoon. If they were on the same route as Seren, it would be easier to get a message to them. Maybe if he escaped, he'd find them.

Water splashed over the edges as Erik raised it to his face, inhaling the rotten odor of a sleeping draught. He wouldn't be doing either of those things if he drank. But his throat ached, and his stomach growled, and Domhnall watched. He wouldn't leave until Erik drank. Erik stared at the cloudy liquid and dark bread. Maybe if kept cooperating, he'd earn Domhnall's trust. Maybe then he'd stop drugging him. Erik devoured the bread and gulped the whole cup down in seconds, praying to The Mother the drug-induced sleep would be deep and dreamless.

The last thing he heard was the *schink schink* of Domhnall sharpening knives.

CHAPTER SIXTEEN

"Did you get my metal printer?" asked Scott, pacing around his smithy, taking swigs from an unmarked bottle.

"Yes." Seren leaned against a counter covered in a grimy cloth and crossed their arms so Scott wouldn't notice how their fingers fidgeted. They had delayed long enough and needed to get the engine fixed, so they could get to NUNES before more Altzis showed up. "You were supposed to stay sober until after you fixed my gear box."

"I fixed it as soon as you left. Where is the printer?"

"It was near the docks. Where are my gears?"

Snorting, he stomped forward and yanked the cloth out from under Seren's behind. Seren stumbled forward, cursing as they caught their balance and studied the glass case the cloth had been covering. The gearbox, along with gleaming new gears, sat in the center of the case like a smug smile. "It's right there. I'll give it to you after I see my printer."

"You can have your machine after you give me those gears." Seren glared into the man's eyes. Seren hired the dockhands to load the metal printer into a cart. The same donkey that helped pull *The Whaler* out of the water was on its way up to the smithy with instructions to go past it to the Mead Maker Inn if Scott didn't hold up his end of the bargain.

He stared. Seren stared back. Reggie's hands inched towards their guns.

"You promise me you brought the printer?" Scott leaned so close that Seren thought they were going to get drunk just from smelling his breath.

"I promise."

He didn't break eye contact. "Do you promise you won't drown us all?"

Seren blinked. "Why would I drown you?"

His lower lip trembled. "I saw you raise the water out of the river and hold it over the city."

"We were being attacked by Altzis," said Reggie. "Your printer is already on the way here. Just give Seren the gears or I am going to smash that damned case and take it myself."

Scott rummaged in his pocket until he found a key, fumbled with it, got it in the lock, opened the case and gave Seren a perfect replica of the gearbox.

"Where is the original?" Seren asked after examining it for a few minutes.

"That is the original. When I use my magic, I can make broken things go back together. I didn't need to make any new pieces"

"Thank you." Seren's throat burned and tears welled up in their eyes. "Barb and her helpers are hauling the machine up on their donkey. It should be here any minute."

"Good." Scott's grimace rose to a smile, but his overweight body sagged onto a stool.

The whole group hovered around in awkward silence as the clopping of hooves grew louder and louder. A donkey brayed. Someone knocked, and Scott answered, "Do you have it?"

"You better plan to help me unload that clunky thing," Barb scolded. "It was a pain in my ass getting it up here."

Reggie snickered, but Scott ran outside, pulled the tarp off the cart and literally hugged the machine, muttering about how he was amazed at its condition for having spent centuries in a salt marsh.

Barb glowered. "When you're done making love to that piece of junk, do you think you could get it off my cart? I have work to do down at the docks."

Seren wanted to run straight down to the marina to fix *The Whaler*, but by the time everyone finished unloading the old metal printer, Seren could barely move. They step and swayed worse than they did when *The Whaler* navigated a storm. Their stomach growled and churned. A burning sensation accompanied the noise. "I need to eat, now, or I'll pass out."

Even as they spoke, they faltered. They'd channeled more magic through their body than ever before, and it took a toll. Mages built up a tolerance and endurance over time, but Seren was young and for the past two years, had been avoiding magic as much as their mother would allow.

If they didn't eat or sleep, they simply wouldn't have enough energy to exist. The edges of everything darkened. David and Reggie rushed to support Seren. The world faded to shadows and blurs. David guided them to the street. Fresh air brightened their vision and sharpened their perception a little more than the burnt air in the smithy, but it didn't fully wake them up, either. Seren let David and Reggie haul them up into the wagon and sit beside them while Reggie told Barb to get them to the Mead Maker.

The ride was a bouncy blur.

"Food will make me feel better." Seren attempted to get out of the wagon on their own and fell. David caught them before their face hit the cobblestones, which morphed into chowder and a hunk of bread.

The food helped, but not in the way Seren wanted it to. After they devoured two bowls of chowder, a dozen rolls, and half a cake, the shaking stopped, but they could barely keep their eyes open. Yawning the whole way, they walked up to their rented room, closed the door, sunk onto the bed, and let a restorative sleep take hold.

Seren dreamed of Erik singing about the lake to a duet of blade and stone. Waking, they searched for Reggie or David. When either of the twins got bored, sharpening knives or cleaning guns was their favorite way to pass the time. They needed a hobby that wasn't steeped in so much violence.

Golden red light stung Seren's retinas. Seren jumped so they were sitting upright on the edge of the bed. The sun had been high when they started their nap, and now it set. They spun around, glaring at David who sat on the floor, honing a hunting knife.

"Why didn't you wake me up?" Seren stood up, digging for their pocket watch to see exactly how late it was. They'd hoped to get *The Whaler* up and running and get back on the way to NUNES by dinnertime.

"You needed the sleep. Even Assana needs to sleep after she works big spells."

"I need to fix my boat." Seren gathered their belongings and rushed down to the water with the twins in tow.

By the time they got down to the boat, waning sun bloodied the sky. Seren patted the boat, trotted over to the engine and began taking it apart. It felt good to have something physical to do. No elemental wills distorted their thoughts as they unscrewed things and replaced broken parts. Nerves shook their hands when they got to the gearbox. What if it didn't fit? They took a few deep breaths before attaching it to shaft. Each piece fit perfectly together. Repairing an engine had never been so easy.

They put the propeller in a bucket of water Reggie reluctantly fetched, pulled start cord and heard the engine sing. "All we have to do is flip her over, put the engine back on, and put her back in the water. Then we can get out of here."

Reggie stared up at the starlit sky. "We are not leaving right now."

David yawned. "You may have napped the afternoon away, but we didn't."

"And none of us have had dinner," said Reggie.

"But we'll be another day behind schedule," pleaded Seren. "And if the wrong people get to the NUNES conference first, they might not even let us in!"

Reggie patted the pistol holstered on their hip. "Opposition will just make getting in more fun."

Seren shuddered. "Reggie, we're supposed to fight with words, not guns."

"They'll let us in," said David. "Ambassador Root and Assana are old friends, even if they only communicate by water messages and hawks."

That was true. Assana had been talking a lot since Root started planning NUNES. He was kind and wise, at least he came across when they spoke through the communication basin. Seren closed their eyes. They had a bad feeling about something, but they didn't understand it. Maybe it was because Freeman was also a close friend of Root and he had attacked two BREAD researchers. "What if Freeman convinces everyone that BREAD is bad, and a bunch of mages attack them?"

"Did Assana tell you to expect trouble on that front?" David asked.

"She said a lot of mages didn't trust BREAD, but she never said they might attack, and seemed pretty surprised by Freeman's actions." Which meant Assana could be wrong about many of the others. She often focused on the good in people and Elementals alike, sometimes to a fault. Seren used to be like that too, but Seren never forgave the Elementals for using Assana to execute someone or the now dead person for committing the crime they did. Assana let it go. What if she was wrong about many of the other ambassadors? Seren wasn't sure if their voice would mater, but maybe there would be other people of their opinion, and together, they could work towards understanding and peace. The sooner they got there, the better.

Seren's stomach grumbled. "I guess we can wait until morning, but we're getting up before dawn and having this boat ready to go as soon as the cursed Thousand Jellies is out of this river."

The twins didn't complain when Seren woke them an hour before dawn. Collecting what few belongings they had left in the room, David and Reggie followed Seren to the boat yard. The workers weren't there yet, but before Seren went to bed the night before, they'd asked Barb for help. They even offered to pay her extra for getting up so early.

The crew flipped the boat over and put it onto trailer. Reggie helped Seren load the hold with the fresh water, berries, and fuel. When they finished, Seren stood at the edge of the boat ramp, staring at the slack river. As soon as the exiting tide conjured a ripple on the glassy surface, Seren unhitched *The Whaler* from the donkeys and summoned a burst of Earth's energy to push it into the water.

Before the twins had a chance to board, Seren ran to the engine, and checked the fuel tanks, refilled courtesy of the donkeys' back ends. Breathing through a grin, they opened the choke, squeezed the fuel pump and pulled the rope. Nothing happened. They pulled it a second time. It sputtered. They took a deep breath, pulled the rope as hard as they could, and were rewarded by the roar of the engine starting.

"Thank The Mother!" Seren patted the top of the engine and smiled. "Are you ready to resume our adventure?"

"We're ready if you promise you won't talk to the engine the whole way up." Reggie stepped into the boat, but David remained on shore, thanking Barb for all her help. Seren's foot tapped while the engine idled, but they summoned the patience to thank Barb again before David boarded the boat.

David glanced at Seren and Reggie with his eyebrows arched before taking his usual seat in the middle. Reggie perched at the bow. Seren slid the boat into drive and pushed the throttle forward, savoring the song of the engine pushing against the current.

"Have a safe journey," shouted Barb from shore.

"I will. And you stay safe here," said Seren.

Looking over their shoulder, Seren saw Barb's mouth move, but the symphony of the wind and engine swallowed her voice. After that, Seren kept their gaze forward, watching for rocks and wrecks that could threaten to break their freshly repaired propeller.

They waved as they passed the creek Great Salt Marsh had dumped them out of and swore they saw the wind blow grass in the shape of a hand flickering in and out of view. They caught glimpses of the marsh stretching on for miles and miles through the buffer of trees and dry-ish land that separated her from the rest of the river.

The thin clumps of birch and peeks at the Great Salt Marsh gave way to a forest so dense the river became a twilit tunnel. Whatever had once been here had been something that angered Mother Earth so much that She not only completely wiped it out but made the land hostile to humans.

"I've never traveled north of here." David sat on the floor of the boat with his back leaning against the bow seat.

"We've heard stories, though," said Reggie. "Ones that make Great Salt Marsh look like someone's friendly aunt."

"Just tell me they don't involve jellyfish," said Seren, eyeing the water in front of the boat. There still wasn't much wind, and the tide had just started to go out when they left.

"No. The river is the only 'safe' way through this region." An impish smile exposed Reggie's uneven teeth. "No one who goes into the woods ever comes out alive."

Seren shivered. "Assana said the woods didn't like visitors—that the trees were carnivorous and that all kinds of predators lived under them, but of course, she didn't specify what kind of predators they were."

Reggie winked. "Someone would have to survive them to know."

CHAPTER
SEVENTEEN

The next time Erik woke, he was on the ship's deck. The after effects of whatever drugs they gave him made his head feel like his brain was melting and prevented him from seeing clearly.

The boat puttered up a narrow stretch of river. Erik's blurred vision contorted the gnarled branches into swaying monsters, creating a tunnel with their tentacles. Very little light pushed past the thick canopy of leaves. Through one tiny crack in the shade Erik glimpsed blue sky and sunlight, but in a few seconds the ship was past it, and the torches and lanterns became the only light source.

"I appreciate how open you have been with me so far," said Domhnall, stepping in between Erik and the brightest torch. It made him appear more shadow than man.

Erik uttered a raspy, "You're welcome."

Domhnall smiled. "Your continued cooperation will help make these lands safer."

The man was too bulky to clean Erik's cell himself sat against the starboard rail, braiding his daughter's hair. It was probably part of the interrogation, even if the girl didn't know it.

Erik didn't believe a thing Domhnall said, but his survival depended on his ability to act like he did without lying outright.

Domhnall took out his knife and whetstone. "The witch's offspring caused quite the ruckus yesterday. Their two body guards wounded several of my men. Would those be Reggie and David?"

"Yes." Erik hoped by several Domhnall meant a lot. "Reggie and David were accompanying them to NUNES."

Domhnall's grin grew. "Martin says you are close with Seren. Tell me about them."

Erik opened and closed his mouth. Words were clumps of food stuck in his throat because he didn't chew them well enough. Even though he didn't want to speak, the *schink schink* of Domhnall's knife lured the words out of him. "I love them, but I don't know if they love me."

Domhnall sighed. "What powers do they have?"

"I'm not sure." Erik's stomach flip-flopped. He reached out to the river, but he only felt a stabbing headache.

"Erik, what powers do they have?"

The *schlink schlink* stopped. Metal pressed against Erik's thigh, tearing his ragged clothing, putting just enough pressure on his skin to make him bleed. It stung but didn't hurt like he thought. Maybe he had a higher pain tolerance than he realized. Maybe his body was numb from the drugs and questions. For the first time since he woke up, some of the piss-his-pants fear that had been bending him to obedience dissipated.

The pressure on his leg increased. Blood leaked out around the knife.

"I don't know," Erik blurted. "They hate magic. They rescued me once in a bubble of air and another time, helped me navigate through a squall. But other than that? I've never seen them use magic. They just don't like to do it."

The knife pulled away.

Domhnall narrowed his eyes. "They used it yesterday in The Port's Mouth."

"I assume they were cornered? In a life or death situation?" Erik didn't want to give away much about Seren, but if he could convince the Altzis to underestimate them, then they would stand a better chance if it came to another fight. But he had to carefully phrase his answers just right, so the words rang true.

Domhnall stared at Erik for a long time before speaking. "My men approached as they rowed to shore. The twins opened fire and my men defended themselves. My men outnumbered them, so it may have seemed like life or death, though the situation was of their guards' making."

Erik nodded. "Then that is why they used magic."

Domhnall narrowed his eyes. "How much training do they have?"

"They don't talk about it a lot." Erik hoped Domhnall wouldn't use his knives to push for more detail where he would have to risk lying or admitting that despite their reluctance, Seren trained several days a week. "I only know when they've trained because it puts them in the worst moods."

"Assana must be disappointed in Seren." Domhnall rested his knife and whetstone on his lap and scratched his chin. "I suppose we'll focus on the few pieces of magic you've seen Seren work."

Erik answered every question as best he could without lying and without giving too much away. He acted like he didn't understand the air magic Seren had used to lift him off a rock and took more credit than was due him when he told the tale about surviving a fierce squall. He shared an exaggerated tale of Seren being forced to represent their mother at NUNES, doing his best to make them sound like a whiny, incompetent teenager afraid of their own shadow. If they didn't take Seren seriously, maybe they'd leave them alone or at least underestimate them.

"You seem awfully eager to tell me about someone you claim to love," Domhnall said as the girl with the braids carried a tray over with bread and two cups.

Erik made eye contact with Domhnall. It was time to gamble.

"When I think about how you say Assana misuses magic, and think about Seren's aversion to it, I wonder if you might find common ground."

"Perhaps." Domhnall took the tray, then handed one cup back to the girl. "Bring that back to the kitchen and fetch some fish to leave in this young man's cell."

Erik ate and drank what they offered. The water left his head foggy. He still couldn't reach the river, but he stayed awake. And that meant he could finally plan his escape.

CHAPTER
EIGHTEEN

The hairs on Seren's arms stood up while the river wound and twisted its way through the forest. It also shrunk. A narrow river meant swift currents, and while there wasn't much wind, the water rushed out of the river, making Seren glad they'd bought extra fuel in the Port's Mouth, even if it did stink up the boat.

They hadn't seen any other boats in a least an hour. The solar barges definitely couldn't make it up here, and the solar skiffs would be slow against this current, especially with tall trees shading a good portion of the river. Maybe they weren't going to be the last ones at NUNES after all, unless everyone else was already there, and the convention began without them.

Seren laid one of Ambassador Freeman's charts out on the console and placed a compass beside it. Right now, they could only go one direction, but that wasn't why they were watching the chart. This part of the river might have calmer waters than the mouth, but it was allegedly littered with rocks and wrecks that could smash the newly repaired prop or rip a new hole in the freshly patched hull.

The chart had steered them around all of the rocks, but they kept a close eye on the water anyways. In the middle sections that the sun reached, they could see all the way to the rocky bottom. Many of the same fish they watched in the lake swam around boulders and between weeds. The familiar sight was comforting, but the piles of bones and rusted metal made them want to puke. Bottom feeders nibbled on the bones, hunting for remaining meat or eating the algae.

Reggie hunched over the bow of the boat. "I wonder how long they've been down there."

"You're going to fall in if you're not careful." David sat in the middle of the boat, hugging his knees to his chest.

Reggie dangled their torso over the edge. "I want to know what killed them."

"Maybe they've been there since The Flood." Seren sincerely hoped Reggie didn't fall in. Assana had cautioned Seren against using magic here, claiming that the land was very much aware of itself and wouldn't hesitate to take over anyone who opened their mind to it.

"Maybe a monster ate them and picked their bones clean." Reggie pushed themselves back into the boat and beamed at Seren.

"Assana told me that there used to be oil refineries and weapon factories on these lands—the kind of places The Mother targeted." Seren kept their mind shut even tighter than normal, but constantly looked back and forth between the chart and the water. They wanted to open up the throttle and speed until they reached the bay, but knew if they did that, they might never make it there.

After two hours of painstaking, slow navigation, the narrow, windy tree-tunnel of a river opened up to a bay bathed in fog. The chart portrayed the bay as a watery heart surrounded by forest, broken up by small towns. Based on what Assana and Freeman had said, the people used the roads sparingly and traveled between towns on boats, occasionally braving the windy river Seren had just come up to reach the Port's Mouth for news and supplies.

Seren planned on getting across the bay before night fell and stopping at the largest town, which straddled the meeting river and bay. That town had an inn and was allegedly more used to guests and travelers than its neighbors. Travelers in Little Port had confirmed its existence but had mixed tales about its hospitality.

Seren tried to plot a course to get there, but fog rolled in from the north, making it hard to tell where they were, let alone where they were going. And as if that wasn't bad enough, the compass spun one way then the other, but never stopped.

"Freeman never mentioned a magnetic anomaly." Seren looked to David and Reggie, hoping the more experienced travelers would have some kind of explanation they knew of.

"I've never even heard that word before," said David.

"Have you, Reggie?" asked Seren.

Reggie shook their head stared out at haze. "At home the fog either rises off water in the morning or it rolls in from the ocean."

"I've never seen it roll in from the direction of land," added David.

"Maybe there is a fog-breathing, magnet dragon out there." Mist muffled Reggie's already quiet voice, making it sound even more sinister, especially since Seren couldn't see them.

Seren snorted. "*Someone* is probably making the fog with magic or science."

"Neither sounds appealing," said David. "Though magic is the most plausible."

A knife sang as Reggie unsheathed it. "Either way, I can't think of a friendly reason for someone to make fog, but I know it would be very useful if I were planning an ambush."

CHAPTER NINETEEN

Fog thicker than any Erik had ever seen hung over the Altzi's boat, pressing them to a standstill. Domhnall told Erik it was a perfect time for more questions since progress towards their destination halted.

Erik opened his mind as much as he could through the narcotic blindfold. Usually, he could feel fog like a fainter version of the water. The drugs skewed his senses and eliminated any hope of control, but he could feel that water around and under the boat. The fog was a void as terrifying as Domhnall. He wasn't sure if it was because of the drugs, or because there was something odd about the fog.

Beads of water clung to Erik's skin. He couldn't even see Domhnall, who lead him by a two-foot section of rope. Erik didn't know the Altzi's leader had stopped walking until he crashed into him and was consequently shoved onto the floor.

Too bad the fog didn't soften the *schink schink* of Domhnall's knife. The frequency of Domhnall's voice couldn't quite get through the moisture in the air, but the knife's sound sliced right through it. "Has the witch ever done anything like this before?"

"Not that I know of." Erik had never experienced fog that pressed down on him so heavily, and he'd sailed through some of the worst fog banks the people of Little Port had ever seen.

"Do you think she could?"

"She made fog dissipate once." Erik recalled a time when a fog bank had settled on Little Port and refused to lift. It was just before his promotion to dock master, and he had to do everything by feel because he couldn't see the boats coming in and they couldn't see the dock. After three days, Assana and Seren came to Little Port, and Assana made the fog leave. Erik had never been happier to see sun and blue skies.

"But could she?"

"I guess, but I don't know if she'd ever want to."

Domhnall's laugh haunted the fog. "It's damned near impossible to see in this. Someone could sneak up on me and I wouldn't know it until their knife slid between my ribs."

"She wouldn't." But Erik had an idea. His hands were bound, but not his arms. He raised them. No one asked what he was doing. He hoped that meant they couldn't see him.

"How do you know? You already said she executed someone."

Erik stood up slowly, "Why would someone who could suffocate you from a mile away bother making fog, so she could stab you in the back?"

"Good point," said Domhnall. "What about Seren?"

"Seren uses magic sporadically and impulsively. They react. They don't plan it." Erik closed his eyes. If he wasn't drugged, he'd be able to feel the fog. He'd know where people were standing based on where he sensed disturbances. But right now, the fog was nonexistent in his mind, and the water was a blurred thought beneath the boat. But earlier, he hadn't felt the water at all. "I can feel the drugs you gave me wearing off. Let them. I'll be able to sense if the fog came on its own or had been conjured by an ambassador."

"My water mage can't even sense the fog, let alone connect it back to any other mage."

Interesting. Erik took a tiny step sideways. If anyone noticed, they said nothing. "Has your mage tried talking to the bay elemental?"

Domhnall sighed. "My water mage can manipulate water, and can repel Elementals, but he has never communicated with any except the one who lives in his pond."

"I've talked to water Elementals all over Valley-Port." Erik took another baby step. "I've even spoken to Atlantik a few times."

"If I let the suppressant wear off, what will stop you from using the local bay elemental to just kill and drown us all?"

"Nothing," Erik admitted. But despite everything that they had done, he didn't want to kill anyone. There were at least a dozen people on this ship, maybe more. Only Domhnall and two of his men had hurt Erik, and if his suspicions were right, not everyone was here by choice.

He wanted to get away. He wanted to see Seren and warn them. After the constitution was ratified, there would be a new government in place with its own justice system. He was happy to let them deal with Domhnall

"Then why would I allow it?"

"Because I'm the only one who can talk to the bay and find out what is really going on." Erik took a step forward. He moved his bound hands up and down.

The silence that followed indicated no one could see him through the fog.

He had been considering trying to ask the girl who cleaned his cell and her father for help, but no one came near his cell when he was awake. And even if they had, he wasn't sure if he would've gone through with it. Either of them might have immediately reported to Domhnall, and if they helped, they might have been risking their lives. But maybe Erik didn't need their help to escape.

He took another step and another, moving towards the starboard edge of the boat. If they'd set him in a different spot than last time, he was in trouble.

"Has Seren spoken with you at all about the constitution?"

Domhnall's voice sounded further away, more muffled by the strange fog. Assuming it even was fog. Erik wasn't sure what else it could be, but unless the other water mage was terrible, he should've been able to feel water in the air. Erik kept moving, bare feet silent on the deck. He stretched his mind as much as he could despite the headache the effort summoned. It was like pushing his consciousness through a tangle of briars he couldn't quite fit through.

"Erik. I asked you a question."

Erik pressed his lips together. If he answered, he risked giving away his position. If he didn't, Domhnall might get suspicious and come after him. Except Domhnall couldn't see him. Erik closed his eyes. He couldn't get through the mental briars that the drugs created, but in his mind's eye, he could see through them. He knew where the water was closest, even if he couldn't reach out and touch it.

He ran.

He bumped into someone small.

She made no sound.

"I'm sorry," he whispered as he pushed by, arm brushing against someone bigger. The person pushed him forward. A hand grasped for him and he crashed into the rail and pushed himself over the edge. He hit the water hard. It stung. It hurt. But then he was floating, weightless and free. He opened his eyes.

The boat was a hulking blur, already moving away. He kicked up and away from the boat until his head broke the surface. He was free and in his element. He was alone in deep water with his hands tied in an unfamiliar bay, unable to access his magic. He could still hear the Altzi boat, muffled shouts and paddles. So he leaned onto his back and kicked away, hoping that either his magic came back, or he found land before he ran out of energy and drown. Drowning would make him just as dead as getting stabbed by an Altzi.

CHAPTER
TWENTY

Seren eased the throttle back until the boat puttered as slow as it could and still make headway against the current. Granted, Seren wasn't sure if they were actually moving against the current or if the water moved around them because the fog was so dense. They only knew the twins were still on board because they could hear Reggie and David finishing each other's sentences as they tried to figure out what enemies could cause this fog and whether they should wait it out or try to press forward anyways.

"Seren could try to clear it with their magic," said David. He had moved close enough that Seren could barely make out the shape of his head and beard.

"I don't know." Seren strained to see anything at all. "If Assana made a fog like this at home, another ambassador wouldn't be able to dispel it without hijacking her connection Earth."

If the compass worked, they could have at least known what general direction they were heading in, but that still spun so fast that it was a blur. Without using magic, all they could navigate by was the movement of the water, which they knew had to be flowing out of the bay.

Seren tightened their grip on the helm, closed their eyes and prodded the fog with their mind. A void stifled an elemental raging below it. They shut their mind shut and opened their eyes.

"As long as we are moving the opposite direction of the water, we should be okay."

"Unless we hit a rock," said David.

"Or a dragon," said Reggie.

David huffed. "We're more likely to hit a rock than a dragon."

"Could technology do this?" asked Seren. "If the scientist can make vests that stop bullets, can they make fog too? Their ships are hard enough to spot in normal weather. Fog like this would make them truly invisible."

"Don't know, but the way they talked about the monsters makes me wonder where the line between science and magic really is," said David.

"But if it is science," continued Reggie, "then you won't be going up against another mage and you should be able to stop it no problem."

"I'm still farther away from home than I've ever been, and Assana said not to use magic while going through the Dark Forest."

"We're out of the Dark Forest," said David.

"And Assana hasn't left her territory since before you were born, and even before you, she never came this far. She went to edge of the forest once and no further," said Reggie.

"You won't know until you try," said David.

Seren didn't want to try. The bay was angry, and they were just starting to feel better, like they could breathe without an invisible hand closing around their throat. Nothing was shaking. The world was steady. Using magic, if they could do it at all this far North, would change that. It would make them tired and sick again, and it would tug them towards home.

Seren picked at their lip. "We could drop anchor and wait it out. This fog can't last forever. Someone would have warned us about it if it was always here."

David put a hand on their shoulder. “And what if it lasts longer than our supplies, or someone attacks? What if someone doesn’t see us and drives into us?”

“We beep the horn at regular intervals just like on a foggy ocean,” said Seren.

“The we are broadcasting our position to enemies. What if something attacks? Like a fog-breathing dragon?”

Seren couldn’t see, but they heard the grin in Reggie’s voice and couldn’t mistake the slap of David face palming.

“Seren, I’m not as powerful as you, but I do use magic wherever I go,” said David. “I’ve never been this far north and west, but I’ve sailed down to Sandy Elbow and back. My magic was the same there as it is as at home.”

Seren clenched their hands around the helm hard enough for the veins to bulge. They picked their lip while trying to come up with a rational excuse to not expose their soul to an enraged elemental.

“We didn’t get up before dawn just to sit out the fog,” added Reggie. “Use your magic or turn around and go home. You’ve been using. Why stop now?”

“We’re a lot further away.” Seren was unsure which was scarier: opening their mind and finding no magic, finding a big, spiritual magnet that would yank them home, or finding new magic, furious and free, that they couldn’t control. When they were in the Great Salt Marsh, and even when they were pulling magic from the Piscataqua River, the self-aware river spirits had temporarily stolen Seren’s will. What if this bay had an even more powerful spirit that would not tolerate seventeen-year-old ambassadors trying to use its power?

Seren’s hands shook and sweated so bad that they lost their grip on the wheel. Tears stung their eyes even though they hated crying. David squeezed their shoulder. Reggie had crawled forward from the bow and stood over Seren, merely a few inches away, which was how close they had to be to be seen in this dense fog. The bodyguard glowered like Seren was a prisoner they needed to interrogate, not a charge they were supposed to protect.

"You got us through an ocean squall and made an army of Altzis shit their pants. You can handle a little fog and the magic it takes to clear it. You can do this. I know you can," said Reggie.

Seren sucked in a damp, snotty breath and nodded. They closed their eyes and fully opened their mind to the magic. Perplexed wrath flooded their senses before they could get a feel for the current and life forces. They'd been right about the bay being sentient like the Marsh and Forest, but they hadn't expected it to be equally confused about the fog as they were.

And the ambassador decides to listen, hummed a deep voice in Seren's mind. It's been awhile since one of your kind visited my land.

There aren't any ambassadors like me here? asked Seren.

There once were, but their line of power ended. Madness drove some to end their own lives and more never passed their gifts on. It is rather unfortunate. Most of the locals cannot properly communicate with me.

You must be lonely, Seren thought at the bay. But if there aren't any ambassadors, then that means it isn't a magician causing this fog.

Anger bubbled under Great Bay's confusion. Images flooded Seren's mind like water rushing back into an estuary as the tide came in. They saw sun blazing in a blue sky, making the calm water glisten. A floating array of mirrors sailed out of the river and into the pristine bay. An unnatural humming made the fish dive deep and the birds fly to their nests. The little mammals retreated to the forests, preferring to risk the predators they knew than ones they didn't. Clouds puffed out of the solar skiff until the temperature had dropped ten degrees, and the bay was cloaked in fog.

Humans in canoes and rowboats pulled in their nets, looked around, and tried to remember which way shore was. Currents picked up and guided them back to land, until the only vessel out on the water was the one making the fog. The bay tried to push it back Dark Forest's river, but it could only expel so much water at once without flooding the forest, which did not want to be flooded. The water hit a wall, and the boat of mirrors stayed in the bay.

Angry, the bay bucked and churned so waves tossed the boat

about. It turned to take the waves head on and rode them out until Great Bay tired and let his waters go still again.

"They don't belong," whispered Great Bay. "But to rid them, I would need to break the Survivors' Accords, and I've grown fond of the people who fish on my shores. If these intruders don't leave soon, if they don't stop their abomination, I will act, and few will survive."

The bay withdrew from Seren's mind, sinking down to his muddy depths.

Seren blinked. The twins were watching, eagerly awaiting news inches away from their face. "Give me space."

David let go of Seren and sat on the other end of the bench and Reggie returned to the seat at the bow. Seren opened their mind further. Great Bay's awareness was still there, but it was leaving them alone to use his power as they needed, much like Attitash, the lake spirit at home, who slept while Assana wielded her power and only woke when Her advice was needed, or She was angered.

Seren pulled the magic into themself, thinking about how they might shape it to dispel the fog. Wind seemed like the most natural choice, but in the memories Great Bay had shown them, wind hadn't blown the fog away. The wind had just gone through the fog, which seemed too dense to move. Seren figured they would have to take out the source of the fog.

"You two restocked your ammo before we left town, right?"

"Of course!"

Seren heard the smile in Reggie's voice.

Closing their eyes, Seren felt the bay instead of seeing it, and pushed the throttle forward. With a tendril of Great Bay's awareness held in their mind, they shared his awareness. They could feel where each living creature was, sense the depth of the water, and the rocks that might rip a hole in the hull. They also sensed the solar skiff sitting on the water like a leach on a leg.

Seren steered the boat towards the skiff at full throttle, and the currents in the bay shifted to push *The Whaler* there even quicker. To their credit, the twins didn't complain or question that Seren was steering with their eyes closed. When they got close to the skiff, Seren shouted, "Blast the horn every ten seconds."

The Whaler's horn honked.

A few minutes later, the hum the Great Bay had told them about buzzed their bones. Confused human energy paced around somewhere.

"It's coming straight for us," someone shouted.

Seren had just enough time to wonder how they knew that before they turned the wheel hard. *The Whaler* swung, gliding past the mirrored panels with a finger's width of space between hull and solar panel. Seren slowed the boat when they were perpendicular to the solar skiff.

Even though it made them gag, Seren curled magic around their throat and used it to project their voice as they spoke. "Please turn off the machine. You're upsetting the bay."

"What?" said a voice Seren recognized from the Port's Mouth. Dr. Fullerton. "Who is there?"

"It's Seren. Please, you have to turn it off. You're in danger."

"Danger from what?" asked. Dr. Fullerton. "The fog is protecting us."

"The Elemental of this bay will sink your boat if you don't turn it off," Seren said. Anger seeped through the magic they were using to amplify their voice. Magic crept down from their throat to their arms even though they hadn't called it there.

There was a long pause in which Seren really hoped would end with them agreeing to turn off their mystery machines.

"I'm afraid we can't do that," said Dr. Fullerton. Seren could barely make out people whispering in the background. "The Altzis are coming. They stole something of ours, and we mean to take it back. They won't see us coming in the fog."

"I'm sorry," said Seren. "The bay doesn't like humans meddling with its weather. It must be turned off and you must leave this bay as quickly as you can. Find a different way to get your things back."

“No.” The word was firm and unyielding. “Now get out of our way so you don’t get caught in the crossfire.”

Reggie placed a hand on Seren’s back. “David and I can go destroy the machine, if that will keep the bay appeased, protect your mind and keep everyone alive.”

“As long as you don’t kill anyone,” Seren whispered. “Just disable the machine and get out.”

Seren took a deep breath. “This is your last warning. Disable the machine or I will.”

“Is that a threat?” Dr. Fullerton asked.

Seren didn’t bother answering. They gathered power from the bay as they backed up as if they were leaving the shifted back into forward and sped up.

“I’ll give you a boost,” Seren told the twins.

The twins leapt off *The Whaler* as Seren surrounded them with bubble of air and raised them up onto the deck.

They landed with a thud, and their calm presences spread chaos into the life forces on the boat. Gunfire triggered pain.

“No!” Seren shouted even though they didn’t think the twins would hear. Their chest tensed. They were trying to save lives, not take them. “Don’t hurt anyone!”

Growing more tense every second the twins were on board, Seren circled the solar skiff until the humming stopped and the twins leapt over the edge of the skiff. Seren caught them in a bubble of air. *The Whaler* hardly rocked as they landed.

“The machine is in pieces,” said Reggie with a wild grin.

David glowered. “A handful Reggie’s reckless shots grazed people, but they should all live.”

Reggie smirked. “I got carried away.”

If words would have penetrated Reggie’s battle-mad skull, Seren would’ve argued, but it wasn’t worth it. What was done was done. Later, Seren could try talking them to make sure it didn’t happen again.

The fog thinned. Some of it rose, some sunk, and some stayed in place. Seren summoned a breeze to help it disperse now that it wasn't being kept so dense by the machine.

"Thank you," whispered the bay. The choppy waters surged then went still, like the bay had yawned. Its consciousness faded from Seren's mind as they pushed the throttle down as far as it would go, speeding towards the mouth of the bay.

Once they were far enough away from the damaged solar skiff to know it wasn't going to catch up and seek revenge any time soon, Seren let go of the magic all together. The compass stopped spinning. Land emerged from the horizon. Seren's hands shook and their stomach growled, but surprisingly, they didn't feel anything tugging them in the direction of home. Just a heavy exhaustion, the crushing weight of failure, and a tiny wisp of magic lingered around their spirit, urging them to keep moving forward.

CHAPTER

TWENTY-ONE

Erik drifted in the fog. He floated on his back with his eyes closed, listening to the ring of water in his ears. He still heard the steady pounding of the Altzi ship's paddle echoing through the water. And it wasn't the only vessel he heard. Vibrations from at least two different engines hummed through the water. Something felt familiar about both of them, especially the outboard. But what were the odds that it was Seren? Outboards were rare in some places, but Seren wasn't the only one who had one.

He tried reaching out to the water, but he still couldn't touch it. Trying didn't hurt as bad. It wasn't like getting stuck in briars in an attempt to barrel through them, but more like getting frozen in icy fog where the air occasionally formed brain stabbing icicles. He was tempted to shout, but worried about the Altzi boat. Plus, Seren probably wouldn't hear him over the roar of their engine anyway.

Rope chafed against his skin. He tried to wriggle his hands free, but they were bound tight.

He alternated between periods of kicking, hopefully in the same direction, hopefully towards land, and when he got tired, just floating. He was almost certain he was in a place called Great Bay.

They'd traveled miles inland, but the water remained brackish, which meant that he was not only at risk of hypothermia and drowning, but dehydration as well. He'd never been here, but he remembered it from maps he'd studied with Seren. There were several ways to get to NUNES, but the quickest was to stay on the Piscataqua river as it narrowed and wound through a once impassable section of forest, then dumped out into Great Bay. From there, they would pass through another section of wild woodland, and then it was easy going through a series of big lakes until they arrived at Ambassador Roots island in the middle of Merry Basin. The downside to going this way was that there were relatively few towns and the forests were too hostile to rely on for food and shelter. At least this bay had surrounding towns and forests that tolerated some humans passing through.

Erik tried to picture Seren's maps. There were basically downs every place a river entered the bay, except for the one they came in on because of the people-eating trees. The rivers were freshwater. And the towns probably had wells, or mages who desalinated the water. Something Erik could do when he got access back to his magic. He only needed to get to one of those towns, get some food and fresh water, and find a place to hide until he got his magic back. Then he'd use the water to find Seren and try to meet up with them, assuming they hadn't gotten too far ahead.

He let his mind drift through memories as he alternated between swimming and floating. Listening to Seren go back and forth about whether or not go. Days they both had off and spent laying on a sandy beach with the toes in the ocean while the sun warmed their face. Debates about what happened to pre-flood religions, about whether the Mother actually cared about half the things people claimed She did (including humans as a species), and how much Elementals and the humans they interreacted with influenced each other. He thought about books.

Assana had a whole library of old texts in her giant tree house, and often traded with other ambassadors via hawk. They had just given him a new book, *The Handmaids Tale*, some horrific imagining of what one author thought the future might look like, not knowing things would get better after the apocalypse instead of worse. At least better for some people. He imagined being a woman in an Altzi community might not be that different from the dystopia Attwood imagined, and to an Altzi, Valley-Port would probably seem like a dystopian nightmare.

A distant echo of gunshots jolted Erik out of his reveries. Shattering glass. Were those screams?

His heart raced, and adrenaline spiked as he pictured a confrontation with Seren and the Altzis. One where they captured Seren and killed the twins. And another where Seren lost control of an Elemental and drowned Altzis and prisoners alike. For a moment, instincts screamed at him to swim in that direction, but sound traveled far on water. The distant gunshots could be miles away.

He kept up his pattern of kicking and floating, but it felt like time had slowed down. Would the fight ever end? He heard something shatter. Something boomed. A humming faded from the water. Shimmer dust fell from the air as the fog cleared.

The good news was that Erik was heading towards shore and about ten yards away from a rocky island crowned with scraggly bushes and trees, and at most, half a mile from the mainland. The bad news was that the Altzi boat wasn't far behind him.

CHAPTER
TWENTY-TWO

Dovetown was the most built-up place Seren had seen since leaving the Port's Mouth. The town itself was an island at the end of the bay. A mismatch of wood and brick houses covered almost every inch of it and spilled over onto the surrounding islands and piers. Catwalks and flimsy bridges connected islands and buildings alike. Solar panels crowned almost all the roofs.

Seren located a place on the map that marked "visitor docking" and pulled up there. No dockhands or harbormasters came to assist them, so Reggie leapt out of the boat and tied it up. Seren checked the fuel. They had burned through more than three quarters of the tank.

They couldn't stop yawning. The magic may not have been choking them or pulling them home, but it still left them drained. Trying to keep their eyes open felt like trying to telekinetically pry open a stubborn clam.

David took the tank out of the boat and walked over to the filling station, leaving Seren and Reggie alone with the boat in case someone came over to collect a docking fee. They watched him walk up to the man and ask him three times before he was allowed to buy fuel. The man hardly made eye contact with David, instead opting to lock his icy blue gaze on Seren and Reggie. Seren shivered under the man's scrutinizing gaze.

David turned his back on the man, frowning, and peering over his shoulder. He held the fuel tank with his right hand while his left rested on the hilt a pistol.

"What's wrong?" asked Seren as David got back to the boat.

David glowered at a rotting plank of wood. A piece broke off as he prodded with his foot. "Generally, in an area that sees frequent travelers, the employees are a little more welcoming to visitors. For a minute, I thought that man wasn't going to sell me any fuel."

Seren frowned. "Did he tell you where we need to pay for docking?"

"He took the fee, but I'm half expecting someone else to come collecting." David pressed the toe if his boot further into the rot, scraping out more soft wood.

Seren glanced back and forth between him and *The Whaler.* "Do you think it's safe to leave the boat here?"

David studied their surroundings and back at that man. "I got the impression we weren't welcome, and if that is the case, sabotaging the boat would force us to stay longer. Why would they do that if they want us gone?"

Reggie winked. "Maybe they figure we won't need a boat if we're dead."

Seren pulled a couple padlocks out of the hold and looped one through the anchor chain connecting it to the oarlock and another between the anchor chain and a cleat.

"You know that won't really stop a thief, only slow them down," said David.

"But that time might be enough for us to stop them, or it might encourage would-be thieves to pick an easier boat." Seren popped the lock closed and stuck the key in their pocket. "Let's go find some food and a bed to sleep in."

The dock groaned when Seren stepped onto it, swaying as they walked, followed by David and Reggie. Even the boards that were the light yellow of new wood bounced like old, rotten planks that could collapse any minute.

They passed people on boats tying up and hauling their catches in for the night, and a few folks who were just venturing out.

"Hello." Seren waved at a random man walking down the dock. It would be easier to get directions to the local shop and inn than wander around searching for it.

The man cast his eyes down towards the water.

After three attempts, Seren gave up. David started saying hi to people. They responded to him nods and muttered hellos, but didn't even glance at Seren or Reggie.

"At least you got some response," said Seren as they passed the tenth boat from theirs. They had one more section of dock left before they got to land. That was when Seren realized they had not seen a single woman yet—all the fishers were men, and so were the dockhands that helped them.

After stepping off the groaning dock and walking by half a dozen closed shops, they passed a group of girls sitting outside a shop front, clad in ankle length, grey, turtleneck dresses. Seren guessed the girls were in their early teens. Their hands shook, and bodies sagged as they mended torn fishnets and sails. The trio of wrinkled ladies watching them had more life in their brown eyes. One girl fumbled her needle and the senior wacked her in the back with a cane.

"Give the kid a break." Reggie lunged forward, but David grabbed her by the arm.

All three crones spat and returned their grumpy gazes to the children.

"What's your problem?" asked Seren.

The old women ignored them.

"They asked you a question," said Reggie.

The women glowered at the girls who were now sewing twice as fast.

"Come on, let them be." David put a hand on Seren and Reggie's backs and guided them away. "Maybe they are afraid of newcomers because they have the kids right there."

"Kids they hit with canes for no reason." Seren's jaw clenched and their face burned.

Reggie's teeth were bared. "The other people on the docks didn't have kids with them."

"They were busy." David nudged Reggie forward.

Seren wanted to believe him. They had little experience with people outside Valley-Port. They didn't know how to deal with people who wouldn't even talk to or look at them. Assana had seemed so confident that the most controversy Seren would endure was about whether magic was safer than science—a topic they were qualified to talk about in spite of their reluctance to use magic. Seren figured if someone who didn't like magic favored it over the technologies that triggered the first flood, then that might make them less afraid of it.

But a whole town ignoring them without giving any reason? How were they supposed to deal with that? How could they figure out what the problem was if the people wouldn't talk to them? What if everyone at NUNES was equally rude?

They'd find out in a couple days if they didn't experience any more delays.

They passed more people on the street and got the same reaction from all of them: whether Seren, Reggie, or David greeted them, the people shook their heads and refused to make eye contact or speak. The women wore plain, ankle-length, turtleneck dresses. Bonnets rested atop their heads, and when spoken to, women hid their face with the bonnets like shy periwinkles retreating their shells. The men, though, wore plain shirts and trousers. None of them wore the leathers and symbols of the Altzis, so that, at least, offered some relief. Being ignored wasn't as bad as being shot at.

After wandering around for close to an hour, Seren and the twins finally found the general store. A bell rung when they entered. The clerk shook his head, blue eyes lingering on Seren's chest for a few seconds too long, evoking a feeling akin to little eels slithering all over their skin. He took out a rag and started wiping a wooden counter.

Seren tried not to huff and puff and rub their arms as they took dried fruit and grain out of oak barrels. They put their bags on the counter to be weighed. The man turned around and started arranging the glassware resting on shelves behind the counter.

"Excuse me, Sir, we would like to buy some supplies," said David.

The man didn't turn around.

"Why are you and everyone in this town ignoring us?" asked David.

"We don't mean you any harm," said Seren, struggling to keep the frustration out of their voice. "We're just passing through on our way north. We need supplies, a night's rest, and then we'll be gone."

The man picked up a plate and wiped it with the same rag he had been using to clean the counter.

Reggie slammed their fist down on the table. "If you don't pay attention to us long enough for us to pay you, we are going to take your supplies without paying for them."

The man pulled a shot gun out from the behind the counter and leveled it at Reggie's head.

They put their hands up. "If you let me pay for it, then I won't steal it."

"I don't want business from someone like you. Get out of this town."

"Like me?" growled Reggie. "What's wrong with me?"

"The sooner you let us pay for the food, the sooner we'll be gone." With his hands raised, David stepped between Reggie and the armed clerk.

"You ain't much better than the other one," he mumbled. "But you are a man, right?"

"That's none of your business." David's cheeks flushed red.

"You got a man's voice at least," mumbled the guy. "You pay."

He didn't lower his weapon.

Conflicting feels warred in Seren like river currents fighting an incoming tide. This man's hate evoked a baffling rage that made Seren want to grab him and shake him. But on a more rational level, they knew that kind of violence was the very thing they were trying to avoid.

Reggie stayed quiet with their jaw clenched. Seren suspected the only reason they stayed silent was because someone held a gun to their head and they were calculating their odds of disarming the man without getting shot.

"Why?" asked Seren, reluctantly opening their mind to the bay. The air in the room crackled with tension, and Seren wanted to be able to defend themselves if necessary and in general, make sure no one died.

"The Mother made men and She made women. It's unnatural for one to pretend to be something else."

The words made them feel like they'd been punched in the chest. Gender was twisty, complex spectrum. Men and women were merely two points on it.

The man turned his gun towards Seren. "You heard me. Now leave."

Tense muscle. Cold seeping through their body. Heart racing. Seren knew they should've just left. They could rely on the land and waters for food for the rest of the trip, assuming it was willing to provide. But the hate in this man's eyes, in his voice, it seeped into the core of their being. They weren't sure he wouldn't shoot them in the back as they walked out. Then one of the twins would shoot him, and who knows what would happen when the gunshots inevitably attracted other people.

Driven by fear, Seren reached out to the elements. Great Bay's steady power rushed to Seren. They closed their eyes, gathering a stream of air currents. Their clothes waved. Papers were whipped up into a cyclone. The man's gun listed away from Seren. "The Mother did not create the concept of binary gender. Humans did that. She doesn't care what our gender or sex is. She even granted her ambassadors the power to change people's sex."

"That power doesn't come from The Mother," he said. "She'll drown you for even thinking that."

The man's hands shook, and his fingers edged closer to the trigger.

"Can we just pay you and leave?" asked David.

"Fifty pieces," said the man. "Steel."

Seren wanted to say something about how outrageous that was, but David handed over the unmarked steel coins. They let go of the power and papers fluttered to the floor like dying butterflies.

"Pick up your stuff and get out."

Reggie slowly bent down and picked up the supplies. Seren helped. They backed out of the shop without taking their eyes off the man's gun. Seren barely dared to breathe until they were back on the street. "Something tells me we won't be finding a room here. We should keep going."

David froze. "Seren, unless we detour, the next town is Merry Basin. Even if we drive straight through, we're a full day's ride away."

Seren didn't slow down. "We'll can camp. I'll ask the trees permission if I have to. Right now, an angry forest seems more welcoming than this town."

"I don't know." Reggie snickered. "We can shoot people. Trees might try to eat us in our sleep."

"Can you stop with the monster talk?" Seren walked faster, fantasizing about pushing Reggie off the docks. It kept them from obsessing about the strange stares they got, but their fists remained clenched and their muscles tight until they were back at *The Whaler*'s helm with fiberglass and water, not rotten wood, beneath their feet.

CHAPTER TWENTY-THREE

Erik picked up his pace, swimming as hard as he could. He could *almost* touch the water with his mind. He sensed anger retreating to satisfaction when he searched for its elemental, but it either ignored Erik's plea for help or Erik remained too drugged to be heard.

Fatigue weighed his limbs. Muscles burned. His throat ached. He needed to get out of the water. Rest. Hide before the Altzis saw. He circled halfway around the island, so it was between him and the Altzi ship, then scrambled onto the rocks until he got to one with a flat enough surface to sit on. A cool breeze made him shiver. He leaned back and hugged his knees to his chest and tried to make himself small. All the docks in this town were tiny and filled with small vessels. Even if the dock had an open berth, the big clunky ship wouldn't fit.

He studied the water. It was shallow from the island in and he saw quite a few rocks jutting up to the surface. If the Altzi ship tried to get to shore, it would break something on the way in.

The paddling engine grew louder and louder until the island seemed to shake. He heard voices, but he couldn't distinguish words.

The ship moved at an agonizingly slow pace. Even when his legs cramped up, he stayed curled up in his little crevasse until it was well past the ended of the houses on shore. Then he slowly climbed down, slipped into the water, and swam to land.

In Valley-Port, if a bruised person in tattered clothing clambered onto a dock, people would've rushed to help whether it was one of their own people or some wrecked sailor Atlantik had spit up on their shore. But here?

Erik swam up the dock that stuck out the furthest, hauled himself onto half-decayed planks, and flopped on his back for a moment, too breathless the talk.

The person stared.

One person staring like that wasn't exactly strange. Not everyone processed the world in the same way. However, there was also always someone who would be the first one to offer help, and then others would follow.

But either no one else saw Erik, or no one cared.

He pushed himself up to a sitting position and slowly got to his feet. "Um, hi. Is there any place I might get some food and fresh water?"

The person was about his age but with blonde hair and freckled, sunburnt skin. He nodded. Opened up the satchel he wore and held out a full water skin. "Where did you come from?"

Erik glanced out at the Atlzi ship, chugging along maybe half a mile offshore, but hesitated to actually answer. Was it shame for having gotten captured? Fear that the people in this village might be Altzis?

The other person's eyes widened as he looked back and forth between Erik and the ship. "If you were their prisoner, it's not safe for you here. They'll moor in the next town over and search along the shore in a smaller boat. They'll ask if people saw you, and most will answer honestly."

"And you? What will you say when they come searching for me?" Erik glanced at the small boat tied up alongside the dock. It had oars and a sail, a fishing pole and a net. A cool breeze ruffled his hair. If he stole the boat and the water this person had, he could stay alive and moving long enough to find Seren. Once he got a little further inland, the water would be fresh enough to drink.

"I can't give you the boat, but I can take you somewhere to hide for a few days." The person held out his hand. "I'm Thomas."

"Erik. He/him pronouns." He shook the other person's hand.

"My pronouns are also he/him." Thomas smiled. "I doubt its coincidence you found my dock in my down out of all the others in this bay. Great Bay must be awake today."

Erik returned the smile. "I'm guessing that's the local Elemental?"

Thomas walked towards the boat and got in carefully. "No one around here can talk to him, but sometimes I can feel him."

"I'm a water mage." Erik followed Thomas into the boat. Normally, he had good sea legs, but days of insufficient food and water had left him weak and dizzy. He wasn't sure if it was actually the boat rocking or a bout of dizziness, but he lost his balance and fell.

"When was the last time you ate?" Thomas untied the boat and pushed off.

"I'm not sure." Erik propped himself up. His sense of time was skewed from captivity. He'd assumed it was morning.

At home, the fog often cleared in the morning, just before the fishers headed out for the day, but as he studied the sky, focusing on the sun and the light now that he wasn't solely focused on avoiding recapture, he realized it was late afternoon. The sun had passed its peak. The light was warm and golden. "That fog took a long time to burn off today."

"I've seen nothing quite like it." Thomas watched a seaweed crowned rock as he rowed past it. "To be honest, when I saw you climb out of the water, my first reaction was that you had caused the fog."

Erik didn't understand that logic, but he didn't was to risk losing

Thomas's help by questioning it. "I can't make fog, and even if I could, the Altzis gave me some kind of drug that suppressed my magic. I need somewhere to lie low until it wears off."

"And then what do you plan to do?"

"My partner should pass through on their way to NUNES. If I haven't missed them, I'm they'll pick me up." Erik wondered if Seren, or anyone, knew he was missing. He was supposed to have the day off but had gone to work anyway because of the winds. When he'd gotten promoted to dock master, the position came with its own housing, so he'd moved out of his parent's house and lived alone.

If anyone came looking for him, Martin could've said he'd gone home, especially if the winds had calmed down. With the time he'd been working, with how run down he'd gotten, no one would be surprised to not see him for a day or two while he rested, but after that, someone would notice.

Erik had no clue how long he had actually been gone for. He didn't know how fast they had been moving, how long he slept for each time he was drugged, and if they woke him once a day or several times a day. When he finally worked up the courage to ask about the date, he found out this was the third day he had been gone. It felt like much longer, but he supposed it made sense that time felt slower when he was miserable, especially if he had been woken multiple times a day.

"So where are you taking me?" Erik asked after a little while of sailing in silence. He was laying down in the boat, so he wasn't easily visible to passerby, and because he was exhausted.

"I'm going to my usual fishing spots, and when I pass by the island my boyfriend and I meet up on, I'm dropping you there," said Thomas. "There is shelter and food. You may as well rest until we get there. I don't arouse suspicion by going straight there."

Erik yawned. The warm sun and the gentle lapping of waves on the hull made him drowsy. "Why are you helping me?"

"I don't like the Altzis," said Thomas. "They've turned my parents against me. Forced me to hide who I am. Made my friends and I scapegoat for all the trouble our village has. They've stripped us of having a voice at NUNES."

"What do you mean, about that last part?" Erik's eyes were getting heavy. But if the Altzis had somehow interfered with a group's ability to take part, he needed to know so he could tell Seren. They could tell Root. Maybe it could get fixed.

"Each individual town along this bay operates independently, but alone, no one town has a high enough population for us each to get a vote, but with all six bay abutting villages combined, we had enough," said Thomas. He paused for a moment, looked around, and cast his line. "But because many of the village leaders had signed on with the Altzi party, we realized the bay towns couldn't join as one state because the chapter we were part of had already registered as one. Some people were okay with that. Others were too afraid to fight it. So now instead of having someone local representing us, one of them is. One of them will be in charge of governing us. One of them will have legal power to enforce their ridiculous rules about conformity."

"My partner's mother is friends with Root," Erik said, struggling to stay awake. "Maybe if he knows you've been coerced, he won't let your population be weighed with the Altzi votes. Maybe he'll send for a delegation from your villages."

Thomas snorted. "Root knows exactly what the Altzis are doing. From what I heard, he was encouraging this kind of consolidation to minimize the number of delegates at NUNES."

"That's bad." Erik fought against exhaustion. That piece of information felt particularly significant, but his tired brain couldn't quite parse out why. "Seren thinks he's an ally."

"Does supporting Altzis make that false?" Thomas tilted he head and peered at Erik.

Thomas's voice sounded distant. Erik's vision and thoughts blurred. He was so tired. So hurt. He could hardly think. "If they knew what those monsters did to me, yes."

Thomas didn't respond, and after a few minutes of silence, the afternoon sun and gently rocking boat lulled Erik to sleep.

"We're here." Thomas's voice woke Erik.

Judging by the sun, maybe an hour had passed. They were beached on a small island that was lower than the one Erik had hid on, but longer, with denser trees and bushes.

"There is a shelter in the middle," Thomas said. "Hurry inside and stay there until you know the Altzi ship is gone."

Erik could hear the paddles churning in the distance. He reached out with his mind, and finally, and was greeted with an expanse of cold estuarine water with branches of fresh water pouring into it from different sides. The currents were slow and foreign. An awareness twined through them all, so focused on something that it didn't notice Erik prod it and draw power from it.

He smiled. Hope. It felt like floating in warm water on a late summer afternoon.

"I'll come back tomorrow and bring more food and water," Thomas said.

"I'll be okay. I might not even still be here tomorrow, if my partner is close," said Erik.

After a quick goodbye with Thomas, he lingered on the edge of the water. He sent his mind into the bay, sensing as far as he could, feeling the shape of the boats on the water. Those moving around bay were unfamiliar. At the largest town at one end of the bay, there were dozens at a dock, but there were too many to pick out details from this distance. He wouldn't know if Seren was there unless he got closer or had help from the bay. But the Elemental wasn't hearing him, and the Altzi boat was gaining on him.

CHAPTER

TWENTY-FOUR

The adrenaline conjured by Seren's close encounter with a shotgun didn't last long. Half an hour north of Dovetown, Seren started yawning. Their eyes blurred, and when they went too long without blinking, they swore they saw Erik's face wavering on the rivers rippled surface.

They rubbed their eyes. The bay narrowed to a windy river, and the houses surrendered to dense trees. There were no warnings on the map claiming that this part of the forest ate people, but like the Dark Forest, there were no roads through it. Seren's head throbbed, and they longed to curl up on a soft bed.

David stared at the chart with his head cocked. "If this is accurate, there should be some coves we could anchor in and be out of the currents."

"But we should make sure nothing else has already claimed said cove before we decide to sleep in it," added Reggie.

Seren nodded, more or less agreeing with Reggie. The only real problem with that plan was that it involved magic. Dull pinks and purples painted the fading blue sky. They wouldn't be able to navigate in the dark without using magic and using it to ask permission to anchor in a cove would be less tiring than trying to sense every rock, wreck, and sandbar.

With a few slow breaths and some spared attention, Seren opened their heart and mind to the Earth, letting her magic flood their sense. A smile seized their yawn as docile, sleepy energy seeped into their mind. The trees were just as sentient here as anywhere else, but like Seren, they struggled to stay awake. A distant, weak thread linked those trees to someone or something bigger.

Picturing themself and the twins dropping anchor and sleeping in the boat, Seren whispered to the forest: "Can we camp here?" It wasn't necessary to speak the question, but Seren felt better doing so because it kept them focused.

A slight breeze rustled a "yessss" through the trees, soon followed by a return of the image they had sent of three people sleeping in the boat, only while they slept, the sky darkened, then lightened.

"We're good," said Seren guiding the boat into the little cove.

"Thank The Mother," said David.

Seren shifted into neutral, and shut the engine off, letting the current swing them the rest of the way into the shallow cove. They darted to the back of the boat, unlocked the engine and titled it up just as the water got so shallow that the propeller would have gotten stuck in the mud. They dropped a bow and stern line. After they secured the boat, they fished around in the small hold for some food and their sleeping bags. Within a few minutes, Seren was wrapped up in a wool blanket, curled up on the driver's bench.

"I'll take first watch," said Reggie. "I did hear a story about this forest once. There were giant bears that were smarter than any human. I just can't remember if they're herbivores or omnivores."

Reggie kept talking, but their words blurred into a senseless lullaby. Seren closed their eyes, welcoming the blissful oblivion of sleep.

It never came. As soon as their conscious mind quieted, it tossed them into some forgotten Hell of a dream vision. Heat, friction, rot, body odor, shouts, grunts, sweat, and steam overwhelmed their senses. Pain sharpened Seren's focus. Metal dug deep into the Earth. Seren screamed. That was skin, not Earth.

This wasn't some pre-flood nightmare seeping into their consciousness from The Mother. It was a prophecy. The Mother yanked Seren's soul out of their body and projected it into someone else's body, and that body was in pain.

Seren tried to take deep breaths to calm themself, but they couldn't control the form they were in. They needed to get out. Envisioning a slingshot propelling their soul outward, they summoned a gale to blow their spirit out.

For a moment, they were free, a bundle of raw energy soaring through the sky until they collided with a gull searching for a meal. They seeped into gull as it squawked, angry that black metal ship with big red paddles scared the fish away. The boat belched black steam as it churched its way up the river. Its paddles stirred up the silt and bones that rested on the bottom, disturbing drowsing Elementals.

"Seren!" screamed a familiar voice. It almost sounded like Erik. But he was back in Little Port, safe. He couldn't be here.

The gull was less conscious than the first body, so Seren was able to make it circled around, but no matter what angle they looked from, they still couldn't see the source of the scream. A man walked to the edge of the ship and dropped a miniature boat in the water. It had white clay bricks and red sticks strapped to it. He used a remote to control it and watched as it carried the explosives down the river. Seren steered the gull to follow boat until it was almost directly above *The Whaler*, where they were sleeping while Reggie kept watch.

Seren woke when the boat rocked hard enough to toss them from the bench to the floor. Pain rocked through their back and cleared their mind. Their heart raced. Every muscle in their body clenched. Trees leaned forward, sinister in the shadows, protecting them from an unseen threat. Reggie crouched at the stern, clutching the edges with a white knuckled grip, and David slept curled up their feet, apparently oblivious to the rough waves.

"Thank The Mother that you're awake," said Reggie. "The river is pissed."

"Not at us." Seren flailed and slithered until they were finally free of their sleeping bag. They stood on the bow, hands clenched into fists.

"Who is it angry at?" Reggie eyed the gun holstered at their hip instead of the writhing currents. One hand crept off the railing towards that holsters.

"Altzis." Seren peered over the edge of the boat, checking the anchor line and finding that it loose but holding. They looked up at Reggie. "Did you adjust the lines?"

"Neither of us touched them."

Seren nodded, suspecting the river had somehow loosened them. "We'll handle this better if we're moving."

"You rested enough?"

"Yeah." Seren hoped they weren't lying to Reggie. A dull ache throbbed in their head. The sky was dark, streaked with gray clouds that hid the stars. They could almost make the moon out through them, but the distortion made it hard to judge its exact position, and therefore the time. Seren reached into their pocket for their watch, but the boat rocked again, nearly knocking Seren overboard. They needed to get out of the cove, so they could take the waves head on.

Seren hauled in the bowline and shoved it into the hold then started towards the stern and crashed into Reggie, who showed no fear of other people, but was terrified of rough waters.

"You need stay out of my way or help."

"Right." Reggie gritted their teeth and sank to their knees, landing on top of their brother.

"What is happening?" David jumped awake, nearly tossing his twin out of the boat.

Reggie crawled, gripping the starboard edge until they ran into the bow, muttering.

A larger wave pushed the port side partially out of the water. Seren leapt forward and grabbed the rear line, hauled it in and dropped it on the deck. They grabbed an oar and pushed *The Whaler* out into deeper water. Seren dropped the oar, eliciting a squeal from one of the twins, and pulled the engine cord once, twice, three times until it finally roared itself to combustion.

They darted over to put the boat in reverse and backed out of the cove. Once in the main river, they turned the wheel. The clouds shifted, and moonlight poured down on the water, illuminating a cat-sized boat filled with white clay bricks, on a collision course with *The Whaler.*

"Is that C4?" Reggie raised their head just high enough to see over the side of the boat.

"Do you know how rare that stuff is?" David popped his head up behind them, practically drooling at the bomb. "So few explosives survived The Flood. Someone really wants you dead, Seren."

Seren reached for the throttle, but as they rounded a bend, they saw the steamboat with the wheels from their dream.

"Seren!" screamed the same voice they heard in the dream and now that they were awake, they realized it was Erik's voice.

How did he get all the out here, trapped on an Altzi ship? Their hands shook. Rage and fear twined around their heart and lungs, making their chest ache. How long had they had him? What had they done to him? Their nails dug into the wheel. Their shoulders shook. They had to save him.

Their anger mingled with the rivers as they pushed the throttle forward, ignoring frantic warnings from David and Reggie, hoping to slide between the bomb and the rocks without hitting either. Fearing they wouldn't fit, Seren drew wild energy from the river, boosting the boat up on a bubble of hot air. They rose high enough to avoid smashing their prop on the rock and to sail over the bomb.

Fire and raw energy roared under them as the bomb exploded anyways. Seren let some heat bleed into their bubble to help fuel it and guided the rest of it around the bubble as they kept willing them forward. The wind blew from the north, but Seren begged the Mother for it to shift directions. A gale screamed behind them, sending the boat shooting forward. Seren dashed to the stern once more, shut the engine off.

"What the hell?" shouted Reggie.

"Did they have a remote trigger?" David's mouth hung open. His lower lip trembled.

"The air bubble itself must have been enough to trigger the bomb," guessed Seren.

"Maybe it registered pressure." Reggie slowly rose to their feet looking around with wide eyes. "Fire proof air bubble. Pretty impressive."

"The Altzis have Erik," said Seren with clenched teeth. "They are going to pay for whatever they've done to him."

"How do you know?" asked David.

"I saw it in a dream." Seren glared at him. "Don't argue that it might have just been a dream, because that bomb that almost blew us up was in it."

Neither David nor Reggie argued. Instead, they began plotting out strategies for rescuing Erik and trying to speculate about what kind of weapons these Altzis would have and how many of them would be wearing vests. Seren heard snippets of the conversation, something about head shots, kneecaps, element of surprise and asses, but most of Seren's focus was on controlling the air bubble and maintaining their connection with a river hellbent on drowning Seren's enemies.

CHAPTER TWENTY-FIVE

June days were long. Erik wanted to nap the rest of the afternoon, but he didn't trust himself not to sleep through the night until the next morning, and he had nothing to use as an alarm to wake himself up. Keeping his mind open to the water, he siphoned what little energy he could from the bay, monitoring the boats and currents, searching for Seren, and poking the Elemental. It seemed half asleep until a burst of anger and fear woke it. It didn't seem to notice Erik latch on any more than a dock noticed a barnacle, but there was more than just the Elemental's anger and energy.

Erik could feel Seren on the other end, angrier and more afraid than he'd ever seen them. He tried to call them through the Elemental, but it was like shouting through a rushing waterfall.

They were so close, but he couldn't reach them.

It was too much.

Logic be damned.

Erik leapt to his feet, rushed out of the shelter and dove into the bay. He'd grown familiar enough with the currents in his hours-long vigil in the tent that he could gather a stream of water around him and use it to propel himself towards Dovetown, towards the place where he had felt Seren, and even if it couldn't talk to him, the bay didn't resist. But even with magic, without a boat, Erik could only swim so fast for so long. He felt the fear and anger recede long before he got to Dovetown and sensed the shape of a boat and the hum of an engine he had long ago memorized to pull out of the dock and speed away. Away from the town. Away from him.

By the time Erik got to Dovetown, Seren was long gone.

The sun burned deep red, low on the horizon, and Erik could barely stay awake.

He didn't see the Altzi boat, but when he stretched out his mind, he could feel it heading into the same river as Seren. Indecision tore through Erik. The desire to rest was the wedge of salt water rushing into the river with the tide, pushing against the flow of fresh water, the drive to find Seren.

He thought of Thomas's words about how the Altzis ran Dovetown.

It wasn't safe.

He swam up to a dory tied to a mooring.

Erik had never stolen before, but he couldn't keep swimming. Cold and tired, Erik worried he already had hypothermia. And Seren was so close. He used the water to steady the boat as he climbed in. He untied the boat and laid down. Rowing would've warmed him, but his arms were too tired. He gathered currents around the boat and sent it towards the river, towards Seren.

Eventually, he had to row because water rushed out of the river into the bay. While he could make a little convection system, so the surface water moved upstream while everything below moved in its natural direction, it was very slow going. As he turned around a bend in the river, he remembered one very important detail he'd forgotten in his half-delirious single-minded attempt to get to Seren.

The Altzi ship was heading in the same direction.

And he almost rowed right into it.

The currents changed as the Altzi water mage blocked Erik's control. A harpoon shot down and slammed into the boat beside him and dragged it to the lower deck of the Altzi ship. Erik scrambled to jump, but a net tangled around him. He wiggled and kicked and shouted as they dragged him on board. He screamed into the water with both words and mind, reaching for Seren, for a drowsing river Elemental. The bay hadn't heard him, but the river did. The water churned as the Elemental reacted to his anguish. The wind picked up. Tree branches groaned.

Help is coming, whispered a voice both gentle and wicked. Vengeance will be our pleasure.

The shouting of the Altzis grew muffled by the sound of water rushing through his ears. He knew fists and feet pummeled him, but he only felt icy water rushing over his body. Liquid dripped in his mouth, and he swallowed, not knowing if it came from the Altzis or the Elemental until his connection to the raging river faded to half-frozen fog suffocating his soul. He screamed as they dragged him in the ship and threw him into the dark hold. He was so close. So close. He kicked at and screamed in the dark, fully expecting to be in there for hours, for days, to die alone in the dark.

Yet it wasn't long before the door opened, and they dragged him out onto the deck, to a sight that filled him with equal amounts of hope and fear. Something that made him smile so big his face hurt, even though he wasn't even sure if it was real.

CHAPTER
TWENTY-SIX

T*he Whaler* hurtled towards the Altzi boat, propelled by gusts howling for its destruction. That same gale stirred up frothy waves. As they rose and crashed, it sounded like they were saying "crush" over and over again. When the wind hit the trees, they screamed as their trunks and branches bent and writhed. The forest didn't form words with its creaks and screams, but the high pitch and minor key made them sound just as angry as everything else. The river, the forest, and the bay all wanted the Altzi ship destroyed.

Seren struggled to separate their thoughts from those of the various earth spirits they were channeling power from. The planet's rage filled their mind, making it hard to remember who they were and what they were doing, other than destroying those threatening their existence. They clung to memories as the tempest of power tossed them about. Memories of the lake, still and steamy on a fall morning, of how Erik's hair always smelled like salt and sunlight, and of their mother, curled up on one of the library's oversized chairs, drowsing while she read a book.

They thought of eating chowder at The Compass Rose, of David and Reggie arguing over a person they both liked but would never pursue, and the way kissing Erik could be so smooth and rough at the same time. Seren clung to the things they loved and used them to hold the raging Earth's power back far enough so it didn't consume them.

The Whaler shot over the boat. Seren released the bubble, allowing it to drop in the water in front of the larger ship. They hit the throttle, surging forward, lifting the bow up and shooting the twins up in the air. Both David and Reggie screamed like babies, but they reacted quickly as Seren surrounded them with an updraft and guided them to the deck. By the time they landed, their guns were drawn and aimed at the Altzis firing at them with shotguns.

Fueled by Elemental rage, torn between the desire to destroy and preserve, to save Erik and go or torment those who tormented him, Seren summoned their own air bubble and lifted themself off of *The Whaler*. They rose slowly, keeping eye on the twins to make sure they were okay. The Altzis were laying out a steady fire, but had poor aim. The twins only fired when they had a clear shot. A few stray bullets zipped towards Seren, but they plucked the kinetic energy and fed it to their bubble, causing the bullets to plop into the water.

They rose higher and higher until they were a dozen feet above the highest tree on the riverbank. Thick cords of energy bound Seren and the river, but they weren't sure who was puppet and who was the master.

They gathered a gust of wind and shot it down at their enemies. The boat rocked. Everyone, including the twins, tumbled over. Some of the Altzis fell overboard, and Seren doubted they would resurface. A wave of crushing guilt rose inside them, but they pushed it away. They had to save Erik no matter the cost. Feelings and emotions could wait. They'd deal with the psychological fallout when they were both safe. Taking a deep breath, they locked up their feelings, gathered Earth magic inside themself and focused on their throat. They spoke, using the magic to amplify the sound waves.

"You have something I want!" Seren's voice boomed across the bay like an earthquake.

For a few seconds the Altzis froze, staring wide-eyed and frozen.

"You took my partner. Give him back, or I will destroy you all."

Reggie snickered. Everyone snapped out of whatever shocked daze seeing a person hovering in the air had put them and started shooting. Half the Altzis fired bullets that bounced off Seren's bubble while the other half continued firing on the twins, who appeared to be running out of ammo. Reggie fired once for every ten Altzis shots. David wasn't returning fire at all.

The wind and waves were still in Seren's mind, urging them to smash the ship. It would be so easy to call a wave and push them to the bottom, but Erik and the twins were on board. Seren gritted their teeth, engaging in a tug of war of wills.

They had to think quickly. There was no doubt that the Altzi ship would sink. Even if they let go of the power, the river was determined to sink it with or without Seren. However, by guiding the river's raw power, they could make sure that it didn't sink with their friends still on it.

The river bucked like a wild horse refusing to be ridden. Tentacles of water lashed out at the hull until it cracked, letting the river get a grip on the boat so they could drag it down. Once the hull was pierced, Seren sensed Erik inside, hurting, scared, and surrounded by metal walls.

Seren raised their arms, summoning walls of water that imprisoned the boat much like its owners had imprisoned Erik. The water formed a wedge speeding towards the boat, intent on crushing it.

Seren spun. They twisted the water into a pillar and drew it under them for support. They aimed micro gusts of wind at the Altzis, knocking them over one at a time until all but their leader had either retreated into the bowels of their ship or surrendered.

The twins held the lead Altzi at gunpoint, while Seren ordered them to bring Erik.

"Why would I give you the only thing keeping me alive?" asked a man who had been leading the battle.

"I won't kill you or your people if you let him go."

"How do I know you're not lying?"

"You don't," said Seren. "But believe me when I tell you I don't like killing. What is stopping me from ordering Reggie to put a bullet in your head and killing my way through your ship until I find Erik?"

The man stared at Seren. "Our wives and children are on board."

"They won't be harmed. I promise." Seren echoed that promise to the river, hoping it listened. "No innocent lives will be taken.

"You'll truly spare them?" he asked.

"Yes," said Seren. They weren't lying. They would let Altzis go. However, they couldn't make any promises about what the river would do. "Bring him up here, and I will release you from the cage and remove my guards from your boat."

"Guss, bring up the prisoner," said the lead Altzi.

CHAPTER
TWENTY-SEVEN

A storm raged inside Seren. As soon as Erik and the twins were off the ship, Seren was tempted to just plunge the Altzi ship down to the bottom of the river, but they'd given their word. They wanted people to trust them, even if those people were Altzi bottom-feeders. More importantly, there were innocent people on the ship, so they focused on lifting Erik and the twins on a spinning jet of water.

It was no easy task. If Seren's attention slipped, David, Reggie, and Erik would fall into the waterspout. The river could revolt and drown both Seren, their friends, and the Altzis. Seren couldn't listen to the shouted demands and insults, or the shots being fired. Apparently, the Altzis didn't care about keeping promises. Seren ignored them, intent on bringing their friends closer until the two water spurts met. Seren lowered three of the four walls and sent the waterspout they were on through the wave of water. Erik stared at the wall, wide-eyed and open mouthed, and the twins wore a similar expression.

"Have some faith," said Seren, grinning as water turned to swirling rainbows on the edge of her air bubble.

"That's the most romantic thing you've ever done," rasped Erik.

Seren's clenched jaw melted into a smile. "You're dehydrated."

"I love you," Erik whispered from where he rested beside them.

"Drink slow." Seren guided a trickle of water through the bubble and into his mouth, and then they lowered one hand, so it rested on top of his matted curls. Seren wasn't sure if the relief they felt at having him safe or if the strong urge to pull Erik inside them and protect him from the world was love, but they knew if anyone hurt him again, they would not show mercy. "I'm not going to let people like that influence the NUNES constitution. I won't let them taint our new government."

Seren could just picture the Altzis policing their states with licensed thugs, beating anyone who tried to exist outside their rigid rules if people voted option three on the law enforcement article and the Altzis got too much power in the government.

"I know." Erik's voice was barely more than a whisper. As his head became a dead weight on Seren's leg, they wanted to scoop him into their arms and hold him while he slept.

"Dammit!" Reggie shoved their gun back together with a click. "We need to stay out of their range. I only have three bullets left in all my guns."

Reggie's cursing drew Seren's attention back to the fact that they were in an air bubble floating thirty feet over the river inside a wall of water that steadily drained their energy. If Seren lingered here cuddling Erik, it would keep draining their energy until they fell asleep, at which point both the bubble and wall would collapse, killing them all long before they got back in range of any surviving Altzis.

Ignoring Reggie's stream of complaints about ammo and unnecessary worries about the Altzis catching up, Seren settled for absentmindedly working the knots out of Erik's hair with one hand while the rest of their being stayed focused on guiding everyone through her wall of water, back to *The Whaler*, lowering the wall of water, and speeding away.

"Do we have to worry about them catching up to us anytime soon?" asked David. He sat on the floor of the boat with Erik's head cradled in his lap. Reggie stood at the bow, keeping watch on what was head of them.

"No. The engines are crippled, and the river wants that ship in the worst way."

"But you said you'd let them go."

"And I did," said Seren. "I begged the river to spare them, but I don't know if it will listen; I'm an interloper here."

"Distance won't stop them from blaming you. Those idiots seem to have their own idea of truth."

Seren nudged the throttle forward. The engine sang, but it was already at full speed. It was not loud enough to drown the screams of the Altzis and their sinking ship. It was too slow to outrun the guilt of having played a role in that destruction.

CHAPTER

TWENTY-EIGHT

Erik woke to a sight he thought he would never see: Reggie driving Seren's boat. At first, he wasn't sure he was even awake, but every muscle in his body ached, breathing set his ribs aflame, his throat felt like sandpaper, and his head throbbed. Panic crept through the pain like poison ivy. He wouldn't dream this much pain. "Seren…is Seren okay?"

"Seren's sleeping." David perched in Reggie's spot at the bow. "Right next to you."

Erik turned his stiff neck just far enough to see Seren snoring on the deck a mere inch away from him. He scooted closer, so their legs and hips were touching. He made eye contact with Reggie.

"But are they okay? They never let anyone else touch that helm."

"They also never use as much magic as they did last night."

Eyes wide and mouth open, Erik turned and gaped at Seren. They were cocooned in their maple-brown sleeping bag, eyes closed and face relaxed. He had things he needed to warn them about, but now that he was here, with them, it was too much to think about yesterday and the day before.

"Seren insisted they could drive straight through until we get to

NUNES, but they just passed out a couple hours ago when the river ended, and a lake began. I think it's a different spirit, one who is less willing to share its power."

"Thank The Mother." Erik lowered his aching head and rested it on Seren's chest where he could feel its steady rise and fall, and hear their heart thud at a slow, relaxing pace. "How long before we reach someplace with a proper bed?"

Reggie glanced at the chart and compass. "The next town is Merry Basin, where NUNES is being held. I'm assuming we'll have decent accommodations since Assana speaks so highly of the host, Ambassador Root. A day if we take turns driving and don't stop."

Erik shook his head as he tried to bury it further in Seren's chest. His cheeks burned with shame as he thought of how easily he had cracked under Domhnall's questions. He bet Reggie or David would've found a way to avoid giving out information. Tears stung his eyes. Bile burned his throat. He clenched his teeth and sealed his lips shut hoping he wouldn't puke on Seren.

Erik didn't hear him move, but in seconds, David was by his side with a hand on Erik's back. "I don't know what they did to you, but when and if you want to talk about it, I'm here. I've been through shit too."

Erik nodded without unburying his face. He hoped Seren would wake up and hug him, but they kept snoring despite his movement. David's arm slid around Erik, sandwiching Erik's body between David and Seren's. Warmth flooded his body, loosening some of the tension, and releasing the flood of tears he had been holding back.

CHAPTER TWENTY-NINE

Seren was still tired when Erik woke them by bawling into their chest. They silenced the tiny, selfish part of themself that was angry at being woken and pressed their body close to his, whispering, "As long as you're close, I won't let anyone else get you."

Erik sobbed. Seren held him closer, regretting how they'd hardly spared him a thought while they were separated. If they hadn't been so hyper-focused on the mission and paid more attention to water and dreams, they might have heard his cries for help. They might have rescued him sooner.

Seren squeezed Erik tighter. His body, warm, solid, and damp with tears of sweat, quaked against theirs as a storm of indefinable emotion battered it. Seren's throat cramped and their eyes watered. They clenched their jaw, trying to hold the storm surge back, but soon, their own sobs were quaking in time with Erik's. They didn't know what the Altzis did to him, but their imagination had plenty of horrid ideas. From now on, they'd keep a closer eye on him, even if it meant using more magic.

Seren didn't know how long they clung to each other for, but eventually, the storm of tears lost its energy. Sitting up, Seren cradled Erik's head in their lap until David told them that they should try to make him eat and drink a little.

Seren propped him up to sitting position. They leaned him against the wall of the boat, afraid he would tip over without the support, and grabbed a flask of fresh water from the hold. When Erik tried to lift it up to his mouth, his hands shook so much water spilled over his face. Seren steadied them with their own, tilting the flask so water trickled into Erik's mouth.

"Eat slowly." David crouched behind Seren with a handful of berries. Seren took one and placed it in Erik's mouth. He chewed slowly at first, but his hands steadied after he ate the first handful, so when Seren gave him a hunk of bread, he ate it on his own.

"I never thought bread and berries would taste this good," rasped Erik after he finished the bread.

"What did they feed you?" asked David.

Erik shuttered. "Moldy bread. Unidentifiable fish."

Anger prickled beneath Seren's skin and their hands itched to feel *The Whaler's* throttle and steering wheel, but they let Reggie keep driving so they could take care of Erik and find out what the Altzis did to him.

After he ate and drank a little more, and his voice started to return, he told Seren snippets of what had happened during his captivity and during his brief escape, and the more he told them, the more they wished they had just drowned the Altzis. If they'd been slower to figure out what happened and rescue Erik, the Altzis would've killed him. Torture, starvation, and isolation were horrible things, and Seren couldn't get the image of him alone in the dark out of their head. Their fists curled, and they bit their lip. The current carrying the boat sped up as the river responded to Seren's anger.

The next time Erik slept, Seren pushed Reggie away from the helm and shoved the throttle forward. The engine roared and *The Whaler* sped on. The river widened as it met up with other rivers, all heading towards the massive lake that was Root's domain. After months of indecision and anxiety, they were almost at NUNES, and Seren wasn't sure what they were more afraid of: more violent confrontations with Altzis and Elementals, or the actual politicking.

As the river widened, Seren caught up to other boats. It was the most traffic that had seen since they left the Port's mouth. Seren had taken the most direct route, which was also the one that passed through the least populated areas. In the end, it hadn't been as quick as they thought thanks to all the obstacles they encountered, but they had no clue what would've happened to Erik if they'd gone a different way.

They passed two skiffs with hulls like *The Whaler's*, only larger with enclosed sleeping cabins. Seren's wake rocked a gundalow, an oblong sailboat with one slanted mast and an almost flat bottom.

That same wake nearly flipped a sailing catamaran already struggling to stay upright in the wind. There were also a handful of smaller wooden boats being rowed, sailed, or propelled by small engines. Some people were downright exhausted. Sweat made their chapped skin shine and yawns frequently escaped their mouths. Some waved at Seren and their crew. Others glared. One couple in a wooden scull picked up their pace, desperate to outrun them before giving up and letting them pass. Seren was not looking forward to seeing how that attitude would play out on the debate floor. Were people even going to listen to each other? How would they convince anyone they were worth listening too?

The river widened. The trees thinned, giving way to fields of tall grass dotted with round thatched-roof huts and teepees. Closer to the water, plowed fields replaced tall grasses replaced. In some, greens like spinach, lettuce, peas, and kale thrived in the sunlight and damp soil. In others, seedlings were just poking their green heads out of the dirt. On south facing slopes, terraced glass houses sheltered tomatoes, cucumbers, and squashes from an unpredictable frost, and the hills that were too steep for green houses had doors that Seren guessed lead to root cellars.

This agricultural hub was able to feed the NUNES conference without leaving its own people to starve in the winter. It wasn't just the lake's connection to dozens of river systems that enabled this area to host, but its abundance of food. Fields marched on miles and miles of similar scenery as the river widened, meeting up with other rivers until it wasn't a river at all, but a lake so big Seren couldn't see the far the shore. Thanks to the steady breeze blowing at Seren's back, this lake looked like a small ocean, writhing with whitecaps.

They'd spoken to Root through water messages back home, and heard good things about his people, but Seren wasn't sure they trusted the people that neglected to mention how cruel the were and who allowed them to take votes from smaller villages for the sake of consolidation. What if Root wasn't the kind, genius of a mage Assana said he was? What if Merry Basin wasn't the welcoming, free place Seren always thought it was? What if it was all a trap? An elaborate trick to get everyone to come together so they could be controlled and forced to change their way of life?

The whipping winds wicked just enough rage from Seren's mind that they dared open it to Earth. They reached out the lake elemental and asked the lake what kind of people lived near.

The lake itself didn't answer. Ambassador Root did.

We're honest people. Like you, we live in symbiosis with the Earth, honoring and supporting Her in whatever way we can.

Seren sighed. Apparently, this lake was more like home, sleeping while an ambassador wielded their power. *Will you welcome a fellow ambassador into your territory, no matter how they dress or behave?*

We do not judge people based on appearances. You are welcome here, Seren, and so are your companions. All are welcome.

All are welcome sounded good on the surface, but what if by

welcoming one group, you're threatening another? If the wolves come, are the sheep really welcome? And if the Altzis were wolves, did that make Seren and Erik sheep? Or were my more like harbor seals, existing in a world so different from the Altzis that they could barely begin to communicate?

Seren didn't have an answer, so they pushed the question out of their mind. While Root was here, it would be good to mention Erik to him.

I picked up a third passenger on the way here. Seren pictured him in their head and sent it with the words. And he is injured.

I know, said the voice. I can feel you all on my lake, and the Sneaky River told me about his captivity and rescue.

Sorry, thought Seren for lack of a better reply. They wanted to ask dozens of questions about Altzis, but they also wanted to see his face when they did so.

You have no reason to apologize.

Right. Seren almost apologized again.

That was a habit they were going to have to break quickly if they didn't want more experienced politicians to walk all over them.

As soon as Seren saw Merry Basin, they knew it was their kind of place. The buildings were organic. Instead of the painted boards that had been slapped on everything in Dovetown, living bark sheathed Merry Basin's buildings. Branches and green leaves wove roots, and solar panels adorned the weave like buttons on a knit sweater.

Giant leaves overhung doors instead of awnings, linking up to one another so people could be sheltered from rain or sun while walking down the street. Even the docks were grown. Smooth platforms of wood crowned gnarly roots that were thicker than Seren's waist. Green bulbs of moss protruded from the wharfs, acting as bumpers for the tied-up boats, and there were lots of boats, even some varieties Seren had never seen before.

Half of the docked vessels were plant-based: hollow tree trunks shaped into canoes still had branches growing out of their sides and stubby roots sticking out of their bottoms. The larger boats had basket shaped root balls for hulls, tree-trunk masts, and giant, leafy sails. Seren assumed they belonged to ambassadors and mages, hopefully ones who were friendlier and more open minded than Freeman had been.

Some solar skiffs were tied up to long, flat sections of dock while others anchored just outside the docking area. They passed a red Altzi steamship. Seren's lip cured up and bared their teeth. Erik trembled.

To keep their anger in check, Seren focused on some of the more interesting vessels. Giant lily pads with tents on their surfaces, boats pulled by teams of oversized frogs, and dragonflies tethered on the island with saddles and bags beside them.

Seren approached slowly, patting *The Whaler* on the side and blushing because it was man-made, a fuel-burning relic from before The Flood. They opened their mind to the Earth in case that was how were expected to find their assigned dock space.

Instead of sensing the rage and betrayal that had plagued much of the land between the Port's Mouth and here, they sensed tranquility: waves gently lapping on shore and trees swaying in the wind. Even more so than in their home, people and the Earth lived together as one symbiotic entity. The island seemed more like one living being than a city. This is what The Mother wanted for her children, not war, destruction, and quests for control. At its heart, bringing this kind of peace all across the Northeast was the goal of NUNES.

Visitors stood out like rose thorns. Some simply vibrated with different frequencies since their power was tethered to a different elemental altogether. Others were utterly disconnected and tainting the peaceful balance like vine borers infesting crops of squash. Seren caught themselves filing the vine borer people aside as potential threats but stopped themself. If they were judging people before they ever met them, then they'd already lost.

Seren felt Root's presence. He didn't send Seren words, but he projected an image to their mind: an empty slip that was just the right size for *The Whaler*. As they pulled up to it, a sandy-haired boy with leaf-green eyes and freckled white cheeks met them. He twined a pliable vine through their cleats and helped them out of the boat. He didn't speak until after he secured the boat.

"Welcome to Merry Basin and the First NUNES Convention. I'm Link Down. He/Him. I presume you are Ambassador Seren McIntyre?"

"I am," they said, shaking the hand he offered. "My pronouns are they/them."

Ambassador. They weren't used to hearing that word paired with their name. It was like adding a sinker to a fishing line meant to have a bobber.

"And you are accompanied by the twins, David and Reggie Strongbow, and the Dock Master from Little Port, Erik Current."

Reggie frowned. "Tell me, how did you know who we all were? We weren't originally traveling with Erik."

"Root sensed the trouble you met downstream. He is waiting for you at our inn with a healer who can attend to Erik."

"Then why didn't he send help?" Reggie voiced a question that had been lurking in the shadows of Seren's thoughts.

Link shrugged. "I have no clue. I'm only a dockhand."

"Thank you. Could you please direct us to the inn?" asked Seren, anxious to be done with formalities and get Erik to a healer. They couldn't focus on what they needed to accomplish with him injured and hurting. And there was so much to do that when they even started to think about it, their breath shortened.

Link smiled. "It's the big round building in the center of town. All streets lead to it."

"Then we'll head right there," said Seren.

"You need not walk," said Link. He turned so he faced the land, where a giant, hollow gourd on wheels waited with two donkeys. "The ambassador feared the walk would be too much for Erik and sent you a cart."

"That was very kind," said Seren. The formal, hyper polite interaction strained their brain.

The twins shifted their weight from one foot to the other, and the only one who looked even a little comfortable was Erik. He smiled, putting nearly all his weight on Seren's shoulders.

Seren couldn't sense anything wrong through the earth and suspected the discomfort they felt had more to do with the hostility they had encountered on earlier travels. After fighting so much and being kicked out of the last town they were in, they had come to expect to have to push and shove their way to the NUNES conference, and now that they'd reached their destination and were being welcomed with no enemies in sight, they just didn't know what to do.

CHAPTER

THIRTY

In a single day, Erik had been transported from dystopian misery to a town as close to a utopia as humans would get without creating the opposite. The organic structures amazed him, but the people made it utopian.

No two were alike. They differed in size, shape, gender, clothing, and skin color. A bearded, rotund man wore a frilly rose dress. People smiled when they walked by him. Several people's genders were unrecognizable. Even though he knew it was none of his business, Erik couldn't help but wonder if they were born that way or used Earth magic to alter themselves.

He kept his mind open to the currents for the whole trip in the carriage. Water swirled around the island, calm and serene. Occasionally, someone pulled them with a gentle thought and mentally petted them for behaving.

"I wonder if people are as nice as everything appears." Erik struggled to sit up straighter, so he could get a closer look at the people they were passing and study their body language.

Was that a grimace? A gossiping smirk? He thought as he passed a cluster of people.

"I guess we'll find out soon enough," said Seren.

Erik leaned back, rested his aching skull against the carriage headrest, and studied Seren. They looked mostly the same as they had the last time they left. Tufts of brownish blonde hair stood up on their head line a crown of feathers, freckles still dotted wind burnt cheeks, and loose wool clothing hid what little softness their body had. However, something about Seren seemed different. Maybe it was the way their shoulders were tighter and straighter, or their hands were curled into fists. An angry determination simmered beneath their gray-blue eyes, and while they weren't pulling power in from the Earth, they weren't blocking it either.

Less than a week ago, Seren had been a reluctant ambassador, on the brink of a maturity that Erik had been patiently waiting for them to discover. Now, Seren seemed closer to it than ever. It excited Erik, but it also scared him. What if adulthood honed more of their flaws than strengths? Would they outgrow him?

"There is a lot to learn on this island," said Erik, breaking the silence that had been lingering between awkward and amazement in an attempt to stop his thoughts from wandering down a dangerous corridor. "If everything goes well with the conference, maybe we can spend some time here after."

"That's a big if, but I get the impression you're right." Seren dropped their voice to a whisper. "The kid who met us at the docks was a little creepy."

"And you're not?" laughed Erik.

"What do you mean?" Seren frowned.

"When you try to be all official and polite, you come across equally creepy as that kid, like you are a child playing dress up in your parent's clothes, pretending to be a politician."

Seren crossed their arms. "Are you saying I'm a bad ambassador?"

He shook his head. "You're a fine ambassador when you just let yourself be yourself. Plus, my impression of your creepy level may be a little skewed after last night. Most people haven't seen you raise waterspouts and walls of water with the flick of a hand. I really don't ever want to get on your bad side."

Seren smiled, leaning down just far enough to kiss Erik on the forehead. He put a hand on their cheek and pulled their face closer to his.

Reggie cleared their throat.

Seren pulled away, blushing.

"Making out with your boyfriend in a diplomatic carriage does not make you a good ambassador."

Erik grinned even though it stung his cheeks. "I'm just making sure I'm still on their good side."

"You are. Trust me," said David.

Erik did trust him, but he also wanted to feel Seren. The heat their skin evoked inside him reminded him that he was alive, that he escaped the Altzis. He didn't kiss Seren for the rest of the ride, but he didn't let go of their hand either, at least not until the cart stopped at the base of a giant tree. He clung to them while they helped him out of the car, but two white-robed people waited with a stretcher that he guessed would take him to whatever passed for a medical facility in this place. Meanwhile, he assumed the mousey girl in the white shirt and tan skirt would lead Seren to the ambassador.

The introductions were polite, awkward, and confirmed Erik's fear. Paige would take Seren to meet the other ambassadors while he went to the infirmary.

"I'd really prefer to stay with Seren," said Erik before Seren agreed to anything.

"You need medical attention, and the ambassador needs to speak with Seren," said Paige.

Seren close their eyes and took a few deep breaths before opening them, leaning forward and giving him a kiss on the cheek. "I don't want to be separated either, but I'm already a day late. My gut says that I need to talk to the ambassadors now. David can go with you and Reggie can stay with me."

Erik took Seren's hand but didn't answer with words.

"You won't be terribly far away from each other," said Paige. "The infirmary is the floor below the meeting area. As soon as the meeting is over, Seren can come check on you."

"Can't I come to the meeting?" asked Erik.

"Can you walk?" asked the healer. "Can you confirm you have no internal bleeding? How is your breathing? What is your body temperature?"

Erik couldn't answer any of those questions. He knew he needed medical attention, but he was afraid. How many Altzis were here? Would they know what the others did to him? He didn't voice these questions, so they stayed inside, strangling him as the healer levitated him onto a floating stretcher.

CHAPTER THIRTY-ONE

Seren hated leaving Erik, but Earth tugged at their mind, urging them to meet the ambassadors. The urgency grew as Seren watched two healers carry Erik away on a stretcher made of branches and leaves. It strengthened when Paige lead them into the base of the tree trunk that marked the center of the island.

"Does everything you make on this island come from this tree?" asked Seren, trying to distract themself from the anxiety buzzing in their chest.

Paige nodded. "The tree is the island, and she lets us grow everything we need whether it be shelters, boats, stretchers, furniture, or docks. The list could go on and on. We even eat some of the fruit she grows, though we also fish and farm on the mainland."

"So does everyone around here have a connection to the tree?"

"Everyone who lives on the island must. The folk who don't live on the mainland, but most of them have some connection to Earth and at least minimal competence at using it. Farming is tough when you can't communicate with the crops and soil."

Seren frowned. "What if someone has a kid who doesn't have that connection?"

Paige shrugged as she led Seren around a bend. "It happens. Root's son didn't have it. He was no exception to the rule that once that child turns sixteen, they leave the island. The parents can stay or go."

Seren slowed, letting a gap widen between them and Paige. "What if they want to stay on the island or really don't want to be separated?"

Paige turned her head and peered at Seren with raised eyebrows. "It's a fifteen-minute boat ride. They can still see each other every day. Most of the parents stay on the island. The only issue we have is with young couples. Some people our age can be extremely dramatic. Root's grandchild was supposed to move onto the island after their father died, but they refused because they loved someone on the mainland. The drama kept us entertained for quite some time.

"This is as far as I go." Paige stopped at what appeared to be a solid wall. "Reggie will have to wait outside in the hall here. The ambassadors are in the council chambers, straight through those doors."

"Thank you," said Seren.

Paige walked away, and left Seren staring at a solid piece of tree bark with no door in sight. They touched the bark, letting it speak to their mind, asking it if they could pass through. They leaned forward and fell through into a round room whose walls were bark, smooth as if they had been under running water for a century. In its center stood a round table surrounded by an amalgam of people who had already managed to segregate themselves.

A group of wrinkled men huddled together on one side of the table, half-gaping at a group of younger men and women who blazed with vigorous energy. Seren was relieved to see that some didn't appear much older than themself. They all wore name tags with their pronouns written below their names. Seren wondered where they got the tags.

Deep belly laughter and musical giggles clashed in Seren's ears.

"That one gets most of us the first time around. We take so much from the tree that it's only fair if she gets some amusement from us," said Root.

His skin resembled aged birch bark and his hair resembled a web that spiders had been weaving for centuries.

"I agree, but this whole thing would be more amusing if I wasn't exhausted." Seren clambered to their feet and extended a hand to the old man. "Ambassador Root, it is nice to finally meet you in person."

He smiled at Seren. "You as well."

The two brown-rimmed black coals smoldering in the center of his face looked like they'd witnessed the creation and destruction of humanity, though Seren knew no man could really be that old. Only Earth was, and Seren wondered how much of this man remained himself and how much of his consciousness he'd sacrificed to Earth to protect his people.

"It is not truly a sacrifice if I am getting something in return," said Root.

Seren shivered, realizing that since their mind was still open to the Earth, it was also laid bare for this man.

"Root said you had a run-in with the Altzis," said a man who resembled a dehydrated puffball with his bald head full of freckles, warts and liver spots.

"I did." Seren glanced at Root, hoping he would spare them the awkward formality of introducing themselves.

He winked. "Well, Mx. McIntyre, I should get around to introducing you to everyone. These days I'm always in tune with the land around me, which causes me to appear absent- minded, though I assure you that my mind is very much present. For starters, the man you described as a dehydrated puff ball is Ambassador Washington."

Ambassador Washington chuckled and shook hands with Seren, whose cheeks were now on fire.

"I'm sorry," Seren stammered, more thrown off by the fact that Ambassador Washington was there in person. Seren had never met him, but when Assana had said he was bound to the largest, stormiest mountain in the North East and would likely send a representative. Yet here he was, as far from his home as Seren was from theirs. "I didn't mean to offend you."

"No offense was taken," he said. "I'm rather fond of puffballs."

"The short man to his left is Ambassador Chocorua, then we have Ambassador Franconia, and Ambassador Sebago." Root paused. "If I haven't told you already, Seren is heir to Ambassador Assana McIntyre of the Valley Port Region."

"It's nice to meet you," said Seren, gaping at a group of men who apparently filled the same role as their mother, wondering if Root had forgotten about the other people. They turned towards the younger two-thirds of the table. "Where are the rest of your from?"

A thirty-something woman with dark brown eyes, curly hair, and skin the color of acorns took the liberty of introducing herself. "I'm Winnie Socks-Freeman, representing my husband and brothers-in-law who are bound to several of the lakes north of here."

"I've met their grandfather," said Seren thinking of the NUNES representative that had traveled to Valley-Port.

"Most people have," chuckled Winnie like she wasn't sure if it was a good thing or not. "These two lovely ladies are Sierra Penobscot and her wife, Lucia Belfast."

"Fast Bell Port is a good two-day sail north of the Piscataqua." Lucia waved at Seren. She was short with dark brown skin. A halo of tight black curls crowned her head. "It's similar in size, yet the river flowing into it is far less hostile."

"You're not the one who has to deal with the river." Sierra chucked and patted her wife on the shoulder. She was tall and lean with copper skin and sleek black hair that fell down to her shoulders.

"The hills aren't exactly tame little puppies either," muttered Lucia.

Sierra didn't reply but based on the arched-eyebrow glares they gave each other, the playful bickering would continue if they were in private.

The other people were a young man from south of the Valley-Port Region named

Mushy Tuk knew of Seren because the twins had saved his life once while they were visiting his territory to buy quahogs. He had red hair and his pale skin was already tiring red from too much sun. A man a bushy brown beard, tan skin, and a fraying flannel shirt that might be as old as Seren's boat, Lard Follard, was from about one hundred miles west of Valley-Port and claimed the Altzis were encroaching on his territory every day.

"Define encroaching," asked Seren.

"When they first came, they set patches of forest on fire then attempted to farm the land. Nothing grew, obviously, so they pretended to realize the error of their ways and asked for help from some of my people. I'm still not sure how they did it, but they kept turning families, convincing them that only one lifestyle was sanctioned by Earth. More than half my people have stayed loyal, but the winning argument on the other side was that I can't produce an heir since I am married to a man, and therefore, I am not a worthy leader."

"I don't understand them," said Arthur, the man sitting next to Eddard, holding his hand. He had similar hair and skin tone but was leaner and clean shaven. "The Mother knows there are more important things than DNA when choosing an heir. Sure, it's convenient if a child turns out to be good ruler material, but we've held on to history in our territory. Passing power down from parent to child didn't always work out for monarchies of old, and it won't work any better for ambassadors."

That comment sparked a conversation of how ambassador mantles could be passed on to people who were not genetic relatives, but Seren couldn't get their head around it. Assana claimed those powers could only be passed from parent to child with few exceptions for nieces and nephews, but Assana also said her power bound her to her territory, and obviously, that wasn't true for other ambassadors. If Assana could pass her mantle of power onto someone else, then Seren didn't have to be heir. Having a choice in the matter all along would've made it more appealing.

As far as they could tell, the ambassadors from the bordering region collectively sent a representative, and those from further regions had come in-person.

"How are you all here?" blurted Seren, hope and betrayal warring for dominance in their mind. "Assana can't leave our region. She has a hard enough time leaving the lake."

Ambassador Washington frowned. It made his already shriveled face wrinkle more. "That is Assana's choice, not a rule imposed on her by Earth."

"Really?" Seren squeezed their hands together behind their back. Had Assana lied to them, or did she really not know?

He nodded. "When Assana was young, she came to visit me on more than one occasion, though I haven't seen her in over twenty years. I requested to visit her once a few years ago when I was doing business in Port's Mouth, but she denied me access to her territory, and I choose not to argue."

"Thankfully, you are different," said Ambassador Sebago, who had eyes and skin reminiscent of maple trees.

"Assana didn't tell me she knew so many of you." Seren was too exhausted to make sense of this new information or even properly react to it. It changed everything. They stared at the floor, watching the waving grains and two big knots that looked like eyes.

"I've never met her," said Winnie.

"Me neither," said Sierra. "Although I did make the mistake of getting into a drinking contest with one of her peace-keepers, Reggie, while visiting Port's Mouth."

"Mistake is an understatement," said Lucia.

"I can imagine," said Seren, irritated at how easy the conversation had gotten off topic.

"This is a discussion we may have after NUNES." Root stood up and his voice boomed through the room. "There are more pressing concerns to discourse now."

"Like Altzis," growled Washington.

"And the sea witches on the solar barges," said Ambassador Sebago.

"They're scientists," said Seren.

Lucia supported Seren. "They don't believe in magic even when it happens right in front of them. How can you call them witches?"

"Turning light into electricity seems like magic to me," said Ambassador Chocorua who appeared to be the youngest of the geriatric group. "And it sure isn't power granted by The Mother."

"Only because you don't know how it works," said Seren. Assana had been hesitant to accept the first solar panels too, but once it was installed and the Elementals approved, so did she. "I think there is a lot we could learn from the scientists, as long as they are willing to learn from us."

The older crowd frowned until they looked constipated prunes.

"Don't tell me you are going to start defending the Altzis too," said Eddard.

Seren snorted. "I'm pretty sure most of them are rotting at the bottom of a river right now."

Root shook his head. "You showed them mercy, and the river followed your example. Their boat sunk, but many who escaped were not sucked to the depths. The river even *helped* the children reach shore."

Seren crossed their arms to mask a relieved exhale with strength. "Then maybe they'll learn to show mercy in turn, and to not hate the people they have to share the Earth with."

The old men shook their heads. Seren looked down and shivered. The eye-like knots on the floor were larger, like the tree was watching, growing more interested in the conversation as it intensified.

"Regardless, that was only one boat. Several are already docked here. A smaller vessel and a larger steamship just passed the wreckage. They will surely report it to their comrades. They practically run Dovetown. You can cut off one head, but another always pops up."

"Which is why it might be better to teach them instead of cutting off their heads," said Lucia. "Seren is right."

"Have you ever met these people?" asked Eddard at the same time Washington asked, "And how do you propose we teach them?"

"I don't know, but can anyone really be that evil?" asked Lucia.

Seren shook their head. "The Altzis I've met are horrible, but Assana taught me to always preserve life, and that it what I intend to do."

"Then you may doom us all," said Ambassador Sebago.

"*You* are going to doom us if you think the right thing to do is just kill your enemies." Sierra stood up with hands balled into fists at her sides. "We are human. We are better than that. Animals don't even do that. They kill to eat. Maybe squabble over territory, but not fatally in most cases."

"That is true," said Seren, taking a step closer to the table they hadn't even gotten a seat at yet. "Don't forget fruitless wars were one of the reason's The Mother pruned so many people from her surface. If we slaughter the Altzis, Earth will see that we are just as bad as them and may decide to rid herself of us once and for all."

The tree groaned. Everyone looked around with a similar wide-eyed expression.

"Earth may consume her fallen," Sierra stood beside Seren, staring at the wall. "But we aren't the judges of each other. We are not exterminators."

Silence owned the room long enough to make Seren's feet twitch and hands twine through the fabric of their shirt.

"The young people are right." Defeat spread from Washington like spores flying from a thrown puffball and no one argued with him.

"We'll break for now," said Root. "Think about what we must do and come up with three potential ways for accomplishing it. Please return here after dinner. I expect NUNES will reach quorum by tomorrow, and we need a strategy to ensure an Earth-friendly constitution. You are all dismissed."

Seren lingered in room as the other young ambassadors left. Then elder men whispered amongst themselves, not including Seren, but not leaving either.

Seren cleared their throat. "Does anyone know where the infirmary is? I'd like to check on my partner."

"It's a few levels down." Root barely glanced Seren's way. "The island spirits will show you the way if you get lost."

"Thank you, sir." Seren backed away slowly, and when Root's attention was back in the conversation, they darted out of the room, through the wall, and crashed into Reggie.

"That thing is just creepy," said Reggie.

"You have no idea," said Seren. "Let's go find Erik."

Their head spun, and their chest ached as they followed Reggie down the hall. They'd been numb and overwhelmed, barely following the conversation but unable to process much of it. Just in that room, there had been so many different people with so many different opinions, and those were only the ambassadors from surrounding states. They'd overreacted almost every time someone disagreed with them, sounding more like the child they were than the politician they needed to be. Their chest ached. They breathed like they'd just swam three miles upstream. They were one inexperienced teenager. How in The Mother's Name where they supposed to make a difference?

They wanted to find a dark little corner, curl up into a ball and cry. Or dive deep into the lake and scream where no one but the Elementals would hear them. But they couldn't do any of those things. Not here. Not right now. Not when everyone was watching them and their right to exist—to live, was on the line.

CHAPTER

THIRTY-TWO

Merry Basin's infirmary was the best medical facility Erik had ever been in, mainly because it did not feel like one. It reminded him more of Seren's bedroom than anything else.

The people who worked there called it Healing Quarters. Everyone wore white garments with a red droplet, a name, and pronouns embroidered on them, though the shape of those garments varied from person to person. The healers didn't talk to each other out loud, only the patients. The healers must have possessed some kind of telepathic connection to each other.

An older patient with a black eye and crooked nose arrived the same time as Erik. Sobs obscured most of her, but he caught a few phrases like, "how could they?" "Why is he allowing them into our home?" and "This kind of thing just doesn't happen here."

Erik assumed she'd been assaulted by Altzis in town for the NUNES conference, even though he had no concrete evidence to support that assumption other than that is seemed like something an Altzi would do, but he knew nothing about the other visitors.

An attendant whispered comforting words to her, then made eye contact with another healer. The nods, flared nostrils, and eye twitches were subtle, but they hinted at a conversation only the healers could hear, especially when one of them walked over with a vial of clear liquid and offered it to the woman even though no one asked them too.

The healer attending Erik introduced themself as Chris. They wore their hair short but had red lipstick that made their skin seem almost as pale as their clothing. "Have you ever been treated by a healer before?"

"A few times," said Erik, thinking of his transition, and of a few life-threatening injuries that had been beyond the scope of the nurses practicing in Little Port. Those times, either Assana had healed him herself, or had one of the three healers in the territory work on him.

"Then you know I will search for your injuries with my essence."

Erik nodded.

"You may speak if it makes you feel more comfortable, but I will sense your discomfort before you find words for it."

Erik wasn't quite ready to tell a stranger about what he went through, so he opted to stay silent while the healer's energy probed his body. It was an awkward fifteen minutes, but when they were done, they declared he had three broken ribs, a concussion, had strained a whole bunch of muscles whose names Erik couldn't pronounce, and was recovering from dehydration and malnourishment. His sores and scrapes had the beginnings of infection.

"I'm going to treat those first," said Chris. "The more infection spreads, the harder it is to wipe out. Plus, if your body isn't fighting the infection, it will be able to lend more energy to the areas that need mending."

"Do your thing." Erik closed his eyes and tried not flinch as Chris laid their hands all over his wounds.

Healing took more energy than almost any other kind of magic, so those who worked them used as much of their patient's energy as possible when mending them. Erik was sensitive enough to feel Chris doing just that: pulling his energy towards the infected sores on his wrist, augmented with their own energy, and burning the infection away.

Even if he hadn't been able to feel the magic, the searing around his wrist would've been enough to tell him it was working. Once it was over, the pain vanished. Chris let him rest for a couple minutes, and then they placed their hands on his ribs and the process started all over again, but this time, instead of burning infection away, they magically welded the fractures shut. By the time they were done, Erik was yawning, barely able to keep his eyes open. For the first time since his capture, nothing hurt.

Chris and David helped him walk from the examination table to a bed that was grown like everything else on this island. The legs were branches sprouting out of the tree, and he guessed the white silky sheets were the by-product of a caterpillar or spider. He tried not to think too much about that and instead focused on how soft they were. He rested his head on the pillow, closed his eyes, and slept.

When Erik woke, he smiled up at Seren, who sat on the edge of his bed with their head in their hands. His smile faded as he noticed their shoulders rose and fell in jagged lurches. There were so many things he needed to tell them and warn them about, but if they were this upset, maybe it wasn't the right time. Maybe they'd already figured out some of it themselves. He hesitated to touch them to let them know he was awake, but then they turned around, and their tearstained eyes contacted his.

"What happened?" he asked, surprised to hear his voice sound strong and clear, not all dry and raspy.

"Nothing, yet. How are you feeling?" Seren traced the edge of his jaw with rough fingertips.

"Tired, but alive. If nothing happened, why are you crying?"

"Frustration." Seren stood up, raising their hands to the ceiling in a stretch then pacing around the room. "I'm not cut out to be an ambassador."

"What do you mean?" Erik watched Seren pace around his bed.

"There were ambassadors from other territories, and I overreacted every time they disagreed with me. I don't know what my mother was thinking by sending me out here."

"You mean there are ambassadors from other territories here, and they can travel?"

"Yes. And they said my mom can travel too, but she chooses not to."

"What do you believe?"

"I don't know!" Seren plunged their arms down to their hips and sank back onto the edge of the bed. "I want to believe them because I don't ever want to be trapped in one place like Assana, but I can't quite accept that she is lying either. She never lies. Mother Earth doesn't approve of dishonesty."

Erik squeezed Seren's hand. "You've been using magic a lot since you left, probably more than you do at home. Do you feel it pulling you back?"

Seren shook their head. "Not anymore. I did at first, but the last few times I used it, I didn't think much about it and did what I had to do. I can feel my connection to Earth wherever I go, but I can't feel home, not even a tiny tug."

"You can't do much about it now. You need to focus on making sure Altzi ideology doesn't infect the constitution. When we get back to Valley-Port, there will be plenty of time to figure it out."

"Unless we fail." Seren squeezed their eyes shut. "What if things get too heated? What if people's world-views are too different to unite? If we end up at war instead of united, it might be the end of humanity, in this region, or the world."

The world was a big place. No one had crossed the ocean since before The Flood and on land, one could only go so far south or west before crossing a magic barrier into a frozen radioactive wasteland. He imagined there were other clusters of protected areas, but he had no clue how many and how far between they were. He looked right in Seren's eyes. "We won't. You're brilliant and stubborn. You'll find a way to get everyone on the same page and work out a constitution that the Mother will find acceptable."

"I'm one person. How am I supposed to make a difference?"

Erik didn't have an answer, so he sat up and pulled Seren against his chest, inhaling the scent of their hair. It still smelled like salt and sunlight.

CHAPTER THIRTY-THREE

Seren felt overconfident and all-powerful when they were hovering over the Altzi's boat, but they felt small and childish as they walked into a crowded dining hall wearing silky pants, a matching shirt, and a thin cloak that felt flimsy compared to the heavy wool garments they'd been wearing for most of the trip. Erik, on the other hand, was enjoying silky brown trousers and a green shirt that the island had given him.

NUNES delegates, travelers, staff, and anyone who just didn't feel like cooking their own meal ate at the dining hall in the heart tree. A person's reason for being there dictated where they sat. The ambassadors all sat at a long table in one end of the hall, and the hostess directed Seren there. The hostess permitted Erik to sit there too, but the twins, much to their complaints, were seated at a lower table with other guards and entourage members. Seren considered arguing, but they decided that conversations would remain more appropriate without Reggie around.

Seren hoped to sit near Sierra and Lucia, but instead, the host plopped them and Erik in the middle of Root and Washington's debate about why some forests and bodies water had drastically different personalities. Root thought the Mother was experimenting on her elemental children, but Washington blamed it on fallen and corrupt ambassadors. Their back and forth had Seren's head aching after five minutes.

"What if it's both?" said Seren, hoping they wouldn't regret opening their mouth. The two men stopped bickering and stared down at them. Seren grinned, glad to have a break from literally being in the middle of their debate. "The Great Salt Marsh and Great Bay are more autonomous than any other place I've been so far. The Great Salt Marsh is wild and wicked like a trickster, and I'd be shocked to hear that any ambassador lived in her lands and maintained their sanity for more than a day. Great Bay, on the other hand, told me his ambassadors had died off without passing on their power. He cared for the people who lived on his shores, but they treated me like shit. I think the Mother gave some Elementals more will than others, but not all the ambassadors worked out. I also think She has been trying to keep us isolated to see what we are like when we don't mix too much."

Neither man spoke for a few minutes.

Seren was thrilled that they were not only quiet, but also seemed to be thinking about their words. Too bad the rest of the room was still raucous.

Delegates chattered all around them, but Seren couldn't pick out specific words over the growling of their stomach. The only thing louder was the Altzi's table. Bawdy jokes and laughter burst from their mouths between swigs of mead. As mean as the men Seren had met were, when with their peers, they were all smiles.

In contrast, the table made up of scientists was quieter. People's mouths moved, but their words weren't audible above the Altzis' ruckus. Seren wondered if they were always that quiet or were just that way because they were uncomfortable in this big, loud hall.

After a few minutes of an awkward pause in the conversation, Seren's pride shifted to anxiety. Maybe they weren't pondering. Maybe they were insulted. "I'm sorry. Did I offend you?"

Washington spoke first. “You passed through The Great Salt Marsh.”

Seren nodded.

Root’s eyes widened. “Did She speak to you?”

“Yeah. She manifested as something almost human and carried on a conversation,” said Seren.

“I’ve heard stories, but when I went there myself, She wouldn’t talk to me,” said Washington. “I just got a general sense that I needed to get out of the area. I haven’t survived two centuries by ignoring those instincts, so I left.”

“Maybe this marsh enjoys the company of attractive, reckless teens more than wise old men,” said Erik, gently nudging Seren’s ankle with his foot.

Both men snorted.

“Did the bay manifest as well?” asked Washington.

“Sort of,” said Seren. The old ambassadors pestered them with questions while they waited for the meal, and much to Seren’s dismay, the men did not cease interrogating when the seared salmon and greens arrived. Seren did their best to answer between mouthfuls, but the men had to repeat their questions sometimes because Serena paid more attention to the food than anything else.

“I’ve traveled through those regions and many more,” said Washington, “but I’ve never connected with any of the Elementals like you have. I have connection and control in my own territory, but outside it I can feel but not manipulate, not even in the wild territories.”

“The same is true for me,” said Root. “I always assumed that when your mother refused to travel, it was because she just did not want to be away from her power, but now I’m wondering if there is something else at play. You aren’t even full ambassador yet, and you can do things we cannot.”

“Interesting,” said Seren between bites of fish, but with all the background noise, they couldn’t grasp the true significance of it. They could hardly think. The conversation lapsed. Seren was glad to be able to focus on eating without talking but worried then they noticed Erik only picking at his meal.

"Do you want any? I'm not all that hungry," he said one of the times he caught Seren looking.

"You need it to replenish your strength," said Seren.

Erik took another bite.

Sighing, Seren returned to their own food, wishing Reggie and David were at the table with them. They would know whether or not to push Erik to eat more.

The rest of the meal was uneventful until Seren was half way through their strawberry shortcake. Root froze with a bite half way to his mouth, and the hair on Seren's arms stood up.

"There is a vessel approaching that should have arrived days ago," whispered Root. "There are injured on board, and I suspect something is wrong with the vessel itself."

A few waves got the attention of his guards without alerting most of the guests, but David and Reggie picked up on the signal and rushed to Seren.

"Is it the Altzis?" asked Reggie.

"The sea witches," said Root.

"The BREAD representatives are scientists," corrected Seren, annoyed that even as they dined in his hall as guests, he still whispered about them in a derogatory tone.

"Oh no." Reggie stared down at their fists. "It's probably the boat we shot up."

Erik stood up so quick he almost knocked the table over. "What did you do?"

Everyone but the Altzis stopped talking and stared at the long table.

David shook his head and dropped his voice to a whisper. "A couple BREAD delegates on their way to NUNES wanted to retrieve something a group of Altzis stole from them, so they set up a trap using some kind fog-generation device. Great Bay told Seren that if they didn't stop it, he would raise a storm to destroy the ship. The women on board didn't believe us, so we disabled their machine, and unfortunately, damaged their ship in the process."

"Was Tav on board?" Erik's fingernails cut crescents into the table and sweat beaded on his forehead.

"Probably." Guilt pressed down on Seren. "I saw them in Port's Mouth with one of the people I talked to in the bay."

He paused and took a few deep breaths. "Seren, I was in that fog. Domhnall couldn't see enough to navigate to so he questioned me on the deck, sharping his knives. I jumped overboard and escaped. I tried so hard to reach you, but I was drugged. I couldn't use my magic."

An anchor of guilt tore through Seren's stomach so hard they almost dropped to their knees. They pried one of Erik's hands off of the table and held it. They knew no words could fix what Erik was feeling, but they still apologized.

Someone cleared their throat. Seren jumped. They glanced away from Erik and found a white-clad woman staring a few inches away.

"A talking bay is a poor excuse for attacking people who are only trying to make peace with you."

"I saved their lives." Seren squeezed Erik's hand and made eye contact with the woman. "We didn't kill anyone. We tried to only damage the machine, and if they had *listened* to us, then the whole disaster could have been avoided."

"Bodies of water can't talk," said the woman through clenched teeth.

"How can you deny magic when you are sitting in a hall grown out of a living tree by the same type of power that allows humans to communicate with Elementals?"

The woman glanced over at Root. "This island is genetically engineered, correct."

"I never said that." Root's cheeks flushed. "I just never corrected you to prevent an argument I couldn't win."

"What is your name?" asked Erik before anyone could argue further.

"Dr. Ulyssa of the BREAD Barge II."

"It's good to see you," Lucia said sheepishly. "Do you still have the spinach plants I gave in exchange for our first solar panel?"

Dr. Ulyssa's face softened. "I still haven't figured out how they continue to grow no matter the season."

Lucia gazed at Dr. Ulyssa with wide eyes. "Magic."

"No." Dr. Ulyssa shook her head. "If you really believe it's magic, perhaps that means you simply don't understand what you actually did."

"Understanding how magic works doesn't make it cease to be magic," said Erik. "Ask Tav when the ship lands. They will give you an accurate account of what happened even if the other passengers are still analyzing the events."

Dr. Ulyssa touched Erik's shoulder with her boney hand. "If you will dine with me and tell me about your connection to Tav, my sisters and I will not take any action against Seren until we have the full story."

Erik's hand twitched as he pulled it away from Seren. He followed Dr. Ulyssa without protest, but took slow, shuffling baby steps, constantly glancing back at Seren.

"He's been through a lot," they said before he was more than a yard away. "And has done nothing to harm your people. Please be kind to him."

Dr. Ulyssa turned towards Seren. "No matter what we decide, he will not be harmed or imprisoned."

Erik walked away slowly.

Seren couldn't shake the feeling Erik had been taken hostage.

"If their ship is already injured, then surely it wouldn't take much to sink it completely," whispered Washington as soon as Dr. Ulyssa was out of earshot.

Seren almost slapped him. "Why in-The-Mother's-name would you want to do something that violent?"

Washington grunted. "They go against everything we stand for.

They want to cut down trees. They'll kill Earth with their science and She will kill us."

"That's not true," said Seren.

"Action matters more than intention," said Root. "Earth feels the consequences of the action, not the intention."

Reggie smirked at the ceiling. "You want to sink them, but you don't have a problem accepting their lights. You *invited* them here."

"The solar lights are one of their least harmful inventions," said Root.

"Do you know anything about how they are made?" asked Lucia, who was staring with her eyes wide and her mouth hanging open. "Do you know anything at all about what those women stand for?"

Neither Root nor the other ambassadors answered.

"They respect the planet as much as we do." Sierra gripped her fork like she was going to stab Root with it.

"Please don't sink their ship." A chill crept through Seren's body. Root just confirmed one of their worst fears about NUNES and he wasn't who Assana made him out to be. NUNES was further on track to disaster than Seren thought, especially if Root hadn't invited BREAD in good faith. "They're annoying, but they can be reasoned with. Give them the welcome they expect and show them that we are neither the enemies nor charlatans they think we are."

Root jumped back like the table had burned him. It shook until the plates and cups clattered to the ground. Its bark surface twisted and changed color, until black knots formed the word "listen."

The ambassadors paled.

"I've never seen that happen before," said Root.

Inside, Seren crumpled with fear. Outside, they straightened their back and squared their shoulders. "Science is not our enemy if it is used correctly. If we further threaten or alienate these people, then they will use their gifts to harm the Earth instead of to help Her. Not everyone has magic. Those who cannot harness the Earth's power need science to overcome illness and other obstacles."

"It's also convenient for reluctant mages," muttered Reggie.

"We won't sink their ship, yet," hissed Root, "But if they do anything to harm Mother Earth..."

"They won't," said Lucia.

"You better be right," said Root.

Seren nodded, praying to The Mother that no one overheard the whispered, treasonous argument, especially while the people Root branded as enemies surrounded Erik.

CHAPTER

THIRTY-FOUR

Erik paced around the dock, strangling his hands behind his back. Dr. Ulyssa may not have bound his wrists, locked him in a cell, or threatened him with knives, but the "conversation" they had in the dining hall had no less of an interrogation than the one he endured in captivity. Dr. Ulyssa put on a kind face, offering to share their food and drink with him, but his stomach churned whenever he tried to eat anything they offered. He could've walked away and dealt with the consequences. No one was forcing him. Yet, he endured it. He needed to help the BREAD representatives unite with the ambassadors. And to do that, he had to find a way to resolve the conflict between Seren and Tav's family.

Dr. Ulyssa appeared calmer than Erik, perched on a bench alone with her back stiff and her long fingers folded across her lap like spider legs. She pursed her lips and observed the lake. Low mist rose off the water as the sun sunk behind the island tree. Long shadows crept across the dock like blood tricking across a butcher block. The shades accentuated Dr. Ulyssa's sharp cheekbones and pointed chin.

Erik shivered. Somewhere out there, Tav and their aunts limped towards Merry Basin in a wounded skiff. If Root's calculations were correct, they'd make it just before dark. Behind the island, deep reds and oranges blossomed in the sky. In the east, those colors faded to cool pinks and purples. Tav and their aunts needed to hurry up.

The aunts put up a front of being arrogant and aloof, but Tav claimed that at their core, they were curious, kind, and fascinated by things they didn't understand. Erik prayed to The Mother that Tav was right. Mostly, Tav was the one who came to shore to trade. He'd only met the aunts a couple times, and they certainly seemed fascinated by everything in Little Port. His plan for getting them to forgive Seren hinged on that curiosity.

The purples deepened across the sky and the still water, but the skiff was nowhere in sight. Dr. Ulyssa stood, frowned at the horizon, and raised a black rectangle to her ear. "There is no sign of them, and darkness is approaching. Ask Seren and their thugs about the damage, again."

She slipped the device back into her pocket and stepped in front of Erik. "So far, this enterprise seems like a complete waste of time. I don't believe Root can sense approaching vessels with his mind, and I detect no sensors or monitors in the area."

"Please just give it a few more minutes." Erik studied the dusky water and sky. If he'd known sooner what Seren had done, he would've begged them to go back and help.

"What is the point? With damaged panels, it is unlikely their batteries will have enough charge to power the engines now."

A disturbance danced on the edges of Erik's consciousness, tugging his lips into a smile. They were coming. "Did you bring the devices I asked you about?"

Dr. Ulyssa nodded.

"Good," said Erik. "Turn them on and see if they pick up anything while I try to help skiff get here."

Taking a deep breath, Erik reached out to the currents swirling around him. Before being shooed away by Dr. Ulyssa, the local dock master had introduced Erik to the currents and taught him the necessary commands. They were easy to remember, more focused mental nudges than words. He felt currents further out than he could at home. The damaged ship rode them too slowly. He pulled it towards him, and it sped up. "ETA fifteen minutes."

Dr. Ulyssa glanced up from a white, rectangular meter and nodded.

Erik reeled the boat in. As the last hints of purple bled into the dark blue of night, the solar skiff hobbled into sight. Its cracked mirrors reflected the flickering light of a row of lanterns that ignited as it approached the docks, illuminating a course for it to follow.

A makeshift sail caught the breeze while Tav steered with a makeshift rudder. Dr. Zhao, Dr. Fullerton, and Tav struggled with a cobbled together rig and boom. They adjusted their sails to head straight for where Erik and the only lit slip on the pier was, not knowing that they weren't actually moving of their own volition.

"Welcome to Merry Basin," said Erik when the skiff was just a few feet away from the dock.

"May we dock here?" asked Dr. Fullerton from the prow of the boat.

"Yes, this spot is reserved for you," he said.

"How did you know we were coming?" She frowned. "Aren't you the dock master from Little Port?"

"I am. The water told me," said Erik. He had yet to convince Tav Elementals existed, but he was close. And once they believed, their aunts would follow. "I've been guiding you across the bay with the winds and the currents. Did you not notice the increase in speed?"

"I did." Tav grinned. They leapt on the dock and shook Erik's hand. "You never came to say goodbye when I left Little Port. Martin said you were sick. What are you doing so far from your home?"

"It's a long story." Erik tossed them a rope he thought would do a fantastic job of strangling Martin. "The short version is I got abducted by Altzis and Seren rescued me on their way to NUNES."

Tav froze. Their aunts busied themselves tying the ropes, refusing to look at Tav or Erik.

"Fools!" shouted Tav while the others kept working the ropes.

Dr. Fullerton dropped her rope and stormed up to Tav. "Octave how dare you speak to us like that."

"If you just listened to other people once in a while, we could have gotten the vests back from the that Altzi ship *and* rescued Erik."

"You mean listen to that delusional child and abandon a plan that would have worked had they not interfered? It's their fault we watched that ship pass by, powerless to stop it."

Dr. Fullerton and Dr. Zhao finished tying up the boat, but still clutched the rope like it was a lifeline.

"I'd already escaped by then," Erik said quietly. "It wouldn't have made a difference."

Though that wasn't entirely true. It might have prevented him from being recaptured. Maybe Seren wouldn't have had to rely on that angry river Elemental to save him. And what if Tav and their aunts lost the fight they planned to pick with the Altzis?

Tav stepped closer to Dr. Fullerton so they were standing nose to nose. "You didn't have to believe them, but they were pleading. You could've turned the machine off and come up with a new plan. You could've worked with them."

"Tav does have a point." Dr. Zhao eased forward and put a hand on Dr. Fullerton's shoulder. "It would have been a prime opportunity to study the young ambassador. We could have analyzed a DNA sample while monitoring sonar and electromagnetic frequencies, temperature and pressure changes, and brain activity."

"And they could've approached in a more peaceful manner," growled Dr. Fullerton.

"That is true," croaked Erik. His skin crawled with fear, but he forced himself to keep speaking. "Seren is young."

Dr. Fullerton folded her arms across her chest. "That is no excuse."

Erik mirrored her pose. "Three people approached a vessel filled with people that had acted rude and hostile towards them a few days before. They were stressed, truly believing that turning the fog machine off was a life or death situation. David and Reggie *are* the closest thing Valley-Port has to thugs. Their job is to protect Seren."

"They showed some restraint," said Dr. Zhao. "No one was killed, and the bodily injuries were easily repairable."

"This was not an act of war," said Tav. "It was the result of arrogance and poor communication on both sides. Do not let it ruin NUNES."

Dr. Fullerton narrowed her eyes. "Are you implying we should just let them get away with shooting up our boat without any consequences."

"Of course not." Dr. Zhao grinned. "We ask for reparation payment—something that will be equal in value to the time we will need to spend repairing the boat.

Tension drained from Erik's shoulders and he swayed.

Tav stepped backwards and put a hand on Erik's back. "There are clearly many things here we do not understand, particularly about Seren and the other ambassadors."

Dr. Zhao's eyes lit up. "Perhaps we could start by asking for DNA samples—hair and cheek swabs."

Dr. Fullerton sighed. "If multiple ambassadors' consent to that, I will agree to stay at NUNES, but I will require something more from Seren."

CHAPTER

THIRTY-FIVE

Assana told Seren that people like Root and Washington would be their biggest allies at NUNES. She hadn't mentioned they were the kind of people who solved problems by sinking ships. Seren could deal with that attitude from Reggie and David. They weren't in charge of anything, and normally, when they weren't racing Altzis to a political convention, they prevented more violence than they caused. Memory of sinking an Altzi ship nagged Seren, but that had been different. The Altzis were going to blow them up. They'd hurt Erik.

The respect Seren accidentally earned merely an hour ago was fading. The elder men sat at a round table with a map in its center. Eddard and Arthur leaned over Root's shoulder. Sierra, Lucia, and Winnie retreated to a corner where they hissed rushed whispers. Seren hovered between the two groups.

"Seren, people like them just can't be reasoned with," said Washington like he was a grandfather trying to explain some difficult concept to his grandchild.

"But they're scientists," sighed Seren. "Reason is their whole existence. The problem is they don't understand our magic, and maybe our explanations of it don't make enough sense to them."

"Yes, so no matter what we tell them, they won't listen."

"That is not what I said." Seren crossed their arms, frustrated Washington wasn't listening and afraid they weren't making sense. The men glared, and the women ceased whispering. Seren took a deep breath continued anyway. "We don't need to make them believe everything now, but if we can at least find the words that might plant a seed, then maybe we can communicate better."

"That is a lot of if."

"Keep talking," said Winnie, leading Sierra and Lucia back to the table. "I want to hear what you have to say."

Seren hadn't planned on saying more. Erik was the one who had all the ideas about getting everyone on the same page, but they could try to explain his plan. "My mother collects books from before The Flood. Erik has read more of them than me and he's also made friends with a BREAD researcher. He's going to frame us as evolved beings when talks to the Clans. Please give him a chance.

"We are higher, more evolved beings than them," said Root. "They never accepted that before. Why will they now?"

"Because we're not saying we are better, just different." Seren still had a lot to learn about the clans, but they trusted Erik's judgment.

"They won't go for it," said Washington.

Seren gritted their teeth. "Erik knows what he is doing. Please have an open mind about this."

"You haven't exactly kept the most open mind either," said Root.

"I agree," said Washington. "We have more experience with these things. We know what we are talking about."

That made their stubborn behavior even more terrifying. What if they were right? What if people were doomed to fight? Half the reason Asana sent them here was because she thought they could help BREAD and the ambassadors get along. But what if they couldn't? What if everyone was just too set in their own ways?

Erik said the Altzis believed that their actions would placate The Mother, not further enrage Her. They believed they were saving people by forcing them into rigid rules. Any human was capable of violence, but it was nearly fanatical beliefs that made the Altzis truly dangerous. "You are acting like Altzis."

"I am not an Altzi," snarled Washington.

Seren stared at him, hoping their set jaw and square shoulders didn't show the fear rattling their insides. Root, Washington, Chocorua, and even Eddard were just as blind as the Altzis. "I didn't say you were. However, you're equally rigid, but with a different perspective."

"You're the one who said we need to act evolved." Washington glared at the map in front of him.

Seren stuck their hands deep in their pockets so no one would see their angry fists. They closed their eyes, retreating into their mind. *What would Assana do? What would she say?* Seren edged closer to the door. This was too much. They needed help. They had no clue where Root kept his basin, but perhaps the Elementals were strong enough to carry a message back home without one. They couldn't do this on their own. Assana should've sent someone more experienced.

They stumbled over a root growing out the floor, opening their eyes just in time to see a branch pop up for them to catch their balance on.

Age does bring wisdom, whispered a voice that almost sounded like Assana. But youth offers fresh perspectives.

Plump buds sprouted from the branches ends, and a tiny green caterpillar inched its way across the top branch. Seren grinned. The lake, or perhaps the tree, spoke to them and not Root. Maybe he was too stubborn to even listen to the Elementals he was ambassador to.

No one else heard the voice, but they were staring at the branch. Seren lowed their finger to it. The silk worm's legs tickled as it crawled over their skin. Some of the Elementals wanted them to keep talking, just like the Elementals at home wanted them to come here in the first place. But what were they supposed to say?

Everyone stared, though Seren assumed that was because the room was literally transforming around them, forcing them into the spotlight.

Just say what you mean, whispered the Elemental's voice in their mind.

They appreciated that this one at least talked to them instead of throwing things at them.

When they finally opened their mouth, the room's walls hummed in the same frequency as their voice. "I didn't mean we need to act superior. I meant we changed and adapted by learning: to respect and live symbiotically with the Earth and the Elementals. We need to show that same respect to different people."

Seren cringed internally at the last two words. It was so much easier to respect the BREAD researchers than it would be to respect a group like Altzis after how they tortured Erik.

"And that includes respecting those who are different from you, and raising up those you think of as lesser," added Sierra. "Different doesn't mean bad. Yes, The Mother gave us magic, so we would need less technology, but the clans have thrived on Her seas for over one hundred years when She could have drowned them at any moment."

"We need to work together," said Winnie.

"You're right." Root's voice cracked like a tree bending in a gale and finally losing its battle with gravity.

Footsteps echoed up the hall, accompanied by a flurry of whispers.

"They're here," said Seren. Had their speech been enough? Had they changed enough minds? Assana certainly would've if she'd come herself. People always listened to her.

Washington raised his chin. At first it looked like defiance, but his expression faded to something like a defeated predator baring his throat to a rival. "I will work with them, but if they prove to be insufferable or hostile..."

The door opened. Erik stepped in with Tav walking beside him and their aunts trailing behind them.

"So we meet again," Dr. Fullerton said. "Erik claims you are some kind of mutant, evolved by accident, not engineered like I thought."

"Mutant?" Seren raised her eyebrows at Erik. "I think you spend too much time reading moldy comics."

A laugh slipped out from behind Dr. Zhao's icy face.

"Mutation does imply accident, but I don't think evolution is accidental." Erik glanced back and forth between Seren and the women. "It's engineered, but not by humans. Earth, who is very much a living, thinking entity, engineers it. The planet is a sentient being."

Dr. Fullerton and Dr. Zhao frowned, but Tav smiled. "My aunts think of you as religious zealots."

Some ambassadors actually laughed at this one. Seren and Erik exchanged knowing smiles. Religion was an intensely debated topic among ambassadors.

Root took a step forward. "Some of us serve as spiritual guides, but it is not our main duty. We hold our positions because we can communicate with the Earth. We are literally ambassadors between the planet and the people living on it. Don't think of Earth as goddess but as a vast, highly intelligent being."

"I bet if you tested their DNA, there would something different about it," said Erik. "Something that could explain why they do things you cannot. Something that allows them to communicate with the planet."

Dr. Zhao walked up to Root, extended her hand, and introduced herself.

"I heard you had some trouble with Seren on the way up," he said taking the hand.

"Yes," said Dr. Zhao. "And my colleagues are concerned that you ambassadors do not respect us. Dr. Ulyssa has even accused you of plotting against us."

"I would never plot against my fellow delegates." Root lied without any visible tells.

Seren literally bit their tongue.

Dr. Zhao continued, oblivious to the conversation that took place before she arrived. “My sisters and I have agreed that if the ambassadors present donate a DNA sample in the form of a cheek swap and strand of hair, we will stay at NUNES and negotiate with good faith.”

“And if we refuse?” asked Washington.

“I consent,” said Seren before Dr. Zhao could answer Washington’s question. It was the least they could do after causing so much damage to the skiff.

“I do as well,” said Winnie.

Sierra and Lucia agreed next, followed by Eddard, Arthur, and Chocorua.

“I also consent,” said Root, “though I hope you will truly on take one strand, as I do not have much hair left.”

“As long as it’s not invasive,” said Washington.

“It’s not,” agreed Dr. Zhao. “Most of our research equipment survived the gunshots. If you let us use some of your electricity, we can run those tests tonight.”

“And then what?”

Dr. Zhao smiled. “If the results show that you are indeed genetically evolved, then we will consider your claim about communicating with a sentient planet as a valid hypothesis.”

“Sounds fair,” said Seren. “I’ll anticipate the results as they may help me understand my abilities.”

“We require additional reparations from you.” Dr. Zhao pointed at Seren. “We will discuss them in the morning.”

Seren sat back and listened as the scientist and older ambassadors engaged in a new debate. Seren appreciated how the scientist could make lights powered by the sun, and now, they wondered what else they could learn from these people.

CHAPTER
THIRTY-SIX

Erik wanted to soak in the tub forever. His scrapes and breaks may be healed, but his muscles and soul ached. Floating in steamy water was heaven that cleansed him of the filth the Altzis left on him. It loosened tension in his muscles and calmed aches. However, the water was cooling.

Hot water was one thing the island-tree didn't make an endless supply. The highest branches stored water. Sunlight heated up throughout, and at the end of the day, people were allowed to use it for baths. As an injured guest, Erik had been guaranteed a warm bath, but he got only one tubful of hot water.

He lingered until all the heat faded and a chill crept along his skin. Then he got out and dried himself with a silky towel made from a thicker version of the material the hospital blankets were woven with and dressed in a loose pants and a shirt that were the same fabric. On bare feet, he walked out of the bathroom and into the bedroom. Seren sprawled out on top of the blankets, still in their formal clothes.

Seren's lip tremble and their nostrils flared. Their hair was tousled, and their cheeks had reddened from days spent out under a sun whose rays were getting more direct as summer approached. After spending so many days in a filthy cell, standing in a room in silken pajamas watching Seren sleep felt like a dream. One he didn't deserve.

Eventually, Erik climbed into bed beside Seren and wrapped his arms and legs around them, snuggling as close as he could until they woke up.

"Did you have a good bath?" yawned Seren.

He nodded. The bath had been good, but his mind had been quiet too long. He'd told Seren the Altzis had hurt him and that they'd asked him about Valley-Port. He talked more about his escape and what he learned from Thomas. But he hadn't said what he'd told them and why it mattered. He'd kept secret the thing he needed to tell Seren most, because telling them would mean admitting how much he'd given away, how easily he chose to protect himself over other people. He needed to tell them, so they could warn Assana. What if the Altzis were planning to do something while people were away at NUNES? "We should talk."

Seren sat up. "What do you need to talk about?"

"The Altzis." He inhaled slowly, trying to calm his racing heart. "I didn't tell you everything."

Seren waited, staring into his eyes.

Erik continued. "They asked me questions about you and your mother. They asked about logistics—where things were, what defenses Assana had and what she could do with her power. Domhnall can sense lies in people, and he had knives. I didn't want them to hurt me more. I told them too much."

"Erik, your life is more important than information." Seren squeezed his hand. "I'm glad you didn't try to resist."

"But I did. When they asked me about you, I tried to lie without really lying. And I escaped. But then they caught me again." Erik couldn't finish the sentence. Fear shook his body and air refused to fill his lungs.

"It's over, Erik. You're safe now." Seren pulled his head to their chest and rubbed his back.

"It's not over," he whispered. "I think they're going to try and invade Valley-Port. What if they communicated with their allies before you saved me? What if they are planning on taking me back or going after Assana while we are away? What if while NUNES is convened, they take over the lands people left behind on their way to this conference?"

"Did they say they were going to do that?" asked Seren.

"No, but why else would they ask me so many questions about Valley-Port's defenses? NUNES would be a good diversion. What if they orchestrated the whole thing?"

Seren frowned. "I suppose it's possible, but the Valley-Port region is well defended. Me, you, and the twins are the only delegates going."

"The twins are the only fighters," said Erik. "And they know about her elemental defenses."

Seren shook their head. "No, Erik. They only know the ones you know about." Seren's lips pressed together and squinted. "Assana doesn't have words to explain everything she can do, and neither can I. Plus, the less people know, the less likely it is that enemies will find out. If you knew more, you could've told them more, but you didn't know, so no harm was done."

Erik put both hands on Seren's shoulders, forcing them to look in his eyes. "I didn't just tell them what I had been told, but what I sensed and guessed."

"What do you mean?" Seren frowned. Their forehead wrinkled.

"Merri and Mac. No one ever told me what they can do or how they could be used to defend Valley-Port, but I know from the time I've spent working with them." Erik sat up and ran his hands through his hair. "I provided details about their personalities and strength. I don't know the other water Elementals as well, but I do know them."

Seren cupped his cheek in their hand. "Erik, even if they know every detail about every Elemental, it doesn't mean they'd be able to get by them all. Maybe they'd be better prepared, but it the Elementals really want to keep the Altzis away, then they will keep them away."

Erik stared, surprised by their confidence, and waited for Seren to elaborate.

They stared into his eyes. "Can you fight a bolt of lightening?"

Erik shook his head, not sure if he understood Seren. "No, but you can dodge if you can predict where it is going to strike."

"Unless the only place it is going to strike is wherever you're standing." Seren smiled. "I'll let my mother know what you told me, but you have anything to worry about."

Erik really hoped Seren was right.

CHAPTER

THIRTY-SEVEN

Seren lay awake in bed while Erik snored, replaying the conversation over and over again. They lingered for hours, fearing visibly violent nightmares plagued Erik, but his sleep looked peaceful. Seren's feet twitched. Imagined ants crawled over their skin. Earlier, they'd meant to ask Root if they could use his communications basin to check in with Assana, but in the chaos of their arrival, they forgot. They hadn't seen one in any common area, but that didn't mean one didn't exist. If they'd left right after Erik had finished talking, they might have found someone awake to ask, but they had been afraid to leave him alone.

This far from home, using a communications basin that had pieces of Valley-Port and a dozen other territories built into it would yield a stronger and clearer connection to home. Most were filled with water from Atlantik, and from hundreds of rivers, lakes, streams, and ponds. For years, people traded vials of water to build a network of basins that could be used to communicate over long distances. The mixed waters, contained in an elemental basin, served as a focus and power booster for ambassadors who used it to communicate over long distances.

That didn't mean seeing Assana from the docks was impossible. It was late, but Assana often had trouble sleeping. She might be awake.

Seren slid out from under the covers, donning a cloak and boots before they ghosted out the door. The hallways were silent, devoid of lit lamps and anosmia-plagued guests. Seren closed their eyes and opened their mind to the tree, following its whispers until they found themself in a spiraling hall that only lead up. Aware it was the opposite direction that actually wanted to, but also that the tree wanted them to go there for a reason, they followed it up and up until they hit a dead end.

The room was round, and the smooth interior bark had more dark knots than Seren had seen anywhere in the building. They tried walking through walls like they had to get into the first conference room, but nothing gave. The floor heaved under their feet until they fell over.

Water and sap seeped through the floor. Seren scrambled to their feet only to be knocked back down by a gust. Wind blustered out of the walls, flattening Seren to floor. The hall's grade steepened. Seren slid headfirst, gaining unwanted velocity with every second. The more they dug their heels in and grabbed for walls, the slipperier the slide became. The Elemental forced Seren away from the place it had initially led them, obeying a ward that overrode its will.

Creating a bubble would be a waste of energy until Seren figured out where they were going. There was literally nowhere to go but down. The bubble would only speed up the process. The door they entered through blurred and vanished. The door had been shut anyway. Seren gathered all the energy they could muster, speculating on what would be at the end of the slide. It couldn't go on forever.

A few minutes later, the tunnel ended twenty feet above the lake. Seren slowed their decent with gathered energy and plopped into chilly water.

They swam to the docks, thankful that the trap had ended in the lake and not in pit of monsters worse than any Reggie could conjure in their tales. The trap was meant to waylay intruders, not kill them. So what was Root hiding that the Elementals wanted Seren to know about?

They climbed back onto the dock. Lights shone from boats at the far end where, but darkness shrouded this area. Remaining would be more private, but they had tripped some kind of alarm. Root might come to investigate who his wards dropped into the lake. Being found here would make it obvious they had tripped it. If he were going directly against the Elementals will, then he was powerful, and it made Seren wonder if he was not only angering them, but also The Mother. Would She notice? Would She care?

Seren couldn't answer those questions, but they did not want to be caught out here alone with Root.

Thinking *The Whaler* might help strengthen the connection to home walked towards it, siphoning the water from their clothing and sending it back to lake. By the time they climbed into their boat, they were dry.

The skiff's wooden seats and fiberglass hull calmed Seren's thundering heart. This was theirs: a piece of home that was practically an extension of themself. They climbed to the bow and held onto the wood and they focused on the water and on home, asking the currents to carry their voice and water to Assana.

Seren sat there, gazing over the edge, letting everything empty out of their mind save their will to see their mother. The gentle rocking of the boat lulled them into a state bordering on sleep and a trance.

"Seren?"

Seren startled. The image of a woman with a frizzy puff of brown hair and dark circled under her eyes flickered. Assana had seen better days, and Seren hoped their lack of communication wasn't the cause of her apparent stress.

"Mom?" Seren pulled their focus together until the image solidified. "I'm sorry I didn't check in sooner."

Assana's sigh conjured ripples on the water, like a tiny stone had been plopped in. "I did try to reach you, but I didn't get my hopes up that you were paying attention."

"This trip has been more of a trial than I anticipated." Seren wanted to share so much that they didn't know where to start.

"Yes. Between your letters, and communications from Great Salt Marsh and Great Bay, I've been able to put that much together. I'm impressed by how you've handled things, for the most part. Sending David and Reggie onto the solar skiff with guns blazing was a misstep."

Seren picked their lip while sifting through Assana's words. Assana had never mentioned communicating with Great Salt Marsh or Great Bay before, yet she just admitted to conversing with them. Why hadn't she? What else did she know?

"Did you know Erik had been captured?" blurted Seren.

"Not until after you saved him. The Elementals' tales contained limited detail," said Assana. "Particularly Sneaky River's tale about the battle with the Altzis.

Seren cocked their head. "When I told the other ambassadors about the Elementals I encountered, they were shocked to hear they had manifested and spoke to me."

Assana bowed her head. "Root and Washington?"

"Yes." More questions bubbled in Seren's throat.

"They're good men, but like all humans, they are flawed. They spend too much time in their own minds."

"How come your power binds you, but others can travel?" The words hurt as the blurted out of Seren's mouth, but they were lighter without them inside.

"No two Elementals are alike," said Assana, "but this is a conversation better suited to have in person."

"Did you know Root considered attacking the scientists?"

"What?" Assana's eyes widened and water rippled around her image. It became so clear that Assana's shocked face almost popped out of the water.

"It's true, and Erik suspects the Altzis plan to invade Valley-Port."

She hardly spoke again while Seren told her about Erik's capture, and the strange first day in Merry Basin. They had just told her about the DNA samples when footsteps made the dock groan.

"Seren?" called Root. "Is that you?"

"Yes," said Seren, struggling to answer and hold the connection with Assana. "I'm speaking with my mother."

Seren didn't look away from Assana's blurring face, but their skin prickled as Root leaned over their shoulders. "Someone tripped a ward near my private office. I fear they may have been trying to break in. I suggest you head back to your room where you will be safer."

"I can handle myself," said Seren, "Plus, I'm not done speaking with Assana."

Root's breath brushed Seren's ear. "I'd feel terrible if anything happened to you. Bid Assana a good night and go inside."

"Thieves are no danger to me." Seren ignored the implied threat in Root's whisper.

"Don't be so stubborn, Seren." Waves distorted Assana's face and wind garbled her voice. "We'll talk tomorrow. It will be less taxing."

"But,"

"Stay safe. Goodbye, Seren." Assana's face vanished, leaving them alone with Root. Assana hadn't technically been there physically but seeing her face and hearing her voice bolstered Seren's confidence. He wouldn't dare attack in front of Assana, but now that they were alone, what prevented him from confronting Seren about the alarm? The Elementals in the tree and lake knew who tripped the alarm. If they had enough willpower to hide that information from him, Seren was safe. If he had gotten in from them, then they were in danger.

"Was anything stolen?" Seren walked beside Root.

"Thankfully not. The wards ejected them from the tree before they found they door, but I'm concerned by how close they came."

Waves rocked the floating sections of dock. The breeze extinguished lanterns as they passed them. Was Root using neutral pronouns because he knew it was Seren, or because he didn't know the thief's gender?

"You seem to have a good bond with your Elementals. Perhaps they can identify the culprit?"

"That is the strange part." Root stepped up from the dock to the island and offered Seren a hand.

They walked past him.

Root caught up. "The Elementals should've been able to show me exactly who entered that hallway, but they only showed a human-shaped blur."

Seren sped to the town's main street. "Can ambassadors mask their appearance from Elementals?"

"Only those who are extremely skilled and powerful."

The shop fronts were dark and closed, and only a handful of apartments showed light through the asymmetrical windows. Seren walked as fast as they could without running. "I don't know the other ambassadors well, but the elder, wiser men seem to be good friends with you."

"Yes, but age and skill are not always as linked as one would think. However, there is another explanation."

"And what is that?" Seren rounded a corner. The Inn was a partially lit beacon above the sleepy streets.

"The Elemental favored whoever snuck in the hall and intentionally hid their identity from me." Root stopped walking.

Seren went a head a few steps then turned around to face him. "Do the Elementals have reasons to keep secrets from you?"

Root shrugged. "None that I am aware of."

Seren took a few more steps backwards. "Well, I can find my way from here. Have a good night, and I hope you catch your thief."

It took every ounce of self-control Seren possessed to walk calmly away without looking back or sprinting. They had not gone searching for Root's office with the intention to steal, and they doubted the complex wards were meant to repeal something as rare and simple as a thief. Root was hiding something the Elementals didn't like, something The Mother didn't approve of. Seren didn't want to think about what would happen if She decided to get involved.

CHAPTER
THIRTY-EIGHT

Early sunlight teased Seren awake, but they groaned and buried their aching head under a pillow. After fleeing Root, Seren had lingered outside David and Reggie's room and almost knocked on their door three times before realizing it was probably better if those two didn't start thinking about Root as potential threat. Seren retreated to their bed and clung to the blankets, listening for any sign of movement outside their door until sleep snuck up and stole them into darkness.

"Is it already morning?" moaned Erik as he rolled over.

"Unfortunately." Seren pushed themself up to a sitting position. Dr. Fullerton and Dr. Zhao were supposed to report preliminary results from their DNA test over breakfast, and if there were enough delegates present to have quorum, then the NUNES proceedings would begin.

"Don't get up yet." Erik scooted closer to Seren and rested his head on their leg.

They ran their fingers through his hair for a minute, but the longer they lingered, the harder it would be to get up and out. After disentangling themself from him and the blankets, Seren dressed in the same clothes that they wore the night before, noting that Erik made no move to get out of bed. Seren washed their face and hands with cool water than trickled out of a root into a wooden basin. When they got back into the bedroom, Erik remained wrapped in the blankets, staring at a wall.

Seren wanted to scoop him up and hold him until he felt safe. Instead, they took a deep breath, crossed their arms and squared their shoulders. “I can’t be late for breakfast.”

“I know,” squeaked Erik.

Seren took a step towards him and froze. Even if they just gave him a small kiss on the head, they weren’t sure they’d be able to make themself leave. “I’ll come check on you if you haven’t come down by the time I finish eating and meeting the scientists.”

“You know they have names, right?” asked Erik.

“Dr. Zhao, Dr. Fullerton, and Tav.” Seren squeezed the door handle so hard it groaned.

“I’ll see you at breakfast?”

“Maybe.”

They leaned their head against the door, crushed by how bad it hurt to see the young man who was always up before the sun hiding in bed. “I love you, Erik.”

“I love you too.” His whisper was a rough sound, like his throat was full of gravel from the bottom of a river.

Seren pushed the door open, darted out and slammed it shut. They counted to ten with each inhale as they put one foot in front of the other, moving away from where they wanted to be and towards where they needed to be.

Apparently oblivious that a meeting with the potential to alter the history of humanity on the planet was about to take place, people went about business as usual. Couples and throuples walked hand in hand, laughing at jokes Seren couldn't hear. Children ran circles around their parents, asking what the special "breakfast dessert of the day" was. Locals strode into the breakfast, but delegates stopped at the long table set up outside.

Paige, the girl that escorted Seren to the Inn on their first day, staffed it. Name badges covered most of the table. A bark sign in sheet covered the other.

"I already signed you in." Paige waved Seren over to the table with an acorn shaped badge. "But you need your name tag."

"Thank you!" Seren walked over and plucked one from the nearly empty row. Their name was printed on the top with their pronouns in parenthesis below it. An image of a tree growing out of a lake filled the middle, and the bottom described Seren's position: Ambassador-Delegate, Valley-Port, Proxy for Assana McIntyre.

"You're welcome." Page smiled. "Let your companions know we have badges for them too."

"I will." Seren stuck the badge to their shirt and stepped into the hall.

Resident families and workers filled the back tables. Independent Villages Association delegates, including members of the Altzi party, occupied the middle tables. Root, the scientists, and the other ambassadors ate at the two front tables, though Seren noted that a few of the older ambassadors were missing.

"Good morning, Seren, have a seat and feel free to eat some berries while we wait for the others to arrive. Morning can be difficult when you are as old as Washington."

"Will they be long?" Seren scooped blueberries and strawberries onto their plate.

"I hope not," said Root.

Seren stuffed their face with berries, bread, and goat cheese while they tried to count the people wearing delegate badges from the different parties.

"Is Erik coming?" asked Tav.

"No." Seren finished chewing. Footsteps creaked the floor, but when Seren glanced up, it was one of the tardy ambassadors. Sighing, Seren made eye contact with Tav. "He's not well."

Tav frowned. "Is there anything I can do to help him?"

"I think he just needs time."

The floor groaned when another person approached the table. Seren hoped to see Erik, but it was just Washington moseying along, greeting various people as he walked by all of the tables, loading his plate full of berries before he even acknowledged anyone at the front table.

"It's about time you arrived," said Root.

The scientists, who were having a conversation among themselves, quieted.

"I'm old," said Washington, "My bowels do what they want, when they want. I trust everyone had a good night?"

Seren and Tav made eye contact, each trying not to giggle as the seniors acted like it was normal to start breakfast by discussing their bowels. The main course came—steaming plates of scrambled eggs and golden toast. People devoured their food, but after a few minutes, Seren couldn't hold their questions.

"Dr. Zhao, did you run those tests?"

The woman swallowed a mouth full of eggs. "Yes, I did."

"What were they?"

"Inconclusive."

Dr. Zhao looked constipated. Tav snickered.

"What does inconclusive mean?" Seren wasn't sure what they wanted the answer to be, but they hoped learning about how and why they could interact with Elementals might help them find a way to make those interactions safer for them.

Dr. Zhao bit her lip. "Your DNA is definitely unique."

Seren stared until Dr. Zhao went on. "Both you and the other ambassadors have some markers we haven't seen before, but yours is even different than theirs, and to be honest, I really don't know what to make of it."

"Does that mean you need to run more tests?" Maybe the difference in their genes would explain why they interreacted with Elementals others couldn't. If it was something they'd inherited from their mom, maybe it explained why Elementals trapped her in Valley-Port while other ambassadors roamed freely.

"Of course!" Dr. Zhao grinned. "I've spoken with my colleagues, and they agreed that if you allow us to run more tests on you, then we will not retaliate or demand monetary compensation about the damage you did our skiff."

"Define more testing." Seren folded their hands on the table so they wouldn't give away their nerves by fidgeting. They hadn't forgotten overhearing Dr. Zhao and Dr. Fullerton speculating about what their brain looked like, but if it wasn't invasive and gave them a fresh perspective on their powers while also salvaging their relationship with these people, then it was worth it.

"We need to examine more DNA samples, study skins cells, blood, but more importantly, we need you to board our barge, so we can scan your brain and observe what kind activity you have when you are communing with the earth."

"Scan my brain? That sounds painful." Seren pictured someone cutting their head open and examining it, though they hoped the scientists meant something else. Seren could feel what lived under the surface of the lake without going in it. Maybe Dr. Zhao had a machine that could do the same thing to their brain. Maybe magic and science weren't really so different from each other.

"It's not, as long as you have no metal in your body. You will lay on a table while a magnetic machine spins around your head and maps your brain. The only danger is that it could rip out a mental implant."

"There is no metal in my body." They'd seen people with piercings but couldn't fathom why metal would be inside someone's body, and they didn't want to risk appearing ignorant by asking.

"Then none of the tests will cause permanent harm, but they will take time since we need to observe a variety of activities multiple times."

Just because "harm" wasn't permanent, doesn't mean it wouldn't hurt. But sometimes magic hurt and people did it anyway. Plus, they were going to be on a barge in the ocean. If it turned out they were lying and actually meant harm, they could ask Atlantik for help. "What else do you want to do to me?"

Dr. Zhao stared up like she was studying a list no one else can see. "Monitor your nervous system."

Seren frowned. "How long? Do I get to pick when?"

"Preferable sometime within the year." Dr. Zhao glanced at Tav.

Tav winked at Seren. "Here is the formal offer. We will forgive all damages if you will spend three months aboard one of our barges consenting to any noninvasive test we want to run on you."

"I'm willing to give you more little cells to study, but three months is much too long. I can't abandon my duties. Assana needs my help."

"I agree," said Tav. "What timespan would you consider?"

"A week." Seren watched the other ambassadors who seemed like they were the audience of a play.

Dr. Zhao shook her head. "A week isn't nearly enough. How about two months?"

"Three weeks." Seren crossed their arms.

"Six weeks is the shortest I'll consider," said Dr. Zhao.

"Do I have to be on board the whole time?" asked Seren. "Can't you bring equipment to me?"

Tav grinned. "It would be fascinating to study Seren in their own environment."

"It's possible." Sunlight reflected off of Dr. Fullerton's pale blond hair. "It would be more work, but the results would be worth the effort."

Dr. Zhao sighed. "I'll allow three weeks on the barge, so we can establish a baseline if we can shadow you for nine weeks after, giving us the originally requested three months of study time."

"You swear the tests are noninvasive?"

"We promise," said Tav's aunts in unsettling synchronicity.

"I will leave the facility in the same condition I entered it, and you will not harm or alter my lands in any way."

"Of course." Tav put a hand on Seren's wrist in a fruitless attempt to calm its shaking.

Seren looked down at the two hands. Tav's fingers were long like their aunts, but sturdier. Seren's were short, stubby, and calloused.

Seren took a deep breath and squared their shoulders. "I will consent to this if we add one more condition."

"And what is that?" sneered Rita.

Seren dropped their voice to a whisper and asked a question. "I want your support when the voting begins."

"Define support," sneered Dr. Fullerton. She'd been quiet so far, which Seren appreciated because she'd also been the most hostile.

"How many other cohorts are there? How much influence do you have over them?"

Dr. Zhao answered. "There are five affected by the NUNES Treaty and we have different relationships with each group. Why does that matter to you?"

Seren closed their eyes as they mentally replayed conversations with their mother and pictured the pieces of the constitution they'd drilled into Seren's head over the past few months. Seren was glad they'd put in the effort in spite of their reluctance because now they knew exactly what to ask for.

"NUNES needs to result in a moderate constitution that preserves freedom while holding people and their leaders accountable for their actions. We must to protect the land without oppressing the people. Vote for as many Option two clauses as possible with the exceptions of items where government power could infringe on human rights instead of protecting them. Persuade the other clans to do the same." Seren paused and sucked in a deep breath. "If you help make this happen, and Assana permits you to observe me at home, then I will agree to your terms, but I will not arrive until early November. Your barge will not go more than twenty miles away from Little Port while I am on it."

Dr. Zhao and Dr. Fullerton watched each other with furrowed brows.

"We will write up a contract as soon as time allows and," said Dr. Zhao. "I assume you have some way of contacting Assana to obtain her permission."

"I do." Seren's nerves plucked their attention away from Dr. Zhao and to the hall. The locals left, and a rainbow of humans filled in the room with a riot of storm-tossed hair, torn clothing, and chapped skin. "And I think we have quorum."

"Just barely." Dr. Zhao traced numbers in the air. "Based on the initial RSVP, two clans and a half a dozen non-Altzi ambassador-less village delegations are missing entirely."

Tav gazed at sun streaming in through a window across the room. "The weather has been rough. Maybe Root will delay."

"I doubt it." Seren gulped down half a glass of water, but it didn't cool the fear burning in their throat. Despite a lack of solid evidence, Seren believed the "rough weather" was Root's plot to delay parties he expected to vote in an unfavorable way. That kind of action was the opposite of democratic. Fear, especially when it stemmed from an angry planet, could spur anyone to unjust actions, but that didn't make it right. Stifling a budding republic and shooting up solar skiffs were wrong no matter what good intentions sparked them. Seren just wished they knew what Root wanted.

Dr. Zhao startled to her feet. "If my calculations are correct, we have the exact minimum delegates present for quorum."

"Expect to start voting today." Seren tipped their glass up for more water, but none remained.

"We'll work on the contract when we are dismissed for the

evening," said Dr. Zhao. "You can sign in the morning, after you have confirmed the details with Assana."

"I'll look forward to it," said Seren, careful to keep their facial features still even though they felt like crawling into a bathroom and puking. They were on their way to making amends for the damaged they'd done, but they didn't feel he relief they hoped for. Root was up to something the local Elementals wanted Seren to know about, and there were still several hostile ambassadors, and they were the people Seren needed to persuade.

CHAPTER

THIRTY-NINE

Since being liberated from the Altzis and arriving in Merry Basin, Erik hadn't thought much about doing anything other than sleeping and recovering. Since enough delegates arrived overnight for quorum, the NUNES proceedings began and Seren was busy. Alone in their rooms with too much energy to sleep all day like planned, he had no idea what to do.

He tried lying back down anyway, thinking his body could use more rest, but the tips of his toes and fingers twitched. Domhnall's voice, accompanied by distant sound of knives, slipped into his mind every time he tried to close his eyes. Sitting in the window seat, gazing out over the village or studying doors and windows grow out of tree bark didn't help much. The distant knife sound sent shocks coursing through his arms, like puppet strings made out of electric eels that raised his fist and shoved them into a wall. Barked scraped his knuckles, but thankfully, nothing broke.

Shaking his head, Erik stormed towards the door. He needed a book. He'd find the library. Pre-flood books, especially whole rooms of them, were rare. Few had survived, and many people didn't care about what world had been like before. Some even shunned that knowledge, afraid it would anger The Mother. However, ambassadors and scholars did care, and where there were powerful ambassadors, there were usually books their ancestors had saved from The Flood. Root was one of the most powerful. There *had* to be a library. Once his mind escaped into a story, there would be no room for Altzi-related memories to surface. The *schink—schink* got louder as he walked towards the door, but he was not going to let it stop him. Once he had a book, it would go away. He slipped his feet into the silky slippers the healers gave him and opened the door.

David sat on the floor, with his back to the wall while he sharpened a knife on a whetstone.

"What in The Mother's name are you doing?"

David paused, peering up at Erik through his matted mane of red curls. "Um, making sure no Altzi scum comes to finish what their buddies started."

Erik glared. "Do not sharpen those near me. The sound—it's just too much."

David's eyes widened. "I'm sorry. I didn't realize. It's a habit — something Reggie and I do so we stay alert when sitting around on guard duty. I won't do it again, and I'll tell Reggie when I see them."

Erik let out a slow breath and unclenched his fists. "Do you know if this place has a library?"

"I don't, but I'll help you look." David leapt to his feet. The knives and whetstone disappeared into his many layers of vests and tunics.

The library did exist, and it was a glorious thing. Fungi shelves grew out of every part of the round walls, and vines with blunted thorns twined into swinging ladders that helped patrons reach the higher shelves.

"You'll have to bring Seren here tonight whenever they get out of the sessions," said David.

"They'll love it," whispered Erik, gazing at thousands of books.

"Can I help you two find anything?" asked a woman wearing a knee length skirt made out of leaves and a deerskin tank top. Her name tag said Libra (she/her).

"I need a book," said Erik, staring in awe at book paradise.

The woman grinned. "Well, you come to the right place. I'm Libra, the woman with the privilege of maintaining this heaven."

"I'm Erik. My pronouns are he/him. I'd like a novel or three to read while my partner is politicking. Preferably romance. Something pre-flood with a happy ending." The genre's predictability and guaranteed happy ever after was exactly what he needed to escape to right now.

"And who are you?" Vines twined about the index finger Libra pointed at David.

"David. He/Him pronouns." He gawked at the numerous shelves. "I'm a friend of Erik and his partner. I'm interested in books on history and music, if you have any."

"I could recommend some titles, or I could give you a tour then leave you to browse."

"A tour would be lovely," said Erik.

"Fantastic!" Libra clapped her vine-clad hands together. "I need a moment to finish shelving one more item, and then I will begin. You can wait at the table behind me with that young man."

She directed Erik and David to a table where a man stared at the table, running hands through a mane of chestnut curls.

David sat next to the man. "It's Arthur, right?"

"Do I know you?" Arthur picked his head up, revealing sunburnt, freckled cheeks. He wore tight deerskin pants and a hemp shirt with one of the acorn name badges Seren had, indicating his name, pronouns, state, and status. His declared him a guest of one of the ambassadors.

Erik made a mental note to ask Seren for one of those name tags.

"We met once when my employer was buying hemp from you." David extended a hand to the man. "I'm David."

Arthur smiled. "You're the one who caught the horse thief."

"Yes." A smirk cracked across David's face. "Though my sibling would probably put horseshit on my pillow if I didn't give them credit for helping too."

Erik took the chair next to David. The three of them made small talk about the island, the weather, and expressing vague concerns and opinions about NUNES while they waited for the librarian. When she returned, two more people followed her, both clad in the silky infirmary issued clothing that Erik wore. One was a young man about his age with skin so light Erik could almost see his veins, hair like corn silk, and piercing blue eyes. A girl, who looked about twelve-years-old, stood behind him, clutching the back of his shirt with her eyes cast to the floor. Their name badges said they were relatives of Altzi delegates.

The girl looked familiar, but Erik couldn't place her until she looked up and frowned. "You're Erik."

Erik froze. Ghosts of manacles closed around his wrists and ankles.

"You have some very dedicated friends." The girl stepped out from behind her brother, inching closer to Erik. "I felt the river help them rescue you. Daddy thought you sinned against The Mother, but if one of Her Elementals wanted to free you, then you can't be as bad as Daddy thought. He says the boss either made a mistake or lied. Maybe a little of both."

Erik opened his mouth, but no words came out. His hands closed into fists and opened again. His breaths were a tide yanked higher and higher by a full moon.

"My name is Clover." She took another step, slowly raising a hand delicate as a water lily but calloused like a smith's.

Erik trembled, but he still stood and took the girls hand.

"I'm sorry my daddy's boss was so mean to you. He never said what he thought you did."

"I—I'm just—I knew things they wanted to know," stammered Erik.

"Domhnall was like mold, rotting us from the inside out." The man scratched the girl's head. "Our people will be better with a less fanatical leader."

Wide-eyed, Clover stared up at the young man. "Daddy said the same thing, but I thought it was just because he gets to be the boss now."

"Maybe both." He turned away from Clover and made eye contact with Erik. "I'm Simon. No words can apologize for what my uncle did to you, but I hope you won't judge me or my cousin by his actions."

Erik's mouth hung open. David stood beside him with one hand on Erik's shoulder, and the other hiding in the folds of his tunic, probably on the hilt of a hidden knife. Slowly, Erik extended a quivering hand towards Simon, just like he did for Clover.

"What in The Mother's name are you thinking?" Arthur yanked Erik away from Simon by his shirt collar. "This probably some ploy to convert you to their cause."

Erik blinked, stumbling until David caught him.

"You should leave, now, while you still can." Arthur strode towards Simon with his chest puffed out and his arms crossed.

Simon stepped forward without blinking. "We just as much a right to be here as you. Leave if you have a problem with us."

Arthur opened his mouth. His hands balled into fists.

Libra dashed over and got between Arthur and Simon. "Nobody is leaving yet."

Libra whistled. Vines snaked across the front doors and rose up between Arthur and Simon. "NUNES is about making peace. It's about unification, diversity, and acceptance. I don't know what kind of history you all have with each other, but you all must stay here, in this house of knowledge, until you come to some kind of peace."

CHAPTER FORTY

The session took place in a room directly above the breakfast hall. A dozen doors lined on the half-circle wall separating it from an oversized foyer. Seren left Reggie at the starboard door, where they would be stationed as general security for the morning. The next door over was guarded by a bulky man with an Altzi badge, and past him, stood a young BREAD representative Seren had yet to meet.

Inside, sunlight filtered through dozen floor to ceiling windows that mirrored the doors. People sat wherever they wanted, which meant in some cases, allies sat next to each other bolstering each other's arguments and threats. In other cases, it meant people shared tables with those whose values were fundamentally opposite of theirs.

Seren wandered around, debating whether it would be better to sit with strangers or people they had met. Strangers would provide an opportunity to learn and exchange information, but the past few days had been taxing, and Seren didn't trust themself to be civil if someone was rude.

When Winnie waved to Seren from a round table with one empty seat, Seren didn't hesitate to take the seat between her and Sierra.

Lucia smiled from across the table. "You looked lost."

"I was." The number of strangers in the room overwhelmed Seren. Some strained to talk over each other, but a many appeared as lost as Seren felt, gazing around the room with unblinking eyes and slack jaws.

They weren't surprised. People from so many different places had gathered in such numbers since before The Flood.

"This is going to be interesting," said Winnie. "A room full of people who are used to being in charge in one capacity or another are going to try to agree on things."

Winnie was right. The session hadn't even begun, and several delegates were competing for the leadership of their tables. The volume increased as more people entered. When it peaked, the doors closed and Root rose out of the floor on a podium. He thumped a staff against the floor until the delegates ceased speaking.

"Welcome!" His voice boomed through the room. "I hope you all enjoy breakfast and forgive me for rushing you. We are already two days behind schedule for a gathering long overdue."

For the next ten minutes, he spoke about the importance of unifying, but never mentioned the anger Seren sensed bubbling under The Mother's surface. Was it out of courtesy to those who didn't believe? To avoid causing fear? Despite his age and power, maybe he hadn't sensed it.

"The first article we must discuss involves how power will be distributed among the leaders of currently sovereign territories."

That is an understatement, thought Seren. They'd seen several drafts delivered by birds over the past year. Each time, the amount of influence a central council would have over individual leaders was drastically changed. Only so much could be done by remote communication. Three different options appeared in dark, curvy letters on the table in front of Seren.

"Thanks to your hard work, we have narrowed it down to three wording choices. This morning, we will vote. The bylaws you all agreed on for this meeting requires a two-thirds majority for an item to pass."

"Two choices would've made more sense," whispered Winnie.

Seren nodded their agreement as they studied the articles. Version one left the leading council as a mere figurehead, existing only to mediate major conflicts between territories, while version three left minimal lawmaking power to individual leaders. Seren favored option two, which allowed the central council to not only moderate conflicts, but to evaluate laws created by individual leaders to make sure they upheld the values on the constitution.

"I'm opening the floor to a brief period of moderated discussion," said Root. "Only one person is allowed to speak at a time. The speaker must remain standing while talking, and not exceed three minutes of speech. Those listening must remain seated."

As soon as Root thumped his staff, a woman with hair the color of marsh muck and a skirt thatched like a sea grass roof stood. "I'm Marsha, Mayor of The Independent Village of Switch Rivers, and I stand for Option one. My people are thriving without the interference of a council. We welcome protection from an invasion, but do not want interference from people who know nothing about our way of life."

"Thriving isn't exactly how I would describe your town." A freckled, pale man with gray hair stood. He wore a blackish green suit that shined like wet kelp. "Call me Rocky. I'm an ambassador from Neck Island, just off the coast of Switch Rivers. The humans in town may be well-fed and happy, but they are taking a toll on the ecosystem. In another twenty years, they'll be starving. This why we need to supervise every leader of territories large and small."

Marsha stood as soon as Rocky sat. "You care more about clams than people. Populations of shellfish and cod are steady. Would you have us starve?"

Marsha sank. Rocky stood. "If you didn't limit your diet, you could cut back just fine. Gulls and rabbits are exemplary sources of protein."

"I'm not making my people eat vermin." Marsha leapt up before Rocky sat. "Do you know what gulls eat?"

Root thumped his staff. "Sit. You've spoken out of turn and must remain silent until we move on to article two."

"We consume gulls." Dr. Fullerton stood and introduced herself. "My colleagues and I have been studying aquatic and gull populations. We've noticed declines in the later and an excess in the following."

Dr. Fullerton sat and Dr. Zhao stood. "Ecosystems are fluid, never the same from one year to the next, however, overfishing is a problem. Local leaders need the authority to set and alter harvest limits to suit their population, but they need some oversight to make sure nearsighted thinking doesn't harm the food supply. BREAD I supports Option two."

"As does BREAD II."

"And BREAD III," said Dr. Ulyssa.

A brief moment of silence followed where most delegates stared at their tables.

Seren took advantage of the break and stood. "In Valley-Port we balance the needs of the people and the needs of Mother Earth. Option three would put us at risk of comprising our balance and values, but Option one allows individual leaders to wreak havoc if they are led astray. We also support Option two."

A person who looked more like a bear in Altzi leathers than a man slowly rose to his feet. "I'm Guss, Mayor of The Independent Village Burnt Falls and acting leader of Altzi chapter A7. I've seen first-hand what unchecked power can do to a man. My people and I support Option three."

Cold sweat dampened Seren's palms. They recognized the man. Hadn't he been on the boat they sunk? Reggie had been on the deck longer than Seren. Certainly they'd know.

"Option three will be our doom." Eddard rose to his feet,

introduced himself, and launched into a tirade about why he blamed centralized government for the first flood. Before he finished, an Altzi as thin as Guss was wide interrupted Eddard. Root didn't seem to notice, or chose to ignore the interruption, and soon, the civil discourse dissolved into chaos.

"This is a nightmare," muttered Lucia. "Why isn't he doing anything?"

Winnie closed her eyes and rubbed her temples. The table twitched.

"Did you that?" asked Seren.

"I tried to make it thump like his staff, so people would stop shouting and listen, but the Elementals won't respond to me."

"Let me try." Seren closed their eyes, reaching out for the elemental tree-spirit, the one who had led them down the hall Root had been protecting. They felt its branches waving in their mind, greeting them like a new friend they were thrilled to have for a second visit.

Every inch of the room came alive in Seren's mind. Vines twined around synapses, sharing sensory data: hands touching tables and feet exerting pressure wood. Heat and moisture squirmed like maggots on a dead porcupine. Their shared awareness seeped from place to place until it surrounded Root's staff. They could've made it jump in Root's hands, but they were afraid of how he might react to Seren being able to manipulate his source of power. Instead, they retreated to the table they sat at, raised it up, and slammed it down.

Silence fell across the room.

"Is there a problem, Ambassador McIntyre?" Root peered down at them, yawning.

"Were you asleep?" asked Seren, stifling a ruder reply as whispering broke out across the room.

"Why do you accuse me of such negligence?"

"People were shouting over each other and going over their time limits. How are we supposed to get anything done with a moderator who won't moderate?"

Root gazed out of one of the windows. “I sensed something amiss on the lake. I must have diverted more attention to it than I realized.”

Eddard stood and glared at Root. “If your duties are so pressing that you let the sessions turn into a cacophony of competing wills, then perhaps you should find a proxy to moderate.”

“I will consider your advice for the next session. For now, let’s vote and see if we can push through Article two before lunch.”

CHAPTER FORTY-ONE

The library was impressive before Erik realized that the mushroom shelves actually rotated deep into the wall, so only a quarter of the library's books were visible at any given time. Now, it was mind-boggling. Erik didn't understand how Libra kept the complex system of organization in her head. Trying to keep track of all her explanations took every ounce of his focus.

David walked beside Erik, staring around with wide eyes and a grin worthy of Reggie's greatest joke. Simon was closest to the librarian, devouring every word she said like he'd been starved for decades. Clover clung to his hands while a smile brightened her face and awe danced in her eyes. Despite the wonders around them, Arthur shuffled behind Erik with his head bowed and his hands in pockets.

"This section is where all our books about music history are kept," said Libra. "The oldest pre-flood editions are on the highest shelves, and they chronologically work their way down. The bottom three rows are contemporary volumes composed by authors from across the North East."

Libra waved her hand. The second row from the bottom pulled

out, slowly spinning in the air in front of her. Bark spines filled the shelves. Libra opened a volume as thick as her face, revealing black ink sprawling over pulpy pages. With another wave of the hand, she brought down a shelf from the middle, and one from high up. The middle shelf contained paper books with printed letters, and the highest one had vellum volumes with handwriting so old Erik could not read it. He longed to touch them, but when he reached his hand out, he found them encased in a perfectly clear bubble of solidified sap.

"We have contemporary transcriptions if you are interested," said Libra, waving their old volumes up to the top shelf.

"I'll wait until the tour is done," said Erik.

"That is a wise choice. Anyone else?" Libra gestured towards the two disks still floating in front of them.

"Can I borrow *Pigs Might Fly*?" David pointed to a paper back with pre-flood factors shadowed against blue sky and pink letters. "I've been searching for a copy."

"Of course." Libra snapped her fingers and the book rose to her hands while vines twined into David's name in the books slot.

"Now you'll have something to do other than sharpen knives outside my door." Erik winked at David, hoping it diffused the bitterness that had crept into his voice.

"Anyone else?" asked Libra.

Arthur and Simon shook their head without looking at each other.

"Well, onto "History of War"." Libra led the group to a wider section of shelves where the wood was blackish red and lacked the shining natural lacquer of the other shelves.

"Why is this section so different?" asked Erik.

Frowning, Libra twirled her fingers through the air until an array of shelves floated down. She raised a tray of newer manuscripts to eye level. "Some argue that war, not construction and technology, woke The Mother into the rage that provoked The Flood. Instead of using advances to help, humans used them for destruction."

Titles like Nuclear Weaponry and The Mother's Ire, Alternative Narratives Doomed Millions, Corporate Greed Killed the Crops, and How White Nationalism, the Alt-Right and Neo-Nazis Triggered the Second America Civil War circled the group.

"Now this is why I have no tolerance for your people." Arthur snatched the last title out of their air and brandished it at Simon. "You do know where the name Altzi came from, right?"

"A lack of tolerance is a lack of tolerance," said Libra. "Each side uses their own moral code to differentiate themselves as good and the other as bad."

Arthur snorted. "So I'm supposed let these guys go around bullying anyone who is different than them?"

Libra crossed "That is not what I said. Have you ever seen Simon bully someone?"

Arthur shook his head. "But I've seen *his people* bully."

"Simon is one person. Not *his people.*" Libra closed her eyes. Erik suspected they were rolling behind her lids. He almost wanted to laugh. How could he have been so scared of Simon and Clover when they had done nothing to hurt him? Especially when Arthur, a person allegedly on his "side" was the one being the ass.

Libra opened her eyes and turned to Simon. "When did you last bully someone or acted out in violence?"

Erik tensed.

"I punched my brother last week," admitted Simon. "But he groped a girl because he thinks anything shy of an ankle-length skirt is an open invitation, and I feared if I left to her to defend herself, worse would've happened."

"To her or your brother?" A small smile tugged Erik's lips upward, remembering how Tina, a fisher from Little Port, had dumped three Altzis into the river when they harassed her with obscenities.

"Her." Simon blushed, bowing his head low. "She wouldn't have been the first girl he assaulted."

Erik nodded, thankful that the other Altzi men he encountered weren't an accurate representation of all their people. Hopefully Simon wasn't an anomaly.

Libra smiled, picking up a book from the middle shelf: a thin volume called *Night* by Eli Wiesel and handed it to Simon. "From the few Altzis I've spoken with, I've inferred that they are not well educated about the groups their name was derived from. I suggest you read this book with a connection to one of their sources—a story told by a victim of Nazi atrocities."

Erik hadn't read either, but he made a mental not to seek them out when he was in the right state of mind. It was important to know the kinds of atrocities humans committed in the past. Some things should not be forgotten, no matter how much the world changes.

Simon took the book. "What is a Nazi?"

Libra took a deep breath. "Nazi's were a political party that murdered millions of Jewish people in death camps."

"That's horrible." Simon frowned, eyes cast down to his feet. "But I don't understand what it has to do the Altzis. Some are pretty bad, but not *that* bad."

"Yet." Libra crossed her arms. "The two groups are not the same, but both are based off of a supremacist ideology and have similar ideas about how a government should be set up. They may not hold the same ideals or persecute all the same groups, but the Altzi founders drew inspiration from the Nazis and supremist groups that came after them."

"And I imagine if they found any of people who refused to abandon their old religions when the Mother woke and flooded the Earth, then they would kill them." Arthur stomped forward and glowered at Simon. "You are part of the damned group, and no one told you where the name came from?"

Simon shrugged. "I was told started calling ourselves Altzis when we ventured out of our territory and saw our values were different from the mainstream in other villages and territories. We follow an alternative path—one that is more challenging than the mainstream but favored by The Mother."

"I wish that were the case," said Libra. "Unfortunately, it is only one facet of the name. I've met Altzi leaders. Most recently, your Uncle Guss. He came here late last night, seeking answers. We spoke about the Altzi's history and the fallacies it's founded on. Fearing the darkness would alienate young members, the inner circle only shares it when—"

"When people move up," interrupted Arthur.

"Yes, which means only leaders have fully bought into that bullshit. But not all of them are beyond redemption." Libra sidestepped between the two men. "Talk to Guss. He disagrees the ideology and hopes to steer his people down a brighter path."

"Thank you." Simon clutched the book to his chest. "I suspect there are more of us who are oppressed by our leaders than those of us who agree with them, though most are too scared to admit it."

"This one is more suitable for someone your age." Libra took *Diary of Ann Frank* off of a shelf and handed them to Clover. "Both of these books are pre-flood, so the technology, culture and context may be hard to understand if you haven't read many pre-flood books, but they will also open your eyes to another world."

"You're wasting your time." Arthur rolled his eyes. "Are we allowed to leave yet?"

Libra laughed. "We have to peruse religion, sexuality, and technology before even reach the many genres of fiction, and Erik requested a romance."

Erik's mind raced as he processed the loaded conversation he'd just witnessed, as he reflected on how much history and culture had been swept away by The Flood, and considered the people around him. A vein bulged in Simon's forehead, just like the one that bulged in Domhnall's.

CHAPTER FORTY-TWO

A lunch break didn't help ease the pressure building inside Seren's head. The metaphysical vines retreated when Seren closed their mind off to the Earth, but Seren swore they left little seeds behind. Tension weighed on the room. With so many people and so many opinions, Seren struggled to think and process everything, but they were determined to at least speak once about each article. They just had to find the right words, and the right moment.

Option two of Article one scraped two-thirds of the vote in the time allotted for three articles. Now, the group discussed how the government's authority would be enforced. It started out calm, but it heated it up when Root slipped in his moderation. The scene reminded Seren of Little Port at high tide when the stripers chased minnows to the surface causing them to literally leap out of the water. Sometimes, a bold blue-fin followed the minnows the air only to be snatched by an osprey.

"No matter what shape this takes, my people cannot afford to be taxed for it." Marsha stood long enough to utter a sentence and sunk to her seat.

"I thought they were doing fine," said Rocky.

"The task force should only include the most competent soldiers." Guss leapt to his feet, drawing attention away from Marsha and Rocky's bickering. "I support Option one."

Eddard sighed so hard it was a miracle he managed to stay on his feet. "This task force should have equal representation of all people. Option one does not allow that."

"Define equal," squawked Marsha. "Some individuals have more power than others."

The discussion was necessary even if it did grow heated. Power was unbalanced between the three factions. Those without the magic of the ambassadors or the technology of the scientists were the most vulnerable part of the population. The new government needed to account for that. Without a moderator to reign it in, heated emotions trumped logic and civility.

Root's attention had strayed far from conversation. His awareness stretched out towards the lake, and knew if they asked him, he wouldn't give a truthful answer. So Seren listened to the discussion with their ears, and they listened to Root with their spirit, only contributing to the discourse when they felt compelled to.

Seren stood. "This task force needs to be respected and trusted. People will not trust it if they are afraid of it."

"If people don't fear it, they won't respect it," said Guss.

"Why do we even need one?" asked Sierra. "My people live peacefully without any force."

"To be protected from people like him." Eddard stood and pointed at Guss.

Guss stood too. "How do you know it isn't your kind people need protecting from?"

"How dare you, who leads a band of thugs, imply I am a threat to anyone." Eddard took a step closer to Guss. Seren cleared their throat. Root winked at them before thumping his staff into the ground. "It is time to vote."

It was a three-way stalemate.

"We didn't spend enough time talking about how this militia is going to be paid for, and that is not clear in any of the articles," said Marsha.

"That is a valid point," said Lucia. "But that is actually addressed in later article."

Marsha rolled her eyes. "You mean the one that proposes to allow the central government to decide on how much they can steal from us?"

"No one is stealing anything." A bald rotund person who had not spoken popped up. "My name is Bo Napper, from the independent village of Miller Valley. I will gladly share my harvest if it means staying safe from brigands and ruffians. Taxes aren't theft. They are funds that our chosen leaders can use to provide needed services."

"It's more like hiring thugs to do your dirty work for you," said Tommy Snyder, a lean man in Altzi leathers. "I run the neighboring village, and his people poach my livestock."

"*You* stole my cow. I simply took it back."

Lucia glanced at her wife, then studied the rest of the room. "This is why we need a functioning central government with a law enforcement and judicial system to support it. My territory may be peaceful, but situations like this require a neutral third party to..."

"And how do you ensure this central government's neutrality?" said Marsha.

Marsha and Bo responded at the same time, and once again Root failed to moderate. Was he actually trying to sabotage negotiations? Or was something else going on? Seren peered around the growing number of standing people to where Root stood with his back to the crowd and his nose pressed against the window.

Further opening their mind, allowed the vines back until the sensed Root diving down into the lake, sucking power in like a root, and sending it out to the mainland.

A thud jerked attention back to the center of the room. The vines writhed in Seren's head, a chair grown out the tree shattered. Marsha, surrounded by chair fragments, lunged at Bo. They each grabbed a chair, swinging. Seren sent their energy surging through the vines, to the floor, and pushing up so the vines took physical form and caught the chairs mid swing.

The two people lunged for each other anyway. Someone screamed. Guards rushed in from the doors. Energy surged from miles under the tree, through Seren's vines, and into their open mind. It mingled with Seren's frustration and memories, blanketing their nerves and taking over their will.

The floor shook. Seren's mouth opened. A slow, creaky voice boomed out of it. "Fools! All of you! Cease your squabbling or suffer the consequences!"

Root rushed Marsh and Bo, but the shaking floor tripped him as he reached the squabble and a rebounding punch landed on his face.

Seren willed the floor to stop shaking as Reggie and an Altzi guard wretched Marsha away from Bo, but it wouldn't stop. Seren tried to pull their mind away from the Tree, but they couldn't. Humans were fighting over ideas like gulls fighting over fish guts. And The Mother did not like it.

Seren worked the knots like they were rope, an overdone knot keeping a boat too close to its dock. The power surged from the very Earth the tree drew its life from. This wasn't an Elemental's rage; it came directly from The Mother.

"Get out my head!" Seren shouted, tearing at their hair with their hands while the spirit struggled against the roots imprisoning it. "I'm your ambassador, not your slave. Force me, and I will not serve you."

The vines and all their magic retreated, leaving Seren panting on the floor, drained and exhausted while silent delegates gaped at them.

"What have you done?" whispered Root. He wasn't looking at the angry delegates. He was staring directly into Seren's eyes.

CHAPTER
FORTY-THREE

A book quivered on its shelf, drawing Erik's attention away from Arthur's scowl and Simon's grin. Its creased spine rendered the title illegible. He tugged it out far enough to glimpse a tangle of muscular limbs over a rainbow bed. Blushing, he glanced over his shoulder. Libra strode away from Clover, who curled up an armchair with a book and a steaming mug of chamomile and lemongrass.

"Have you ever been in love?" asked Libra as she crossed from the brown floorboards into the reddish pink ones that denoted the "gender, sexuality, and romance" section of the library.

"I am in love," said Erik, hoping Seren was doing okay.

"Me too." Arthur stared at the ceiling.

The floor grumbled. More books shook. "What about you, Simon?"

His smile twisted. "Not with anyone my father ever approved of."

Arthur rolled his eyes. "Did she refuse to spread her legs for him?"

Simon's smile vanished. His open palms clenched into raised fists. "*He* never even met my father."

"He?" Arthur blinked. His mouth opened and closed.

An ear-shattering groan obscured the word. The whole room quaked. Erik grabbed onto a shelf to keep from falling over. Books toppled over him, pushing him to the floor regardless.

"Clover? Are you okay?" shouted Simon.

Clover's scream pierced the groan.

Simon leapt up, showering Erik with more books as he tried to run to her.

"I've never experienced this before," said Libra. Her steady voice didn't betray a hint of fear.

The tree groaned louder. The shaking intensified. Simon threw himself on top of Clover, shielding her body with his.

Fearing the quake would trigger some type of large wave, Erik mentally reached out, feeling the water around them, getting ready to help the locals calm whatever wave came of this. Nothing quaked beyond the tree. The waves of pressure and sound were muted enough by the time they reached the water, so they did little more than stir a few log-seized swells.

The tree was furious. The lake was angry. Earth poured fury through them to the Tree's central halls where the NUNES delegates were supposed to be working on their constitution.

CHAPTER FORTY-FOUR

As soon as the quake ceased, panicked voices clashed until Root thumped his staff. An aftershock rumbled the floor, sending people scurrying, and in some cases, rolling, to their seats. They waited in silence with closed eyes and white knuckled grips on the table. In some pre-flood books, people went to door ways to weather quakes because they were supposed to be sturdy structurally. Maybe these people never read those books. Perhaps they knew that this tree had nothing in common with the pre-flood structures because they didn't even crawl under the tables.

That wouldn't have helped anyway. The tree was quaking, not the earth, and the tables were grown from its wood. If the tree wanted to kill someone, it could turn the table into vines and strangle them. Even the strongest ambassadors in the room couldn't stop The Mother if She truly wanted to destroy them.

When the shaking ceased, whispered speculation broke out. Seren stood ousting vine fragments from their mind and squeezing their hands together so they wouldn't claw their skin in a useless attempt to make it stop crawling. "The Mother, and her Elemental Children, do not want to see us fight amongst ourselves. Discussions and debate are wonderful things, but we can't let them escalate to violence."

Silence clung to the air for about three seconds before Guss broke out into laughter. "And *you* are telling me this why?"

Seren opened their mouth to ask the man if they knew each other, and slammed it shut when they realized he had been on the Altzi ship they rescued Erik from.

Seren sank to their chair like a boat dragged to the bottom of a river. Their hypocrisy was an oversized anchor. Earth seethed when her human children fought, but She raged when they hurt each other while hurting her. The violence Seren committed on the river had been sanctioned, if not driven by an Elemental, but they still didn't want other people knowing about it. It was utterly hypocritical, but those without a connection to The Mother wouldn't realize the duplicity was Hers more than it was Seren's.

Guss nodded and sat down.

Sierra stood. "I motion we table the enforcement discussion and move to the tax options. We will be able to make better decisions if we know what kind of funding and supplies this central government will have."

"I second that," said Guss.

Root thumped his staff. "Motion approved. We will spend the next hour disusing Article seven, and then we will vote."

Lucia stood. "Even though this item doesn't name specific amounts, it establishes a process for determining how much the government will be allowed to take, and in what form they may take it."

Seren tried to focus, to shake off Guss's comment and the quake, but Root watched them through silted eyes. The chills it evoked made Seren feel like their skin was experiencing its own personal quake.

CHAPTER FORTY-FIVE

More delegates and their staff arrived throughout the day, some before and others after the quake. People and their nervous energies packed the dining hall. Boisterous voices blended. Erik struggled to focus on Seren telling him about NUNES. He managed to understand most of their agreement with Dr. Zhao and Dr. Fullerton, and as much as liked Tav, he only knew a couple of their aunts. Images of Seren trapped on a boat mingled with his own trauma, and he caught himself trying to talk them out of the agreement.

"Erik, it will be fine." Seren slid closer so their legs were touching. The leaned in and whispered, "Plus, we'll be in the *ocean*. Atlantik will save me if anything happens."

"Maybe you should ask Her first," Erik whispered. "Just in case. What if they drug you like the Altzis drugged me?"

Part of him felt ridiculous for saying that when he was the one pushing Seren and the scientists together. Part of him wondered if the Atlzis had made that drug on their own or got it from someone with more advanced chemical knowledge. One couldn't assume everyone in a group meant well just because a few of its members did, just like you couldn't assume everyone was bad based on a few bad members.

"I'll try to reach out to her tonight," said Seren before changing the subject to disastrous debates. They said something about conversations that got too heated and a snail's pace leading to a grudging consensus about taxes being collected in the form of natural resources, produced goods, and currency. They lost at something about a tithe of region's production. Seren's lips kept moving, but Erik didn't hear their words.

With so many knives scraping on plates, his mind strayed to his time aboard the Altzi ship. Domhnall's voice remained an incoherent presence in his mind, not there but not gone. His wrists itched and stung, even though healing had cleansed the infected wounds. Food didn't taste like much, but his head swam with fatigue and hunger. He shoved fish and greens in his mouth. It didn't help.

The more he thought about it, the more he was convinced the Altzis were going to invade. Domhnall was dead. The survivors from his ship were here, and not all of them were evil, transphobic scumbags. Seren stopped worrying, but they shouldn't have. For all he knew, Domhnall could have been working covertly with a more violent and fanatical group of Altzis. His subordinates might not be aware of his invasion plans unless they had a role in it.

He had warned Seren, and they had warned Assana. She had the land on high alert. It was enough. It had to be. Seren was needed here, adding whatever small voice they had to what they were starting to fear was a fruitless attempt to unite people. According to the dreams Seren told him about, an Altzi attack would be the least of their concerns if people maddened The Mother by not coming to some kind of agreement.

Seren's foot brushed against his. "How are you doing?"

Distant thunder rumbled. Some of the voices died down, but not all of them.

"I'm okay. Just tired."

"And lying."

Erik shrugged. "Isn't that what people do?"

"You should eat."

Seren's plate was licked clean. They slid their foot between his feet. Over the noise of chewing and clattering and chattering, snippets of conversation wound their way into Erik's ears.

"Isn't there someone, I don't know, younger who could be Root's proxy? Maybe a grandchild?"

"I'm surprised Sally isn't here."

"Still blames Root for their dad's death. Hasn't spoken to him in years."

"Him not letting their partner live on the island doesn't help."

"Tell me what you're thinking." Seren's voice drew Erik away from the conversation he listened in on.

He sighed. There were too many things in his head and too much going on outside it. "I need to get out of here."

Seren squeezed his hand. "Where do you want to go?"

"Let's go outside and see if we can reach Atlantik, and then maybe check in with Assana." Erik stood, but his feet tangled with Seren's, so he stumbled, knocking over a half drank glass of mead and mashed potatoes.

Seren stared at the mess until the floor absorbed it. "I could use some air."

Erik followed Seren to the dinning hall's exit, but instead of going straight through the passage that would've taken them directly outside, Seren took a right into a narrow opening Erik had not noticed before.

"Where are we going?"

"Taking a short cut." Seren didn't look back at. They pressed on, silent, occasionally running their hands along the wall.

"Are you sure you know where you are going?" asked Erik. The further they went, they further they moved away from outside. The only water he sensed was what flowed through the tree's roots.

"Just trust me," whispered Seren.

Erik trailed Seren, jogging to keep up with their steady strides as they wound through narrow, woody tunnels that could've once been the island tree's veins. The tighter and darker the space got, the tighter Erik's lungs and muscles became. The walls glowed purple and green, courtesy of the fungi growing on them. Erik's jaw clenched. His body ached like he carried a hundred pounds on his back.

Finally, the vein dropped them out into a wider hallway. He sucked in a deep breath, thankful his lungs could expand without hitting a damp wall, and he could see by more than the light of bioluminescent fungi. He followed Seren down ramps and stairs made out of gnarly roots. They went descended until they were well below the water level.

It swirled around them, pressing the root, seeping into the outer walls but not the hollow core, unless he counted the condensation feeding the glowing mold that had reappeared. They kept going until they hit a dead end: a translucent membrane acting as a semi-permeable porthole overlooking the blackness of the lake floor. Something ancient, a primal force that made Merri and Mac seem like domestic kittens, churned on the edge of his consciousness. He didn't dare open his mind to, afraid he'd lose himself in its vastness.

"Seren?" He reached out and took their hand, but they didn't respond. Their eyes were dilated and unblinking as they gazed out into the darkness. "Seren? Are you okay?"

He thought of how quiet they'd been on the way down here. Had this power been calling them? And if it already had its roots dug into in their head, would it release them?

CHAPTER
FORTY-SIX

The intensity of The Mother's energy overwhelmed Seren. Raw power washed over them like a storm surge battering the Little Port jetty until the sharp edges of Seren's nerve endings smoothed out enough to process it. After being overtaken by The Mother, Seren wanted answers. The Tree and the Elementals led them here, but they, along with the entire region felt small: just slivers of an omniscient being too large for Seren to truly comprehend. How could they hope to stand up to a being so vast?

If Erik hadn't grabbed their hand, Seren might have gotten lost in The Mother's vast glory and never returned to their body.

"Something is happening," yelled Erik. "Snap out of whatever trance you are in."

Seren blinked. Water pooled around their feet and the fungi glowed an angry red. A blur of a person approached, pushing his will on the stubborn elemental that took its time implementing the security protocol: ejecting the intruders to the bottom of the lake where the pressure would kill them long before they could swim to the surface.

Pulling Erik close, Seren pulled the root's remaining air into a bubble like the one that made *The Whaler* fly. They reinforced its walls with a tiny thread of The Mother's pure energy.

"Are you sure this will hold?" asked Erik as Seren lead him through the membrane, just before the root filled with water and shot it forward like a sideways guizer.

"Yes." It had to. Any amount of doubt could hurt their concentration enough for them to fail. As soon as they were through the membrane, they floated just above the bottom of the lake. Hundreds of roots as wide as houses sucked nutrients from the lake bottom, while more smaller roots hung firm in the water, absorbing it to the humans it sheltered.

"It's beautiful," said Erik.

Beautiful did not do it justice. Down here, they felt everything above and around them for miles and miles, and the more they let their awareness flow into the lake, the further they could feel. Not far behind them, Root was smug. Probably happy to be rid of Seren, so they stopped stumbling places they shouldn't and interfering in whatever schemes he was plotting.

He can't feel you, whispered the voice that Seren had heard shortly after meeting Root.

He would be shocked when he found them alive and chipper at the NUNES conference or sensed them return to the island. They'd worry about that later. Right now, they had two messages to send.

Seren stretched their mind until they reached the edge of the lake and found the river that had been so angered by the Altzis.

I need to speak to Atlantik, they thought to the river, and the river connected them to Great Bay, and he connected them to Great Salt Marsh who brought them to Piscataqua who finally brought Seren's consciousness out the ocean, to Atlantik.

Seren had spoken to the ocean a few times before, to seek safe passage home during squalls that broke out. She'd never declined to help before.

Atlantik's fluid voice sung in Seren's mind. *Child, you never contact me from so far away.*

I know you do so much me for me already, but I must ask something of you.

Must? Or desire?

Both.

Ask.

Seren mentally played out the conversation with the scientist.

I will do as you ask, but you must not shut me out when you cross my waters.

Ignoring the tightness in their chest, Seren sent their agreement and their gratitude and intentions down the series of Elementals and their bodies of water, letting it flow out into Atlantik. Seren didn't stop there. They pushed their spirit further along, in through Little Port and down the river until finally, they were back home, swirling through the waters of Attitash.

"Seren?" Assana's voice was loud with surprise.

Seren stared up at their mother from the inside of a goblet.

"Hi Mom. How are things going?"

Assana's eyes widened. "Nothing is out of the ordinary here."

"No sign of anyone encroaching or planning an attack?" Seren tried to not be freaked out by the fact that they weren't just talking to Assana through the lake but her beverage.

"None. And the Elementals have scoured Valley-Port and the surrounding areas. Johnny Wind left Little Port for the first time in several decades to inspect the coast up the Port's Mouth with some young people he's been tutoring. Not an Altzi or intruder in sight."

"That makes me more suspicious," said Seren. "What if they found a way to hide themselves?"

"If they had an ambassador that powerful, surely The Mother wouldn't have allowed their flawed ideology to continue."

"Ambassadors can go bad," said Seren. "Root just tried to kill me."

The clay goblet fell to floor and shattered. From the puddle, Seren watched Assana flee the room. Seren's spirit slipped from water to wood, traveling up into Assana's communications basin.

Assana stared in wide-eyed, open-mouthed shock, like a tree frog frozen mid peep, while Seren told her about everything from the suspicious room to being ejected from the bottom of the Tree.

"Watch him," said Assana. "Gather evidence. Make allies. Don't make accusations until you know others will believe you. Don't directly move against him until you can win. Be careful. Do what you can to minimize the damage. Don't tell anyone other than Erik, Reggie, and David. I'll contact the other ambassadors, including Root, individually, and see what I can ascertain."

"You could come," said Seren.

"Even if I could convince the Elementals to let me, that would raise suspicion," said Assana.

"By the time you'd get here, I'd have proof."

Assana shook her head. Her face contorted, and her jaw clenched. "I'm needed here. If he is planning something, I need to protect our home. The Mother is with you. I trust in Her to keep you safe."

"I miss you," said Seren.

"I know. I love you," said Assana. "But you should go before Erik has a heart attack. You may appear to be unconscious."

"I love you too," whispered Seren as they pulled away from the basin, traveling miles in seconds until their spirit snapped back into the body.

"Thank The Mother!" Erik collapsed onto the bubble floor. "Are you, all right?"

"I spoke with Atlantik. And Assana."

Erik made a noise that was a cross between a sigh and a laugh. "I thought you passed out."

"Assana said you would say that." Seren squeezed his hand.

The bubble raced to the surface, propelled by currents Erik commanded. They brightened, and Seren could just make out lightening cracking across the sky through the lake's blurred surface.

CHAPTER

FORTY-SEVEN

Erik wouldn't have slept at all had David and Reggie not taken turns keeping watch throughout the night. The little sleep he snatched was restless and fragmented. In his dreams, Domhnall and Root fluidly morphed into each other. The island tree turned into an enormous, writhing squid and swallowed him whole. He was actually happy when the thunder rumbled loud enough to shake the room and yank him from the nightmares.

Seren tossed, turned, and muttered to themself in a sleep that a few words or nudges wouldn't wake them from. It wasn't peaceful, but Erik hoped it was deep enough to help them recover the energy they expelled.

Jolting upright, Seren woke when the black of night faded to a slate gray morning and peered around with a wild, confused expression.

Erik thought having them awake would make him feel less alone and less anxious, but his heart beat faster and his chest hurt more. "I need to do something today."

Seren's gaze settled on him. "What do you want to do?"

Yesterday, between the library and dinner, Erik had snatched a few hours of reading, but he'd struggled to make his mind focus on the words. He needed to do something that used his body, something familiar. "I wish I could go to work. What are the odds they'd let me help out at the docks?"

"The docks are overloaded, and the hands will need all the help they can get making sure the visiting vessels don't float away." Seren got up and stretched.

"How you do you know?" Erik followed Seren out of bed.

Seren walked over to the washbasin and splashed their face with cold water. "I'm still connected to the tree on some level."

Unsure how he felt about that, he placed a hand on their shoulder. "Do you think that they will accept my help?"

"Of course." Seren turned around and smiled at him. "What are you going to do?"

"Secure my alliance with The BREAD representatives, and then I am going to try and figure out who could be working with Root, and what-in-The-Mother's-Name he is even trying to do."

"Do you have a plan?" Erik took over the washbasin when Seren vacated it.

"Not yet."

Five minutes later, Erik jogged to keep up with Seren on the way to the dining hall. The scientists were already there. Instead of sitting at the front table with the other ambassadors, Seren took a seat next to Dr. Zhao.

Root sat in his usual spot next to Washington, but he didn't spare Erik a glance. Maybe he didn't really know it had been him and Seren down in the base of the island. Perhaps he did know, but didn't want them to know he knew.

After exchanging rushed pleasantries, Seren asked Dr. Zhao the contract and read it while munching on fruit.

Erik sat next to Tav. "Your aunts won't hurt Seren, right?"

Tav shook their head. "Everything they want to do is safe, and I'll be there to make sure curiosity doesn't override their moral code."

Erik snorted. "I was hoping for a 'oh, they're really kind and would never hurt anyone, especially Seren.'"

Tav paused their eating and arched their eyebrows. "If you haven't noticed, they aren't exactly the warm and fuzzy type, but they respect Seren and were impressed by how they handled themself during the sessions yesterday."

Seren scribbled their signature on the document and handed it to Dr. Zhao. "I'll see you in the sessions soon."

Seren waved by to Erik and strode across the room without letting him know where they were going.

Tav put a hand on Erik's shoulder. "You have nothing to worry about."

"From them," said Erik as lightening reflected off of the water in his mug. It seemed like Seren had patched things up on their own, but he wondered if he could seal it tighter, make sure it didn't leak.

The harbor was chaos. People bailed out boats and tightened ropes as waves lashed them. The mossy bumpers prevented the piers from scraping or digging into the boats, but the pressure of constantly getting whacked against something solid wasn't great for the hulls. Dockhands scattered throughout the chaos, lending aid where they could. Some stood on the far ends of the wharves with their eyes closed and hands outstretched, trying in vain to stop the currents.

"This is just what the skiff needs." Tav growled and picked up their pace.

Erik stayed on their heels. The dock master and dockhands' wills had no effect on the currents thrashing against the dock. This far inland, the rise and fall of the tides should be negligible to someone who wasn't sensitive to them, but they were rushing in like they did in Little Port's jetty. Either Root was trying to scare people as part of his scheming, or Mother Earth was very, very angry.

"How can I help?" Erik leapt onto the damaged skiff right behind Tav.

"We need to finish patching the holes." They handed him a canister of shimmering putty. "Just brush it around the interior of the whole. You don't need to fill the whole thing. The material will expand."

"Anything else I need to know?"

Tav frowned. "Don't get any on your hands. Uncured, it's extremely flammable. If you can do anything to keep us from rocking, that would be great."

Erik stared down at the putty jar. "I can probably manage both if you don't talk."

"The works for me." Tav picked up their own jar and brush and set to work on the starboard hull.

Erik closed his eyes for a few minutes and opened his mind, getting attuned to the rhythm of waves slapping the boat. The people attempting to push it back were throwing their energy against an impenetrable wall of The Mother's wrath.

Unlike Erik, these people were used to gentle lake currents that only got stirred up when the wind whipped them, but Erik had lived his entire life in a port where fresh and salt water waged an internal war in the river. He knew he couldn't just halt a current this strong. If he were on duty during a Nor'Easter at home and needed protect docked vessels from a storm surge, he'd create a convection system where he channeled the current down up and around, so it wasn't slamming at the boat all at once.

He slid his will over a wave and pushed it down below the surface of the boat, let it expend energy, looped it down, around, and back in the direction it was heading, only with the lower currents. He wasn't really moving the water but redirecting the energy that stirred it.

At first, it took all his attention, but once the repetition faded to a subconscious ritual, he opened his eyes and patch holes. The boat wasn't still, but boats never were. The violent tilting calmed to a gentle sway that Erik could effortlessly step into. His mind was completely occupied by the two tasks, and for the first time since his abduction, Erik was completely at peace.

CHAPTER

FORTY-EIGHT

"Are we really going to sit here and debate whether or not the government will have any say in who marries who while a storm is battering our ships?" asked Marsha. Her hair was plastered to her face and her left leg bounced even when she stood.

"What is there to debate?" Seren glared at the three options on their table. One forbade the government, both at the local and federal level, from interfering in any kind of marriage, and this was one of few issues where Seren planned to vote for Option one. In Valley-Port, marriage was a commitment people made to each other, and if people wanted to end a marriage, that was their business. The only time Assana ever got involved were in rare abuse cases. Two granted local governments power to approve or deny both marriage and divorce. Three gave it power oversee who married who. "I don't understand why the government should play any role in people's personal relationships."

"Woman can't be impregnated by other woman," said Guss. "Men can't carry babies. The survival of the human race depends on heterosexual relations."

Lucia stood. "There are plenty of people who enjoy the company of the opposite sex. It's not necessary for everyone to have children."

"There are ways for same-sex couples to have children," said Dr. Zhao. "My wife and I chose not to have children, but my sister and her wife have a healthy child."

"That's...unnatural," muttered Guss.

Silence stifled the room. Arguments warred in Seren's mind. Should they reprimand Guss or just let it slide? Was there more that needed to be said, or would it be better to move this to a vote while the debate lulled?

"I motion to move to a vote," said Marsha.

"I second," said Seren.

Root thumped his staff on the floor. "All in favor of Option one, raise your hands."

Everyone save a few Altzis, three non-Altzi villagers, and Ambassador Washington raised their hands.

"Option one passes," said Root. The assault of rain dulled to a pattering, and the next rumble of thunder was quieter than the last.

Guss stood up suddenly, looked around like he'd heard something no one else did, and excused himself from the meeting.

Seren watched him rush out the door, but very few other people did.

"The next item on the agenda is Article six, which we skipped in an attempt to get to taxes quicker," said Root. "This pertains to citizen's right to bear weapons."

The floor swayed, as if it was a retina and the tree was rolling its eyes.

CHAPTER

FORTY-NINE

A scream, followed by shouts, thumps, and splashing, ripped Erik from his calming work.

"What was that?" Tav dropped their brush in a bucket of water and screwed a lid on their jar of sealing putty. Erik did the same and followed them up to the deck. His concentration on diverting the waves slipped. The boat rocked. The rain had slowed to a steady shower, but the wind blew harder, whipping up larger waves than before.

Some of the dockhands managed to replicate Erik's system of steadying the waves, creating calm areas for smaller vessels and sailboats that would flip if they were moored or out in the storm. Captains of larger vessels moored their boats far enough to be safe from the docks but close enough to make it back in a dingy.

Another burst of shouts and splashes rang out. Erik let go of his calm section of water and sprinted towards it the chaos. An ironclad Altzi steamship capsized about ten yards away from the furthest dock. People rowed out to it, trying to get others into their boats, but the waves were tossing the prams around.

A couple dockhands rushed closer. They exerted their will on the water, making the convection system they copied from Erik, but they didn't quite do it right and created a maelstrom that sucked someone further under. They let go and the person surfaced. They tried again, and this time ended up with a calm surface, but strong downward currents that still pulled people under. It was almost what Erik had been doing to keep the water calm with the boat, but people weren't as buoyant as boats.

"Let me help before you drown them!" Erik skidded to halt on the edge of the dock. "Stop trying to pull people into the boats."

Before anyone had a chance to question him, he threw his will out into the water, creating a much wider and slower convection system. The change of the surface wasn't instant, but slowly, the waves calmed. Water pushed up on the people, helping them stay afloat while it pulled them to the shore.

The men in the tenders rowed against the current, trying to reach the flipped vessel. Someone shouted. "They're still people on board, and it's sinking quick!"

People, including Simon and Clover, rushed to the edge of the docks to help pull others out of the water. The rowboats weren't making progress. Erik widened the system, but the stupid ship wouldn't budge.

"My dad left the NUNES sessions, so he could help Uncle Buddy get the ship off the docks. Buddy picked us up after Domhnall's paddler sunk." Clover's voice was high pitched and frantic as she perched on the edge of the dock, straining to see the sinking ship. "I know daddy wouldn't leave the boat until everyone else was safely off."

Erik bit his lip. Guss was the large man who guarded his cell. Who dragged him to Domhnall and back? Who sat by braiding his daughter's hair while Erik suffered Domhnall's interrogation? He deserved to suffer in the sinking ship.

"Please, help him," pleaded Clover.

Erik sunk to his knees. He didn't know Clover well, but she was a child. Innocent in spite of who her father was. She was kind. Her cousin was kind. No matter who her father hated, Erik didn't doubt he loved her, and she loved him. Letting Guss die would mean subjecting Clover to the grief of losing a parent. She was young. She might get over it in time. Or she might not. She might hate him and everyone like him for choosing to let a man die when he could have saved him.

"Mother help me," muttered Erik. He took off his shirt and pants, leaving only his undershorts on and dove into the lake.

"Erik, what are you doing?" Reggie's voice echoed from someone where in the crowd. They'd slept in since they took the last watch and sent David to guard duty during the sessions. They must've just woken and come looking for him.

He created mini currents to push the few people still struggling in the water close enough to swim to shore, then let the lake resume its chaotic state, only creating a small current to hurl him towards the ship. Someone splashed into the water behind him. Probably Reggie being their reckless self.

As much as they complained about boats, they were an excellent swimmer, especially when they boosted their muscles with Earth magic, and caught up to Erik's stream. Reggie swam beside him before he let go of the current and climbed into the sinking ship.

"There are people inside, and I can't haul it shore. Anyone who could is probably still in the NUNES sessions and wouldn't make it in time."

"Damned Altzis," muttered Reggie, but they didn't try to talk him out of helping. They climbed into the boat, scrambled ahead of him, and hauled away debris that got in their way.

Reggie freed a young boy trapped behind a bookcase, and a woman whose foot was crushed by a supply crate. A man who had refused to leave her side helped her up to her feet and took her weight as they hobbled through waist deep water.

"Who else is onboard?" asked Erik.

"Guss was trying to get a few people out of the engine room. Everyone else made it off."

"There is one window still above the water," said Reggie as they proceeded to describe how they came in. "But it's a long swim to shore."

"What should we do?"

Reggie and Erik stared at each other, each waiting for the other to answer. The boat lurched and dropped. Water rushed in behind them.

"Run!" The man scooped up his wife and ran further into the ship, yelling as he ran. "There is a metal door that should seal the water out of the engine room. This ship was built for brief periods of submergence and underwater combat, but the stabilization and air filtration systems haven't functioned in a long time."

"By a long time, he means *centuries*," said the wife.

Erik, Reggie, and the little boy followed him.

"This isn't going to buy us much time," hissed Reggie.

"We need Seren," said Erik.

"They're halfway across the island, and if you haven't noticed, we are in a metal tub of watery death."

Erik didn't waste energy on a reply. He sent his spirit out through the water, to where the island tree's roots sucked it up.

CHAPTER FIFTY

Seren stood to make a case about why the central government should be able to fluidly impose limits on harvesting non-food resources and clearing land, but the words never came out of their mouth.

An invisible void sucked air from their lungs, like the room suddenly sunk to the bottom of the lake without adapting to the pressure. No one else reacted. Seren's legs ached, and so did their head, like they were trying to control too many things at a time, straining the ability.

Was Root doing this to them?

If he was, it took no effort at all. His face and posture were relaxed. His words were garbled like they were hearing them through water.

People did notice water seeping out of the wood beneath Seren's feet. Sierra bent down to touch it. Lucia watched. Spots floated in front of Seren's eyes as the water took shape, forming the word "help". Each line of each letter held blurry images of Erik and Reggie. They swam, searched a dark space, and ran from a wall of water until they sealed themselves in an engine room.

Delegates rushed to Seren support as they swayed, asking garbled questions. Seren closed their eyes, ignoring the people as they traced the water through the floor, down the roots of the trees and out to lake, where it seeped into a metal deathtrap of a boat where Erik and Reggie risked their lives to save a few trapped people.

Focusing in on Erik, they thought *I'm coming* and prayed to The Mother they could save him.

Seren ran faster than they had ever run before. Their feet and heart pounded. Their lungs burned. The closer they got to the docks, the clearer the scene grew in their minds eye: Erik and Reggie struggling to free Guss from a tangled heap of metal while the ship sunk deeper and deeper into the lake.

The lake and all Her power flooded Seren until the image of the metal hulk dropping deeper and deeper while drifting further out filled their mind. Seren grabbed it with the lake's power, but the lake tugged back. *The ship is mine.*

My friends are on board. Locked in a tug of war game with an Elemental, Seren sprinted, pouring more of their energy, their will, and their need to save their friends into the action.

Roots rose out of the floor to trip Seren, but they felt them growing and leapt. Spirit vines snaked into their mind, trying to get control of Seren's body.

Help me save them, please! I'm asking, not forcing like you did to me. Seren poured love of Erik and Reggie down the vines. They played memories of Erik selflessly aiding ships and of Reggie risking their life to stop people from hurting the Earth.

The Elemental resistance let up, but it didn't cease completely.

Seren reached the edge of the dock, fell to their knees, and toppled into the water, letting their body and soul merge with the lake, bleeding thoughts of Guss slowly transforming the Altzis into a safer group of people.

You can have the boat as soon as I have the people, pleaded Seren.

They lake ceded enough control to Seren for them to lift the boat up just above the surface. A group of people clambered out of a hatch into the lake. Seren let the empty boat go and grabbed the people in a bubble of air while the lake crushed the hulk of metal that had somehow angered it.

Seren dropped the people onto the docks, climbed out of the water themself, and laid on the wet planks, panting while they struggled to disentangle their thoughts from the chaos of the lake and people around them.

Reggie's laughter, sharp as their knives, sliced through the tears, sighs of relief, and confused shouts. They plunked to the dock beside Seren. "Now I that is the closest I've come to dying yet, and I was trying to save the Earth-forsaken enemy."

Thunder rumbled, and the rain picked up.

"Sometimes, you are incredibly thick." Seren pushed themself to their feet.

Erik hovered a yard away, looking back and forth between Seren and Guss. The later sat on a bench, crying with and clinging to his daughter.

Clover broke away from her father and threw her arms around Erik's waste. "Thank you for saving my Daddy!"

Erik smiled and ruffled her hair.

Guss hobbled and clapped Erik on the shoulder. "You could've let me drown. Should've, after what my people—after what I did to you."

Erik's smile didn't fade, but a few tears mingled with the water soaking his cheeks.

"I owe you my life, Erik. You are a good man, and Domhnall was an idiot for thinking otherwise."

Seren glared down. Reggie still laid on their back, alternating between coughing and laughing. "You're wrong, Reggie. Guss and the Altzis are not our enemies. You don't have to like them or forgive them, but they're not the enemy."

"Then who is?" Reggie sat up, wiping rain out of their eyes.

Seren stared out at the stormy lake, realizing this was going to be as calm as the weather got for The Mother knows how long. Maybe the enemy wasn't a person, but the idea that someone could be other enough to be considered an enemy.

"Clear the docks!" shouted Winnie, charging down through the crowd with Root in tow.

"Retreat to the island and seek shelter!" Root's voice boomed over the docks as people rushed towards shore. "Bomb incoming. Evacuate the area."

People surged to the ladders leading from the docks to the island.

Seren didn't move. They'd used a bubble to protect themself from a bomb before. Maybe they could save the docks. Most people fled the dock, but Erik, Guss, Clover, and Reggie, and a couple who appeared injured all stayed close to Seren.

David wormed against the crowd that bottlenecked until he broke free and sprinted towards his twin. "Of course, the sensible people are running from the bomb and you are lounging in the place it is supposedly going to hit."

"The docks are pretty big," said Reggie. "But since Seren isn't moving either, I suspect they have plans to stop the explosive."

"I have to figure out where it is coming from first, and I would rather not have to protect a whole group." Seren watched Erik and the four Altzis who were slowly making their way to groups clambering up ladders and gangplanks. "Help them, and if you hear any useful information from anyone, have Erik send me a message."

"You don't need me to send a message." Erik walked from the Altzis to Seren. "Clover can do it."

Reggie frowned. "Are you sure you trust—"

"Yes." Erik folded his arms. "My abilities can help Seren. Your strength can be put to use getting the injured off of the docks."

Reggie opened their mouth to protest, but David put a hand on their shoulder and steered them towards Clover, explaining how he met her in the library with her cousin.

"What's the plan?" asked Erik.

"I'm not sure." Seren searched for Root. He wasn't with the thinning crowds near the places where the dock connected to land, and he wasn't helping the stragglers get there. When Seren searched with their mind, they sensed him out on the water, and could just make out a tiny speck of him floating in the distance, probably in a bubble.

Seren made sure their thoughts were walled away or hidden in their mind before they reached out to Root. He hadn't reacted to seeing Seren alive after they were expelled from the root, but that didn't necessarily mean he hadn't been behind it. Maybe he was a good actor.

When their mind found his, Seren asked what was going on. Root didn't reply with words, but with an image of a rowboat with the Altzi's symbol pained on the starboard side. Barrels of explosives filled the boat, which sped towards the island like it had a motor, even though didn't have one and neither of the two people on board were rowing.

A man held a gun to the head of a younger person. They had the same eyes and jaw as Root.

"Seren?" asked Erik.

"An Altzi has a hostage and boat full of explosives. The hostage looks like they might be related to Root," Seren sensed fear and victory, but couldn't tell who was feeling what. Someone manipulated currents to speed up the boat, but Seren couldn't tell who the power came from.

"Erik, can you sense who is controlling currents? I'll bubble us closer."

Erik squeezed Seren's hand as they gathered air around themself and Erik, slowing lifting them off of the docks and gliding them out over the water.

"Root is trying to alter them and meeting resistance," said Erik. He frowned, and his eyes widened. "The Altzi has the same ability as me."

"Great." Initially, Seren assumed that since the Altzis were so cruel, they didn't have any connection to the Earth because The Mother just wouldn't allow it, but they kept meeting more and more Altzis with abilities.

"Seren, what should we do?" asked Erik.

Seren blinked. "Can you help Root?"

"Get me closer?"

Seren pushed towards Root and the speeding boatload of explosives.

CHAPTER

FIFTY-ONE

Danger crawled over Erik's skin and screamed in his mind. No matter how hard he commanded the currents, he couldn't wrestle them from the grip of whoever controlled them. At first, he thought someone was forcing the other person to control them at gunpoint while Root tried to stop it, but as they got closer and his mind more attuned to their surroundings, he realized it was the other way around.

"What in The Mother's Name?" he said out loud, feeling around to make sure he was right.

"What?"

"Root is in full control of the currents," said Erik. "This is a set up. We're not supposed to stop them, but it's supposed to seem like we tried."

"Are you sure?" Growled Seren, shaking their head at Root's timing. The next article they convention was supposed to vote on set up the court system. It was late because Root was being a bad moderator again.

"I can feel the way he is messing with the currents. The boat with the explosives is heading straight towards Tav's solar skiff." Erik shuddered, thinking about how some of the mages seemed so afraid of science and technology. "I think he wants to blow it up and blame it on the Altzis."

"He doesn't like or trust either group," muttered Seren.

"No, but it's not that personal. The material Tav and I were using to patch it is very combustible. It will amplify the explosion." Erik wobbled around with his arms flailing not sure what he was really standing on. Standing in an invisible bubble of air disoriented him.

He diverted a sliver of attention from controlling the tides, brushing images on the water in a message to Clover, begging her to warn Tav or any BREAD researcher she saw that someone was trying to blow up the boat.

Mist curled into messy words. "Who is doing it?"

Erik drew a question mark in the mist and sent it back to her. He couldn't accuse Root without evidence people would believe and telling people it was a boat with an Altzi symbol wouldn't be much better.

The bubble jerked. Erik fell and was certain he would splash in the water, but a burst of hot air caught up and bore his weight up, making his backside a little too toasty for comfort.

Taking a deep breath, Erik stretched his mind out as far as he could. Tav's aunts had been at the NUNES proceedings, and Tav had followed him out when the Altzi boat sunk, but he had lost track of them. He found where the currents hit the roots of the solar skiff's slip and sent his consciousness upward.

Merely feet above the tides, his senses were raw and disoriented, but they weren't as dulled as he expected. It was like trying to see through murky water. Everything was shadowed and blurred, but he wasn't completely blind. A dozen life forces hovered in or around the solar skiff as well as the ones near it. "Seren, the solar skiffs are full of people. Either they didn't get the message about the bomb, or they are trying to save their ships."

"Damn him. What the hell is his endgame?"

"Power," breathed Erik. It was the only thing he could think of. Maybe Root wanted to set everyone against each other, so they would think their attempt at democracy failed. Then he could step in and "save" everyone by uniting them under his rule. Or maybe they'd just be too busy fighting each other to notice him somehow taking over. "What if he doesn't want a democracy. What if he wants an empire?"

Root shot out of the water and grabbed Sally with his bubble. Seren caught a few glimpses of his voice in the air as his bubble dissipated and both he and Sally sank into the water.

"Help!" he cried out. "I'm all out of energy."

Sally swam towards him and tried to keep his head above the waves while the treaded.

"You don't feel like you're out," barked Seren.

Erik squeezed Seren's hand. Energy exuded from Root, pushing the boat onward and fueling the lake's waves.

Seren held their course toward the boat, saying, "If you hadn't pointed it out, I wouldn't have noticed."

"Noticed what?"

"How he is doubly manipulating the currents."

"So he is faking needing help?" Erik hoped Seren would say yes, so he wouldn't feel guilty about leaving him to fend for himself in the chop.

Seren snorted. "He is plugged into the lake's power source. There is no way he is burnt out if I am still going."

"Are you worried about what others will think of you ignoring him?"

"First, I'm going to stop that bomb."

"I still can't affect the currents." Erik threw his mind against them to no avail over and over.

"You don't need to. Brace for impact."

Erik didn't know what Seren meant by brace for impact, but he doubted it would be pleasant. He wrapped his arms around their waist and held on tight as they sped towards the boat head on.

Seren's body tensed under him. The man driving the boat wasn't much older than Erik. His eyes were wide, and his hands shook.

An arm of water yanked the man out of the boat. The hostage's eyes bulged as the boat kept speeding ahead, on a collision course with Seren and Erik.

Root's shouting became fainter. In a few seconds, Erik would be able to reach out and touch the boat. Sweaty palms made his hands slip, so he bunched the fabric of Seren's shirt in his hands.

"Don't worry," Seren said. "I did this right before I rescued you, but it might be easier for you if you don't look."

Erik shut his eyes. A few seconds later, a thunderous boom made his ears ring until he couldn't hear anymore. The bubble quaked and sweltered. Sweat poured off his skin, which ached like it had been exposed to the sun and whipping winds for days. Seren growled. The bubble shot up then plummeted back down and whipped around. Erik thought he should just trust Seren and keep his eyes shut.

He opened his eyes.

He regretted it.

He and Seren were inside a ball of flames.

CHAPTER
FIFTY-TWO

It was hard to see through a ball of flame, but thankfully, Seren didn't need to see. Their connection to this lake grew stronger every second, and with it, their ability to sense where even the tiniest pebbles were and how they interrupted currents of both water and magic. Nevertheless, Seren bled energy out of their bubble until they had a window to see out of.

The excess energy formed a flaming tether, and the end of it, a shovel of fire insulated by air and water. This scooped Root Sally and closed the ball around them. Seren used the remaining energy to propel them towards shore and plop down in front of David and Reggie, who were last off of the docks behind Tav and their aunts.

Root stood and dusted himself off, but Sally sat on the ground, rocking back and forth. He didn't bend down to comfort them, but a healer rushed to their side.

Like rest of the people, David and Reggie stared with wide eyes and open mouths. Seren's expression wasn't much different. Elemental power whirled through their mind, making it hard to separate their thoughts from the lakes. The struggled to feel anything save the world around them.

"What in The Mother's Name is going on?" asked Reggie.

The crowd broke out into a cacophony of speculation. Seren dropped themself and Erik into the heart of it.

"You are mad!" shouted Root. "What the hell were you thinking?"

"Why are you yelling at Seren for saving you?" asked Reggie

Seren squeezed Reggie's arm but glared at Root. "I saved your life and Sally's life. I stopped a bomb from blowing up what is left of the already damaged solar skiff. I even caught the perpetrator who wore Altzi garb and drove one of their boats."

David's hands flew to one of his hidden pistols.

Guss pushed off a bench and growled. "Who? When I took charge of Domhnall's ilk, I ordered them to cease their ridiculous acts of violence."

"He's not an Altzi. The idiot was pretending to be one so we could get rid of those damned witches who want to put Earth on a leash and..." Root stopped talking, blinked, and shook his head.

A cacophony of surprised gasps and harrumphed agreements burst from the crowd.

"I mean, he hates them both. He wanted to kill them so they won't put Earth on a leash and —"

"We want no such thing." Dr. Zhao cut him off. She pushed her way out from behind a group of onlookers with her colleagues and Tav in tow.

"You say," snarled Root.

"We want to make life better for everyone, not only those with DNA that lets them manipulate energy and minds alike," said Dr. Zhao

"I don't manipulate minds," said Seren.

"Yes, but it appears that he can," said Dr. Zhao. "And I suspect there is another, less competent mind-bender in the crowd."

"Dr. Zhao, Dr. Fullerton, Tav, I assure you, this is all a misunderstanding. I can explain," said Root.

A dozen people snorted in the crowd. Their chatter and whispers got louder, making it hard to focus on Root.

"I'm sure you can," said Dr. Fullerton sarcastically. "You don't trust us and or you just don't want to deal fairly."

"The whole thing was a set-up to destabilize NUNES before it begins." Seren didn't even try to sort out their knowledge from the lake's. "But I made sure he didn't pull it off. We can confirm when the person he hired to play an Altzi gets to shore."

"How is he getting to shore?" asked Tav.

"The lake will deliver him for me." Seren smirked. The lake carried him on a current, proud as a cat brining a mouse home to her human.

Dr. Zhao gave them a skeptical look, but Tav returned the smirk. "Can we see how this works?"

Seren nodded and led the group to the water. The man who'd posed as an Altzi arrived on shore, drenched, and shaking. "Where am I? What happened?"

"This is him?" asked Reggie.

"What in The Mother's name did you do to me?" The man turned on Root, baring his teeth.

Seren stepped between them and raised a hand-shaped spurt of water behind the boy. Their ears rang like they were under water. They floated on the lakes power, unsure if the cold anger surging through them was theirs or not. "Tell me who you are and why were you in that boat?"

"I'm Tony." He pointed at Root. "The last thing I remember is getting into an argument with him. *Last night.* Then I was soaking wet, surrounded by all of you."

Seren frowned. "You don't remember driving the boat?"

"I just told you I didn't."

Seren conjured a hand of water, raising it higher and higher over Root. "What did you do to him?"

His mouth opened and closed even though no sound came out.

Seren turned to Tony. "Has he ever done anything like this to anyone else?"

He frowned. "There are rumors, but no proof."

"He is lying," said Root. "He is trying to ruin me."

Seren lowered the hand closer to Root, who waved his arms and shouted, trying to get the hand to back down and failing.

"Tell the truth," whispered Seren. They willed the hand of water to grab Root's torso. It morphed into a liquid snake squeezing the air out of his lungs, just how he'd been squeezing its will with his for so many months.

CHAPTER

FIFTY-THREE

Erik couldn't take it. Seren transformed into his Altzis captors while he watched from a few feet away, and they were oblivious to his reaction. He hoped that cold, calculating expression was the result of an Elemental in their mind, not just them. But he wasn't sure. Root's eyes bulged as he gasped, his hands shook, and Erik guessed if Root wasn't already drenched, a wet spot would've grown around the man's crotch. Seren hadn't used knives like Domhnall, but the concept was the same: cause pain and evoke piss-your-pants fear until the subject talks.

"I was acting in Earth's best interest!" shouted Root.

Erik backed away, but he could still see glimpses and hear the conversation.

Seren loosened the water just enough for Root to breathe, but not enough to ease the visible fear. Their voice was gravely, like a stone wheel grinding grain. "So you admit that you misled this boy here? And attempted to trick him into harming people?"

Root didn't respond.

Seren and their water turned to the young man. "What is your name?"

"Tony."

Erik wanted to puke. He wandered further and further away, not really looking where he was going until he could no longer see, hear, smell, or sense his surroundings. He wandered down winding hallways, passed doors that were locked and doors that weren't. He peeked in vacant guest rooms, storerooms, and offices. He wondered what was behind the doors that didn't open, but he wasn't sure he really cared to find out. He went higher and higher into the tree until he couldn't go any further.

The hallway ended. At first, he thought it was a dead end, but when he stared until his eyes watered, he could see the faint outline of a door—the secret passage Seren told him about.

He had not talent with wood magic, but something nudged him forward. A current rushed around his ankles, guiding him towards the door, urging him to open it.

He froze. Breathing became a battle. He fought to open his mouth and pull in enough air to fill his lungs then push it out again. The current shoved his feet forward like a pelting stream. The emotions strangling him were more like the wall of water Seren had threatened people with, but instead of menacingly hovering in the air, it pummeled him over and over. He was drowning. Unable to rise about the tide, he sank to his knees, crying.

He escaped one enemy, but more lurked in places strange and familiar. Even if the individuals who hurt him had drowned, there were other people like them. Many were among the Altzis, but today, he realized Seren was capable of the same violence if they felt like it needed to be done. Seren's brass determination saved him, but after being a victim, how could he look them in the eye, let alone love them? Still, the thought of not seeing Seren was a rip tide, sucking his drowned soul further out into a dark, stormy sea.

"It's not really Seren," he whispered, begging himself to believe his own words. "It has to be the Elementals."

At some point, his mind found its way back to shore and he realized he was on his knees, sobbing in front of a door. Through the blur of tears and his raw, exposed soul, he could see it clearly: a circle, almost like a hole that would form naturally allowing a squirrel or some other critter to make a home in the tree. Wood darkened by rot hung on rusty steel hinges. It was the first time Erik saw anything like it on the island. He didn't recognize the symbols etched into it. They were all lines and sharp angles. Some almost resembled letters, but Erik couldn't even make sense of those.

Curiosity pushed his anxiety aside as he stood up, walked towards the door and traced the runes with his fingers. It opened without him pushing it, revealing what appeared to be part office and part laboratory. The desks and shelves were grown like everything else on the island, and they were laden with books and papers.

Erik recognized the basin of water in the middle of the room. Assana had one like it, except hers was rough granite, not a bowl grown out of tree bark. He watched it for a few moments, knowing he had just enough of an affinity for water to be able use it to send a message to Assana and tell her more about the depth of Root's recurring treachery.

Erik took a step forward, then another, only hesitating because he knew he wasn't supposed to be in this office. Root admitted to a violent plot before Erik left, but Seren tortured him. Under that kind of pressure, he would say anything to save his own skin. Erik had said anything to save his own skin. Root might not be as guilty as Seren thought. And the instance they nearly drown under the tree? That didn't incriminate him. They trespassed and might have tripped an alarm designed to keep malevolent intruders away from all the raw power stored down there.

Erik looked around, with his eyes and mind, trying to make sure he wasn't missing anything. That is when he saw the metal lab bench. With so many books were stacked on it, he almost missed the little machines, vials of liquid, clay bricks, gears, wires, powders, and other little bits of machinery he couldn't name.

Root was an ambassador with magic powers most people would

only dream of, but he made explosives and read books that the grown parts of his office instinctively bent away from. Erik peered at the spines of the books. Some were titles he had read about, others were foreign. Other books had titles written in unknown alphabets.

Letters littered the center of the table. Erik sifted through them, hoping they would help him glean more about Root's intentions than the books would. He skimmed the beginning, middle, and ends until he saw his own name in one: a report from the Domhnall documenting what "useful" information Erik disclosed. There was a dozen addressed to him, discussing logistics and defensives of various towns and also complaining about how far humanity had strayed from the way The Mother wanted it.

Root hated how people in his territory used their connection to the Earth to fully morph their gender, or worse, just a little bit. Sally, in particular, was guilty of this. Like the Altzis, Root believed people should not use The Mother's power to change their bodies even though so many of his people did it with no visible consequence. He kept this hidden from his people in fear of them revolting and usurping him before he was in a position to truly hold them all.

His children were dead or powerless, but his grandchild, Sally, posed a considerable threat. Their power rivaled his, and the people loved her. Sally and he disagreed on issues beyond gender, and many times, they pushed him to retire and let them take over.

Erik froze, torn between whom to warn first. He wanted to rush down and warn Seren, but warning Assana would be much easier from up here. The basin of water made the decision for him. It rippled like a breeze storied it, and Assana's face, creased with worry, appeared on the water.

"Ambassador Root, how are the NUNES proceedings fairing?"

"Assana," gasped Erik. "Thank The Mother!"

Assana's head tilted, and before she had a chance to voice any questions, Erik launched into a rapid-fire explanation of what had transpired since Seren last spoke with her. Her expression grew more strained with every word.

"His betrayal is deeper than I thought." Assana closed her eyes. "This is the unrest I've sensed. The Elementals were trying to warn me, but he must have blocked them from revealing his whole plan."

Erik shivered. Assana had a reputation for being one of the most powerful mages in the Northeast. Erik had felt her power first hand and been awed and terrified by it. If Root was stronger, had more control over the Elementals, did Seren really stand a chance?

"He must be stopped." Assana opened her eyes and held her chin high. "The Mother will see this level of manipulation as a betrayal. And if he uses Her Elementals and Her power to start a war and to raise himself up above all other people and ambassadors, She will be...enraged. Provoked to a wrath we may not survive."

"What do I do?" Erik's heart raced. His lungs ached like every breath of air was icy water.

"Tell Seren. Tell David and Reggie. Tell his grandchild. Tell as many people as you can," said Assana. "Make sure the Elementals know you are trying to help. Beg The Mother for mercy."

"Will it be enough?" Erik stuffed the letters in his shirt with a quivering hand.

"I don't know," Assana whispered as her image faded from the basin. "But you must hurry!"

CHAPTER
FIFTY-FOUR

"He's a traitor!" shouted Root. "A powerless piece of fungus that impregnated my grandchild, Sally, with his weak seed. *He* convinced them to move off the island and live a peasant's life."

Sally leapt to their feet and slapped him across the face. "You were trying to kill us. I can still feel you in my head, stuffing my consciousness into a box and making me a puppet. You tried to kill me and destabilize NUNES in one stroke."

"I would never harm you! I had the power of the lake watching over you long before I reached you in person."

"Lying scum!"

Root yelled back, but Sally kept shouting at him. It was impossible to understand what they were saying. Their churning emotions fed into the lake, stoking its choppy rage. Seren's head ached. All the intense, negative feelings barraged their brain. Murderous rage. Fearing Root and Sally would inadvertently kill each other, Seren called the water hand back and used it to push the two people apart.

Root collapsed. "It seems I am the one forsaken by my own Elementals."

"They are not things that can be owned." With a wave of their hand, Sally wrenched control of the water away from Seren. Pressure faded from their mind. Sally released Root, only to turn the water into a noose that hauled him up by the neck. "Tell me how my father died!"

"He drowned!" shouted Root.

"Obviously." Sally tightened the noose. Part of Seren wanted to fight for control of the lake and make Sally stop, but part of them was so fascinated by the scene that they couldn't do anything but watch.

Finally, Root caved. "I conjured a storm while he was out fishing and attacked his boat with wind and waves. He had a choice: master his power or die. Unfortunately, he failed to take hold of the magic and drowned."

Seren's throat tightened, like the collar of magic they were always aware of back home had returned. Anger at Root's cruelty bubbled in their throat, but relief dominated it. Assana never resorted to measures that extreme when forcing Seren to train. They crossed their arms. The story was tragic, but nothing could be done about it now, so Seren focused on the positive. Even if they couldn't fully prove Root planned the explosion, he *had* just admitted to murder.

Root collapsed into a heap of sobbing apologies. The crowd of bystanders whispered amongst themselves, but Seren couldn't focus on what they were saying. The lake's anger had finally retreated, now that Sally had harnessed its power.

The wall of water holding Seren's feelings at bay fell, and they were assaulted with an indecipherable wave of emotion. They reached out to take Erik's hand. He was gone. They searched the crowd, but they didn't see him.

"So what are we going to do with Root?" Reggie's voice interfered with Seren's search.

"There are no prison cells on the island." Sally straightened their shoulders and brushed off their tunic. “There are some on the mainland, but I don’t trust those to hold him.”

“Keeping him close by might be better anyway. Can you contain him in an office or guest room?” asked Guss. “At least until we all finish negotiating the constitution and can hold a proper trial?”

“I can if the Elementals respond to me, but if they’re loyal to him...” Sally shook her head. “And if they’re not loyal, if they’re angry enough, I might not be able to stop them from killing him.”

Seren scanned the crowd while they spoke. “Twice they led me to places he didn’t want me to go, but they couldn’t resist enough to not trigger his alarms and traps.”

Sally snorted. “His office is probably the most secured room on the island. If I can alter his wards, it will hold him well enough.”

“Then lead the way,” said Guss.

It took Reggie and David seconds to bind Root’s hands and haul him to his feet. Along with Seren, Guss, and Dr. Zhao, the twins followed Sally. Seren kept searching for Erik on the way, but no matter which direction they looked, they couldn’t see him. Dozens of reasons for his absence ran through their mind, ranging from him being recaptured to having run away because of how Seren and Sally treated Root. In all the scenarios, he was hurting, whether it was Seren’s fault or someone else’s.

CHAPTER

FIFTY-FIVE

Seren's eyes stung and their throat ached like they swallowed a bunch of fishing tackle: hooks, sinkers, floaters, and lures. Since they'd noticed Erik's disappearance, every muscle in their body coiled up as tight as a dock line straining against a storm surge.

"Erik, where have you been?" Seeing him was a change in tide. The current shut down and the line went slack, but when Seren threw themself on him, hugging as hard as they could, and his only reciprocation was a light pat on the back, they knew that they'd caused his disappearance.

Erik whispered in Seren's ear, telling them about letters he'd found in Root's office.

"I knew he was still hiding something," muttered Seren, stepping away. Their hands curled into fists at their side, appalled at how Root betrayed his own family and gaining a better understanding of why the Elementals were so angry.

Erik froze and backed away from Seren.

"What?" Seren hands were fists and their eyes were a winter storm.

Erik took another step back, whispering "You're turning into our enemies."

The words were barbed hooks, lodging in Seren's chest and twisting around them.

"We found your lost boyfriend and it seems like you are the reason he left," said Root "Are you satisfied that I did not have anything to do with his disappearance?"

"I never actually accused you of making him disappear." Seren crossed their arms, shoving their feelings away. Erik had a point, but Root was dangerous, not just a threat to them, but to *everyone*. "Let's go."

"Do you really want to lock me up in my own office?"

Seren swallowed the first response that came to mind, one that would make them sound like the kind of enemy Erik had just accused them of becoming, and instead, chose to ignore Root.

David and Reggie pulled him forward.

"The place is a disaster. I don't spend much time in it and really am embarrassed by some of its contents."

Seren stared at the smooth wood walkway.

"You just got caught in a murder plot," said Reggie. "You're lucky we're bringing you there instead of throwing you in some dark, worm infested hole."

He blushed, folded his hands and gazed at the floor. "You don't understand. It's quite embarrassing."

"Well, that is your damned fault," barked Sally.

"I'm an old man with strange tastes for pleasure."

"Perhaps there is more incriminating evidence you don't want us to see," said David.

"Or an enormous pet spider waiting to trap intruders into a web." Reggie chuckled to themself. "Maybe he has a tank of flesh dissolving jellyfish he feeds his enemies too."

Seren wouldn't be surprised if there were some kind of monster waiting there, though they hoped there wasn't. Root stopped abruptly and muttered a few curses under his breath. A damp chill made the hair on Seren's arms stand up.

"Keep moving." Reggie pushed Root ahead, and he laughed as he resumed walking.

Seren followed Sally up flights of stairs and through winding hallways. Moisture tickled the back of their neck as they entered the spiraling hall they'd been ejected from the other day. Something was going to happen, but what? Being able to read Root's thoughts or do something other than making waves and bubbles would've been incredibly useful.

In the current situation, the best they could do was pay attention to their surroundings and keep their mind open to the magic, even if it did leave them vulnerable to The Mother's whims. The Elementals creaked their support, glad Seren had finally acted against their unwanted master. But not even the Elementals knew what was coming next.

Energy shifted. Power surged towards Root from the depths of the lake. Sally tugged on it, trying to pull it away from him. He must not have been trying very hard earlier, because this time, he took it from her with little effort. The walls became molten. Seren tried to grab the power, but it was a slippery eel slithering out of their grasp before they could get a good hold of it. The liquefied wood stretched out towards the group.

Reggie pulled a gun, but before they squeezed the trigger, a vine snapped out of the fluid wall and yanked the gun out of their hand. David and Dr. Zhao drew their weapons, but the same thing happened. Roots snaked out of the wall towards all of them. The group bunched together. Erik's back pressed against Seren's. When roots twined around Guss, he roared like trapped bear, but his action only made the vines tighten faster. Seren kept trying to yank Root's power away, but it wasn't working.

"You're approaching it wrong," whispered Erik. "Go for the power at its source, not where he is holding it."

Seren nodded, remembering that while they avoided using their magic, Erik embraced his and had a career because of it. His talents were limited to water, but he had more experience with the process of actually using that power.

Seren reached down to the heart of the lake, past the place where they had been earlier and down to where those roots pulled energy from Earth Herself. Power trickled the roots towards Root, amplified by the island as it went. Seren didn't touch that thread directly, but first pulled their own rivulet of power, just a little bigger than his. Magic wound its way up through the island and the tree at its heart, and Seren dove back down for another and another. They dropped down a fourth time and tied two of the three threads around the one that Root had pulled, tying lines of power into the tightest knot so it cut Root's off from the source.

Seren opened their eyes. Root panted and stared at Seren. His arms hung limp and the wall was solid albeit warped. Grinning, Seren used the thread of power they still had to liquefy the walls around him. Waves of wood snapped out and formed cuffs around his hands, feet, and throat.

With a snap of their fingers, Seren severed the cuffs from the wall.

"David and Reggie, would you please make him move so we can get to his office?"

Seren followed Sally, but Erik didn't move. Guss and Dr. Zhao strode past him. He stared at Seren like a deer trying to decide if the human it saw would ignore it or eat it.

"Erik?" repeated Seren.

He shook his head and walked.

David and Reggie hoisted Root between them.

"He's heavy," complained Reggie.

"I'd help if my leg wasn't wounded," said Guss.

Root laughed, but he didn't fight.

When they got to the top of the tree, Sally paced around the dead end. Erik, with his chin high and shoulders straight, walked right up to what at first appeared to be wall, traced his fingers and pushed. A door appeared as it opened.

"Impossible!" shouted Root. He wiggled and flailed, but he couldn't get out of his bonds.

"Show Sally the letters I gave you," said Erik.

Seren handed a letter to the Sally who passed it to Dr. Zhao and Guss after reading it. Sally's cheeks darkened when they read a second letter. Their eyes widened. Their hands shook. They moved their hands like they were going to throw the letters at him, but thought better of it and slammed it down by their side. "You arrogant, ignorant, stupid asshole!"

"Whatever you think is in those papers, it's not true. I love you. I would never do anything to hurt you."

"Except kill me or ally yourself with people who would rather kill me than live on the same planet as me?"

"It was fake—just a way to get information out of them!" pleaded Root.

Guss shook his head, muttering something about Domhnall being an idiot and getting people killed. Dr. Zhao's lips pursed, but the rest of her expression remained neutral.

Sally stomped over to his desk, read more letters, glowered at books, and yelled incoherent curses. During the chaos, Seren sidestepped to the basin of water and used it to contact Assana.

"Seren, thank The Mother! I've been so worried about you."

"I'm fine," they grumbled, "but I was right about Root."

"Erik explained when he contacted me a few minutes ago."

Seren snorted. "He tried to kill his own grandchild. He named and shaped the Altzis. Even his own power is turning on him," said Seren. "I can use it like it's my own, and when his grandchild draws from the well, power flocks to her and flees him."

"So you've stopped running from it," muttered Assana.

"Mom, I'm telling you that your ally is trying to turn NUNES into his own little empire. He tried to murder me a few minutes ago when

I caught him. And you are worrying about me deciding to actually use my magic?"

"Where is he now?" asked Assana.

"Restrained."

"Let me see."

The twins dragged Root into view of the basin. A mini, water-sculpted for of Assana's rose out of the basin. "Why would you betray us?"

The room went silent. Even Sally stopped cursing and rummaging through things.

"I didn't betray you," he said.

"Oh really." Assana raised her eyebrows. "Please explain."

"I'm doing what you and some of the other ambassadors refuse to do. You claim to be working in Earth's best interests, yet you ally yourself with NUNES and scientists who want to put the whole damned planet on a leash. You abuse your power. You've led your people astray. They need me to lead them back to the right path."

"And what path is that, Root?"

"One where people accept what The Mother gave them and don't try to change. One where people share the same beliefs, so they don't risk war over meaningless arguments."

Root narrowed his eyes. "I've studied history. Many efforts were made to cleanse humanity, but they all failed because people were too soft. Most rulers didn't have the stomach for it and waged wars on those who did. They did so much damage for nothing. The Mother took matters into Her own hands."

"And murdered billions of people for wars that would've never happened if people respected each other and valued humanity's diversity." Sally stepped towards Root with a look reminiscent of a blizzard. "People don't need be the same or believe the same things. They just need to respect and appreciate each other."

"You're delusional," said Root. He turned towards the basin. "Assana, tell your child to unbind me, or I will make them do it."

Seren arched an eyebrow at Root. "And how do you plan force me to unbind you?"

"This is your last chance," he said.

"I'd like to see you try."

Root's cackling scared Seren the most. Even when it seemed he was beaten, if he could break out into such deep, crazed laughter, then that meant he had something else hidden up his sleeve. Seren opened their mind as wide as they could, and felt Erik, the twins, and Sally doing the same thing, even though some of their talents all lay in more narrow areas.

The room shook. Something moaned deep in the tree.

"Cut him off at the source!" screamed Assana. "Dive as deep into the well as you can. Work together. Cut him off and make sure The Mother knows what he has done. Beg Her and the Elementals to shun him, so he will not be able to use it to harm you."

Seren grabbed Erik and Reggie's hands. Erik's damp hand held Seren's lightly, but he didn't pull away. David and Sally took hands, and Guss closed circle. Dr. Zhao lingered just outside, fiddling with a device. Seren closed their eyes and ordered their energy to follow Sally's down deeper into the lake than Seren had ventured before. They could feel the others all around them, spiritually clawing their way forward.

Sally fumbled, unsure where to go. Even though Seren had little experience with this kind of thing, they took the lead because they could sense the core of power under the lake just like they could feel sun warming their skin on a sunny day. The group boosted Seren's strength and helped them stay on course. The other times Seren had drawn power from the lake, it was calm and serene. Now, it churned like a storm had it all riled up.

Root's presence was down there too, gathering strings of power to him and wrapping himself in them. He formed a metaphysical octopus with tentacles of power writhing around, trying to swat away Seren's attempts to grab power. They charged the giant cephalopod head on, each fending off a tentacle, attempting to reach the three that were too entwined in the tree's roots to fight.

Root couldn't focus on fighting three fronts, so he directed his power towards Seren. Cold darkness coiled around them. If it happened to their physical body, they would have suffocated, but it was their spirit he strangled, and that hurt in ways they never expected: a stab in their chest and a pressure in their head. Could metaphysical trauma actually cause some kind of a heart attack or a stroke?

Seren screamed, both in the real world and in their head, pulling power not from the lake and the ground below it like Root did, but from much deeper in the Earth, in a place where territories didn't matter, a place where if one went in with an open mind, they could possible talk directly with Earth Herself.

Down here, Seren bared their soul to the vast being they called The Mother, showing all their flaws as they begged for help overcoming their adversary.

They were stubborn.

Narrow-minded.

Childish and spoiled.

They tried to be the kind of good Assana was, but they failed more often than they succeeded.

But they loved Earth and Her children.

Seren not only wanted to keep the world clean and wild, but they wanted it to be a place where humans could be fluid, evolving in infinite directions. Seren knew they weren't perfect. They didn't deny that they'd shunned their connection to The Mother, but they were certain with all of their being that Root was a monster who'd lead the Earth and all Her children to ruin.

Seren didn't express this in words. They projected feelings and memories from their soul to the gargantuan ball of energy that made up Mother Earth.

They waited.

Silence reigned.

They waited more.

Raw, raging energy exploded in Seren's mind. Brains and bones melted to molten rock, flowing towards some unknown end. As detached as Seren was from their body, they still felt Earth quake as it severed ties with Root and flooded Seren's mind with the excess power created by the action. It was too much. They already bore a connection to one Elemental power source. They couldn't handle another.

Yes, you can, said two voices in unison, familiar and alien.

Miles away, Assana dove down to the same core, and joined Seren as a bystander encouraging them as they pleaded with Earth. The other voice wasn't really a voice at all. Seren perceived the idea as words, but it was so much more than that.

It was a sentiment power pumped into their soul, telling them that they were capable of more than they gave themself credit for with half the restrictions they expected. Seren saw themself traveling to places that looked familiar and strange: land where the earth was pink and orange, forest lush with alien vegetation, and arid desert with yellow sand that stretched on for miles.

Seren was a true ambassador, not merely a go-between Attitash and the people of Valley-Port, or even just the people of NUNES, but a medium between Earth and humanity.

An overwhelming sense of agreement washed over Seren. Earth intended for all ambassadors to be Her channel of communication to all people, but somehow, many of them had misunderstood that and clung to their territories, which were meant to be home bases, places to return to and recharge, not places to hide in or lord over like monarchs of old.

Root tried to raise himself up above the others. He wanted to rule them, and he encouraged their squabbling, so they would think they needed him. Humans like him led others astray. They started wars and destroyed out of selfishness. For decades, the people around him were oblivious to it, and remained that way until they were on the brink of a war.

Something small burrowed down into the core, interrupting The Mother's wrath. Sally clawed and dug through bedrock until they floundered around like a child wielding magic for the first time. Seren wanted to hand the new power over to the person who should've inherited it, but Earth yanked it back to Seren.

They are untried spawn of the traitor.

Again, words registered in Seren's mind, but they were accompanied by something older, something more primal.

"But I'm the one who's going to stay and take care of the island," said Sally aloud and mentally. Images of walking around, talking, and healing danced around in the ether.

"I have no intention of lingering here much longer," added Seren, followed with images of them traveling to all of the places Mother Earth showed them.

My decision is made.

Yet, Seren noticed that The Mother took a sliver of power and wound it around Sally giving her what Seren suspected would be just enough power of her own to be able to hold her place as a leader on the island.

This is a trial for you.

Reluctant gratitude emanated from Sally to Mother Earth. Sally appreciated what The Mother gave, but they wanted more.

You must clean up his mess.

Images of people shouting and men plotting in small rooms filled their mind. Pictures of a war between ambassadors wrenching the earth apart danced across their consciousness.

This must not happen.

"I promise it won't," said Seren. "I will do all I can to restore peace."

The Earth shook. The rains of a new flood are falling. The delegates of NUNES have until dawn to prove they are capable of cooperating by finalizing the constitution. If you fail, you, the delegates, their people, and their land will all drown. I won't risk survivors harming me again.

"But that's not fair!" Seren scrambled to put together an argument that would defend humans.

If you want what I showed you, then you will make it happen. The Mother ejected Sally and Seren from Her core. Their spirits flew up, side by side, through bedrock and water, until they were both once again grounded in their bodies.

Root gaped with his mouth hanging open. He looked around, trying to figure out why whatever he tried to do didn't work. Footsteps shook the room. Dr. Fullerton and Tav burst through the door with guns drawn. David and Reggie drew their pistols.

"Don't fire!" shouted Seren.

A beam of red energy flew from Dr. Fullerton's gun, hitting Root in the leg.

The twins held their aim, but they didn't shoot.

Root collapsed, crying out and clutching the smoking hole in his knee.

Sally broke away from the circle and rushed to their wounded grandfather's side.

"Get a healer!" They laid one hand on his knee and another on his head. No one moved. Root's pained shouting stopped as he passed out in Sally's arms. "I made him sleep so he won't suffer, but if I try to repair the damage, I might not do it right and his knee will sustain permanent damage."

"He planned to kill us all, including you," said Reggie. "He deserves a little suffering."

Seren closed their eyes, melding their mind with the surface of the tree's power, using it to write a message on the wall to alert the healers. Healers left their quarters and moved towards the office. They weren't the only ones heading higher into the tree. Fear and curiosity had sent others scurrying about like squirrels before winter, trying to figure out what shook the tree and if their leaders were okay.

Opening their eyes, Seren stared at Sally. "The healers are on their way. If your town laws are anything like mine, you are in charge now, and your people are afraid. They need to know the truth."

Sally ran their fingers through their hair. "You're right, but I don't think you all should be here when they do. People like Root. He might even have allies who knew his plans and might try to harm you."

Seren knew they should say or do something, but they had no clue what they should say or do, let alone feel. Assana's image had faded from the basin, so they couldn't ask her for guidance. "Do you need us to do anything?"

Sally shook their head "Get the delegates back in the hall. I'll meet you there shortly. We have a deadline."

CHAPTER

FIFTY-SIX

Erik's eyes flew open when Seren dropped his hands. Seren swayed; he rocked along with the whole room. He took a step, wobbling like a drunk.

Erik clenched his jaw, determined not to puke.

Seren and Sally spoke, but their voices were garbled. They moved around. People came in. Erik ducked as shots were fired. They shouted and moved, but part of Erik's soul lingered deep in the lake where The Mother's heart thundered against the muddy lake floor, sending sound waves up to the surface where the water took their shape.

Thunder shook the office, pushing Erik's soul closer to his mind. Lighting illuminated the office. Root lay wounded on the floor. Seren and Reggie stormed towards Erik.

"That was wild," whispered Reggie as they brushed past him. Jolting pins and needles rushed into his limbs.

Seren grabbed his shoulders. "Erik, I need you and David to go down to the docks. Anyone trying to ride the storm out must abandon ship and get inside. We have until dawn to finish the constitution or The Mother will drown us all."

Half formed responses opened and closed Erik's mouth like a scallop propelling itself across a bay floor. He managed a "yes" before David yanked him out of the office.

With each step, Erik steadied, and his spirit settled into his body. Everyone else seemed to have snapped back from the incident like it was nothing, but Erik couldn't quite shut out The Mother's pounding heart and the waves it stirred up.

"You look as confused as I feel." David held open a door that lead out of the winding hall and onto a staircase. "I felt Seren pulling strength from me, but nothing else. Did you get a sense of what actually happened?"

Erik nodded and shook his head.

David laughed. "You okay?"

"I was there. I could see and hear them battling, but I couldn't quite reach them. I tried so hard, got so close, but I couldn't help. I just...became the water."

Erik tried to describe exactly what transpired, but he struggled to find words that explained what witnessing people's souls battle over an infinite heart of power was like. He still fumbled over words when they reached the docks. Erik's teeth ground and opened his mind to the currents in an attempt to gauge how serious this storm was.

He regretted it.

The lake's too strong tides had strengthened, pulled high and angry by the moon. The winds teased the waves, taunting them until they reached for the moon, trying, and failing to knock it down and gain their freedom.

It teased him too, calling him tiny and weak, daring him to join the waves in their quest to wrench the moon from the sky.

Your partner challenged our old master, whispered the wind. They won. Why not challenge the moon with us?

Erik shook his head and slammed his mind closed. "This is not going to be fun."

David squeezed Erik's shoulder. "What do you need me to do?"

"Get *The Whaler* running.

David arched his eyebrows.

"Don't tell Seren." Erik winked. "Do get a team people to usher everyone inside while I venture out on the water."

Wind howled louder than *The Whaler's* growling engine. It didn't do much, but whatever energy it expended pushing the boat was energy Erik saved. His convection system was a liquid version of the tread from a pre-flood tank, carrying *The Whaler* over waves and against the angriest surges the wind stirred up.

All but three boats had banded together in a vein of relatively calm water. Local dockhands manned the perimeter boats, maintaining that calm area. Erik shouted to them, telling them that the storm was getting too intense, but even when his boat was only about ten feet away from one of theirs, it still seemed no one heard him.

He reached with his mind to the calm area, stretching it out so it included his boat. One of the dockhands nodded, and the boats slowed down enough to let him slip between two. Once inside, the wind slowed and the air warmed.

"How long have you been alone out there in that little skiff?" Arthur leaned over the edge of a log catamaran. His partner, Eddard, sat cross-legged in the middle with his eyes closed and his hands resting palm up on his knees.

"Not long," said Erik. "You all need to get to shore. The storm is going to keep getting worse."

"How do you know?"asked Simon from a red boat, three away from the Gundalow. "We are doing okay right now."

"Eddard, Lucia, and Sierra can't keep the winds calm forever, even if they do keep switching off," said Winnie who stood alone on an oversized lily pad. "The dockhands are tiring too, and all my talents lie in soil and flora, so I'm pretty useless out here."

"We'll lose our boats if we leave them," said Simon.

Winnie grunted. "That is better than losing our lives."

Erik rubbed his hands together, hoping a short version of the truth would be enough to convince them. "Did you hear about the bomb threat?"

Five people spoke at once.

"Earth is enraged one of Her ambassadors was behind it," said Erik. "There was a struggle for power. Root lost, and The Mother gave Seren an ultimatum: we have until dawn to agree on a treaty. If we fail, no one will survive the flood that ensues."

CHAPTER
FIFTY-SEVEN

After sending messages all over the island instructing delegates to gather in the hall and residents to shelter in the highest parts of the island, Seren headed down the docks with Tav. A spark of anger flared when they realized Erik took *The Whaler* out, but the thought that taking another boat would've meant thievery tempered it. The boats still tied up weren't doing well anyway.

With a slew of ambassadors and water mages, Erik's group made slow but steady progress towards shore.

"That is definitely Dr. Ulyssa." Tav pointed at a solar skiff barely staying afloat as it veered towards an Altzi paddler that was doing a seesaw impersonation. The winds appeared to have forgotten the laws of physics and were blowing from opposite directions, pushing the two ships closer and closer together.

Tav held a gray square to their mouth and pressed a button. "Ulyssa? Do you hear me?"

Static crackled back at her.

"Can you communicate with them?" asked Tav.

"Only if there is another mage on board."

Tav put a hand on Seren's shoulder "Is there anything you can do to save them?"

"Yes. But you should get inside with the others."

Tav shook their head. "I'll wait here and help Erik get people to shore. I may not have magic, but I am strong. I can hold ropes and lift people if I need to."

"I'm sure they'll appreciate the help." Seren closed their eyes, gathered air and water around themself and stepped off of the docks.

Seren caught an updraft and rode it until they had a bird's eye view of the three ships that were out on their own. They flew to the furthest one. Chocorua stood alone in an oversized canoe surrounded by his own bubble of calm water. Seren's bubble merged with his and they landed on the deck. They gave him a quick, abbreviated explanation of Root's treachery.

"That is not good," he said, gaping at the rain as if he only just noticed it.

"Seriously. You should get to shore."

"I thought I'd be better on my own." He shook his head and watched the group of ships clustered together. "But they could use my help getting to shore."

"Can you bring the paddler with you?" Seren pointed to a struggling Altzi ship.

"Yes, but should I?"

"Did you listen to anything I told you?"

"The Mother wants us to unite." Chocorua studied his weathered hands. "Consider it done."

"Thank you. I'll take care of the solar skiff." Seren leapt back into their own bubble and rose on a gust, shooting towards the solar skiff. It strayed even further from the group, and awkwardly rocked from Port to Starboard. Women scurried from machine to machine struggle while Seren thought about how to best help. Before they made up their mind, it flipped.

The time for thinking was over. Seren spotted Dr. Ulyssa and swooped down, scooping her out of the water. "How many were on your boat?"

"How? How are we flying?" asked the drenched scientist paced around Seren's bubble.

Seren repeated the question.

"There are eleven of us," said Dr. Ulyssa, looking at everything but Seren.

Seren scanned the water and plucked another seven people out. Their muscles burned, and each rumble of thunder sent shooting pains through their head.

No one floated on the churning water. Seren reached out with spiritual tentacles, feeling for human life forces.

One unconscious mind floated just beneath the waves.

"Just great," muttered Seren.

"What?" asked someone. "Do you see them? There are still three people unaccounted for."

Rubbing aching temples, Seren listened to the rebellious waves and currents. If they dove into the water themself, they wouldn't be able to maintain the bubble, so they pressed the currents into submission just long enough to propel the unconscious woman to the surface and into the bubble. Water evaporated from her skin as she passed through the flickering orange membrane.

Two women rushed to catch her, checked her pulse, and laid her on her side. She coughed up water until she could speak, "Ginger and Oleander are stuck in the skiff!"

Seren wanted to scream. The skiff's panels barely poked above the water. When Seren probed it, they found two very alive, very panicked souls trapped in the head.

"If I leave this bubble, it goes away and you all fall back into the water." Seren made eye contact with Dr. Ulyssa. "I can lower you onto the boat to get them out partially raise the vessel."

"Do it," she said.

"Stay quiet and do exactly as I say, when I say it." Seren closed their eyes, partitioning their attention so part of their mind stayed focused on keeping the bubble and the nine scientists it held afloat. They focused the rest of their attention on the waves and currents around the damaged solar skiff, creating an upward spout of water to push it back to the surface. Wind nudged the bubble closer and closer to the skiff until the two nearly touched.

Seren pointed to Dr. Ulyssa. "Go help your colleagues get to the surface of the skiff. When you return to the surface, do not move. I'll pull you all back to the bubble."

Dr. Ulyssa nodded and climbed onto the skiff. Wind whipped her hair. Hail pelted her skin. She slipped through an opening and vanished from Seren's sight, but not their mind.

The wait was the hardest part, keeping the boat and the loaded bubble afloat. Currents and waves raged against Seren's will, clamoring for blood like sharks circling a wounded seal. Sweat streamed down Seren's temples and pressure built in their head until their vision blurred, and they saw spots. It felt like being under ten miles of water, not hovering then inches above it.

Seren barely managed to stay upright.

The woman emerged from the barely floating vessel with a bundle in her arms and two shaking teenagers close behind. They perched on the broken bow, staying as still as they could while being rocked by waves and pummeled with hale.

Seren mustered a tendril of energy and hauled them into the bubble. Their sisters embraced them as Seren yanked a gale to blow their bubble towards the island. It was a quick trip. Seren plopped the woman down in front of the hall and rose up once more to make sure no one else was in immediate danger. As far as their tired eyes could see, everyone had either reached shore or the vein of relatively calm water.

Seren floated themself to *The Whaler* and plopped onto the deck behind Erik.

CHAPTER

FIFTY-EIGHT

Erik tensed when Seren's hand brushed his shoulder.

"The other ambassadors and I are going to pool out power to get to shore quicker. Do you want me to patch you in?"

Erik chewed his lip. It would be convenient to be able to telepathically communicate with the ambassadors who helped maintain the calm current, but he'd need to go through Seren's mind to manage it. After seeing them interrogate Root, Erik wasn't sure he wanted to let them in his head.

Seren stepped away and closed their eyes. "It's okay. I forgot. I'm being thick."

Erik grit his teeth and grabbed their wrist. "Patch me in. Things will be smoother if you do."

"OK," croaked Seren. Their consciousness slipped into his until the raw energy of a raging bonfire burned his mind and bolstered his power. It was nothing compared to what happened a few seconds later when Seren fully opened up their connection to Mother Earth. A supernova of raw, perpetual energy consumed him. He felt like an ant under a human's boot, frozen, and unsure how to exist in the face of something so massive.

No wonder Seren feared this power.

He shuddered. All that energy, in the hands of someone willing to torture another human for information terrified him. How far could Seren be pushed? How much pain and destruction could they cause if they believed they were doing the right thing?

"Are you okay?" Seren's voice echoed from another world. They squeezed his hand, pulling him back to reality and anchoring him there, away from the power and the cyclone of what-ifs.

"I think so." He retreated to mass of energy's outskirts. If he survived past dawn, then he'd worry about Seren could do with their newfound power.

Mentally reaching out, Erik siphoned a tiny thread of energy to replenish his diminishing strength and analyzed the area around him. Ambassadors and dockhands strove to keep the vein calm. More ambassadors worked from highest parts of the island, doing their best to shelter the main building and the people it housed from winds, lightening, and hail.

As tempting as it was to take more power, Erik didn't dare try. The mass of unending energy fueled the storm and taking too much might burn him up. The siphoned trickle sustained him long enough to help direct the fleet to shore before the storm caught on to his actions and started fighting back. Pulling energy from it became just as hard as manipulating currents and without that borrowed power, Erik and Seren were close to empty.

Erik shivered when Seren stood up. They'd been unpredictable these past few days. Thankfully, they only projected their voice and didn't raise a wall of water or summon a tornado.

"We can't get the rest of you to land with your boats. I can fly you to safety, but you will need to abandon ship." Seren pulled one last blanket of power from the storm and rose up a few feet in the air. Sierra, Lucia, Chocorua, and Eddard did the same.

Lightening forked towards a mast, but Seren intercepted it, using the electricity to expand the bubble.

Each ambassador filled their bubbles with as many people as they could, whether it was three or ten, and repeated the process until only Erik and two dockhands remained.

"That's everyone." Seren crashed into Erik as they landed, knocking him away from the helm. "The hall is the safest place now until the ambassadors there are depleted. If the storm isn't over by then, we're all doomed."

"Then let's go before you collapse." Erik hoisted Seren to their feet and wrapped their arms around them. The two other dockhands leapt on board. Seren created one last bubble that lifted themself, the three passengers, and *The Whaler* up into the wind until it leveled with most of the tree house roofs.

"Is this necessary?" Erik glared at Seren. Other people liked their boats just as much as Seren liked *The Whaler*, and frankly, moving it wasted of energy. If they failed, the boat would sink no matter where it was, and Seren wouldn't be alive to care.

The bubble bobbed and shook, narrowly avoiding light post and an awning. Erik clung to his seat, counting heartbeats for the remainder of the shaky flight. On the ninety-third pulse, they crashed into a bush outside the conference building. The dockhands ran inside like spooked rabbits while Seren and Erik stumbled like they were drunk, coming home from a Little Port tavern.

CHAPTER
FIFTY-NINE

Seren barely had both feet in the door when Winnie grabbed them by the shirt. "Thank The Mother you are here. It is chaos inside."

"And I'm supposed to do what?" Seren blinked, barely able to stay awake. "With Sally moderating and without Root sabotaging, people should be politer."

"You're the one that exposed Root's schemes and defeated him. Sally says *you* have his power and need to moderate."

"I'm the youngest, least experienced person here." Seren wobbled behind Winnie and crashed into Sally.

Sally ran a hand through frazzled hair. "I can't hold their attention. Delegates are terrified and taking it out on each other, and the Elementals won't respond to me like they did to you. If you can be louder, maybe you can get them to stop yelling. I need you to take over."

Spots grew on the floor like bread mold. No one else looked at it. Was it a message? Or a hallucination triggered by extreme fatigue?

"We need to reform!" shouted a man with an Altzi logo on his sleeve. A dozen men thumped their chests and shouted in approval.

He glared over at a table full of scientist. "Maybe if we burn one of the witches, The Mother will be placated."

"Maddock, The Mother doesn't want any more bloodshed," said Ambassador Freeman, leaning heavily on a cane. It was first Seren had seen of him since arriving to NUNES. "The storm won't stop until we find common ground."

"Then the sooner you see those witches need to die, the sooner The Mother will be placated," said Maddock.

"You're being ridiculous." Guss sat on a bench with his leg propped up and bandaged.

"Yes." Freeman grunted. "I don't like the demands they've made or the machines they build but killing them will not solve anything."

"It will solve everything," said another Altzi flanking Freeman.

"Buster, back off," growled Guss through clenched teeth.

Buster inched closer to Freeman.

Freeman didn't flinch. "How can you think that? Has The Mother told you this? I doubt She speaks to you much after you burned her forest and tried to plant corn where ancient trees once stood. If The Mother wants anyone burned, it's you."

Buster got right up in Freeman's face. "Watch what you say, old man, or you may be the one who gets burned."

Simon leapt to his feet and yanked Buster back. "No one is getting burned."

Maddock and three goons flanked Dr. Zhao. "You should leave before we make you."

Dr. Fullerton mustered her iciest glare. Tav stood, but Dr. Zhao put her hand on their shoulder and guided them back to their seat.

David and Reggie got between Dr. Zhao and the group threatening her. "They are staying right where they are."

The group lost their resolve when they saw the gun tucked into Reggie's belt and the knives strapped to David's hip.

The moldy spots plaguing Seren's eyes rose up. Blue-green bread mold danced with the fuzzy white stuff that grows on the compost all summer. It swirled around feet, taking on more color until it looked more like puke than mold. The spots darkened, sucking light from the room. Swaying like a sick tree, Seren leaned against a wall for support.

"How do we know you ain't causing this storm to force to agree to your terms," yelled Marsha, standing nose to nose with Washington.

"I'm not! I spent the last two hours trying to shelter you from it." Washington backed away bumped into another woman as Marsha advanced.

"Maybe we should test that theory by tossing you and a few others out."

"That isn't even a theory," said Dr. Zhao, who was flanked by Tav and Dr. Fullerton. "It's merely a claim you pulled out of thin air."

"I thought you didn't believe in The Mother." Marsha turned her anger-flushed toward Dr. Zhao.

"We believe in science and have no evidence one person can cause a storm. The idea that the entire planet is actually a sentient being is still being explored."

"What can we do to make it stop?" asked Clover. Her blonde hair was charred at the ends and the side of their cheek blistered.

Across the room, a glass shattered on a wall. A fist slammed into a face. David and Reggie rushed to break up the fight just as another one broke out.

Civil discussions escalated into screaming matches.

The babble, combined with Seren's headache and fading consciousness, made Seren question their decision to pull dozens of them from flaming tents and writhing waves.

Now you understand, whispered The Mother's distant voice.

"Don't be ridiculous," Seren latched onto whisper, pulled power from it to sustain their drained body, and projected their thoughts down the vein they pulled power from.

Annoying doesn't mean people need to die. They have the right to voice their opinions and debate with each other, but if they are shouting and throwing punches, they are never going to find common ground. This group just needs a firm moderator to help them focus.

The spots dissipated. Seren pushed off the wall, steady on their feet. They were in no way the most qualified person in the room to lead, were pretty sure they were among the least qualified, aside from some of the Altzis, and technically, they weren't even an adult. They spend most of their teenage years fishing and playing coast guard, not defending the territory, just saving the people who got stuck on its waterways. They'd done all they could to avoid their mother's lessons on magic and politics.

"I'm useless." Seren fell back against the wall.

"It's raining harder," said Erik.

Seren nodded. That was obvious from the unceasing patter of precipitation battering the hall's roof.

Erik crossed his arms. "It isn't going to stop."

Seren shrugged. "It will when everyone comes to an agreement, or we're dead. At this point, the latter seems more likely."

"I can feel the water getting closer." Erik paced circled around Seren, huffing like a smith's bellows. "If it goes on long enough, this whole island will go under."

Seren reached out, squeezing Erik's shoulders.

"Don't touch me. Do something." Erik turned his back on Seren and stormed into the chaos.

Thunder louder than any they'd heard yet shook the hall, silencing people just long enough for Seren to bolster their voice and shout, "The storm won't stop until we stop fighting."

"And what does the storm have anything to do with us?" asked one of the scientists who Seren had not met yet.

Seren opened their mouth to answer, but Dr. Fullerton beat them to it. "The planet is a sentient being."

"Dr. Fullerton, don't tell me you believe that nonsense."

"It is not nonsense, Dr. Helios." Dr. Zhao stood beside Rita and took her hand. "We have hard evidence to support our hypothesis, and plans to test it further."

"A hypothesis isn't proof," said Dr. Helios.

"I know," said Dr. Zhao. "I admit there is a lot more to explore before we can accept it as fact, but it is a viable hypothesis."

"Even if that is possible, how can a human talk to a planet? Many ambassadors speak about the Earth like it's their God."

"We will be able to give you a more conclusive answer this time next year, but our preliminary analysis of ambassador DNA samples showed that they possess unique genetic markers," said Dr. Fullerton. "We suspect that brain scans will reveal an enlarged pineal gland that is most active when engaging in an exchange of energy with the planet."

"Can you measure these communications?"

Dr. Zhao grinned. "We haven't tried yet, but we plan to."

Whispers broke out all across the room, but before they escalated, Dr. Helios spoke again. "You really examined their DNA?"

Everyone from Dr. Zhao's skiff nodded.

Dr. Zhao spoke. "We analyzed oral DNA samples, blood, skin tissue, and hair. We watched them levitate without a device and manipulate air and water. At first, I thought they genetically modified while some of my colleagues hypothesized they were a cyborg. However, our current hypothesis is that their abilities are the result of a natural occurring mutation. Ambassadors are the next phase of human evolution."

"It is a sound hypothesis," said Dr. Ulyssa. "My colleagues and I would've drowned had Seren not flown over to us in their orb of energy. They possessed no machinery. I checked. When I pulled my colleagues off the sinking ship, I grabbed a few instruments because I feared high levels of radiation. They were a little above normal for a human, but still safe. I also observed an exchange of energy between Seren and their surroundings."

"I need to think about this." Dr. Helios crossed her arms.

"Then think," said Seren. "But don't let it interfere with our constitution. A few hours ago, we left off mid discussion of Article ten when a bomb threatened our boats and friends."

Silence followed, occasionally broken by whispers as Seren strode to the podium. "Our previous methods off debate were slow but through. Unfortunately, the clock is ticking. I will allow thirty minutes of debate for each remaining item. If we get through one item quicker, then the left-over time can be allocated to another."

An hour later, they agreed on Option three for the judiciary article, which gave territories power to establish their own courts, but also gave the central government's high court power to overrule any decision to lower courts made. And they also had settled on Option two for natural resources, leaving regulation mainly up to local governments with some oversight from the central government.

A policy for approving acceptable energy sources went equally quick, but decisions about weapon policies, law enforcement and rules for contact with the world beyond NUNES' borders took more time. Thankfully, a group of locals kept the delegates supplied with bread, cheese, sweets, and tea so they could push through the night.

Seren guessed it had to be getting close to dawn by the time Erik approached the podium whispering, "We have an hour before the water reaches us."

Seren glanced over at the list. "We have three items left."

Their stomach sunk when they read them. While they expected the health care article to go quickly, they worried the other two would be hotly contested. The first, Article Twenty, was titled "Research and Development." Option three made anyone planning do any kind of experiment, magical or scientific, go through complex review process with the local and central government. Option two put approval at the digression of local governments, and Option one meant no government oversight or involvement.

Dr. Zhao spoke first. "Initially, my colleagues and I whole heartedly supported Option one, but after seeing how unchecked power poisoned Root, and even led him to build explosives capable of mass destruction, we believe Option two is safer. However, we still hold that Option three will halt progress to a point that will hurt everyone."

"My clan takes no such stance," said Dr. Ulyssa. "We must not be limited in what discoveries we can make. If this planet is as alive and fickle as some of you claim, we need to have the technology to fight back if it ever does try to kill us. There should be no government interference in research."

Several people responded at the same time. Seren couldn't understand any of their answers.

Thunder roared, and the tree shook so hard that glasses topped, and a light fixture crashed from the ceiling.

"We are running out of time," said Erik.

Seren raised a dozen chairs and slammed them down like a judge's hammer.

"Silence!" Seren amplified the sound waves of their voice. "Only one person may speak at a time."

Sierra stood. "Permission to speak?"

"Granted," said Seren.

She smiled at the crowd. "The Mother wants us to thrive peacefully, and if allowing experimentation can result in a more consistent food supply and healthier population, then I don't see a problem with it."

Erik stood when she sat. "I agree. Science has a lot of potential to improve our lives, and I do not believe anyone would've survived in the middle of the ocean for centuries if The Mother was opposed to their lifestyle."

Several ambassadors' showed their support. Marsha protested, but Guss cut her off. "If these experiments don't hurt The Mother and leave me with a full belly, then I am all for them."

"All in favor Option one?" Seren asked when the allotted time had passed.

Two thirds of the scientist and a couple ambassadors raised their hands.

"You may lower them."

"All in favor of Option two?"

A majority of hands shot towards the ceiling.

"All in favor Option three?"

Fewer hands shot up.

They held their breath while they counted and didn't let it out until they were certain it had passed.

The health care article came next, and it seemed to be one of the few things almost everyone agreed on. Option two passed, which meant it would be managed at a local level, the central government would set up a fund and committee to make sure everyone had access to doctors and healers.

The last item made Seren's stomach flutter with fresh nerves. The first time they'd heard of it, they were shocked it was even up for debate. The idea that one person, let alone government, thought they could have any level of control over someone else's body horrified them. However, the reality was that there were people who sought to control others, who would try to stop someone from altering their body with magic, whether it was because they were transgender or had a different reason. By putting the issue of body modifications on the ballot, they could protect people's rights at the constitutional level.

Option one would mean no government entity could legally prevent anyone from altering their body by magic or science for any reason. Option two left relevant laws to the local government, and Option three left it up to the federal government. Seren had never discussed this issue with anyone from BREAD, but they knew the Altzis would likely fight for Option two, so they could prevent any kind of transition or alteration in their town.

As Seren announced the final item, Erik edged closer to them, standing less than an inch away from them. He took their hand. It was the first time he had willingly touched them since they had crossed a line while interrogating Root.

This issue was personal to both of them. Erik had transitioned. At the moment, Seren didn't have any plans to alter their body, but they hadn't ruled out the possibility either.

They both stared out at the room, daring anyone to challenge them.

Dr. Fullerton stood. "Harmony between mind and body is essential to good health and being able to transition across the gender spectrum is a human right that must be defended. I support Option one."

"I agree." Dr. Zhao stood as Dr. Fullerton sat. "Every individual should have full autonomy of their own body. Option one is the best way to ensure that."

As soon as she sat, one of the Altzis, Tommy Snyder, stood. "Those kinds of transformations are dangerous and insulting to The Mother. She made us each the way we are for a reason."

"I disagree." Guss stood, and many of his fellow Altzis stared at him with wide eyes and open mouths. "I once felt as you do, Tommy, but now I see that line of thinking is wrong. It was an excuse people like Domhnall use to blame other for their problems and to be cruel."

Tommy shook his head. "What you say about Domhnall might be true, but that doesn't mean The Mother approves."

"She wouldn't have granted Her mages the power to alter bodies if She didn't want them to use it." Guss stared at water seeping under the door jam. "In the past few days, I've met several people who have transitioned or modified their body in some way. Two of them saved my life. Domhnall, on the other hand, is rotting at the bottom of a river because of its Elemental. Domhnall's hateful ideology is what The Mother disapproves of, I support Option one."

Some gasped, glared, and stared down at shifting feet. The scientist smirked. The puddle at the door's threshold grew.

A smile wavered on Erik's. "I've read that before The Flood, there was a high suicide rate among trans people because they were often denied the ability to safely transition. I've heard that is also true in some areas now where they don't have access to magic or medicine that would allow a transition."

Seren took his hand. They had things to say too, but as moderator, they felt like they shouldn't.

Thankfully, Sierra had something similar to add. "In territories like mine, suicide is rare. One of many reasons is that our care from out healers is free and includes aid with transitions for anyone who asks."

Seren raised their hands. "All in favor of Option one, raise your hand,"

Water licked the feet of those who were closest to the door.

All the scientists raised their hands, not flinching as water circled their ankles. At least half of the ambassadors raised their hands. Those who didn't climbed the chairs as water reached their knees. One by one, the villagers who Erik saved raised their hands. Standing on a table, person from the Altzi party who called Erik a hero raised his hand, and soon, others followed.

"All in favor of Option two?"

Only a few hands went up as waves knocked on the door.

"Option three"

No one raised their hands.

"Then Option one passes. No government, local or central, shall prevent a person from altering their for whatever reasons they deem it necessary."

Erik made eye contact with Seren, and then they both stared down at the water, still rising above their knees.

"All in favor of passing the constitution with the agreed options, raise your hand."

Erik's hand shot up instantly. The scientists, still ignoring the water, followed suit. All the ambassadors raised their hands, whether they were hip deep in water of standing on tables. The villagers did with few exceptions, but the Altzi party was divided and many shouted in protest despite Guss's glares.

"Silence!" yelled Seren.

"All in favor of further modification, raise your hand." Half the Altzi party raised their hands high.

Seren counted. "We have a two-thirds majority in favor of ratifying the constitution as it is now. I hereby declare this document to be legal and valid. The first NUNES conference is officially dismissed."

Frantic mumbling broke as more people climbed on tables, searching for a way to escape the rising water.

Seren closed their eyes, sending their mind down to depths of the Earth.

I did what you asked. Spare us!

You did indeed, said Mother Earth. Open your eyes.

The doors to outside blew open and all the water rushed out of the room. The bottom half of the doors were wet, but the water receded fast, exposing a foot of land for every two or three heart beats. All along the road, people opened doors and stepped onto damp roads. Some even fell to their knees and kissed the ground.

Gray ruins of clouds tumbled across a vibrant blue sky, and double rainbow created a bridge from one shore of the lake to the other.

EPILOGUE

Seren found Assana passed out on an oversized armchair with an open book resting on her chest. It was an old, cloth bound edition whose spine said *There and Back Again* by J. R. R. Tolkien. Seren picked it up carefully, surprised to see it was a novel, not the one of the histories or social science texts she usually studied. She'd left off on a chapter titled "Out of the Frying Pan and Into the Fire."

Seren flipped to the beginning of the book and realized it would've been an antique before The Flood. It wasn't the oldest book Assana had, but it was up there, an old one usually kept shaded and dry, spending more time on the shelf than in the hands of readers.

"Seren," yawned Assana.

Seren leaned down and hugged Assana. They were going to ask why she was so tired, but they suspected they already knew. "You sheltered your people from the storm."

"Just like last time," said Assana. "And all the times before."

"Is that why you don't leave?" asked Seren. "Ambassadors from all over left their territories to go to NUNES. They were the leaders themselves, not their children or representatives. Why can they travel and not you?"

"Power and security come with a price," said Assana. "Not every ambassador is the same."

Seren frowned. "When I first left, I couldn't use my power without feeling like I was choking or being pulled back home. Later it stopped, and The Mother told me region did not limit my power because it came directly from her."

"That is true," said Assana.

"Your power comes from the same place." Seren stood up and crossed her arms. "I felt you there when we fought Root."

"That is also true. Please put that book down before you damage it."

Seren handed it to Assana. "Why were you reading it?"

"The same reason as always: for insight and understanding."

Seren waited for Assana to elaborate.

"Our power comes from The Mother, but it is filtered through our minds. The Elementals influence us, and we influence them." Assana put a bookmark on the chapter she left off at and gingerly placed the book on an end table. "I got hurt when I traveled, and Valley-Port suffered in my absence. Here, I control everything. Here, I can keep the storms at bay no matter how violent they get."

Seren frowned. "So you just choose to never leave and let me believe it is your magic?"

"It's not so simple." Assana stared down at her book's creased spine. "Sometimes the line between my will and theirs is blurred. They will not let me leave any more than I want to leave, and when you take over my power... I cannot say whether the consequences of my mistakes will trap you here or not."

Seren scratched their throat. "So when I felt that choking sensation, it wasn't the magic doing it."

Assana shook her head. "It was you."

That explained why it stopped, eventually. But there were so many other unanswered questions. "If the world scares you so much, then why did you send me out into it?"

Assana stood. "Someone had to go, and you'd been talking about leaving my territory for years."

"And that justified making me do something you're so afraid of?"

Assana smiled as she shook her head. "Not all. Valley-Port is safer when I'm here. You were as afraid of your power as I was of the world. You stopped making progress in your training and hardly heard anything I tried to teach you. You could not have cared for Valley-Port if I left, but by representing me out in the world, you grew. You probably learned more about your magic over the past two weeks than you did in the past two years."

"It's true," said Seren. "I used my magic and realized how bad it can be out there."

"What else did you learn?"

Seren thought about the question before answering. They could easily list a hundred things, but their mother didn't want to hear about every little development. She would in time, but that wasn't what she was asking right now.

Seren smiled when they realized that there were three big things that encompassed all the smaller ones. "First, I learned that there is a lot I don't know and should know. Second, I learned that no matter how terrifying my magic and the world can get, I can handle it. Third, I learned The Mother isn't some benevolent being with who always has humanity's best interest in mind."

"Then your trip was a success," said Assana. "You can fill me on the rest over dinner. Right now, I'd like to get back to my nap. That storm was the worst one I've fought since you were born."

"I love you, Mom." Seren walked out of the library and back down to the docks, where David and Reggie munched on nuts and used their arms and full mouths to narrate some epic part of the trip to a group of entranced children. Reggie got so into describing whatever detail they embellished they fell off the dock, right into the lake.

Seren laughed so hard they couldn't breathe. There was still so much they didn't know, but with enough time and adventures, they would learn. And there would be plenty more adventures to come.

Ratifying a constitution was only the first step in uniting NUNES. Some Altzis had turned out to be decent humans, or at least learned the error of their ways, but only a fraction of them had been present in that voting hall on the island.

Seren's challenges were far from over, but they could handle whatever trials Earth brought them, and that they wouldn't have to face them alone. One day, when Assana was warped and gnarled with age, Seren would lead Valley-Port and accept all the responsibility that came with. Until then, they had lots of exploring and education to undertake.

No one expected Erik to show up for work on his first day back in Little Port, but he didn't know what else to do. He'd rested enough on the ride back. He'd gotten the best sleep on a mat on the floor of Seren's boat while the splash of water and the hum of the engine drown out any memories of his days in Altzi captivity that his brain dare conjure, and the hum of river Elementals at the edge of his consciousness chased dreams away. Sitting around and resting more left too much time for thinking. Too much quiet for unwanted thoughts and memories to creep into his mind.

The usual chaos of a morning on the docks soothed him. A cacophony of voices and shouting joined the squawking gulls and the music of songbirds. The sun shone, and the river was calm. Add to that the saws and hammers of people still repairing sections of dock, and it drowned out the spectral s*chink schink* haunting his ears. And once he opened his mind up to Merri and Mac, the swishing and splashing chased away remaining hints of it.

Once all the usual folks were out of their slips for the day, Erik went about inspecting everything. Boards broken or twisted from the storm surge had all been properly replaced, but he found frayed ropes that needed replacing and mooring balls that had shifted. With the Elementals' help, he got those all back in place by the time the boats that used them would be back. When breaktime arrived, he grabbed his lunch and got in his own dory and rowed out into the river. Studying at the town from this distance, it appeared the same as it had when he left. Had he not spent the day half-listening to stories about the wind, rain, and storm surge, he wouldn't have believed that the storm had hit Little Port.

Many folks had told him the only home destroyed was Martin's. Lightning struck a tree, knocking it down and setting his house on fire. He didn't make it out. The tale didn't offer Erik any closure or relief. It made him sick, like seeing Domhnall bloated, half-eaten corpse at the bottom of Sneaky River along with half a dozen others. The Altzis were humans who deserved to live as much as him. They were grossly misguided. He would've rather seen them live and test out the new courts that would be established now that the constitution had passed even though it would be some time before those courts were actually set up.

As he rowed inland with the last flow of the rising tide, he saw very little evidence of damage. An occasional tree had a fresh break or had toppled, but not as much as he expected. Down by the river, houses, both built and grown, had weathered the storm without damage. When he got to his favorite lunch spot, he was surprised to see Seren there. They wore loose capris and a short-sleeve shirt. Their bare feet were in the river.

"Today's the warmest one we've had this year." Seren smiled up at him. "And everything feels so calm. After all the chaos, the violence, it's surreal."

Erik nodded. "It is surreal."

Seeing Seren still conjured mixed feelings. He felt the same longing to be near them he always had, but it was tempered by a fear of their power. He sat down on the rock a few feet away from them. "I'm surprised you're here."

"Why?" Seren peered down at the sun- kissed water shimmering as it gently lapped the rock.

"I thought you'd be busy filling your mom in on everything and making plans." Erik looked everywhere but at Seren. Just where the rock met the flatter, muddier section of river bank, a fiddler crab stood on the edge, waving its large, fiddle-shaped claw at another crab. Across the water, a blue heron stood still where water met tall grass. An osprey circled overhead.

"She wants me to go back for the next session." Seren's brow furrowed. They picked apart a piece of dried out seaweed.

"When is that?" Erik knew the constitutional convention had only been a start. A lot of work was needed to get the central government running. Once a justice system was in place, its first task would be to try Root and investigate his accomplices.

Eventually, there would be elected officials from all the territories that would gather regularly to vote on budgets and policy. More should've set up at the end of this session, but with all the damage from the storm in Merry Basin, it hadn't been practical. Plus, it sounded like other places were hit worse than Valley-Port. People had wanted to go home and make repairs.

"From the end of July into August," said Seren. "I should be back by mid-September. Then I'll be here for a month or two and off to the solar barge in November."

Erik nodded. Seren being away so much would certainty give him time to process things, but he wondered if it would also be the end of their relationship. And when he thought about it being over, his stomach churned as much as it did when he thought about Seren interrogating Root.

"There's something else." Seren turned and met Erik's eyes. "Since there is so much to plan, and will be less voting in the July session, Sally was asking for two delegates."

"Does Assana have someone in mind?" Erik tried to picture who might go. Johnny Wind was the wisest person in town, but he never left Valley-Port and would claim he was too old to make the trip. Tina lead the fishing fleet. The manager from Compass Rose could certainly negotiate like a politician.

"You."

Seren's words cut off his thoughts and sent his brain spiraling.

"Me? Who'll run the docks?" Thoughts slid around in Erik's head and didn't come together.

"Merri and Mac told Assana they'd accept Tina in your absence."

"Does she really want two teenagers going?"

"Technically, you won't be a teen by then." Seren sighed. "The Elementals are demanding I return for The Mother only knows what reason. And Assana says your connection with Tav, Dr. Fullerton, and Dr. Zhao will help things go smooth. You're empathetic. Skills you use calming rowdy Elementals might come in handy too, except you might calm people, not currents. With words, not magic. Assana also said something about not trusting people who actually want the power that comes with politics."

"Do I have a choice?" Erik's brain churned like the river on a stormy, full moon night. He'd need time to figure out if he wanted to go or not.

"My mother says you do." Seren studied at the muddy riverbank where the tide quickly receded, and the two crabs had written the word "Go" in the sand with the sticks clutched between their claws.

"But your mother isn't the one charge," said Erik, surprised by the smile growing on his face. "She's an ambassador. A messenger."

"No one controls the Elementals," said Seren. "But sometimes, they control us and they're less likely to try when we listen to them."

"And we listen to them, they are more likely to listen to us in return." He'd figured that out quickly when he started working on the docks. If he listened to Merri and Mac, they listen to him.

Seren smiled at him. "So does that mean you're going?"

"I know there are more qualified people in Valley-Port, but if the Elementals, you, and Assana all believe I have something valuable to contribute, then I'll do it." Erik scooted closer to Seren. "And I think we will make an excellent team."

"Balance." Seren placed their hands between them, palm up. "We balance each other."

"You're right." Erik's smile grew. Even though they'd survived, they'd passed the constitution and convinced The Mother to let them live, Erik had still been feeling like they'd lost. The fact that certain laws were needed at all was a failure of humanity to accept people for who they are.

But it wasn't a loss so much as an awakening. Valley-Port may be a peaceful, accepting place, but they were merely one tiny dot on the map.

He hadn't lost.

The game only just beginning.

ACKNOWLEDGMENTS

The road to get *Earth Reclaimed* from an idea in my head to a published book was a long one and there were so many people who helped me on the way there. I owe a big thanks to Artemis, Merisa, and Janice who, early in the drafting process, read my early chapters and helped me brainstorm. Thank you to the beta readers who read the draft when it was still in its early stages: Megan, Eve, Hannah, Courtney, Gillian, Barbara, and anyone else who read even part of my draft. I've lost contact with many of you, so I'm not sure you'll see this, but if you do, thank you! The draft wouldn't have gotten this far without your help. Thank you to Beth Phelan for creating #DVPit, which helped me find my publisher. Thank you Aurelia Leo for believing in this book enough to publish it. I also want to thank my editor, Lesley, for helping me see how much better I could make this book.

Thank you to my critique group (Natalie, Katie, Robin, Bill, and Seri) for helping me work through some significant changes I had to make during edits. Thank you to the wonderful folks in the Reading Excuses forum who gave me feedback on the revised version of my opening chapters. I also owe a big thanks to my friends from Pitch Wars for all their encouragement even though this book was unrelated to what I was working on in Pitch Wars. Thank you to the folks who sprinted with me in discord. You helped me stay focused and motivated. Thank you to my family, my spouse and parents, for always supporting me and my writing. Of course, thank you to

Goose, my meowditor, for hitting my face with your fluffy tail while I try to write.

About the Author

BIO: Sara Codair is a community college English professor, and is an author of speculative short stories and novels. They partially owe their success to their faithful feline writing partner, Goose the Meowditor-In-Chief, who likes to "edit" their work by deleting entire pages. You can follow Sara and Goose's writing journey on twitter and instagram @shatteredsmooth.

Made in the USA
Columbia, SC
26 November 2021

49769170R00209